A PLACE OUTSIDE THE WILD

DANIEL HUMPHREYS

For Tara, who got me writing again.

Prologue

Miles Matthews survived the apocalypse because of his third job.

Unlike many of his fellow graduates, he'd been able to get a job after graduation. The position in the IT department of a local pharmaceutical company wasn't a world-beater, but it was a start.

The work wasn't all that difficult and the pay was decent enough for a single guy living on the cheap. All things considered, post-college life started out well. But like all things that seem too good to be true, it wasn't long until harsh reality reasserted itself.

Once the recession hit, his full-time job with occasional overtime became a 28-hour a week proposition. To make things worse, his seven-hour shifts weren't consecutive. His schedule called for him to work Mondays, Tuesdays, Thursdays, and Fridays. "The beginning and end of the week are our busy times; we can't sacrifice staff," his boss proclaimed. If Mr. Novak had noticed his own low-hanging hypocritical softball, he didn't let on. As far as Miles could tell, management hadn't taken much of a hit, if any. It was a hard lesson to learn for someone just under two years out of college. In the business world, when times get tough, IT takes the hit.

For some reason, they hadn't covered that in any of his coursework.

After a few months of attrition, Miles was the most tenured IT staffer. The others had found positions with other companies or moved on to different fields.

In the end, Miles had Wednesdays and weekends to make up for his lost pay. It wouldn't have been a big deal, except for the payment on the brand-new Jeep and ballooning student loan repayments. There went dating. On the bright side, the rent for his childhood bedroom was low. Miles wasn't dumb, but even he could admit that foresight wasn't always his strong suit. One quality that he *did* possess was that he was in no way, shape, or form a whiner.

Things were tough now but this was just a situation to which he had to 'react, adapt, and overcome'. Uncle Pete's catch-phrase had been eye-roll worthy when he was younger. Now it made much more sense.

Weekends weren't a big problem. His uncle was more than happy to let him help out in his shop, and that was even less real work than his IT career. Stand around and shoot the breeze, drinking coffee and run the cash register once in a while? A piece of cake, but not quite enough to restore his budget to its former splendor.

After some searching, he found a part-time gig running the front desk at a motel. Just off the Interstate, it was far enough away from the city to be cheap.

Despite the limited hours, it was his most difficult job from a labor aspect. His job title could have been clerk, bellhop, alternate housekeeping, and general gofer. In those terms it wasn't worth the pay, but jobs weren't falling out of the sky.

From a mental standpoint, it was boring. The weekends were the motel's busiest days. The weekday nights that Miles covered were usually a wasteland. On the bright side, he was pretty much his own boss. He read a lot of books and perused job-seeking websites. The coffee was lousy compared to his other jobs, but it had enough caffeine in it to keep him awake.

Lack of extracurricular — translation: 'expensive' — hobbies stunk. But he was making steady progress on digging himself out of the hole. It was an ascetic life to be sure, but Miles forced himself to take the long view.

Wednesdays were usually dead and this one was no different. Only a quarter of the motel's forty rooms had occupants, and no one had checked in since Miles had clocked in at noon. A few hours after that, he'd turned off the lobby television. All the news was talking about was the flu outbreak that had dragged much of the world into sick beds. When the same stories began repeating every hour, Miles figured that he didn't need the noise. He had a painter's mask and a jumbo bottle of hand sanitizer behind the counter in case anyone came in coughing. He wasn't in any sort of mood to hear about the crisis for the next nine hours. The latest Larry Correia book was a more worthy investment of his time.

He was a few pages into the second chapter when the two-way radio sitting on the desk chirped. A breathy, panicked voice shouted. "Miles! I need help in room 17!"

Miles shot to his feet and threw his book on the desk.

On his way out of the office, he snagged the radio and brought it close to his mouth. "On my way, Celia," he responded as he trotted through the glass doors. The layout of the chain motel was simplicity itself. Rooms 1 through 20 were on the right side of the motel, 21 through 40 were on the left.

Every few months, tweakers would pay cash for a room and use it to cook a batch of meth. It often didn't work out for them. The chain restaurants on either side of the motel were popular cop hangouts, and they usually made a cursory check of the vehicles parked in the lot for warrants. Sometimes the maids happened upon them first. This was most common when the vagabond cooks neglected to hang their "Do Not Disturb" signs. On the bright side, the cooks were more bark than bite when confronted. Usually. The rest of the time they needed a little more reinforcement to sit down and wait for the police to arrive. The motel had a strict zero-tolerance policy regarding armed employees, but Miles already had two other jobs. He wasn't about to trade his life to keep his third.

Toward the rear of the motel, one of the housekeepers stood several feet back from the door to room 17. It was almost as though she were afraid to get any closer. He heard a high-pitched scream, but it wasn't the housekeeper. She stood with an open jaw and a shocked look on her face. Miles doubted she could have screamed if she wanted to. As he came up to the room, he eased Celia to the side. She didn't resist, but raised her arm and indicated the interior with a trembling finger.

As Miles looked there was another shriek. Just inside the door, another housekeeper lay face down and spread-eagle on the floor. The source of the high-pitched screams was a balding, heavyset man. He stood on the threshold of the bathroom with a towel wrapped around his waist.

"What happened?" Miles said to Celia, though he kept his eyes on the man.

After a moment, she regained her wits and replied, "I was in the next room and I heard a thud. I came out and Rita was lying on the floor. I don't know if he hit her or . . ."

"I didn't touch her!" the heavyset man said in a shrill voice. "I came out of the shower and she was standing there *bleeding* out of her damn eyes! She hit the floor and I screamed." He edged back into the bathroom. "Oh God, she has it, doesn't she?"

"Her eyes?" Miles muttered. He began to move into the room, but there was a tremendous crash back in the direction of the office. Startled, he turned and looked in that direction. It was tough to make out any detail, but it seemed as though there had been a wreck on the state highway in front of the motel. For a moment all was silent, and then the screaming started, from the road this time. After a beat, another scream sounded, from a different direction.

"What the . . ." Miles began, but a much closer scream cut him off. He spun back around.

Celia was bent over Rita, and she was trying to pull the younger women up for some reason. No — Miles blinked and tried to reconcile what he was seeing. No, Celia was trying to pull *away*. Rita had her teeth clamped on the older woman's fleshy forearm. Blood streamed down the bottom of Rita's face and joined the twin tracks from her tear ducts. The most frightening thing of all wasn't the gore. It was the slate-gray nothing that stared at Miles from what had once been a pair of rather beautiful blue eyes.

"Holy sh. . ." Miles started. With a final, Herculean effort, Celia tore her arm away. Flesh stretched and then ripped with a sound like damp cloth tearing. Celia screamed again. The blood that had been streaming turned into a torrent as one of the arteries in her forearm opened to the

11

air. The older woman staggered back and fell. Before Miles knew it, he backed away. The man in the towel screamed again, retreated all the way into the bathroom, and slammed the door.

Thanks for the help, buddy.

Later, the thing that would most stand out to Miles was just how surreal it had felt. He would remember blurs of blood, the screams, and the dead gray eyes. He would never remember drawing his concealed pistol.

The Kahr 9mm was small enough to make the slightest bulge under his polo shirt, and he'd never fired it anywhere but the range. He fired three times now, without a thought. The ingrained instincts of hard-earned muscle memory saved his life.

In the time it took him to draw his pistol, Rita had staggered to her feet and closed within arms-length of Miles. The first two hollow points went center mass and were ineffective. Later, Miles would reflect on the irony of that. He'd seen enough horror movies to know the game, but here and now he was still on a learning curve. This course was pass-fail, and to fail meant death.

The pistol tracked upward with the recoil of his first shots. As the bridge of the Rita-thing's nose crossed his sight picture, he fired again. The gray eyes changed hue and the body stiffened and fell to the ground in mid-step. Miles forced himself to look away from the shattered ruin of Rita's head as he stepped toward Celia. She groaned and turned her head to look at him. Miles met her look, then recoiled. There was still a tinge of warm brown to her eyes but as he watched hints of steel gray crept into the surrounding white. Blood welled at the corners of her eyes and began to trickle down plump cheeks. "Run," she whispered.

Miles began to raise the pistol, then hesitated. Defending himself was one thing, but this would be cold-blooded murder — wouldn't it? He shook his head with a start and moved to obey Celia's last command. Miles ran, digging for his car keys.

As he ran, the crescendo of chaos returned to his ears — more screaming, from the highway. The squealing of tires. The impact of another wreck. Then, from the south, the rapid pop-pop-pop of gunfire. After a moment, more screams sounded. If anything the sound of gunfire escalated. "Police?" Miles wondered aloud. The sounds could have originated from the Waffle House in that direction.

He reached his Jeep. The welcoming flash of the lights as he thumbed the unlock button on the fob prompted a shout of elation. He yanked the driver's door open and jumped inside. Without thinking, he thumbed the door locks and locked himself in. For a moment, he juggled the pistol in his right hand and the keys in his left. Finally, he dropped the pistol on the passenger seat, transferred the keys to his other hand, and cranked the engine. The self-doubting voice in the back of Miles' head whispered, "It won't start." The reassuring roar of the Jeep's V6 shut that self-doubt down.

Before he put the Rubicon in gear, a figure leaped in front of it and slammed both hands down on the hood. Miles flinched and grabbed for the Kahr. As he leveled it at the figure through the windshield, the figure backed up and stuck both hands toward him. "Wait!" the figure shouted, and Miles blinked. The man was disheveled, soaked in blood, and wild-eyed, but Miles recognized him.
Derek Garcia and Miles Matthews had run in different circles in school. Despite that, it was a small enough school

13

— and town — that they knew of each other. They weren't friends by any stretch of the imagination, but they weren't enemies, either.

Derek's black Lewisville PD uniform was much the worse for wear. A spray of blood had washed across Derek's chest and stained his name tag and badge. The right sleeve of his shirt had separated at the shoulder and revealed the T-shirt underneath. Miles hesitated. He didn't lower the Kahr. "Is it yours?" he yelled.

The other man looked puzzled for a moment, but then he looked down and saw the blood on his chest. He grimaced and shook his head.

"Are you bit?" Miles shouted, his tone growing more frantic. This time, Derek shook his head without hesitation. "No!" the other man shouted. He turned to look over his shoulder. "For God's sake man, let me in the damn truck!" Miles swallowed and nodded. He thumbed the locks again, and Derek slid around to the passenger side and climbed up in the Jeep. When he closed the door Miles locked it again.

"Derek, what the hell is going on?" Miles demanded. The other man stared at him. He saw something of the same shock in the police officer's eyes that he'd seen in Celia's. Before Rita. Before . . . Miles shook away the memories. He didn't have time for them now. He popped open the center storage bin and pulled out the spare magazine for his pistol. The small size came at a disadvantage when it came to ammunition capacity. The Kahr only held seven rounds if you kept one in the chamber. As Derek spoke, he exchanged the partial magazine for the full and tucked the partial away.

"Drive," Derek demanded, running shaking hands through his hair. "Just drive."

Miles nodded.

Miles drove.

//BEGIN INTERCEPT TRANSCRIPT
30-OCT-2019 0255EST
CALCULATED GPS COORDINATES [REDACTED - SI/TK]
TYPE OF INTERCEPT: HAM
INTERCEPT FREQ: [REDACTED – SI/TK]
SUBJECT CODE NAME: "UNCLE PETE" (FILE 002-2134)

CQ, CQ, CQ, this is KG3BBX. Anybody out there, over? [LONG SILENCE] All right, kiddies. Pull up a chair and listen. It's story time. Of course, if you're hearing this you probably know it already, but back off. It's my dime. You can talk next, if you're out there.

The Brazilian flu went through civilization like a tidal wave. We went from the first 'oh by the way' reports on the nightly news to the Emergency Broadcast System going off while I was trying to drink my way through the baseball playoffs in twenty-six days. Mankind went from zero to Mad Max in just shy of a freaking month. I used to joke that the world would end when the Cubs won the Series, but the end of the world didn't even extend me that small courtesy. Ah well. They would have lost anyway. [LAUGHS]

It's a no-brainer why it spread so fast – international flights, world travelers who couldn't be bothered to take a sick day, yadda yadda yadda. The flu took a ride on every plane, train, and automobile — great flick, by the way —

that radiated from those travel hubs and spread from there. If you didn't catch the first wave of the sniffles, you were lucky. Maybe about 10 percent seemed to have a natural immunity. Include me in that. All things considered, I'd rather have won the Power Ball. [LAUGHS] Initial symptoms were mild, which they say contributed to the lack of concern about it. After about 72 hours, though . . . I'm not a disease guy, I just know what I've seen in movies and heard on the news, but at that point the virus spread to the brain, causing seizures, comas, and in some extremely rare cases death. They say the death part was about 10 percent of the population. It's hard to even think about it. Go to a party with a couple dozen people, if you can find them, and imagine two or three of them just keeling over dead, boom. In a lot of ways I think they were the lucky ones. But, hell, I'm just a crazy old man talking to himself in the depths of the night. You know all this already, or you should. Feel free to interrupt me if you have something better to talk about. [LONG SILENCE]

So the coma patients pretty much overwhelmed the medical system, there were hardly enough beds to go around. In the rural areas it wasn't too bad; folks had families, and doctors could usually be persuaded to make an informal visit. The cities were bad then. I shudder to even think about what they're like now. So this went on for a while until one day, like flipping a switch, they woke up.

Sort of; I don't know if you can really call them alive, for God's sake. I mean, some of the folks around here decided to get all scientific and stuff, and they tell me they couldn't find a pulse or anything. They're morons for even trying, you ask me.

So they woke up. And they were [STRONG EMPHASIS] hungry [/EMPHASIS]. You'd think that might have been something the folks in Asia might have mentioned, given that they ran into it a good two weeks before the rest of the world, but I guess there was just too much damn static to pick up the real, solid information. By the time the first coma patients in the old US of A started waking up, it was too late. I don't know if Uncle Sammy was locking down the information for our 'protection', but we've got a few former . . . hospital employees in our group. Not trying to be cagey, but who the hell knows who's listening to this. Anyway, the medical people thought the stories were a bunch of crap. The worst part, of course, wasn't the coma patients — it was the people who never even realized they were sick until the virus reached some sort of, I don't know, critical mass. Right around the time the coma patients were getting up for dinner, people all over the world were dropping dead where they stood — then standing right up a few minutes later. By the time it hit here, small town USA, it was too late. Of course, we had enough business travelers among us that our outbreak kicked off the same time as places like Denver, Boston, Louisville, and Minneapolis. I had a lot of ham buddies out there. Can't reach a one of them now — anybody listening out there? [LONG PAUSE, STATIC ON TRANSMISSION]

Jeez. Old Uncle Pete, all alone in the radio wilderness. Maybe I'll hook up my stereo and blast some tunes later. I've thrown the rest of our protocol out the window, might as well see if I can bring the FCC down on my ass. Maybe they'll bring some grub. You out there, Uncle Sammy? I'm partial to spaghetti and meatballs if you feel like dropping off some MREs. [LONG PAUSE, STATIC ON TRANSMISSION]

Anyway, if you've seen . . . I can't call them . . . you know. Everybody else around here thinks it's a pretty funny joke, and they try to drop as many nicknames as they can come up with, like we're in a movie or TV show. I watched that stuff with my nephew, I guess. Never wanted to live through it. If you've seen them, you know what I'm talking about. They're not right. If you haven't seen them, trust me when I say that when you do, run until you can't run no more. Until then, keep quiet and keep your head down. I've been to war. I've seen things that no man should have to see in a lifetime. But nothing has ever scared me as deep and as hard as the things outside the fence. Anybody out there? [LONG SILENCE] To hell with it. KG3BBX, out. //END TRANSCRIPT

Chapter 1

From the journal of Miles Matthews
March 3, 2026

My daughter does not laugh.

It's our fault, of course. From the day she was born, she has been shushed at every noise no matter how innocent or joyous. Years of small, silent moments — anger, love, praise, and discipline conducted in hushed speaking tones. It was hardest when she was a baby, in the first years after Z-Day. She didn't know any better, but we did the best we could. With the walls and the fence, it was enough, but noise was always a concern. Sometimes I wonder if the difficulties we faced made those around us reconsider children. Even if that wasn't the case, she is one of the youngest in our community. It was hard enough raising a kid before. Having to worry about them making an errant noise just means that hardly anyone is having children now.

In the beginning, we never thought that we'd come this far. For a while, we thought that life moving forward would be little more than blood and teeth with a generous helping of terror.

The strange thing, of course, is that we were perhaps the best-equipped generation to face this crisis. We'd grown up with zombies — dancing zombies in music videos, stumbling ones in horror movies and exploding ones in video games. The fact that our 'zombies' were mostly different from anything Hollywood had ever envisioned didn't change the circumstances. The rules are still mostly the same. Stay quiet and out of sight. Don't waste your time with anything other than a head shot.

Don't get bitten.

The funny thing is — well, maybe not funny. Humor has taken a decided turn for the macabre in the last eight years. The odd thing is, almost every zombie movie I watched as a teenager or streamed at work while I was doing server maintenance had one thing in common. They all stopped at pretty much the same point — an indeterminate future, with our heroes heading toward the unknown.

We live in that unknown.

We still don't really know what caused the outbreak, though we have our conspiracy theories and debates. No matter the cause, there is one fact that can't be denied. There is a half-life to human flesh. No matter how infernal the engine behind its reanimation, at some point it gives out.

Eight years of freeze and thaw, stumbles and falls, and battles against a population of survivors particularly well-equipped for this disaster. Let's just say the zoms aren't much of a threat anymore. Not like they were in the beginning, anyway. It's an empty world out there, as best we can tell. Which is where the funny part of it comes into play.

Why do I say that's funny?

I never really thought a zombie apocalypse would be boring.

He hadn't slept well in years; when something grabbed him, his eyes opened immediately. He shoved his hand under the pillow in search of his pistol even as he searched for the source of the touch. In a sea of shadows, he made out the small form beside his bed and relaxed. Even though he knew for a fact that his home was a safe place, his initial reaction was still a defensive one. At least until he was awake enough for recognition.

"I'm hungry," Trina whispered. "Is it time to get up?"

Miles squinted in the darkness and found his watch. He never wore one before Z-Day — like many of his generation, he'd used his phone to keep time. Now his phone was worthless and a watch was something to depend on once again. He angled the face and noted the dull reflection off of the glow-in-the-dark hands. "Yes, it is," he said to his daughter, and levered up on one elbow to give her a hug with his free hand. "Good morning."

He threw the covers back and sat up. His jeans had been clean yesterday, so they were still good for today. Pulling them on, he hunted in the dimness for a clean shirt. He'd long been in the habit of sleeping partly-dressed in boxer briefs, socks, and a t-shirt. You never knew when you'd have to be up and moving in a moment's notice. It had been a long time since he'd needed to do so, but it was a hard habit to break.

After a moment of hunting in his laundry basket, he pulled on a clean shirt and buttoned it. "How long have you been awake? Did Mommy tell you bye?"

"Yeah. She said not to bother you until it was almost time to go to school. What were you doing last night?" Miles grinned as he stood and headed for the bedroom door. "Aren't you the curious one? Didn't your mom tell you? It's not a big secret."

"Just a meeting," Trina replied as she followed him on swift, silent feet. "Grown-up stuff. It sounded lame." Outside of the bedroom, the house brightened. They'd boarded up the bedroom windows years ago, and as with his sleeping habits, he was leery of change.

"Maybe a little lame," he conceded. "We're finally going to name the town Wednesday night. The kids get to vote — that's something, huh?"

"I guess. Why does a name matter? We never had one before."

"Well," he began, then paused to consider his words for a moment. "Maybe it *doesn't* mean much. But in a way, I think it means we're starting to think about the future. Maybe we're the only ones who will use it. There's always the chance that one day we'll meet other people. When they ask where we're from, what are we supposed to say? 'The fenced-in area on County Road 300'?" He reached down, grabbed Trina around the waist, and tickled. "Does that sound good to you?" He hoped for a giggle, a laugh, something.

No such luck; she flashed a wide grin and wriggled out of his grasp. "I guess, but you know what sounds better?"

"What's that?"

"Pancakes!"

Miles shook his head. "I don't know if you're lucky. Let's see." The modern appliances in the kitchen always struck him as incongruous. Without a working infrastructure, none of them were usable. The gas stove had lasted longer than the refrigerator, but the propane had run out as well.

These days the stove served as a stand for an alcohol-fueled camp stove. Even then it didn't get much use. The town was still small enough to make a common cafeteria the most efficient way of feeding everyone, but the communal breakfast tended toward gray and runny. As such, many people tended to make their own. His wife, Tish, had the early shift at the clinic, but she'd left them a meal somewhat better than oatmeal.

He waved his hand near the side of the coffee pot and smiled. It was still lukewarm. The microwave over the stove had long ceased to produce popcorn, but it still worked to keep food warm. He opened the door, and sure enough, a plate of pancakes sat inside.

What little wheat they grew went for bread. As a result, the ersatz 'pancakes' were an unfortunate mix of Bisquick with roughly-ground corn meal, to stretch out their supplies. On the bright side, they had good egg production, and a yellow mound of scrambled eggs sat by the pancakes. Miles still would have given almost anything for a dairy cow or two. Or bacon. His mouth watered at the thought, but he pushed it aside. Might as well wish for the world to be back to normal. Mankind had held on at the brink of extinction.

As far as they could tell, pigs hadn't been so lucky. The zombies would eat anything they could catch; penned livestock was effectively a buffet.

He piled up a trio of cakes on a plate for his daughter and drizzled a healthy dollop of syrup on top. That, at least, they had plenty of. He made himself a plate and poured a cup of coffee. "Water?" The eggs and pancakes on his daughter's plate were disappearing at an impressive rate. Trina's immature palate declared them to be 'great'. In his opinion, the pancakes were flat, gritty, and a bit on the bland side. The eggs weren't bad, though they could have done with some butter and seasoning. He doused them in pepper and tried not to sigh.

Breakfast shouldn't be so depressing.

"Yes, please."

A bucket of ice in the bottom of the fridge kept drinks cool and the seals kept insects out of anything stored inside. They had to make ice in one of the central buildings that had solar power, but there was enough to go around, at least.

The door opened with a soft sucking sound. The sound drew out, too long for normal, and Miles grimaced and rubbed his forehead with the ball of his fist. Inside the refrigerator, the fat guy from the motel that he'd left to die grinned broadly, his eyes gone steel gray.

He closed his eyes. *One, two, three. Not real, not real.*

Miles opened his eyes again and tried to still the pounding of his heart. The interior of the fridge held nothing more ominous than food. Demons thus banished, he forced himself to adopt an air of normalcy. He poured a glass of water from a pitcher into a cup for Trina and sat down with his coffee and food to eat.

Miles finished his eggs and ate the pancakes with mechanical precision. He forced himself to ignore the taste and texture. This was fuel; no more, no less. The coffee was decent, though it would have been better served with a touch of cream and sugar. Their supply of it wouldn't last forever, but eight years in they still had stacks of scavenged, sealed cans.

He spent most of his time watching his daughter and trying not to think about intermittent hallucinations. It wasn't like they had a plethora of psychiatrists.

As tedious as life was, at least there were some things in the world that made him look forward to a brighter future. Trina caught him staring and wrinkled her nose at him. Miles chuckled.

There was a rap at the door and she flinched. As it opened, a tall figure leaned inside and intoned in a deep voice, "Is it safe to enter?"

Miles laughed, and Trina said, "Grandpa!" She jumped out of her chair and ran over to him to share a quick hug.

"Finish your breakfast, girlie," Larry Vance intoned. He swept her up for a quick squeeze and then deposited her back into her chair. "Glad to see your daddy decided to get up."

Miles rolled his eyes in an exaggerated fashion. "Trina, tell your grandfather that some of us have more responsibility than others. And I only have those responsibilities because Grandpa refused to accept the nomination. I hope he's not getting senile in his advanced age."

"All right, truce," Larry said with a grin. "I think I've bitten off more than I can chew."

"Grandpa, do you want pancakes?"

"No, I'm just fine, Trina. I hauled up a bit of breakfast for your Uncle Pete this morning and watched the sunrise." She turned back to her pancakes. Miles pushed his own plate away with a grimace and took a sip of coffee. He raised his mug and cocked an eyebrow.

"Thanks," Larry said, and moved over to the pot and poured himself a mug. "I need to talk to Charlie one of these days and see if he can find me a new Thermos. My old one is starting to leak."

Miles chuckled. "I'm sure he'll make you a deal." Charlie Maddox was a notorious altruist when it came to scavenging for the good of the town. He was also a notorious pirate when it came to 'special' favors. In Larry's case, though, Miles thought the other man was liable to make an exception. They'd all been through a lot together, and that counted for something, these days. "You stop by the office?"

Larry nodded as he sipped his own coffee. "I did. Slow night. Jimmy Taylor's sleeping one off, and we've got half a dozen noise complaints. Miss Jaid is in a tizzy about those, of course."

"Great," Miles rolled his eyes. He got along with most everyone, but Jaid Sims had always rubbed him the wrong way. In high school, she'd run with the popular crowd. Miles had been an odd duck, preferring to hang with the farm kids and computer geeks, despite being on the basketball team. Most of his friends had looked at her with stereotypical nerd-cheerleader adoration. Miles himself had always thought something was off about her. That hunch was only cemented after her crew spent most of a school year making his best friend's life hell. Sticks — his long-time best friend — had put forth an epic rant on the subject when he learned that Queen Mean Girl had been one of the few survivors to make it out of Lewisville after Z-Day. His ire had turned to humor when Jaid had made it obvious she was now head of the Miles Matthews fan club. If she noticed his lack of interest, she didn't seem to care.

And of course, thoughts of Sticks turned to other things and . . .

Larry noted his grimace. "Who came to mind?" Such was the form of conversation, eight years AZ. Streams of normalcy interrupted by memories of loss. Everyone dealt with it in their own way; some with better function than others.

"Sticks," Miles said with a sigh. "Da — dang," he corrected, looking at Trina out of the corner of his eye. "I miss that skinny little jerk."

The other man smiled. "He was a good kid." He fell silent for a long moment, then continued. "Pete also mentioned that he saw Alex hiking out to the south fence with that Ruger of his. I figured we'd swing down that way after we drop Trina off at school and see what sort of field trip he's on."

Trina perked up. "Miss McKee says that Alex is a stubborn boy."

"Indeed he is," her grandfather agreed. "And that's not always a bad thing, but rules are rules for a reason."

"Always be quiet," Trina intoned, "and don't draw attention." Miles frowned as he looked at her. He wanted to say something, but words failed him at the moment. Instead, he smiled as she made eye contact. "Daddy, will Alex get in a lot of trouble?"

"No, no," he replied. "We'll just talk to him. He's not in any trouble." *I hope.* He glanced at his watch. "Ready to go?" She was out of her chair before Miles could even register the nod. She scrambled to the back door and strapped on a worn backpack after removing it from its wall peg. Miles' AR-style short-barreled rifle hung on a pair of higher pegs. This put it out of Trina's reach even if she'd been standing on one of the kitchen chairs. He brought it down, chambered a round, and put it on safe.

"Guess I'm done with my coffee," Larry complained, and Miles laughed.

"Fill up your Thermos," he suggested.

In short order, they were out the door and onto the porch. Miles held the door for his father-in-law and pulled it shut as the older man stepped through. He didn't bother to lock it. There wasn't anything inside that was easy to steal except clothing. If thieves managed to haul his gun safe out without heavy equipment, he'd let them have it out of sheer respect. Of course, even if someone *did* break in the list of suspects would be predictable and short. *One of the few benefits to having such a small population.*

The top of the tallest grain bin that loomed over the house wasn't visible from the ground. Miles waved anyway as he slung his rifle over one shoulder. Trina imitated his actions then blew an exaggerated kiss. He smiled and hoped that Pete had seen it.

Trina skipped ahead to the end of the gravel drive and turned right to head toward the school. At one time, it had housed the tractors and combines for the farm. Since it was the largest building within the community it was now used as a combination cafeteria, school, and meeting hall.

Miles gave his daughter a few steps to draw ahead as Larry fell in next to him. "You try and talk him into coming down for a bit?"

"I swear he just makes me go up that damn ladder to screw with me. Yeah, I tried. Tried is the operative word."

"He's not scared."

"I know that, son. Pete's just . . . focused. It's like part of him thinks that if he's not watching over us all the time, something bad is going to happen."

Miles glanced up. "He's got to sleep at some point, even he knows that."

"I think he naps in the daytime, or when his trainees are around." Larry frowned. "At night, I guess, he's up the whole time. Says he doesn't trust the wall guys to do their job without him being there to nag at them."

"Was he like that when you guys were in the service?" Larry grunted and gave a sad smile. "No, not really. He was serious, but he was never much of a worrier. He usually left that to me. He's been through a lot, even before things fell apart."

"Yeah," Miles replied, then trailed off for a moment.

"Thanks for picking up those noise complaints. You'd think with me being Town Marshal and all they'd let me pick my own secretary."

Larry snorted. "You and I both know that she's Norma's eyes in the station. But, let's be honest. Of all the career paths available for those of us around here, which would you rather have Jaid in? You think she'd volunteer to work in the cafeteria, or stand a post on the wall?"

Miles barked a laugh. "Yeah, no. It was bad enough having her be a babysitter back in the day, and that was with Martha riding herd on her."

"It could be worse, she could actively dislike you instead of being aggressively interested."

"You are an evil, evil man. Especially considering I'm married to your daughter."

Larry laughed. "What can I say? I need all the entertainment I can get. Watching you squirm under the attention of our secretary qualifies."

Miles shook his head. "I don't think Tish would be quite as amused, Pops." He shrugged. "Who knows, maybe Jaid will get the point that I'm married and not interested. It's not like there's a shortage of guys around who wouldn't jump at the chance." He glanced around. A crew was working in front of one of the storage silos, and a few folks were walking toward the school along with them. None of them were close enough to overhear. "Anyway, on a more serious note — that thing we talked about last week? I talked to him, and he went for it. When the salvage crew comes we should have a better line on where all the garbage is coming from."

Larry shook his head and sighed. "Ain't a thing new under the sun. Sure as we've got drunks stumbling out of Tom's bar every night, there will be folks that take it to the extreme. This area was a hotbed for meth abuse before the dead started chowing down on the living; why should it change? We can talk till we're blue in the face about the dangers of drugs. That doesn't change the fact your wife and Doc Scott have the coma patients in the clinic. You and I both know we turn a blind eye to the few funny-looking plants in some of the greenhouses. But that's because pot's useful for other things than smoking. If you'd told me ten years ago I'd be taking this sort of attitude about drugs, I'd have laughed myself silly. There was no place for it in the service, but let's be honest, this ain't the service."

"Funny enough, they issued meth to soldiers in World War Two. Well, the Nazis, anyway."

"That's not funny at all, history boy. Besides, the Nazis lost."

"Exactly. The last thing we need is for somebody to freak out and start ringing a dinner bell for those things out there." He sighed. "It's bad enough with alcohol, but at least most of our people just get sad and quiet when they drink."

"You don't have to convince me." Larry pulled some slips of paper out of his pocket and waved them. "Just you wait. I think one of these noise complaints is promising. We might get a line on who our Jesse and Earl are."

"Jesse and *Walt*, Pops. I know we've got those disks, don't tell me you forgot the names of the characters already."

"Well, like you said — I *am* getting old," Larry grinned. "And you *are* going to be paying for that remark for a while, don't you worry." He waved a hand as they approached the side entrance to the old equipment barn. A tall, slender figure stood outside and leaned against the metal wall with the door propped open.

"It's about time you showed up, Trina Matthews!" the slender woman said. "I thought you were skipping school today."

Miles' daughter turned, favored him with a goodbye kiss, and scampered inside the door. Larry leaned in and gave Val McKee a quick hug. "You doing all right, girl?"

"Can't complain, Mister Larry, can't complain. Howdy, Miles."

Miles smiled; he couldn't help it, Miss McKee was just someone you liked. She could go from stereotypical school teacher to mother bear at the drop of a hat. The few children in the community that hadn't been born inside of it were there because of Valerie McKee.

When Miles and a few others had realized that there were survivors in the local elementary school, they'd gone in with guns blazing. They saved the day, but the tall, slender woman in front of them had ensured that there were children left to save. Her frail appearance was misleading. A tipsy Larry had said it best, not long after the rescue. "Val McKee survived the zombie apocalypse because she brooks no nonsense." Coming from a retired Marine Gunnery Sergeant, it was the highest of praise. "Hey, Val."

The interior of the converted building was bustling. Half of the room featured rows of tables and a serving line. During town halls, they dragged a podium out into the middle of the room. Low conversation and the clink of silverware filled the air. The servers and diners plowed through breakfast, and Miles was glad he'd eaten at home. It smelled particularly unappealing today. The other half of the room served as a school; colorful mats lay on the concrete floor. Rows of shelving filled with salvaged books, movies, toys, and games defined the borders. As Miles watched, Trina slipped her shoes off at the edge of the mats and scampered into the classroom area. There were perhaps twenty kids and around that many adults. Most of the adults sat on the mats and stared off into space. The children playing and moving past the sitting adults elicited little reaction. A few had distant smiles on their faces as they watched the children burn off energy before school started. Miles took a moment to watch the scene, then glanced at his daughter's teacher.

"This is safe, right, Val? You'd tell me if there were concerns, right?"

She gave Miles a sad smile. "It's okay. It's good for the older kids, too, Miles. Sometimes I think Trina is one of the lucky ones. She was born after the worst of it — she doesn't have the same memories as some of my first kids."

Across the room, Trina climbed into the lap of a kind-faced woman in her mid-40s. Her eyes remained fixed on some unseen point front of her, and she began to rock from side to side. As she hugged Miles' daughter, her lips began to move, forming the words to a silent song. Trina smiled at Miles and Larry as she rubbed the arm of the woman holding her.

Val followed their eyes. "Betty doesn't talk, but when your daughter's around she *sings*, Miles. It's not perfect, but it's what we have."

Miles shrugged. "That's our world now, isn't it?" He turned to leave but turned back after a moment. "Val, does Trina ever laugh in class?"

She hesitated. "Not as much, but she's happy, Miles. She's a real leader, too. Likes to stick up for others." She glanced over at Larry and winked. "Reminds me of a few guys I know." Val turned and studied the classroom for a long moment. "I'll be the first to admit that this is unconventional, but I think it's helping. I really do. Some of us just dealt with Z-Day better than others. Give them time. They'll come back. Charlie did."

Chapter 2

The silent man knelt in the driveway as he studied the house.

At one time it had been a brilliant white. After eight years without maintenance, the paint was closer to dirty dishwater than eggshell. The external appearance was of little concern to the silent man. His intent eyes flickered from window to window. He assessed the condition of each in turn and studied the faded drapes behind with just a bit less interest. The contents were far more valuable than the structure.

The front door was a solid, albeit weather-worn slab of wood. The shine of the brass doorknob and lockset was dull but remained intact. He had yet to determine whether the house remained occupied, but it was secure outside.

Crunching noises shattered the silence. The sound announced the presence of two men as each walked around a different side of the house. They wore heavy canvas overalls and leather jackets despite the hint of spring in the air. Heavy boots and leather gloves capped their extremities. Like the home, their clothing showed the wear of long years.

The silent man's own clothing was similar enough to that of the other men to consider it a uniform. His own hands were bare, and he carried a Bowie knife in a scabbard strapped to his left leg. Vivid red scars encircled his right hand, twisting around his palms and down his fingers. The damage to his pinkie was such that it hung at an angle. The digit was stiff, unyielding, and almost completely sheathed in scar tissue.

Despite the scars, he flexed and released the fingers on his right hand. It was a habit gained in physical therapy intended to maintain dexterity. By now, he'd been doing it so long it was an unconscious reflex — almost a nervous tic.

The two newcomers flanked the silent man and crouched down. He glanced at each in turn and cocked his head to one side in a silent query.

The larger of the two spoke. He was a balding, well-tanned man with a salt and pepper beard that spilled over the open collar of his jacket. He towered over each of his compatriots and weighed more than the two of them combined. Not much of it was fat — his build was more wall than pear.

"The back door's shut and all the ground floor windows are tight on my side. Corey?"

The other man, younger and clean-shaven under a mop of sandy blond hair, nodded in agreement, "It was tight on my side, too."

The silent man considered this for a moment and then gave a slow nod. He raised his eyes to the second story of the house. Finally, he turned to look at the larger of his two companions. The silent man swept his hand across the lawn, indicating the knee-high grass. It had risen after months of compression under snowdrifts.

"No tracks. No crawl trails, either," Dalton offered.

The silent man gave a faint smile. Like the younger man, he was clean-shaven, but he had a lined face that seemed inclined to dourness. The addition of a smile to his expression made him look more melancholy than amused.

He gave the big man a pointed look and then jabbed a finger at Corey. Dalton showed bright white teeth in the graying forest of his beard. His own expression was much more on the cheery side, giving him the air of a maniacal Santa Claus by way of Harley Davidson.

"All right. Kid, did you check for crawl trails?"

Corey bristled, as though the concept of the question itself insulted him. "Seriously? Come on, Dalton. This ain't my first rodeo." He looked to the silent man, who cocked his head and made a 'go on' motion. "Yes, I checked. How long are you guys going to keep up this 'haze the new guy' garbage?"

Dalton grinned again. "Don't get prickly, kid. Just checking your eyes and what's between your ears. The Wild doesn't have much forgiveness in it. Best to learn that before you have to face real consequences." He turned and regarded the area surrounding the house. Before Z-Day, it had been a high-end subdivision with a dozen Craftsman-style homes. Each home lay on the outer side of a circular lane. Inside the circle was a decorative pond. The flowers and landscaping around it were overgrown with weeds after years of neglect. In a way, the overgrown roses and perennials still held a raw beauty worthy of appreciation. The stench of rotting flesh from something half-submerged in the pond forced any study to be a quick one, though.

A heavy wooden fence surrounded the entire addition. Despite the years of neglect, it stood straight and firm. The solid construction was a good omen for the construction quality of the homes. A thick forested area sat outside the fence at the back end of the development and overgrown cornfields flanked either side. The surrounding greenery lent the area a secretive hush and absorbed any echoes.

A low, decorative stone wall held down the addition's southern border. That wall transitioned to the more conventional, and taller, board fence at either corner. The faded white house was the first home on the left, and close enough to the stone wall to use it as a fence on that side.

"You're good, kid, but not so good you don't have things to learn. If you don't want to listen, that's fine. No hard feelings, you can find another crew or another line of work."

Corey considered the older man's comment and nodded. "I'm listening."

"It's hard to pick up tracks on a paved road, but biters tend to wander. We can see by the lack of trails or tracks that there ain't any in here moving about, at least not recently. The grass is your friend, so use it." Dalton jerked a thumb over his shoulder. "Our ride will keep it that way long enough for us to pack up and boogie." The decorative stone wall lacked a gate, but the faded yellow school bus parked across the drive blocked access to the road. The low wall wasn't tall enough to serve as a long-term barrier. It *would* serve as an effective temporary blockade if biters outside the perimeter discovered them, though.

"This place is creepy as hell," Corey murmured. "It's like nothing ever happened here. Where are all the people?"

The bigger man grunted. "Flu put a lot of people down before things fell apart, kid." Corey had been just shy of nine years old on Z-Day and presumably occupied with other things than the news. He nodded in understanding, and Dalton continued.

"They're still here, more than likely. Keep quiet and hope they don't realize that *we're* here before we get a chance to work our way around the block. Keep your head on a swivel and don't get too comfortable. Things have a way of biting you in the ass — hah! — if you aren't paying attention. Just move slow and do what we tell you to do. You'll be fine. This is the best job around, anymore. Definitely beats —" The silent man cut off Dalton's speech with a sudden, authoritative wave of his hand. The big man nodded and turned back to Corey. "That's it then, kid. Start fetching totes — Charlie's going in."

The hinges gave a muted squeak as Charlie opened the door. With one ear aimed inside the house, he tucked the lock release gun into an inside pocket of his leather jacket. It was amazing what one could find in the back of an abandoned police cruiser.

He turned to Dalton. The big man leaned against the house to one side of the door. Charlie nodded, and Dalton handed him a pistol with a small flashlight clamped under the barrel. The rifle that Charlie had been carrying was already slung over the big man's shoulder. It was too long and bulky to maneuver in close quarters.

He inspected the action of the handgun with the familiarity that only comes from long practice. Satisfied, he withdrew a black cylinder from another pocket on the inside of his jacket and screwed it onto the pistol's threaded barrel.

In a world bereft of machinery, other sources of unnatural noise like a gunshot could carry for miles. Like

Dalton had told Corey, this was about taking their time. The longer they went without discovery, the more salvage they could claim.

He took a moment to ensure that the sound suppressor was secure and nodded to the other men. He stepped inside and closed the door.

As expected, the house was well-built and remained tight. In a way that was both good and bad. Charlie had lost count of the number of homes he'd searched in the last few years. Some held up while others leaked like crazy. He'd walked through homes with shattered windows, broken pipes, and collapsed roofs. He'd picked his way through jungles of mold and rot, and scenes of long-past horror. Such was a scavenger's life; anything to keep the community going.

The search wasn't so critical now. They were self-sufficient — anything the salvage teams found now was a luxury. Alcohol, books, canned food, and spices had become ancient artifacts. These were the treasures of the new age.

The art to the science of what the salvage teams did lay in knowing what lasted and what didn't. Beer was almost always a lost cause; soda was iffy also. Canned foods, even past the expiration date, were fine if they weren't bulging or rusty. The items with the most utility tended toward small and compact — soap, hygiene products, vacuum-sealed dry food, and bottled water. Thus, the totes outside.

The dry food, in particular, required careful inspection for rodent damage. If the house was tight, it was generally good. Hard liquors and wine in bottles were always worth scavenging, and usually worth quite a bit in trade. A cattle farmer named Tom Oliver was running a pretty brisk business with the community's first bar and grill. He was still working out the kinks in his home brew beer, so 'real' alcohol was always appreciated to fill in the gaps.

Books, audio disks, and movies they took without question. Given that these articles didn't last forever, even duplicates were something to cherish. They enforced gentle care with an almost manic fervor, but wear was unavoidable. Paperbacks, in particular, tended to be a bit creaky at their age. The binding was already falling apart on many of the items in their library. There had been idle talk of starting a print shop to salvage, bind, or even reprint damaged books. It was a pipe dream for now — none of the survivors had any real experience in that line of work.

Charlie was particularly fond of books. While this house was a great environment for books to endure, that usually meant things deadlier than books had also endured.

The living room was clear. All that his flashlight revealed was dust-covered furniture and a long-cold fireplace. He strode across the room and pulled the curtains open to let more light in. Dalton and Corey were still hauling armloads of storage totes across the lawn.

Charlie turned and studied the layout of the room. The bottom floor was open concept. The back wall led to the dining and kitchen area while a short hallway off of the entryway led to a pair of closed doors. He guessed they were most likely the garage and a closet or powder room. A staircase bifurcated the lower floors and led to the second-floor landing.

When in doubt, take the path of least resistance.

With slow, careful steps, he reached the end of the short hallway and placed an ear against the first door. Silence.

Charlie stood motionless for half a minute before reaching down and testing the doorknob. It turned without resistance. He paused again, turned the knob, and pushed on the door.

The beam of the flashlight revealed a well-appointed garage. A bright red minivan sitting on four flat tires occupied one of the two slots. A workbench, tools, and various clutter filled the rest of the space. There looked to be some interesting material inside, but Charlie didn't move. He swept the beam of the flashlight across the breadth of the garage with his free hand tight on the doorknob.

Nothing stirred save for the motes of dust that danced in the beam.

Charlie pulled back and cocked his head to one side. He lowered the pistol and tapped the sleeve of the sound suppressor on the door jamb. Knock. Knock. Knock.
Silence.

He nodded to himself in silent satisfaction and eased the door shut. Reaching inside of his jacket, he withdrew a Magic Marker from an inner pocket. He removed the cap and drew a large black circle on the door for Dalton and Corey's reference. He'd hammered into them that his marks were not holy writ, so they'd still proceed with caution. But generally, such a mark indicated the room was clear for them to salvage.

After sitting so long, the cars they found were no longer drivable, but they did merit some attention. During salvage, they retrieved the vehicle registration forms from the vehicles and stored them.

Back home, a database of found vehicles provided a listing for potential repair parts. While it was rare to find an exact match, many manufacturers used common parts across product lines. The community's vehicles, for the most part, tended to be diesel as they could run on biofuels and oils. Those had been a minority before Z-Day, which made the ongoing search for parts critical. If they couldn't find an exact match, they could usually make it work with shade tree engineering.

As needed, a specialized salvage crew would descend on garages and strip needed components. They relied on crews like Charlie's to catalog details. But most important, they depended on the teams to ensure that interior spaces were clear.

Once Charlie and his team stripped everything of value from the room, they'd slash an 'X' through the circle. This saved them the time of looking through rooms that were already scavenged.

He turned and gave the opposite door a cursory study. This door hinged outward, which called for a different clearance method. He wedged one boot in front of the door and eased it open. If anyone or anything attempted to rush out, his foot would stop the door and give him time to recover.

Nothing rushed him, and the flashlight revealed nothing save for a dry toilet bowl and a pedestal sink. He settled the beam on an opened package of Charmin on the floor between the two. He made a subtle, almost satisfied grunt. A tight house meant no mice or critters inside, which meant nothing digging through the goods. After eight years, toilet paper was a luxury like none other, right up there with tampons and ammo.

Door closed, circle.

He considered his next move. Some of the other teams, he knew, would consider the ground floor cleared and move on to the second. Charlie was more exacting. You never knew where a person would try and hide, especially if bitten. He'd once opened a pantry door to find a biter crammed inside, unable to escape. Rare, perhaps, but the margin for mistakes wasn't what it had been in the old days.

So — kitchen it was.

Like the rest of the first floor, it was open-concept, with a single mass of tile across the kitchen and dining room. A desk sat in one corner with a halo of envelopes surrounding a closed and long-dormant notebook computer. Beneath the desk, Charlie took note of a ten-ream box of paper and grunted in satisfaction. Paper was always a good find. It was typical to find at least a few homeowners who had worked from home in these nicer additions. Pens, pencils, markers — all went into the totes and onto the bus. Their electrical grid was too inconsistent to run larger desktops, but Charlie and his men scrounged every laptop and tablet they found. They'd been doing this long enough that there was a plentiful stock of power adapters, so even if they couldn't find every accessory there was a reasonable chance they'd be able to power the devices up. In a worst case scenario, laptops were still good for parts.

There were dirty dishes in the sink, but time and the dry air had reduced whatever had stained them into dust. Plates were too bulky and common to be a major need, so he ignored them as he went through the cabinets one-by-one. Salt, pepper, and spices were a highlight, as were a few bulk packs of Kraft macaroni and cheese still sealed in the plastic wrap. It tasted pretty awful with powdered milk and no butter, but the younger kids seemed to like it.

They aren't old enough to know the difference.

As was typical, there wasn't a huge stock in the kitchen. Too many people before Z-Day had made frequent trips to the grocery, with large stockpiles mocked as paranoid.

What was that show, about the preppers? Sheila . . .

His hand froze as he reached out to the next cabinet door. That was a bad mental window to look through during the best of times, never mind in the middle of a run. He spoke for the first time, and his voice was harsh in his ears, like two stones rubbing against one another. "Focus," Charlie managed. The word came forth with a Herculean effort that testified to his reasoning for keeping quiet. Speaking was hard, it *hurt*, and he'd lost the capacity for whispering as well.

His voice carried, and from above, he heard a noise as something shifted in response to the stimulus.

The creak of the ceiling and his self-admonishment were more than enough to bring him back on track.

There you are. I wondered when you'd come say hello.

Charlie turned away from the kitchen and moved back to the living room. He turned to face the staircase and waited.

The noise came again as something moved above, the floor joists making their slow creak of complaint.

He waited across the space of a dozen heartbeats and then stepped forward to place his foot on the first step. He kept his foot on the outside edge. The treads should be tighter over the nail, quieting his steps. Charlie's eyes remained on the landing. He cradled the pistol in a secure, two-handed grip and kept the barrel low with his finger off of the trigger. Survivors were rare, but they did find them from time to time. It wouldn't do to shoot one in the darkness just because he thought they were something else.

Another step. The stair gave a squeak of complaint under his weight, and the rustling ahead grew more insistent. The pitch remained the same, though, as though it weren't coming any closer. Charlie refused to let himself relax.

His head crested the landing. Gloom shrouded the second floor. There was a vague slice of light ahead of him, coming from an open door at the end of the hall. He could see just enough to give him the idea that he was looking into the master bedroom. Again, the noise, and this time he could tell that it originated from that room.

A few more steps and he stood on the landing. The short hallway ahead of him had closed doors on either side along with the open door. Based on the different color and decor he guessed they belonged to children of each gender. He took a few steps forward, just in front of the closed doors and studied the entrance. With his eyes there, he tapped the doors on either side of the hallway with a knuckle.

On either side, silence. Ahead of him, noise.

Good enough.

Charlie stepped forward, quicker now. He raised the pistol as he went. The entrance to the master turned right. He eased inside and rotated, sweeping the bedroom in front of him with the pistol light.

Dust floated in the beams of light coming in through the cracked curtains. There was more than enough illumination for a quick study of the room. A skeleton in sweatpants and a white t-shirt lay on a king-sized bed in a corona of used tissues. He'd kicked the covers off before dying, and the remnants of his rot stained the sheets below him. All that otherwise remained were the bones and a faint, sharp stench.

The biter lay on the floor in front of the bed. She was wearing nurse's scrubs, stained here and there with what might have been blood. Had she turned sometime after the man in the bed had died, and never left? Was she bitten at work, making it home only to die there? Charlie would never know the story of this house in full, though he could make guesses.

In undeath, she'd walked, across the width and breadth of the bedroom, from window to window. Whatever sounds she'd heard outside had drawn her, though she was unable to do anything but watch. A worn track in the carpet testified to the literal march of time. Finally, she'd collapsed when the unknown force that drove her limbs failed. She saw Charlie now, though, and reached for him.

They didn't rot. They didn't die, either, but without food they wasted away. This biter was little more than a skeleton covered in desiccated skin the gray color of a storm sky.

Darker, almost black traces of veins marked that skin here and there. Its remaining muscle tissue was enough for slight, vague jerks of its limbs, as it tried to rise, to hunt. To feed.

For Charlie, the eyes were the worst part. The cornea and pupil were gone; the entire sclera had turned a silvery-gray. It was as though someone had installed stainless steel ball bearings in her orbital sockets. Though Charlie couldn't see where they were looking, he knew without a doubt that they focused on him with predatory intensity.

Charlie let the barrel of his pistol fall and flicked the switch to turn off the light. He regarded the figure on the floor for a moment, then sighed. He lay the pistol on the bed and moved to the side of the biter. Kneeling on the floor next to it, he placed a gentle hand on its forehead. The skin was cool and smooth, though dry. The thing tried to bite, but the strength of its neck muscles wasn't enough to drive past the gentle force Charlie applied to hold it to the ground. With his free hand, he slid his boot knife out of the scabbard and brought it forward. "I'm sorry," he rumbled.

His apology wasn't for the punch of the blade into a skull that should have lain still long ago nor was it for the ransacking of a home. This apology was for someone who wasn't even there. If there was anything left of the person that had been there before, perhaps she would understand, and carry that message with her, Charlie thought. If not, then no harm done. If in the end, it was for naught, perhaps it would be enough to help him sleep content in his own failings.

Chapter 3

From above, the influence of civilization on the landscape of the world was undeniable. The lines of roads and bridges and the checkerboard patterns of fields and lawns were still evident. But the years of neglect weighed heavy, and the wild reigned.

The last vestiges of mankind's final harvests lay choked in weeds or grasses. In the first year, unchecked by the hand of man, the deer population had exploded. In the years after, that population crashed. This came both from the loss of the surplus food supply and the ferocious culling conducted by their natural predators, who had experienced a population boom of their own.

That boom led to the migration of species that might not have happened in a world steered by the hand of man. For the first time in centuries, the wolf spread from the southern reaches of Canada and the northern rust belt and strode the ground of the Midwestern United States. The deer weren't as close to being extinct as mankind, but they huddled deep in the expanding forests all the same. Their freedom of movement saved them; with few left to care for them, mankind's herd populations starved to death in their pens, or provided easy meat for the resurgent predators.

Roads buckled and cracked, undone by the heat of summer, the cold of winter, and the methodical spread of tree roots. Bridges fell — washed out or collapsing under their own weight as support structures rusted.

Here and there, mankind endured. But more often than not, civilization was reduced to areas that could support walls.

Like the pioneers before them, they faced a world outside their door that was neither of their own creation nor friendly to their continued survival.

The southern fence wasn't much to look at compared to the rest of the perimeter. It consisted of cemented, eight-foot steel posts placed at regular intervals. It had taken two layers of chain link to span the entire height. A stabilizing bar interleaved the upper and lower sections, and twisted wire every few inches kept the assembly together. It looked impressive, but it wasn't the community's first line of defense.

The real defense was in the creek.

After centuries of ongoing erosion, the creek sat eight feet below the surrounding pasture. The banks held a near-vertical slope, and only intermittent growths of weeds sprouted from the damp earth. Footing was uncertain at the best of times, and chunks of the bank slipped into the creek with every rain. The rock formations that had given Stone Creek its name were long quarried. All that remained was thick, viscous clay.

Alex Worthington knew none of these facts on an intellectual level. His understanding was one that came from long hours of contemplation and consideration. The fence sat far enough from the edge of the creek that it wasn't susceptible to ongoing erosion. This created a viewing angle that blocked any inspection of either bank from ground level. All he got from his position behind the fence was the vague sense of a slight depression in the ground.

To the east and west, the creek meandered back and forth. This provided scant glances down into the depths when he chose to make the study. Once or twice he'd had the urge to scale the fence for a closer look, but he'd been able to resist it. His current position was familiar and comfortable. The wall guards would see him in short order on top of the fence, though that was a reason he'd never admit to himself. Teenage bravado refused to allow it.

He was short for 12-going-on-13; skinny, dark of hair, and tanned beechnut brown. He wore dark brown hiking boots, a pair of often-patched jeans, and a faded Captain America T-shirt. The stock of the .22-caliber rifle lying across his legs was just a bit less worn than its owner. Despite the wear, the rifle was well-tended and completely functional.

Defiant of the slight chill in the air, Alex sat with crossed legs on the ground just behind the fence. He conducted a silent assessment of the pasture on the other side. The only clue to his focus was the restless motion of his eyes as they flickered back and forth in a narrow arc. The grass around him stirred in the wind.

At once, a new, almost furtive sound came from across the creek. It was different enough from the whisper of grass on grass to bring a smirk of recognition to Alex's face. He stuck a pair of fingers in his mouth and whistled. The noise shifted in response, moving from a slow whisk-whisk to a rapid shuffle.

One could almost say that the noise sounded *excited*.

The crest of a balding head rose up behind a hillock on the opposite bank. Many of the bald patches went to the bone, and all was the gray of dirty dishwater rather than the expected white.

The grown-ups had all sorts of names for the gray people surrounding them, but Alex preferred his own. He'd been too young for zombie movies on Z-Day. Biter had just never made sense to him, so he went with his own appellation.

Alex opened his mouth and called out, "Come and get it, creep! Bring any friends?"

The noise struck the creep like a lightning bolt. He wasn't a moaner, which was too bad. That made sense; as he crested the rise Alex spotted the torn-out gouges in the thing's neck. It was a wonder it was still up and at it given the size of that freaking hole. Alex marveled at the dimensions of it. Anything the creep swallowed had a better than 50-50 shot of just plopping out onto the ground. And, he noted, as the thing came into view, there were — *whew!* — still a vestige of pants on it, though exposure to the elements had left them shredded and rotten. Looking at creep junk was pretty much the only thing that made him feel in any way queasy.

Alex shouldered the .22 and lined up the sights on the creep's forehead. It was an easy shot, maybe 30 feet, but the rounds were small and took just the right placement to do the deed. He forced his excitement down and squeezed the trigger.

The .22 cracked, and almost immediately a slash opened up on the creep's left cheek. There was no blood, but the wound revealed whitish-gray bone and a few upper teeth.

Faint, silvery lines coated the revealed flesh. There was no blood, but then again, he hadn't expected any.

"Damn it!" he hissed, quick and under his breath. Despite the adolescent thrill that ran through him at the use of the forbidden word, he still couldn't bring himself to use a normal speaking tone.

He adjusted his aim, compensating for the slight jerk of the creep's head with each step. It must have been stumbling forward on a broken ankle. It walked like the drunks that spilled out of Tom Oliver's pub every night at closing time. Another crack and this time there was a solid pock of impact. The creep's head jerked again, and then again and again as the 40-grain bullet did a ricochet jitterbug inside of its skull and pulverized the remnants of its brain. Strings cut, it collapsed to one side.

Lowering the rifle, Alex stifled a grin and cocked his head to one side, listening. All was quiet save for the whisper of grass. "Damn it," he muttered again. It must have been a loner. If there had been any others, the cracks of the gunshots would have brought them in. He settled down and prepared for the wait.

Behind him came a slow, soft clapping. Alex jerked to his feet and just avoided tangling his legs up in the rifle. He spun around.

As his luck would have it, Larry Vance and Miles Matthews were strolling up the path from the gravel road that paralleled the fence. The older, bigger man had a half-smile on his face as he headed in Alex's direction. The younger man – the town marshal, he reminded himself, whatever the hell that was – looked more serious, and had his hands tucked into the pockets of his Carhartt jacket.

"Correct me if I'm wrong, Mister Worthington," Larry boomed, "but isn't today a school day?"

Alex shrugged. Mr. Vance was a larger than life figure in the eyes of the youngest members of the community. One of the earliest memories Alex had was of Mr. Vance and his friends making their way into the school and taking Miss McKee and the children to safety out of the classroom the teacher had barricaded them in. He couldn't remember his mom and dad, but he remembered Larry Vance shooting anything and everything that staggered toward his preschool class.

It had been like, well, Captain America saving the day.

Then again, superheroes weren't real, were they? The monsters had been and still were.

"It's stupid," Alex said finally. He turned back to the fence and waved his hand. "What does algebra have to do with this?" He looked back at the men and tried not to sneer.

Larry glanced at Miles and shrugged. "You have any input, son? Can't say math was ever my strong suit."

Miles grimaced, and Alex watched the town marshal study him for a long moment. "Maybe you're right, kid," he said, and Alex's jaw dropped in surprise. "They don't care about algebra if I had to make a guess. Don't care about much of anything, if they even have any concept of the notion. But that's not the point."

"So what is?" Alex demanded. "X minus 10 equals whatever — who gives a crap?"

Miles smiled this time. "It's not about the Wild, Alex. Pretty soon all of this will be over. Pretty soon, we might not even need fences."

Alex frowned as he considered it.

Miles continued after giving him a moment to mull it over. "Don't get me wrong, some of the folks in town won't take too kindly to not having fences. If I had to guess, there will always be something. Even if it's to help make people feel at ease. But . . ." he trailed off. "You guys ever learn about the Dark Ages?"

Alex shrugged. "I don't know. I don't like history."

"Here's the thing – civilization took a pretty big hit on Z-Day. At some point, we'll be able to move forward in some form or fashion. But what Larry, and Miss McKee, and guys like me have to remember is that we have to keep you younger kids – no, younger *people* – in the loop. If we have a chance to survive long-term it's going to fall on your shoulders. So we have to make sure that you have an understanding of how things work, of how to survive for a time when we're not around. That way, when *you* have kids, there will be more to their lives than scratching in the dirt for subsistence. Art, science, industrial farming methods – and yeah, algebra, those are tools for tomorrow. You may not see the need for them *now*, but trust me, they'll come in handy someday."

Alex rolled his eyes. "If you say so; I don't even remember half the stuff the other kids talk about."

The marshal looked at him for a long moment, and then finally said. "Tell you what; I'll make you a deal. You quit cutting class and popping zoms on the sly, and I'll talk to Pete about letting you up in the Crow's nest. You can get a little bit better idea about what we have around here." He nodded toward the unmoving creep on the other side of the fence. "Lecture over, but I have one question – why do you think we don't have folks out doing what you were doing right here?"

Alex opened his mouth, and then closed it. For a long moment, he didn't know what to say. Why *didn't* they have people out on the flanks taking care of roamers? It would make things easier on the scavenging parties. They already had machine guns up in several locations to protect against hordes. What made this different? Finally, he said, "I don't know." The admission was only a little embarrassing.

"You're too young to remember, but after the end, when the Air Force took out the bridges, we thought we were golden. Yeah, it stunk, because it cut us off from a lot of potential salvage, but that was something we could work around. So for a while, we didn't have a care in the world. Our noise carried, and yeah, those bridges were out, but it didn't take long for zoms to start stacking up. After a while, they walked right across piles of their own fallen to get to us. The walls weren't as tough as they are now, and we lost a lot of good people." Alex opened his mouth to say something, but Miles cut him off. "Don't apologize, it's all right. We have scouting parties that conduct frequent checks of the creeks, but they use hand weapons to keep things quiet. Your rifle isn't that big of a deal, but gunfire still attracts them — even if it takes a while. That's why we made this little detour on our way to . . . well, something else. It was on the way, and we knew somebody had been up to something." Miles stepped closer to Alex and knelt so that their eyes were on the same level. "So, what do you think? We have a deal? Can you try it my way?"

Alex thought about it. Trade some algebra for getting a chance to climb up into the Crow's Nest and meet *the* Pete Matthews? Oh, yeah. *So* worth it. He stuck out a hand. "Deal."

The grain bins towered over the rest of the settlement. Three of them were of a like size, just under six stories in height. The trio clustered around the final bin, which was both larger in diameter and almost twice as tall. Auger pipes and catwalks ran from the large bin to the smaller in spider-web fashion. This allowed an inspection to begin at any of the bins and move over to any of the others. The original agricultural contents were long exhausted, but the empty space was still useful.

They'd converted one of the smaller bins into secure backup housing. The interiors weren't much; several stories of stark space constructed out of lumber with I-beam cross members. This was enough room to hold the entire population of the settlement inside on a short-term basis. There would be nothing in the way of privacy, sleeping room, or restroom space, but it was zombie proof.

The only exposed entrance was accessible at the top of the tower, just off of one of the catwalks. Recognizing that they might face other, more intelligent enemies, the survivors had taken further precautions. They'd welded covers to the bottom of the safety cages halfway up the ladders on the side of each bin. The theory was that the last person up the ladder could pull up the cover behind them and secure it from within. It was possible to climb up the safety cage. The survivor who'd designed the covers had deemed that would take 'more bloody balls than brains.' Even so, it would be slow going, and simplify defense from above.

The remaining bins served for general storage and warehousing. Crews sorted scavenged goods from the outside world and stored them in a semi-organized fashion. The settlement had some access to electricity via scavenged solar panels and wind turbines. It wasn't enough for a true grid, but it was enough to provide power for a small hospital and freezers. Insulation around the freezers reduced the power load and created a large cold room. This space provided long-term storage for perishables. In the fall, the cold room burst at the seams with fruits, vegetables, and meat. By early spring, much of that excess was a distant memory.

That lack of food was the reason for re-purposing structures rather than building more efficient ones. The ground space on the interior of the fences was more valuable as gardens and farm fields. If anything they should have been tearing buildings down, but so far they'd found a use for them. They'd built cabins in some areas poorly suited for growing. Those in charge of farming had raised a fuss about even those small encroachments.

It would have been a colossal pain to haul everything up to the top of the warehouse with mere muscle power. As such, the survivors had cut large openings into the base of each of the warehouse silos. Only one of these openings was convenient to the outdoors. The other openings oriented toward the other silos. They'd poured intervening walkways of concrete, then walled and roofed them with heavy timbers and layers of sheet metal. The heavy construction of these covered hallways was, if possible, more robust than that of the silos themselves.

This was only one aspect of the security-consciousness that had gone into the design. Heavy, barred gates sheathed in more sheet metal capped each opening. In the event of a breach of a hallway, doors at either end could secure the breach. For now, though, they were convenient pathways to move supplies between storage rooms. While the silo improvements were impressive, the survivors' final construction project was far more ambitious. The survivor's referred to it in hushed tones as 'the Crow's nest.'

For Pete Matthews – the Crow – it was home.

The Crow's nest was a circular platform centered over the rounded top of the tallest bin. It had a peaked roof sheathed in rippled aluminum, though the sides were completely exposed to the elements. Welded steel pipe formed a short railing all the way around, with larger pipes ascending at the cardinal points and center to support the roof.

The floor of the platform was open and planked in wood. An access hatch offset from the center support led to a ladder that traversed the curve of the grain bin's dome and intercepted the catwalk.

An old Army cot, metal folding chairs, workbench, and a propane heater were arranged around the rest of the center support.

At the moment, three figures stood under the roof while one sat in a wheelchair. Each looked outward, in different directions.

This high up, the wind was brisk, but not so brisk that the quiet murmur of one of the observers was inaudible. "Contact northwest."

The seated observer turned his chair and raised his binoculars. "You are correct, young lady," Pete Matthews said after a moment. He lowered the binoculars and examined each of the standing observers in turn. None of them were far into their teens, and they were there for a reason just as important as observation.

Up in the Crow's nest, class was in session.

"Range," Pete muttered as he rolled next to the observer who'd spotted the movement. He set the brakes on his wheelchair.

The speaker was a petite, slender girl with a freckled face and brilliant green eyes. In the end, those eyes were all that mattered – to get up here, the Crow only took the best.

The girl looked out again, studied the terrain, and then commented.

"1000 yards? It's between the bent tree and the rusty gate."

Pete examined the girl's sector once again and nodded once in affirmation. "Good eyes, Cara." He paused for a moment of consideration. "Vinnie? Drop at 1000 yards. Three-three-eight."

The boy rubbed his chin for a moment. "Two hundred sixty-two inches. But it's a trick question, sir, you're zeroed at a thousand on the Savage."

Pete barked a short burst of laughter. "Right you are. Grab it for me."

Vinnie grinned and grabbed a rifle that was almost as tall as he was from where it leaned against the rail. With slow, careful steps he brought it to the Crow. There was a reverent sense to his movements, as though he carried something priceless and irreplaceable.

That's not all that far from the truth, Pete thought.

He shouldered the Savage 110. They'd modified a bipod to rest on the guardrail, which worked quite well with Pete's sitting height in the chair. The rails would be knee-high to anyone of a normal height. This made the selection of sharp-eyed, shorter youngsters for the training class even more fortuitous. Anyone taller was at constant risk of tripping over and experiencing a ten-story fall.

On the bright side, heights didn't bother Pete much.

"Bruce," he said. "Wind?"

The third student was a bit taller than the rest, tan, athletic, and towheaded. A trio of scars ran down the side of his face and marred his otherwise handsome visage. The old wounds made Pete feel old. He could remember when they'd been cuts on the terrified child in his best friend's arms.

"No cross wind," Bruce said after a moment where he'd been studying flags hung every twenty feet or so on the perimeter fence. "Wind is at your back."

"Good," Pete agreed. He peered through the rifle's Leupold scope, and their visitor jumped into sharp focus. Without looking, he flipped the safety off. "You know what the big irony here is, kids?"

For a moment, none of his students said a word. Finally, Cara — always the bold one — said, "What's that, Captain?"

Pete offered them a crooked smile. "I've got five thousand dollars' worth of scope, rifle, and suppressor. I'm shooting five dollar bullets at a refugee from a zombie movie, and I'd trade it all for a cold Diet Pepsi." When there were no laughs, he muttered, "Tough crowd," and pulled the trigger. *Do they even remember dollars?*

Cara's zombie was in decent shape. Decent for values of eight years post Z-Day meant an intact shirt and pants, ragged shoes, and more than half of its flesh on the bone. Despite that, it moved with slow jerking steps that aimed it toward the settlement.

At this point, Pete didn't care what caused them to keep walking and eating. They were just targets in need of service. In the end, one of the best things about the Crow's nest was that it kept him out of the mess below. He'd once proclaimed to Larry that it was ironic that a people-hating grump such as himself should have to live so close to hundreds of useless examples of humanity.

Larry had laughed and laughed until Pete flipped him off.

As the trigger clicked home, everything worked to mechanical perfection. The trigger unlocked the hammer, which unleashed the tension of the firing pin. The pin struck the primer at the base of the cartridge. The impact detonated the primer and ignited the charge of gunpowder. The explosive gases created by the gunpowder expanded. The brass case that contained them channeled the force outward. This forced the mass of copper-jacketed lead to move in response to the building pressure behind it. The rifling cut into the barrel's interior lent it a twist as it moved forward. A blink of an eye later, the bullet left the barrel, rotating in space as it shot forward. The suppressor attached to the end of the barrel caught the expanding gas in a series of baffles. As the bullet exited the suppressor, the trapped and slowed gases followed. The resulting subdued noise was still audible at close range but the report was much reduced.

It's never as quiet as the movies, Pete mused as he watched the target through the scope. But it was better than the alternative. From this high up, anyone at ground level would hear next to nothing. He worked the action and chambered another round after the spent brass ejected. With his eye on the scope, he sensed rather than saw one of his students kneel to retrieve the brass. Later, they'd pop out the spent primer, resize and trim the case, and reload it.

Waste not, want not.

Meanwhile, the bullet shot forward at 3,000 feet per second. The pull of gravity acted upon it as it flew and changed its flight path from a straight line to a ballistic arc. Pete's point of aim, based on a straight line, would have been far above the target. The adjustments in the scope compensated for this drop; velocity did the rest.

Just shy of two seconds after Pete had pulled the trigger, the upper half of the zombie seemed to *explode*. The 250-

grain bullet struck it in the upper chest, and the bullet mushroomed as it slowed. Hydrostatic shock transmitted through desiccated flesh; a halo of bloodless meat blossomed in the air.

Separated from the spine, the head rolled in the air as it described a short arc that ended a few feet behind the staggering zombie. For a moment, as though unaware of what had happened, it took a step, lifted its foot to take another, and then fell to one side in a heap of lifeless meat. *Four* seconds after impact, they heard the vague *splat* sound, and the kids around Pete cheered.

Despite himself, he smiled. *I may not have my legs,* he thought, *but I'm sure as hell good for something.* Eye still to the scope, he grimaced as he saw the zombie's mouth and jaw working, despite the fact that it was no longer connected to the rest of the body. "All right, class," he muttered. "Let's see who can hit the leftovers. Vinnie? You want the first crack at it?"

After all, Pete mused as the teenager retrieved his own rifle and returned to the railing, *they* are *here to learn.*

Chapter 4

In life, the two zombies stumbling across the county road had probably run in different circles. The larger of the two, formerly male, wore the tattered remnants of bib overalls and a flannel shirt. His smaller partner — once female — had dressed for exercise. The yoga pants and top she wore had borne up to the ravages of time better than the big one's bibs. Score one for synthetic fabric, perhaps.

Despite any differences they may once have had, they stood united in a new cause. Feed. Propagate.

As one, they shuffled toward the source of the noises that had caught their attention. If they recognized the shape and color of the school bus blocking the way, they gave no external indication. It was merely an obstacle in their path. The drive to feed was implacable; they would seek an opening unless another opportunity presented itself. They were nothing if not patient.

A figure stepped out into the road in front of them. As one, their heads swiveled to study the new source of movement, but the presence of one of their own kind was not enough to dissuade them from their path toward the bus, and the sounds of life behind it.

The new figure was tall, bare of chest and foot, and clad in ragged khaki pants. If not for the pallor of its skin and the flat nothingness of its eyes, it could easily be mistaken for being alive. As the other two began to move past, the new figure raised a hand, palm-out, as though performing crossing guard duties.

An inaudible command passed, and the two fell to a stop. The new zombie eased forward and circled the pair. His flat gray eyes flickered across their bodies. The farmer was largely intact; the only wound on his body was a blackened bite mark on one forearm. His feet were clad in heavy work boots.

The exerciser was in far worse shape. A multitude of bites pockmarked the bare skin of her back. Her light running shoes had fallen to shreds, worn away by the passage of her feet over countless roads.

The new zombie came before them, decision made. Hand still up, it reached out and brought its palm close to the farmer's face. For a moment, the other zombie stood still, as though uncertain how to react, then it snapped into a more upright posture. Its head jerked slightly back and forth, as though it were a punching bag for a set of invisible fists. This continued for a moment, and then the farmer fell still. The new zombie lowered its arm, turned away from the tableau, and walked back into the woods across the road from the bus. With no hesitation, the farmer followed, and soon vanished into the undergrowth.

Left behind, the exerciser lacked the capacity to care.

Despite what had just happened, her goal remained clear, and she resumed her move toward the school bus.

Feed. Propagate.

Charlie stepped off of the porch and onto the grass as Corey and Dalton began to haul totes inside. The older man had been working with Charlie long enough to know the plan from front to back. It would take longer for Dalton to pause every so often to explain their methods to Corey, but that was all right. They had nothing if not time.

It might have been more efficient for Charlie to begin scouting the next house, but that violated one of his core rules. Unless necessary, he never went into an unknown space without backup. There was no guarantee that any other biters would be as emaciated and weak as the first one. They were, to his frustration, as different as the people they'd once been. Some wasted away to nothing, some hibernated, and others just walked from place to place until something caught their attention.

For that reason, Charlie remained outside while the others began assembling the salvage. Several teams had lost people in the past when the noise of a crew inside a home drew attention from outside. Charlie took a fierce pride in never having lost a team member. They'd had some close calls — usually due to rookie mistakes — but in the end, everyone had come home.

Satisfied that the others had everything squared away, Charlie slung his rifle over one shoulder and stuck his hands in the pockets of his coat. The wind was picking up, and despite the welcoming brightness of the sun, there was still a cold bite to the early spring air. He stepped forward, and if not for his weapons, he might have been a homeowner taking a morning stroll through the neighborhood.

He turned to move between the stone fence and the side of the house. He kept his eyes to the left as he went and surveyed the road. It remained clear, and he relaxed as he rounded the rear corner of the house and turned once more. The only fences in the addition were those around the perimeter, so the yards themselves were continuous. Charlie wondered if the people who had lived here had liked each other. Were there community cookouts, or groups of kids scampering through the yards?

Such thoughts always led to the wrong place, and he jerked his head to the side and tapped his knuckles on his temple. What had gone on before wasn't important; he needed to focus on the moment at hand. If not for the benefit of his own safety, then for that of Dalton and Corey.

The yard of this house was empty save for a pair of sagging lounge chairs. The waterproof finish hadn't stood up to the test of time. The wood was showing vague signs of rot while streaks of rust streamed down from the fasteners.

Charlie moved on.

The next house in line had a large play set with several slides, swings, and ladders to a second story. It was in almost as poor of shape as the lounge chairs, but as Charlie's eyes slid around the yard he saw something of greater concern.

A pair of large French doors led out of the rear of the second house onto a broad paved patio, but that wasn't what drew his attention. Past the doors, off what was likely the kitchen, was another door. And where the other rear doors remained shut, this door wasn't even in the frame — it lay, cracked and splintered, a few feet from the doorway. Half on the patio and half on the grass, it lay right next to the grill just outside the kitchen door. Charlie licked his lips and tried to will away his growing sense of worry.

Even in the best of times the biters couldn't break their way out of a house. It was one of the things that made his job so dangerous. A walking corpse too weak to break out a glass window on its own was going to be stuck inside until it gave up the ghost.

This was something different, though. How recent was this? He eased forward and slid the sling off of his shoulder as he moved. He gripped the rifle in both hands and clicked the safety off.

He hooked his toe under one corner of the door. A slight flex of his leg and the entire thing slid sideways. The part resting on the patio made a dull scraping sound, but he ignored the noise for the moment.

The strip of grass that had been under the door was a bright, healthy green, even though the weight had crushed it. This was recent, maybe even in the last couple of hours. Charlie raised his head and the rifle as one, aiming into the house. Some of the windows had the drapes drawn, but the interior of the kitchen was visible. Inside, nothing stirred.

He turned and noted for the first time a few slight divots in the grass just past where the door had landed. They looked, if anything, as though someone had landed on the sodden ground and left the impressions of their heels. Continuing the turn, he let his eyes follow the line described from the back door to the side fence. The grass rippled in the breeze, and he saw no evidence to show anything had walked across it in recent hours.

If the lawn had recovered, the smears of mud and grass on the fence remained to tell a different story. They began about a quarter of the way up and continued for the entire height of the fence.

As crazy as the idea was, it looked as though someone had run through wet grass and mud and scrambled over the fence.

That doesn't make sense.

If it had been a survivor, why make for the fence? Why not left or right, if evading pursuit? And if they'd fled, why wasn't there any sign of the pursuers? They hadn't left any tracks, and the part of the tile floor inside that Charlie could see was pristine. Nothing from outside had walked on it in years.

So — what? Someone blasts open the back door, does a long jump across an eight-foot concrete patio, and then climbs an even higher fence?

Charlie had seen some crazy shit since everything fell apart, but that was crazy with a cherry topping. There had to be a more rational explanation.

From behind him came the slapping sound of flesh on stone. Charlie spun and brought the barrel of his rifle around. When he saw the source of the noise, he barked a short laugh. This, at least, was something he could understand. A wandering member of the infected population had found them.

It had been a woman once, though most of her long hair had fallen out in clumps. The absence revealed leprous patches of graying skin or exposed areas of bone. The rest of the body wasn't much better. Though no wounds were immediately visible above the top of the fence, rotten scraps of cloth draped its shoulders.

Questing hands reached over the top of the stone fence, and one arm slapped down as she clawed at Charlie. Not for the first time, he wondered how well they could see out of the blank gray orbs their eyes had become. In this case, depth perception was not a strong suit, given that he was a good twenty feet outside of her range.

He put the rifle on safe and slung it back over his shoulder. "There you are," he rumbled, and ignored the pain in his throat. Charlie took one step closer, and then another. As though excited, both arms began to slap the top of the stone fence and her mouth opened wider than seemed possible. For a moment, Charlie imagined that he could hear the creak of tendons in her face.

The biters didn't make noise, of course — that was one thing the movies got wrong. It made logical sense considering there seemed to be no real need for them to breathe. Of course, there wasn't a logical reason for them to eat the uninfected, either. In that regard, Charlie had long since stopped questioning the reality of his situation. A typical corpse rotted away in around a month out in the open, so said the doctors, and here was a typical example of the infected. It was doing just fine after dozens of months.

The docs had also had noted that once killed, they rotted away at an accelerated rate. Whatever it was that kept them going was staving off decay, somehow. In the early days, they'd smelled of excrement and blood, but years of exposure to the elements had washed the stench away. The lack of decay meant that the older ones didn't smell at all, which made them all the more dangerous — quiet, odorless, and unwavering.

Charlie moved closer, pausing after each step. "Beautiful day today," he murmured. "Was a long winter."

The biter's teeth clicked together as she strained over the top of the fence. She wasn't much of a conversationalist, but that was just fine by Charlie. He much preferred the quiet. Just out of arm's reach, now. He raised his own hands, palms up in mock supplication, and took another step.

Her hands contacted his own, first one, then the other. Her fingers scrabbled over his bare palms in a frenetic fashion, as though she were so excited that she didn't know what to do. Finally, they clamped down, vise-like. Charlie stood still. She jerked once, twice, trying to draw him closer. Despite his resistance, his boots began to slide across the grass. It wasn't so much that she was particularly strong, it was just that what little strength she had, she exerted at full output without ceasing.

He took a step and her fingers quested up the sleeves of his jacket, seeking a better grip. Her jaw opened wide, and Charlie got an up-close and personal look at the inside of her mouth. The strange, gray traces that filled the eyes and lined the skin were more evident inside. They lacked any sort of advanced medical facilities to test just what the gray shit was. It was pliable, difficult to cut, and seemed to strengthen the tissue. It corded muscles, tendons, and anchored teeth when they might have fallen out as the body dried. Whatever 'it' was, it was likely either responsible for, or a symptom of the plague, but they didn't have a definitive answer either way.

Charlie reached out, avoiding her questing arms, and brought his hand up underneath the gaping jaw. The skin was dry, almost leathery, and he felt the play of tendon and muscle under his hand as he gave her throat a gentle squeeze.

I could let you have a bite, you know. I know you'd like that.

The scars lining his fingers and the back of his hand whitened as he squeezed harder. Bone rubbed together under his grip. Her own hands had found his shoulders, now, and he sighed. Even stymied, with his grip keeping her from achieving her purpose, she'd never quit. Like the walker in the bedroom, she was single-minded and robotic, only responding to certain stimuli. He looked into the storm cloud orbs of what had once been a living, breathing person with hopes and dreams. Maybe she'd once had children like

Charlie had. The only reason he stood here instead of on the other side of the fence was sheer luck.

Sometimes in his darkest hours, he wondered if it had been luck at all.

He found the knife with his free hand and brought it up. Charlie pushed her arm with a delicate grace and brought the tip of the blade to the thin bone at her temple. There was still no change in reaction — she would not abandon her quest to reach the meat before her.

Without a word, Charlie drove the knife home.

The east and west walls were both taller and more robust than the fences on the flanks. This design had come about in simple recognition of geography. There were no helpful terrain features here to depend on. The east and west border crossed ruler-flat farm fields and the two-lane highway that cut through the center of the settlement.

The initial construction was on utility poles. In his former life, Gary West had driven a pole truck for the phone company. When Z-Day came, he knew where to access stacks of unused utility poles, and had the keys to the equipment used to plant them. In those days the zombie population was more, well, *problematic*, so the people putting the wall together had to be on a constant lookout.

The closest major city to the eastern border was Cincinnati. They'd rushed to erect the first line of defense on that spot, parking vehicles and piling debris to form a temporary barricade. Though the much-smaller town of Lewisville, Indiana was closer to the west, rivers and other natural obstacles slowed foot travel from that direction. In the early days, the zombies trickled in from the west. They came in *waves* from the east.

The temporary barricade gave them enough breathing room to complete the first wall, and then they repeated the process to the west. The walls were far enough apart to provide them with a decent amount of interior farm ground — encompassing several homesteads as well as the farmhouse where Miles and Pete lived.

The west wall was right at a thousand feet wide. The creeks spread apart as they traveled, and as a result, the east wall was several hundred feet longer. The perimeter the fencing and walls defined was shaped like a squared-off airplane wing. With telephone poles planted every four feet, it had taken just shy of six hundred poles to form the basis of the walls. The sheer number had cleaned out the phone company depot, and then some. In the end, they'd ranged far and wide, cutting down poles with chainsaws and dragging them back to use as horizontal members. Even then they'd lacked enough raw material to complete the walls to their planned ten-foot height.

The survivors were scavenging lumber yards for outdoor-rated wood when the military began their air campaign to sever Interstate, highway, and access road bridges. Blocked from many of the locations they'd planned to raid for materials, they hadn't known whether to worry or celebrate. As Miles had told Alex, it should have been the former.

A quarter of the survivors died when the swarms overran the incomplete walls. Even then victory created a vicious cycle. Defensive gunfire attracted more zombies, which required more gunfire, which attracted still more. There was a *reason* Trina was obsessive about noise; she'd grown up in the aftermath. But they'd endured to make it *to* the aftermath, Miles reminded himself. They'd learned from it. They'd completed the walls and the fences. They'd identified low spots in the surrounding creeks, installed their own make-do bridges, and gated them off to prevent easy access.

After the extended period of terror and mayhem, there was something almost like peace.

Many of the survivors tended to cluster together. Miles didn't know if it stemmed from a desire to huddle up in the event of another wall breach, or something else. It was a practice that came about in an organic fashion rather than from some decree. In the case of Val's older 'students', it made more sense for them to bunk together if only to make caring for them easier.

In spite of that tendency, there were still some who preferred living in relative isolation. Many of the wall guards, for example, had made use of the wall to form the initial construction of small cabins and shacks. These were generally sited around the bunkers located every few hundred feet — six on the east wall, and four on the west. If nothing else, it made rotation easier as guards who weren't on shift could take the opportunity to nap or prepare a meal. Many still lived in 'town', but quite a few chose not to. It worked and hadn't caused any serious problems, so they went with it.

Henry Flanagan was one such survivor who preferred to be a loner. He was also one of the few who lived on the wall but didn't guard it. Henry was a farmer, and a pretty good one. The greenhouses and fields he tended were in much better condition than the ramshackle cabin he lived in. Miles would have made a significant bet that the only straight wall in the home Henry had built was *the* outer wall itself.

What was *not* up for debate was the fact that most of the community regarded Henry as an irredeemable pain in the ass. If not for his skill at producing fruits and vegetables, none of the other survivors would ever have dealt with him. This morning Henry had a legitimate reason to be that pain.

"How am I supposed to fix this?" the older man demanded, waving his hand at a small greenhouse. The door hung on a drunken angle by its lone intact hinge. If that wasn't enough, whoever had damaged the door had also shattered the glass on the side of the door lock. The hole itself was large enough for most people to fit through, so Miles didn't understand the reason for the rough treatment of the door. Then again, the more experience he got with law enforcement, the more he realized that people who broke the law were most often dumber than a box of rocks.

Miles lowered his head and rubbed his mouth with one hand to keep himself from laughing at the absurdity of the situation. "Larry?" he managed.

The other man shook his head. "Good grief, Henry, get the stick out of your ass. You act like we're the ones who messed up on your crops. Talk to Jim Piper, he'll pull supplies from storage so you can get fixed up. Hell, if you ask him the right way I bet he'll get a work crew out here to help."

"Oh." Henry deflated a bit. "Well. All right, then. I guess I'm just mad at myself, fellas."

Miles' moment of levity had passed. He managed, with perfect seriousness, to say, "Did you hear anything?"

Henry had the good grace to look embarrassed. "Well, if I'm being honest, no, I didn't. I traded Tom Oliver a bushel of sweet corn for a six pack of his home brew. I was three sheets to the wind not too long after the sun went down.

That stuff has a real kick, and I can't hold it like I used to, you know? I went outside to take care of some business just before dawn and saw the mess. I hit up one of Gary's guys down the way and he radioed in a report."

"We've all been there, Henry," Larry said.

"Oh, you bet," Miles said. He was not completely successful at keeping the mirth out of his voice. "Henry, if I'm guessing right, I bet there were a few folks who saw you bartering last night."

"I'd say that's so," he allowed, then gave Miles a wary frown. He had the look of someone trying to figure out if he was the butt of the joke. "Tom opens up a little after five and I walked down a bit after that to make the trade. My first crop came in and I decided to treat myself."

Miles walked over to the greenhouse and glanced inside. The thief had trampled most of the stalks of corn; the vast majority were missing the cobs. It hadn't been a big plot, but considering their bland diet, any change of pace was welcome. "So, somebody sees you make your trade. They put two and two together and realize you've got a greenhouse of sweet corn ready for harvest. After dark, they come around, bust their way in and pack up all they can carry." Miles' voice trailed off as he looked down. "And track dirt from the plots right out the front door and across the field."

"You're kidding," Larry said and moved up beside Miles. He leaned his head back and laughed as he saw the tracks. Henry's plot of land was a few hundred yards south of the county road. Henry had let the grass grow for hay, and that plot stretched a good bit west. Beyond that, the fields opened up behind what had once been Miles' next door neighbor's house. Instead of moving on the paved road, Henry's corn thief had dragged his haul through the hay field. Even though it was just over ankle height, the path was clear as day hours later.

Miles nodded to Henry. "Talk to Jim, he'll get you set up. And we'll see if we can't get at least some of your corn back for trading, all right?"

"Works for me," Henry said. *The grumpy so-and-so actually sounds grateful.* Miles chuckled. *Time to catch a thief.*

Chapter 5

"So. I got to ask. Donnie says you've *never* had a cheeseburger. He's messing with me, right?"

Vir Singh lowered the binoculars and gave his questioner an annoyed glance. Joey Bennett was twenty years old; short and skinny with a messy thatch of black hair. A not-insignificant crop of acne flowered across his forehead. *"Excuse* me?"

"Umm. You're Indian, right? He said Indians don't eat beef. You guys worship cows or something."

Vir gave a heavy sigh and turned back to the binoculars. He resumed his slow study of the warehouse across the highway. "Yes," he said. "I was born in India. And Hindus regard cows as sacred. I do not, as I am Sikh." He reached a hand up and touched the blue fabric wrapped around his head. "Hindus do not wear the *dastar*, what you call a turban. I can eat all the cheeseburgers I want, when I can get them."

"Oh."

Joey was silent for a long moment. Vir heard him take a breath as though to ask another question, but none was forthcoming. He lowered the binoculars and looked at the young man. "What now?"

"So, uh, if you were born in India, why don't you sound like Apu . . . um." Joey had the good grace to blush. "Never mind."

"I attended secondary school in England. I also went to uni at the Imperial College of London, where I earned a degree in structural engineering. As you were rather young when our world fell apart, you may not know that India was once a part of the British Empire. Many of my countrymen speak with a similar accent. 'Apu' from The Simpsons is a ridiculous stereotype." *Of all the relics of the past, someone had to scavenge those bloody stupid cartoons.*

"Right. I'm sorry I asked."

Vir stared at the young man for a long moment, then said, "Joey, there is no problem with an honest question out of ignorance. In that, you are more refined than Donald, who made an assumption due to his preconceived notions. If you have questions, feel free to ask. I do not mind discussing them. This moment is perhaps not the best time to do so." He nodded toward the road. "We need to be watching out for biters, not talking." The boy gave him a jerky nod and turned to look out the windows on his side of the room. "Hey," Vir said, finally, then winked as Joey looked back at him. "I know you boys think I'm a bit aloof, but I'm not nearly as big of a stick in the mud as you think I am. Once we get back to civilization, we'll tip a few back, all right?" Joey's color returned a bit and he grinned. In the ensuing silence, Vir resumed his study of the landscape. He tried not to think about how far from safety they were.

The I-275 bridge spans over the Whitewater River were long destroyed, but in a way that was a boon for their current mission. The land on the west side of the river had been farm ground before Z-Day, with houses few and far between. The northward trek had been a far easier movement than it would have been had they crossed the river and taken surface streets through the suburbs. Those neighborhoods were still infested with biters. Vir was no coward — he'd stood more than his fair share of watches — but the thought of that trip left his mouth dry. Their ultimate goal was north of the city, and they were able to get close to it while remaining somewhat safe.

The warehouse complex was north of the city proper — and just across the river. After some debate, the council had agreed that this run was worth it. They'd authorized the usage of a pair of six-wheeled cargo trucks; spoils of war courtesy of the Indiana National Guard. When they'd left the settlement at the break of dawn, materials and tools filled the beds of the trucks. The trip to the crossing had been the easy part; they'd spend much of the morning laying logs and securing them in place at a shallow spot.

They'd made it across the temporary bridge with ease unloaded. The thinking was that the cargo they were intending to return with would be bulky, but it wouldn't be *heavy* enough to cause an issue.

The house they'd chosen was just off the river and perfect for the job. Nestled in a lot thick with trees, the driveway doglegged in such a way that the house was invisible from the road. They hadn't even had to clear it, Vir marveled — it had been empty when they arrived. Wherever the homeowners had been in the last days, they'd never managed to make it home. There was some interesting salvage inside, but the real gem lay a few hundred yards away.

The industrial park was full of nondescript two-story warehouses. The three on the near side of the road consisted of a restaurant supplier, a company which had sold water filtration systems, and — right in the middle — a distribution center for a pharmacy chain.

One of Vir's new teammates had worked there in a temp job, and he'd told enough stories that the mission had been green-lit. Two hundred thousand square feet of bandages, toilet paper, feminine hygiene products, vitamins — all ripe for the picking. Sure, some of it would be useless after sitting for so long, but still more would be fine. The most difficult parts were prioritizing what to take first and being quiet enough that repeat trips were workable.

Soft footsteps sounded behind them on the stairs that led up into the loft space they'd set up in. Vir and Joey abandoned their study of the warehouses and turned to look as Buck, the head of the salvage team, joined them. Curtis Buckner was a tall, trim man in his late forties. Even after eight years of rough living he kept his beard and hair close-trimmed. His eyes glittered with wit and charisma. It was safe to say Vir had liked him pretty much immediately. There was a solid and dependable aura about 'Buck' Buckner. He was the type of man who would not have seemed out of place running a construction site or a corporate boardroom.

"Gentlemen," he murmured as he crested the top of the stairs. "What's the word?"

"Looks clear, so far. I've seen a couple of solo acts, but there's no sign of any larger numbers out there," Vir replied.

"Same for my sector, boss. Just one biter, and it isn't even movin' much," Joey reported. "Just kind of stands by one of the warehouses and wobbles in the wind."

Buck nodded. "Hibernating, most likely. Good. Light loads only, gents, we'll leave most of our gear here in the meantime. We're going to go for it. The exterior doors all look closed, so we're presuming light to zero presence inside."

Vir frowned but said nothing as Buck turned to leave. He pulled the strap of his binoculars over his head and laid them on the couch that he'd been using for a support. The loft was set up as a home office and den. An L-shaped desk and computer took up one half of the room. The rest held comfortable furniture arranged around a television. He picked up his backpack and unclipped a small tactical pouch from it, then placed his backpack on the couch next to his binoculars. The pouch held extra loose shells for his Mossberg pump-action shotgun and extra magazines for his sidearm. Vir clipped the tactical pouch to his belt, on the opposite side of his holstered pistol. He nodded to Joey. "Ready?"

The younger man shrugged. "I don't know," he whispered. "This ain't my first rodeo, but this is a hell of a lot more nerve-wracking than what I'm used to."

Vir smiled in what he hoped was a comforting fashion. Sometimes his beard made the expression look fiercer than he intended. "Stick with me, Joey," he promised as he picked up his shotgun from where he'd laid it beside the couch. "We'll get through this together, all right?"

"Sounds good," the other man said with a wan smile, then moved toward the stairs. Vir cast a look over to the row of warehouses and frowned again. This was his first time out with Buck's crew, but he felt nervous as well. The team leader had a reputation for being cautious and patient, and he was being neither at the moment. Vir shook his head slightly to clear his thoughts. He slipped a hand under his jacket to ensure his *kirpan* was loose in its sheath. The presence of the long knife was comforting, as always.

He just hoped he wouldn't need it.

"You ever think this is the start of something worse?" Larry mused as they pushed through the ankle-high grass.

"What, people stealing corn?" Miles thought about it, then laughed. "Not really."

"Thieving, making meth. Heck, even Alex going off the reservation and playing sniper games instead of going to school is a little troubling." Larry adjusted his gun belt and shrugged. "We've got a bunch of folks that have spent damn near ten years on the edge of death at every waking moment. That's got to leave some psychological scars, right?" Larry sighed. "I don't know. I just wonder if we're not waiting for the other shoe to drop and someone to snap under the pressure. Maybe I wouldn't be so worried if we didn't have so many people content to just sit and mope instead of actually, you know, doing something to make things better."

Miles was silent for a long moment as he rolled it over in his head. "I read a magazine article, before. It said that disaster relief organizations always planned on bringing fewer people than they needed when traveling to recovery efforts, because there was always a given percentage of victims that couldn't just sit there, they had to *do something*. Remember right after it all went down when we started putting up the fences? Guys like Gary, and Jim Piper, they were chomping at the bit to get it done, to not just sit around. Hell, even Miss Martha would have been out there pounding nails if we'd have let her. By that same regard, there's a nasty little secret those organizations knew, too. After the disaster is over and they're packing up to go home, there are usually a significant number of people they have to force out of the shelter because they don't *want* to leave. It's worse for us. Take out those who aren't capable of work and we're split down the middle. For every Gary West, who damn near lives on the wall, we've got someone else with a primary focus of waking up before they shut down the breakfast line at the chow hall."

"So what do you suggest? Forced labor? I might not go along with that for certain historical and ethnic reasons, mind."

Miles grinned. "Hey, I should suggest it at the next council meeting. Maybe they'll fire me and elect someone else."

His father-in-law chuckled. "No, I'm serious here, son. There's a reason why people picked you for this job. You think about things at different angles than everyone else. Sometimes that's what we need — an opinion that doesn't run in line with the status quo."

"Well. Here's how I see it, then. You worry about waiting for the other shoe to drop, I worry what kind of world I'm leaving for my daughter. Because the way it's set up now, it could morph into some sort of neo-feudalism or sharecropping setup. If you're worried about me bringing up forced labor now, in a few more years people will be clamoring for it. What we've got right now is a commune more or less. Everyone gets food and shelter, clothes as needed, and generally aren't forced to work for any reason other than peer pressure. Someday, when people aren't so scared of what's going on outside, they're going to start looking at what's going on *inside*, and they're going to resent the shirkers. There are people that are still freaked out by the whole "zombie apocalypse" thing, and who blames them? But knock on wood if I don't think we're seeing the light at the end of the tunnel. Yeah, they should have rotted away to nothing long ago, but they're getting there. And once that threat isn't hanging over our head, human nature is going to snap back, fast.

"Yeah, there's some semblance of an economy, but it's for luxury items or pretty trinkets the scavenger teams bring back. And even then that exchange is on a barter basis — it's not based on any official currency other than Tom's quarters. It's basically bushels of corn for beer, or a basket of fruit for an iPod recharge."

"How do you *create* an economy, though? Do we start printing bills? Force people to work to pay for things?" Larry shook his head. "You know who that sounds like."

Miles stopped walking and stared into the distance. "Yeah, it sounds one heck of a lot like . . ."

In the early days, the number of survivors had been few but loud. The night Miles recalled had been a prime example.

"Grant's on the warpath tonight, isn't he?" Sticks had whispered.

Miles glanced over at his best friend and tried to hide his smirk. The subject of their disdain marched back in forth in the center of the Quonset hut they used for meeting space. If they got any more people they were going to have to shift things into the equipment barn. At the moment, it was standing room only behind the folding chairs.

Grant Johnson had been a City Council rep before things went to hell. As far as Miles could tell, he hadn't quite figured out that his position was meaningless without, you know, an actual *city*.

How did this jackass even get elected?

". . . Even if we are to discount the actual danger involved, how can we justify outright theft from a legal standpoint?"

"Danger? Is he coming with us? I feel safer already," Sticks whispered. Miles bit off his snort of laughter and tried to look innocent as a couple of people around them looked for the source.

"Don't you think we're getting a little too far into the weeds?" Pete called out. "Legal? For better or worse, the law is just a set of books that will molder on the shelf if people like us don't try to preserve it."

Grant turned to face the other man. "You're wrong. At some point, the government *will* be coming back, and we're going to have to answer for what we've done in the interim."

"Then where are they?" shouted someone in the audience.

"Look," Grant said. "I'm sure that rural Indiana isn't high on the priority list. But at some point . . ."

"Look," Pete interjected. "The power's been out for weeks, but I've been able to run my HAM set a bit. There're people out there, sure, but they're alone. If there's any semblance of government or organization out there, *they ain't talking*. So we need to do what we can to survive this thing. Call it salvage, call it stealing, it has to happen."

"You crazy coot! You think you're in charge? He who has the food makes the rules, is that it?" Grant spat.

Pete laughed. "Don't look at me. If anything, Larry's in charge. He's the one with all the guns and ammo, he can get all the food he wants."

Miles realized he'd fallen into silent reverie and finished, ". . . Grant Johnson before he tried to take over." A handful of people died on both sides of the issue during the nascent coup. The one most important to him being Sticks.

Larry grunted in agreement. "Yeah, I try to keep that little stain's comments in the back of my head. That's why I've pushed to distribute food production to as many people who want to farm as possible. It's also why I keep fighting all the proposals to centralize weapons storage."

"That would be terrible in the best of times. If things start going south, the last thing we want is someone claiming sole ownership of an arsenal. It's hard for a knight to lord over a peasant when the peasant can shoot him out of the saddle with a longbow."

"Always with the history, kid," Larry laughed.

"You know you love it. I think I picked up most of it by osmosis from you and Uncle Pete over the years." Miles kicked at a rock in the field. "You know what I don't get, though? What's our corn thief get out of this? Nobody has a working fridge. If he starts showing up at the depot for buckets of ice Jim's going to get suspicious. Can't eat it raw. So he cooks it? No way. He'd have to live in one of the bigger houses to do it with any privacy. People are too nosy to cook outside without someone up in your business." He counted names off on his fingers. "I know nobody in our house did it unless you're ready to confess your dastardly deeds." Larry shrugged and shook his head. "Didn't think so. Val didn't do it, and none of her kids are strong enough to haul what looks to be a pretty full bag all this way. How many people does Tom have living in his place now, six? Seven? And they're all solid, either work with him on the farm or Gary on the wall. Maybe I shouldn't jump to conclusions but I don't see any of them stealing a bag of sweet corn." Miles sighed. "Sometimes I wish Derek was still around. He had a better mind for this crap than I'll ever have."

"So maybe he didn't steal it to eat, he stole it to trade. Which begs the question, who was at Tom's bar last night — the thief, the guy trading for it, or both?" Larry paused for a moment and rubbed his chin in thought. "When we get done, we need to run over to Tom's and see if he can remember who all was there last night when Henry came in. And I'll go you one further, Sherlock. If the guy who stole it can't cook without the neighbors coming up and saying, 'howdy fella, where'd you get the corn?', how in the world is the guy he's trading it to going to get any use out of it? Unless, say, he's got somewhere outside of the fences to bring it to."

"You think they're cooking the meth outside the fence?" Miles considered it, then observed, "Ballsy."

"Like you said, we're seeing the light at the end of the tunnel. It's not as dangerous out there as it used to be. We've gone over every building inside the fence with a fine-toothed comb. By definition, the lab has to be somewhere else."

"Yeah, but *where*? We stripped all the usable material out of the houses around here. There's nowhere left to hide."

"Yeah. I guess."

Miles frowned. The slide marks were fading as the day got warmer, but remained visible enough to see that they ended near Martha Bradley's old horse barn. They didn't have many horses left, so they'd converted the building into apartments. Upstairs, they'd quartered the hay loft to provide larger spaces for families.

Downstairs, they'd stripped out the half-walls between the stalls. New walls made single apartments out of each pair of stalls. Insulation, wall panels, flooring, windows, and doors furthered the transformation.

While it would be generous to describe the construction as rough, the rooms were tight. The entire building stayed warm in the winter with the addition of a wood-burning stove on the lower floor. The center aisle of the barn was still dirt, due to a shortage of concrete. They'd hauled in enough gravel to ease drainage and prevent it from becoming a sloppy mess when it rained or snowed.

For a moment, Miles felt as though he were slipping between past and present. He'd played in this horse barn as a child when his family's next door neighbor served as a periodic babysitter. Miss Martha, as everyone called her, had been just shy of her ninetieth birthday on Z-Day. She'd been stubborn enough to reach the ripe old age of ninety-four before passing away.

Martha's contributions to the initial core of survivors were almost indescribable. She'd provided them with advice and know-how that would have been quaint or irrelevant in a world of electricity. It was funny, in a way. The little old lady had been more valuable to the prospects of the survivors than a dozen younger and presumably more capable souls.

Of course, it's been like that since, well, forever.

There were always people willing to work, and those who avoided any sort of responsibility. There were those who knew how things worked and those who knew little more than the latest reality TV stars. The end of the world had just made the distinctions between the two types that much more obvious, and the stakes that much higher.

The power had stayed on for almost a week after Z-Day. Though they'd considered the consequences ahead of time, the sudden loss of water had caught them flat-footed. Even though they had well water, those wells were useless without electric pumps. It hadn't been an oversight per se; far safer to say that it had been further down the list than other, more critical points of survival.

It would have been a fatal mistake if Miss Martha hadn't pointed out that her windmill-powered well pump was working just fine, thank you. "Why don't you boys do the same thing for the other houses?"

Old, sure. Physically limited? Yes.

Useless? Not in the slightest.

Was it a solution some of the survivors would have thought of on their own, at some point? Maybe, maybe not. Miss Martha had approached Z-Day with the same unflappable attitude that she took toward life. It was the perfect demonstration of leadership. In a way, she was the cornerstone of the entire community.

And to this day, behind the home that Miss Martha opened up to Miss Val and her group of terrified students, that windmill stood. It wasn't an official memorial. But every survivor knew the story — the lesson, even — of Martha's well pump.

The trail ran past the windmill and ended at a graveled area just outside of the converted barn's door. Larry gave Miles a thumbs up and moved to pull it open. The entrance to the barn consisted of a pair of glass French doors to brighten the place up in the daytime. There were four doors on either side of the entryway, and the staircase to the second-floor apartments climbed the back wall.

Miles eased inside and slid his rifle off of his shoulder. He kept the barrel pointed at the barn floor and flipped the safety off. Gravel crunched under his feet as he stepped to one side of the entrance. Larry shut the door behind them with delicate grace. There were footsteps and muted voices from above, but otherwise, the interior was still.

Miles glanced at the floor, trying to discern a pattern in the gravel. There was a thump from above accompanied by the muted giggle of a toddler, and Miles frowned. He considered the weapon in his hands and shook his head. It was a bad idea; especially in such a small area with so many people around. He flipped the safety back on and slung his rifle. He felt, for a long moment, a deep sense of shame.

You aren't a real cop. A real cop wouldn't have made that mistake.

And of course, he wasn't. Oh sure, he had the title and the responsibility. The extent of his official training consisted of behaviors borrowed from old TV shows and the little he'd picked up from Derek Garcia before he'd bought it. As with anything else these days, sometimes they just had to make do with what they had. For better or worse, a computer geek and retired Marine were the closest thing they had to a professional police force.

So act like it. He turned to Larry and raised a finger to the ceiling, then lowered it and indicated the pistol the other man held at low ready. His father-in-law pursed his lips as though he'd bitten into something sour, but he finally nodded and slid the pistol back into his holster.

"Tasers," Larry muttered. "Or night sticks, at least."

"I'll talk to Charlie," Miles turned back and examined the ground again. With the gravel, there were no tracks to follow; scuffs here and there could have been anything.

One of the doors to Miles' left opened and a stooped figure in worn bib overalls shuffled out. What little hair he had left stood out in proud white tufts just over his ears. As he closed the door to his apartment behind him, he regarded Larry and Miles with a placid expression.

"Mornin', gents," Ronnie Cartwright said in low but strained voice. He was one of the original members of the community. His own family farm had been just outside of their current borders, but the pitted geography of his fields made a wall there a tough proposition. When they had begun consolidating, the survivors had dragged him, kicking and screaming, out of his own homestead. He'd later admitted he was glad the decision was made for him — alone, he would never have survived. Ronnie had helped with farming knowledge and labor in the early going. Although the latter had become more difficult for him in recent years, his mind was still as sharp as ever.

The knowledge of a man with decades of experience as a small farmer was priceless. That work entailed everything from bookkeeping to equipment repair, on top of the core know-how of his profession. Much like Martha, Ronnie Cartwright had been a Godsend.

"Hey, Ronnie," Miles murmured. "Hear anything out of the ordinary last night?"

Ronnie opened his mouth to answer, but his only immediate response was a quiet wheeze. A flash of embarrassed annoyance crossed his face. He held up a finger as he hauled a handkerchief out of the back pocket of his bibs and brought it to his mouth. His coughs were far more authoritative; deep and wet and somehow resonant. It wasn't a healthy sound, and Miles had a vague, unsettled moment of panic.

The feeling was one that had become all too familiar as time went by. It was the sense that someone before you was not long for this world because the only care available was the medical equivalent of duct tape.

As Ronnie coughed into the rag and wiped his lips, a door to an apartment on the opposite side of the building flew open. "For fuck's sake, old man, it's not enough that you cough up a lung all hours of the night, you have to do it like a damn rooster in the morning, too? I'm trying to sleep, asshole!"

One of Ronnie's eyebrows arched in response. Miles turned, and as he did so he felt the urge to sigh in exasperation. Because he'd had a suspicion in the back of his mind all along, hadn't he? It wasn't like he didn't look at everyone around him and sort them into categories as he went about his day-to-day business.

It would have been unkind to say that Chris Naylor was a waste of space. When provided with the proper motivation, he was a determined worker. He'd contributed as much sweat as anyone to the building of the wall. But when the pressure was off, well, he just kind of drifted. If Miles had to sum him up in one phrase, "works well under constant supervision" would have been it.

Miles met Chris' bloodshot eyes, then glanced down. He was clad only in a pair of ragged boxer shorts. A black athletic bag of the type used to carry hockey equipment sat on the floor next to his bare feet. The top was open just enough for a few tassels of sweet corn to poke through. Miles looked back up, and he couldn't help it. He laughed.

You dumb ass.

Chris' eyes went round with shock. He blurted, "Oh, shit," and slammed the door.

There was a long moment of silence. Finally, Ronnie spoke as he shuffled toward the exit. "Well, I'll leave you boys to it."

Miles turned to look at Larry. The other man looked as though he was on the verge of laughter, himself. "He's not serious, is he?" Miles jerked a thumb at the door to Chris Naylor's apartment.

"I got nothin'," Larry said, then guffawed. "After you, boss."

"Oh, brother," Miles said as he tried the knob. Locked, of course. They'd used metal exterior doors for the apartments. In the event the walls were ever breached, these could suffice for temporary shelters. Zombie-proof, sure, but to somebody living? Time to find out. He stepped back and eyed the doorknob. He lifted his right leg and kicked, slamming his boot just beside the door knob. The jamb creaked. If Chris had engaged the deadbolt, this was going to hurt.

"Here, alternate," Larry said, then slammed his own boot into the door. Miles followed suit, and they fell into a rhythm; boom boom, boom boom. Doors opened around them as curious neighbors looked to see what the fuss was. After several kicks, the door burst open with the crack of splintering wood. The interior was dim, despite the window in the opposite wall. As Miles' eyes adjusted, he realized why, and the urge to laugh bubbled back up.

The windows in each apartment were about eight feet off of the ground. This was low enough to admit light and air, but high enough to make it difficult for anyone or anything to push inside. Chris had placed his bed right under the window. He'd used it to boost himself up and out through the screen — until he lost his balance and began slipping outside. His legs were pointing straight up in the air, waving back and forth as he tried to slow his fall and avoid face-planting on the ground outside.

Miles stepped across the room in a pair of long strides and grabbed a leg. He pulled down, and he caught a glimpse of the other man's head outside as he did his best impression of a human teeter-totter. The sudden shift planted Chris' crotch on the lower frame of the window, and he emitted a piercing shriek. Miles winced.

Larry stepped up on the opposite side of the bed and grabbed the other leg. "Stop wiggling, you idiot!" he roared, and tugged inward.

Chris shrieked again at the renewed assault on his crotch and began to struggle even more. "Don't kill me! Don't kill me!"

Miles and Larry pulled again, and Chris slid further inside. He turned as he came in, putting his back to Miles. At once Larry let go and leaped back. "Damn it! He pissed on me!" Miles kept pulling. Finally, Chris slid out of the window and bounced on the bed. He rolled onto his stomach and curled up into a fetal position with his hands on his crotch. He groaned.

Larry roared. "We're not here to kill you, you lush! We're here to arrest you!"

Miles stepped back and took it all in. Finally, he composed himself enough to speak, and said, "Get some clothes on, idiot. Where the hell were you going to run in your underpants?"

Muffled: "I didn't think it that far through."

"News flash," Larry spat. He rooted through the debris on the floor until he found a grimy t-shirt. He began wiping his arms and chest. "Why the *hell* did you piss on me?"

Chris sat up, wincing as he shifted positions. "I drank a bunch of beer last night and I've been sleeping it off. I haven't had a chance to go yet."

Miles concluded his own search of the floor and threw a shirt and pants at the other man. "Get some clothes on. You can sleep it off at the station." He glanced up at Larry and grinned. "You get any pee on your handcuffs?"

The other man glowered at him. "One day, boy. One day."

Chapter 6

Tish Matthews — formerly Vance — regarded her patient as she scrubbed in, and tried not to sigh.

Todd Jenkins, you are such a typical man.

After putting up with the pain in his side for three days, he'd waved off his shift on the wall and come to the clinic. These days, 'suck it up, buttercup' was one of the most common prescriptions. But sometimes there were things that needed addressing. Appendicitis was one such problem.

During moments of perverse self-honesty, Tish would often note that Z-Day was not without its health benefits. In the old days, doctors had taken to throwing antibiotics at everything, to the extent that the efficacy of said medicines had dropped. Most of the time Tish and her crew didn't have antibiotics to use after major surgery, much less for garden-variety infections.

After the first few years, those predisposed to any number of chronic conditions had passed on. At this point, the remaining survivors were a damn hardy bunch, and even when they were sick they tended to shrug it off. In that light, Tish could understand Todd's attitude, even if she didn't agree with it in this particular case.

Though he had taken longer than he should have, Todd was here now. Unfortunately the best and only available treatment was one that had gone out of common use before Z-Day. On the bright side, it was a procedure that had still been common enough to teach. Even better, it was one Tish had observed — though not performed on her own.

Her surroundings were not dissimilar from the inner city hospital at which she'd been a resident before Z-Day. If she squinted, she could almost convince herself that she'd stepped back in time and into a modern medical facility. The floors were shiny, off-white linoleum. Fluorescent lights shone down from in the ceiling, and there was a vague odor of bleach in the air.

It was all a mirage, of course.

It was ironic that Grady Scott was the only official 'doctor' in the community. He was a DDS and a self-described comedian. For this procedure, he was playing the roles of surgical assistant and anesthesiologist. Tish would have handed dental surgery off in a heartbeat. In this instance even Frannie Ferguson — their lone RN — was more familiar with an appendectomy than the dentist. That wasn't saying much, of course. Yeah, sure, Tish had assisted on a few appendectomies during her short-lived residency. They'd been laparoscopic, using small fiber optic cameras and minute incisions.

This was butchery in comparison. Her reference books indicated that the doctors had performed the first successful surgery of this type in France way back in 1735. That should have given her hope. Hell, that had been more than one hundred years before Lister proved the value of sanitary medicine, and she recalled a long-ago class discussion about a Russian doctor who'd performed the surgery on himself in a remote Arctic post. Maybe he could have empathized with her position; she doubted that the French guy back in the day had "only" had a dentist and an RN on hand to assist.

Buck up, girlie. Whining changes nothing.

On the bright side, Todd didn't have much fat to cut through. Few of them did, after all this time. Call it the zombie apocalypse diet plan. Tish made the first incision, surprised at how steady her hands were. She licked her lips and murmured, "Forehead."

Grady stepped forward and blotted the sweat off her brow. Once he was clear, she positioned the clamps and spread the incision.

And, wouldn't it just be her luck that a nice, thick blood vessel was running right across the surgical cavity from the top left to bottom right. She held up the scalpel. "Hemostat."

Grady took the scalpel out of her hand and replaced it with a scissor-like pair of locking forceps. He stepped back and placed a couple of fingers on Todd's throat, careful not to dislodge the gas mask.

No more heart monitors — yet another relic.

"Look on the bright side, Tish," Grady said. "At least your patient isn't screaming bloody murder. We could be doing a root canal right now."

Tish smiled, then glanced at Frannie and winked. "I get enough smart-alec remarks at home, buddy. None of that from you."

He chuckled. "Aye, aye, Captain."

Tish dug at the tissue under and around the blood vessel to free it. She edged the blades of the hemostat around the vessel and moved it to the far left side of the wound cavity. She locked it with a slight click, and then laid it aside to rest on Todd's stomach. "Another."

Grady placed it in her hand, and she clamped off the opposite side of the vessel. This left the inner strip of the blood vessel between the pair of clamps. "Scissors."

They were getting into a rhythm now; Tish was thinking less about her worries and more about the task at hand. She snipped the blood vessel in the center. A little bit of blood came out, but not much — the clamps were nice and tight. "Frannie, warm up the cauterizer. I'm going to go ahead and ligate the ends."

"On it."

"Chatty Cathy in the house," Grady observed with a chuckle. Tish smiled under her mask but neither woman gave a noticeable reaction. They were well-accustomed to Grady's incessant commentary.

She handed off the scissors in exchange for a length of sterile suture thread. Their supplies were close to exhausted, which added to the pressure. The stitches had to be right the first time. She hoped that Buck's salvage crew would find some in the medical warehouse. The clinic put stitches in often enough that she could almost do them in her sleep. There was a lot of dangerous work on a farm, and that wasn't even counting the added danger of the Wild.

She looped the thread under the right-hand hemostat in an attempt to make the knot as close as possible and thus not waste as much. She made the first tie, then repeated it. The thread dug into her gloves as she pulled with all her strength. Frannie stepped back up to the table with the portable cauterizer.

"Hand it off, and then remove the hemostat to your right," Tish instructed.

"Okay."

As directed, Frannie released the hemostat, ready to snap it back down if the knot failed for some reason. It was good, and Tish let out a breath she hadn't even realized she'd been holding.

"Cauterizing," Tish murmured as she leaned over. The small handheld unit had a needle-like extension at its tip. Using the knot to hold the cut blood vessel steady, she held the heated tip against it. There was a slight, sizzling hiss, and she held it there for a three count. "Good." She handed the cauterizer over. "Scissors." Leaning in, she trimmed the surgical suture. "Same on the next one. How's our patient?"

"Heart rate steady, he's sleeping well," Grady reported.

Tish and Frannie repeated the process on the opposite end of the blood vessel. So far, so good.

"Scalpel." She deepened the incision and revealed the taut fibers of the oblique muscle. Here, she had to change the orientation of the incision to be in line with the fibers of the muscle. This allowed for faster healing and a better recovery than cutting across the grain. The problem though, was that the fibers were *damn* tough.

Finally finished with the cut, she placed another set of retractors in the new incision. "Grady, I may need you for this one. Pull it slow, but as hard as you can."

He nodded. There were no jokes now — they had fallen into a good, compatible rhythm. Unasked, Frannie took up Grady's former position near the gas mask.

The open obliques revealed the transverse abdominis muscles. These fibers ran perpendicular to the oblique, in line with the original incision. Tish and Grady repeated the process after she made another cut, adding another set of retractors. Below the muscle was a translucent white layer of tissue.

"Peritoneum," Tish breathed. "We're in the homestretch, Grady. Forceps."

She pinched the tissue to draw it away from the intestines below and not damage them when cutting through the seal. The peritoneum served as an organic satchel, keeping the abdominal organs together while lubricating them with a serous fluid to reduce friction from the movements of the abdominal muscles.

She made her final cut, a small line in the lifted-up section of membrane parallel to the axis of the main incision. Tish took a deep breath and handed the scalpel off to Grady. "Cross your fingers, kids," she said. So far the interior looked clean and free of pus. If they were in time, the appendix hadn't ruptured, and the risks of infection were not so high.

She swept her index and middle finger inside of the opening, searching. *There you are!*

Tish withdrew her fingers out of the incision with them hooked. This drew the appendix — it looked, for all the world, like a worm attached to the end of the large intestine — out of the incision in the peritoneum. At its base the organ was slim and a pale pink, but it bulged to twice its size in the middle and from there was a bright, angry red.

The rest of the surgery was a blur. Tish isolated the inflamed portion of the appendix from the large intestine by clamping it near the base with another hemostat. She tied off blood vessels in the membrane that ran between the large and small intestines and the appendix itself as she cut through the connective tissue. Once this was free, she knotted a stitch around the base of the appendix, below the hemostats. "Do the honors, Grady," she said. "Cut it."

He leaned forward and cut above the knot and dropped the infected tissue into a specimen tray proffered by Frannie. "Think Todd will want to take a look at it?" he mused.

"Bronze that sucker," Frannie said. "We need to hang it on the wall of Tish's office."

"Ugh, no thanks," Tish said. She cauterized the appendix stump and began tucking it down into the base of the large intestine. Though she'd sutured the stump, to avoid excess friction during healing, she needed to tuck it away inside a pouch of flesh. The pouch was then purse-string sutured to keep it secure.

If anything, completing the surgery was the trickiest part. Tish had a natural elation from removing the appendix, but she had to remind herself that she had to repair every bit of damage she'd created, one step at a time on the way up and out of the abdominal cavity. It was nerve-wracking, and she realized with a start as she began to lower the curved suturing needle into the surgical cavity that her hands were shaking.

"Let me suture," Frannie offered. "Take a moment."

Tish gave her a grateful nod and stepped back. "Thanks," she said. She wanted nothing more than to scratch her nose, but then she'd have to scrub in again. After a moment, she forced herself to ignore it. Thinking about the itch was just making it worse.

"A resident, a nurse, and a dentist walk into an operating room . . . What kind of joke is this?" Grady announced. Tish laughed, and Frannie smiled as she continued stitching.

"A successful one, I hope," she replied. "I assisted on a total knee back in the day. The surgeon was an interesting guy, he liked to have "One Piece at a Time" by Johnny Cash on repeat during his procedures."

Tish shook her head. "If I did maybe a hundred more of those I'd feel comfortable enough to do something like that. Once you've got each step of the procedure down it tends to just flow." Frannie pulled, then knotted and cut the suture.

"Done."

"I'm good now," Tish said. She took her place back at the table and eased the peritoneum back up and over the intestines and began stitching the incision closed. This was a methodical, time-consuming process as the stitches had to be quite small to be certain of a good seal.

Layer by layer, stitch by stitch — they moved with methodical, machine-like precision. Surgery was a dance with death at the best of times. Maybe their current situation made things a little more difficult with lack of resources, but the challenge had always been there. Speed, in this case, killed.

Finally, the surgery was complete. The long row of stitches running down the McBurney's point on Todd's side proclaimed where they'd been and what they'd done. *Look on my Works, ye Mighty!*

If all went well, one day he'd be an example they could use for the next generation. "Here it is. The first appendectomy we did after Z-Day." The great irony to that, of course, was that if they made it that far, this landmark would be unknown to many and appreciated by few. Tish could live with that possibility if it meant a world closer to what they'd had before.

"Nice work, people," Tish said as she removed her gloves. "Now, let's all pray that Buck and the guys bring us back some goodies because the cupboard is starting to look a little bare."

"Listen up," Buck said. "We're burning daylight, and I want to get started." The salvage crew clustered between the pair of Army trucks, awaiting their orders.

Donald Grayson gave a lazy wave of his hand before speaking. "You think that's the best idea, boss?" Buck's second-in-command was of average height and build with a thick beard and retreating hairline.

"I do indeed, Donnie. We've been watching for hours and seen next to no activity, but we can't count on that to last. We're going to move the trucks over to the dock and start loading them up. Things stay clear, we'll hoof it back over to the house and hole up here for the night."

A handful of voices interjected, and Buck raised his hands to calm them. "Yeah, yeah, not a good tactical decision, I get it. But these damn Army trucks are loud as hell. I'd like to reduce the number of times we fire up the engines as much as possible. So. We hoof it across the road unless you feel like crashing out in the warehouse. There should be plenty of cotton balls in there if you want to make yourself a pillow." He grinned.

The voices that been complaining moments ago began chuckling. Vir had to smile, himself. Buck exuded confidence and was able to push that same confidence onto his people. It was one of his strong points. He turned to one of the two women on the crew, his wife, Allie.

"Babe, I want you to take Joey and Melanie. Try to control yourself around the womenfolk, Joey-boy." Most of the group chuckled roughly. Joey turned a bright pink. "Vir, you're with Donald and me. Let's saddle up, cowpokes."

Vir walked around the front of the truck Buck headed for and opened the passenger door. "I call shotgun, newbie," Donald called as Vir began to step inside.

He resisted the urge to roll his eyes. Instead, he gave a tight nod and replied, "As you will." The truck didn't have a rear seat, and the two front seats consisted of narrow benches with a gap in the middle. Vir was going to have to balance a cheek on either side and hope they didn't go over too many bumps. On the bright side, the truck had an automatic transmission. He wouldn't have to worry about an errant stick shift hitting him in the crotch. He wedged his Mossberg behind the front seats and sat. After a moment of thought, he braced his arms on the headrests to keep from flopping around.

Buck frowned as the other two men climbed up into the cab with him. "Donnie, you called shotgun. You get to take out the roamers as we pull in."

"Whatever, boss-man," Donald said. Vir kept his face blank.

Buck cranked up the truck's big diesel and all three of them winced. The exhaust systems were well-maintained, but still loud. When it came to quieting such big engines, there was only so much you could do. Their best bet was to keep the duration of operation to a minimum. In that regard, lighting the engines back up only when they were ready to go made a strange sort of sense. The sound of the engines would rile up any biters in the vicinity. When the noise stopped, they'd fall back into their quiescent mode until roused again. It was contrary to every standard operating procedure they'd refined over the years. If you weren't behind secure walls, stay mobile. In this case, Vir could understand the logic. Even if the thought of a thousand-yard walk from the warehouse back to the house made his skin crawl. Maybe he should have brought his rucksack along after all.

Buck put the truck in gear and headed down the driveway. He glanced over at Vir and commented, "So what do you think so far, Singh? You like scavenging better than wall duty?"

"It is not as tedious," Vir said in a dry tone. "Thus far, I have no complaints."

Donald grunted a laugh from the passenger seat. "You're an interesting cat, fella. Most of the wall guys seem pretty content to sleep in a warm bed every night instead of bunking out in the Wild."

Vir gave him a tight smile. "Are you familiar with the tenets of Sikhism, Donald?"

The other man gave him a wary glance. Vir's arms tightened as the truck bounced over the railroad tracks near the end of the drive. On the bright side, he didn't lose his balance. It would have been a little comedic given the serious nature of what he was about to say.

"Well, can't say that I am, fella," Donald replied.

"In my faith, there are five principles. These consist of honesty, equality, fidelity, meditating on God, and never bowing to tyranny. It occurred to me that, in a way, we exist under the tyranny of the dead. There are none of us free to live our lives as we choose. We cannot go for a walk on a beautiful day such as this without a weapon at hand, or a companion to watch our backs. There is honor in standing watch on the wall, so that others might rest well in their beds. But to be Sikh is to be a warrior." Vir shook his head. "The community has provided a safe harbor for my wife and children. How can I call myself a true warrior if I'm not willing to defend it?"

The other two men in the truck were silent for a long moment. Buck made the left turn into the industrial park and Donald let out a low whistle. "Well damn, son. I thought you just wanted to pick up some extra coffee rations or something. Here you are, all philosophical and shit."

"The first of the five principles — honesty," Vir intoned and winked. "That doesn't mean I don't tell jokes, by the way. And I adore cheeseburgers."

Buck burst out laughing. "Hell, Donnie, I may have found your replacement. He's made me laugh more today than you have all week."

"Funny, boss," the other man muttered. He slid a pistol out of a holster on his hip and a suppressor from a pocket on his tactical vest. He assembled them and leaned out the window. "Come get some, rotter!"

One of the biters outside the warehouse had zeroed in on the sound of the diesel engines. It staggered through the empty parking lot in their direction. Donald waited a moment until the range was close enough, and squeezed off a pair of rounds. One round hit the biter in the chest and the other hit it in the head. It was enough, and it collapsed like a puppet with cut strings.

"Going to walk back later and police that brass?" Buck said as he steered around the corner of the warehouse and headed for the loading dock. There were a couple of dirt-encrusted sedans parked in the back lot. A semi with a faded store logo on the side of the trailer sat in front of the docks. "The Crow will have your hide if you don't bring back reloading materials."

"Fuck that cripple," Donald spat, and Vir raised an eyebrow.

Interesting.

Buck laughed again. "I'll note for the record that you didn't say that *anywhere* in that old boy's effective range."

"Yeah, yeah, yeah. He can give me crap on his next salvage run. The way I hear it, he drinks more coffee than the next ten people inside combined. As long as I'm being Starbucks for his ass, he can kiss mine."

Buck pulled the deuce-and-a-half to a stop. He waved his arm out the driver's side window to beckon the other truck forward. It pulled up beside, and he said, "Back up to the dock on the other side of the semi-trailer. Give me a space between."

His wife flashed him a thumbs-up. She pulled her truck into a tight, three-point turn, and backed out of sight beyond the trailer. "Game face, Donnie," Buck mumbled, and the other man nodded. The team leader glanced over at Vir. "You good to go, Singh?"

"I am ready," Vir replied, and the other man nodded. He took his foot off the brake and pulled the truck forward. Shifting into reverse, he executed the same maneuver as his wife and backed up to the dock. He slowed as they neared the pads at the dock but the truck still jerked as he pulled into them.

"Oof," Buck muttered. "Let's do it." He opened the driver's side door and slid out. While Vir waited for Donald to get out of the way, he took a moment to retrieve the Mossberg. He lay it down in the foot well and stepped down to the ground. Once down, Vir grabbed the shotgun and slung it over one shoulder. Donald was already clambering up the side of the dock. Vir made an annoyed noise in the back of his throat. *Bloody hell, I'm starting to wonder about these people.*

Ignoring the dock, Vir eased the truck's door shut and moved to the front of the semi. Keeping most of his body out of sight, he peered around the front of the truck and studied the industrial park. For a long moment, there was nothing, but he finally detected slow movement. He grunted to himself in satisfaction.

"Hey! Quit lollygagging, fella!" Donald called out. Singh turned to him and gave him a hard stare. He said nothing in reply, but brought a finger up to his lips. The other man purpled in anger.

Vir turned back and looked back around the front of the semi. Still just two. They staggered toward him at a pace more languid than the norm. Perhaps the end of the trucks' movement and sound had confused them, but he knew they'd home in at some point. Once they were paying attention, the smallest of sounds attracted them. He needed to take them out of the equation. The shotgun was too loud, and the team had not bothered to give him a suppressor to go along with his handgun. Fair enough. He waited a moment to ensure no more came out of the woodwork, and then he stepped out to meet them.

The men who stood guard didn't have much use for guns. Oh, they had them in abundance, in the bunkers spread across the eastern and western walls. Gary West had designed and built those walls. Now he led the men and women who guarded them — and what he had hammered into them above all else was the need for silence. No suppressor was perfect. This was particularly true of the field-expedient ones they'd fabricated to increase their supply.

The obsession with noise control ended in the face of larger hordes. For those, they had several 'appropriated' National Guard heavy machine guns. Vir had only been on the wall for one of those engagements, and he'd been glad to have the noise. Even so, as soon as the majority of the horde was out of action, they'd reverted back to quieter methods. As Gary put it, "Our first job is making sure the wall stays secure. Job one-A is making sure we stay quiet while doing it."

Which made it a position well-suited for Vir. Growing up in India and the United Kingdom he'd not had much exposure to firearms. He'd learned quite a bit out of sheer necessity. Though he'd never become more than a middling shot with a rifle, he was quite good with a pistol. Like many others in the settlement, he carried one with him at all times. But the go-to weapons for the men and women on the wall were as old as mankind itself.

The materials might be different, but the sturdy iron-pipe spears were effective enough. As a result, when it came down to it, Vir felt odd killing a biter with anything but a blade.

The closest was the second one he'd spotted. It was in good condition; still clothed though the garments were sun-faded. It'd been a man once, and from the clothing perhaps a delivery driver. Perhaps even the driver of the semi he'd lurked behind, if not one of the other parcel companies. Vir unslung the shotgun and ensured it was on safe. He ducked under the biter's questing arms, then hooked the stock of the Mossberg behind one leg and pulled. Off balance, it tumbled onto its back. Vir kept one eye on the other biter as he dropped a knee onto the first one's chest to pin it. He drew his *kirpan* from its sheath. He aimed and with a grunt of exertion stabbed the blade into the thin bone at the thing's temple. It jerked as though Tasered and fell still.

Vir pulled the blade out, stood, and waited for the next one. It came on, heedless of the fate that had just befallen its compatriot. Its half-life ended in the same fashion. As he stood, Vir looked down and noted the filth on his *kirpan*. He wiped it several times on one of the biters' trousers before securing it back in its sheath.

He waited a moment, but no more were forthcoming. He gave a slow, satisfied nod, and turned on one heel to walk back to the parked vehicles. The rest of the team stood watching, having moved out from the loading docks, and all looked stunned.

"There now," Vir said. "No need to look gob-smacked. Just covering our six, right?"

After a pause, Buck cleared his throat. "Right. The show's over, let's get a move on."

The team turned and moved back to the docks. There was a metal staircase between the two trucks. Vir hid his smirk; the staircase made Donald's climb onto the dock even more ridiculous. Some of his mirth must have shown — the other man gave him a hard look as he stepped up. *Well, there's an enemy I've made today.*

The loading dock had two types of bays. The slot the semi-trailer occupied allowed it to back into the wall of the dock. It was possible that the exterior doors of the trailer were open on the inside of the warehouse, but they'd need to get inside to be certain. The rest of the dock had a shallow walkway at the edge of the roll-up bay doors. Vir reasoned these doors were for smaller, local haul vehicles. This dock was a bit shorter than the area intended for semis. The difference was such that there would be a few inches of drop off into the bed of their trucks. An inconvenience, but the tailgates would function as acceptable ramps once lowered.

All the roll-up doors remained closed. A metal access door stood in front of the personnel staircase. A sign on the door read 'Authorized Personnel Only' in faded red letters. An electronic access card reader sat on the wall to the side of the door handle. The lights on it were dark, to no one's surprise.

Buck tried the handle, then shook his head. "No such luck today. Joey, grab the Halligan tool out of the back of my truck." He stood back and studied the door for a moment, then accepted the tool as Joey returned.

The Halligan tool was like nothing Vir had ever seen before. The combination of crowbar and pick-ax on steroids topped a long, thick handle. Buck inserted the curved blade of the tool into the seam between the door and jamb and heaved. For a long moment, nothing happened. Buck redoubled his efforts, and metal gave a dull groan. He removed the blade, inserted it at a lower point and repeated the process.

The metal of the jamb and door crumpled with each iteration. Finally, the latch was free, and Buck tugged the door open a bare six inches. Satisfied, he turned and handed the Halligan back to Joey. "Stow this and grab some tow straps. We'll need to hold the door shut from the inside." He looked at Vir and winked. "Need to cover our six, right?" The rest of the group, save for Donald, shared a quick laugh. "Everyone get ready," he said.

Buck wedged the heel of his boot against the door to prevent it from coming open, then pounded on it with the palm of his hand. He continued for a ten-count, stopped, and then pounded for another ten-count. He peered inside the gap. After a moment, he cocked his head to one side and said, "Huh. Weird." He moved his foot away from the door and pulled it the rest of the way open. "I think we might be all right, people."

The interior of the warehouse was well-lit, to Vir's surprise. Skylights in the ceiling at regular intervals allowed for plenty of natural light. The towering rows of shelves cast shadows galore, but the interior was navigable. The group stepped inside, pulling the door shut behind them as they went. After a moment of study, Joey looped the tow strap around the door handle and a support track for one of the roll-up doors. With the strap ratcheted tight, the personnel access door could only open a few inches.

Inside, back-to-back desks sat in the dead space between the doors. Workday litter was still spread across the tops, as though the occupants had left a few moments ago. A wheeled cart sat next to each desk. Each cart had a pair of flat decks with low rails — to keep cartons from sliding off, he assumed. As Vir looked down the warehouse, he noted a handful of long-dormant forklifts and more of the carts. The most overwhelming part of the interior were the rows of shelving. Each unit was perhaps six feet wide and stretched to just below the ceiling some forty feet above. Palletized cardboard boxes overflowed the shelves, with the excess piled on the floor. Other than that clutter, the warehouse looked pristine.

"All right," Buck whispered. "Donnie, you used to work here. What's the layout?"

The other man looked up and down the length of the warehouse. "There are two sections — cold storage, and the part we're in now. Cold storage is down at the far end of the building. I wouldn't bother with anything in there. If it needed refrigeration it's gone bad a dozen times over by now. It doesn't look like things have changed much since I left." He pointed at the row in front of the personnel door. "The narcotics and other controlled substances are in a restricted-access cage down there. We'll have to use the Halligan or a set of bolt cutters to get it open. The rest of the general pharmaceuticals are down at the cold storage end. Antibiotics, anything that required a prescription but wasn't a painkiller, that sort of thing. General goods throughout, anything over the counter is at the opposite end." Donald paused. "It's kind of a cluster, but management would go on and on about how efficient the layout is. All I know is, I walked my ass off when I worked here."

Buck slapped the other man on the shoulder. "Good deal." He turned to the rest of the crew. "Allie, you take Melanie and Joey and head down to the other end. You've got the antibiotic list?"

"You know I do."

"Yeah, yeah," he winked at his wife. "We're loading the first truck with the high priority pharmaceuticals and vitamins. Sorry Joey, you'll have to wait a while for your Vicodin fix." Everyone chuckled save Vir, who kept his face blank. "Donnie, Vir and I are going to start loading up the vitamins. Once we fill the first truck up, we'll start loading the second with toilet paper and lady stuff."

"Thank God," Melanie muttered. "Those makeshift pads are terrible. And don't forget the baby wipes."

Buck grinned. "Take your time, folks. We're going to strip this place to the bones, and it's not going to get done in one go-round." He glanced at his watch. "We've got a couple hours of daylight, let's see if we can't make a good dent on the first truck. Let's move like we got a purpose!" Buck turned back to Donald as the other three headed toward the far end of the warehouse. "Donnie, lead the way. Vitamins, ho."

Buck held back for a moment as Donald headed toward the front of the warehouse. "You good, Singh?"

Vir glanced over at the other man, then turned back. His eyes flickered back and forth from in front of him to the empty aisles on the right. The loaded shelving blocked much of the light from the skylights and the gloom in the aisles was quite heavy. Their noise should have attracted anything in the warehouse, but Vir hadn't survived this long to let his guard down now. "I am good," he muttered. "Just a little wary."

Buck frowned. "Relax, buddy. This is going smooth as silk."

"That is exactly my concern. This close to an urban area, the population should be much higher. Why is it not? The truck driver might have been one of the biters outside, but there are two more vehicles. Where are their drivers?"

"If they're in here, maybe they walked until they gave out. We'll find them in some random spot, struggling to get up. I've seen it before."

Vir considered it for a long moment. "Perhaps you're right," he admitted. "It has been a while since I've been outside the walls. It is possible I'm just nervous."

Buck clapped him on the shoulder. "That's the spirit!" Ahead, Donald had stopped a couple of rows before the warehouse wall and he stood, rubbing his chin. "What's up, Donnie?"

"It's one of these, I think, but I'm not sure."

Buck considered for a moment, then said, "All right. I'll take the far aisle, you take the next one in. The cases have labels, right?"

"Exactly."

"Okay, Vir . . . Ah, crap. We didn't bring a cart. I'm not hauling this stuff by hand. Go grab one of those carts and we'll start ferrying this stuff to the door."

Vir nodded and began walking back the way they'd came. After a moment, he glanced over his shoulder and noted that both men had already stepped into the aisles. Shadows danced as each clicked on flashlights and began to scan cartons. Turning back, Vir began to move, then stopped once more. That sound — what had that been?

Turning back around, he cocked his head and strained to listen. *There.* A ripping noise — cardboard?

Vir turned into the aisle next to Donald's and crept down it. He paused every few steps to peer through the gaps in the shelf stock. He was halfway down the aisle when he saw the glow from Donald's flashlight. It seemed low, and after he shifted to get a better look, he realized the light was resting on the ground. A torn-open box sat on the floor nearby. Despite the light, Vir couldn't make out the labeling through the shadows.

The suspicion that arose when he'd heard the sound deepened. *Why is he tearing boxes open? It's simpler to pack and haul them intact.*

Stepping at a languid pace, he scanned the lower shelves until he found an area missing a good bit of its material. He crawled up onto the lower shelf and wormed his way through. It was slow going, and awkward, but he made it through with little noise. As he breached the other side, he turned to get a better look down the aisle.

Donald knelt in front of the opened cardboard case with his back to Vir. As he pulled the individual boxes out of the case he ripped them open. Vir was unable to read the labeling, but he could see that each box contained bubble-packs of pills. Once they were open, Donald transferred the foil bubble-packs into an olive-drab duffel bag. The growing pile of debris to his side bore testament to his progress.

Vir didn't recognize the bag, but it looked to be quite collapsible. It was possible that the other man had rolled it up and concealed it under his jacket on the way inside. He glanced down at the floor to make sure it was clear, then extended his legs, and stepped down with care. He paused for a moment to see if the other man sensed his presence. Oblivious, Donald continued to transfer foil packs into the bag. Vir reached down and eased his sidearm from his holster.

He tip-toed forward with excruciating slowness. Around fifteen feet away, he brought his thumb up and snapped the Beretta's safety off. Donald stiffened at the sound.

"That seems to be quite a lot of decongestant," Vir mused. "Do you have a particularly bad case of hay fever?"

Donald eased around and met Vir's eyes. The look of anger he'd been giving Vir before had faded into placid calm. "You're right, fella. You do have a pretty good sense of humor."

"Stand up," Vir said, pantomiming the motion with the barrel of his pistol. Nice and slow. Hands up." Donald followed his instructions. "You know, in all honesty, I rather wish I'd made that bet with Miles. He was quite certain that Joey was the culprit. The activity seemed to heat up ever since he joined your team."

Donald gave him a crooked grin. "Nah, he's just a dumb kid. Didn't make sense to involve him. He'd be liable to mention it to the wrong person, and boom, out go the lights."

"I don't suppose I can convince you into a bit of a chin wag, maybe give me a name or two. Unless, you're the chef, of course."

"I ain't talking," Donald said with a sneer. "Not to you, not to Miles, and not to that asshole Larry."

"Oh, I don't know. I hear that Pete sometimes comes down and provides assistance with interrogations. Must be something he picked up overseas."

The other man shrugged. "I have nothing else to say. So what's your plan now, hot shot?"

Vir reached into an inner pocket of his jacket and drew out a set of handcuffs. Miles had given them to him when

Vir had finally agreed to the job. "I tie you up, we find you a cozy spot somewhere, and we get this sorted. You can ride in the back with the supplies. Once we're home, you and Pete can chat." A cold circle pressed into Vir's neck just above his collar, and he stiffened.

"Sorry, son, but I don't think that's in the cards just now. Gun. Hand it back, how was it? Oh, right. Nice and slow."

Blasted idiot, Vir raged at himself. *Having so much fun playing at being a policeman you didn't think this was more than a solo act.* He passed the gun back, and Donald's grin widened. Small wonder the man had been so complacent. For a moment, Vir considered going for his shotgun, but no way was he faster than Buck's trigger finger.

"Back against the shelf, over there." A hand pushed at his shoulder, and Vir moved to comply. His new position against the shelf made a neat triangle of himself, Donald, and Buck. He gave the team leader a questioning look.

"Oh, don't look at me like that." Buck engaged the Beretta's safety and handed it to Donald. The other man stuck it in his waistband. "It's not like I'm forcing people to smoke the crap. The fact of the matter is, there isn't much left to distract a man from his troubles, these days. Now myself, I'm partial to a good bottle of Scotch now and then. One of the nice things about this job is I get first dibs on pretty much anything I find." Buck chuckled. "Hell, if I'm being honest, maybe I'm just bored. If nothing else, at least being an outlaw is *different.*"

"What's the play, boss?" Donald said. "Can't just plug him. Sheriff Rick will know something's up if we bring his secret agent back with a bullet hole."

Buck frowned. "Donnie, what was he thinking? Climbing up to the top of the rack like that. Damn shame, he missed one step and fell the whole way down." He glanced further down the aisle and pointed at a wheeled utility staircase. Buck offered Vir a joyless smile and said, "Get to climbing."

A high-pitched shriek filled the warehouse. A crescendo of gun fire followed, along with another sound that Vir couldn't identify. It sounded like a hundred people clapping, as fast as they could, but with no rhythm.

Ignoring Vir, Buck and Donald turned and sprinted toward the end of the aisle. When they reached it, they hesitated for a moment, and then Buck shouted. "Door!" The pair of them sprinted back toward the entrance.

The clapping noise continued, though the gunfire had ceased. Vir sprinted to the end of the aisle and turned to look.

For a moment, he couldn't believe what he was seeing, to such an extent that he froze. At the opposite end of the warehouse, a broad sea of biters surged forward. They filled the entire aisle, packed in like sardines. To make matters worse, they moved faster than any of the dead Vir had even seen. Feet slapped on the concrete floor in a discordant rhythm as they surged forward in a wave of dead flesh.

They aren't supposed to be that fast!

At the door, Donald and Buck struggled with the tow strap. The two men shouted at each other until Buck finally pulled a knife from under his coat and began to saw at the strap. Vir glanced back at the mass of dead, then back at the two men, and knew right away that they weren't going to make it. Donald looked, and the other man must have thought the same, because he drew Vir's pistol and began to fire.

Donald might as well try to stop an avalanche with a fire hose. Vir forced himself to turn away and sprinted back down the aisle. He heard a pair of screams over the sound of running feet, but they were both cut off in one disheartening moment.

Vir leaped over the pile of debris Donald had left in the center of the aisle and continued running. His Mossberg flopped around on his back, and he grabbed the sling with one hand to keep from dropping it. The shotgun would be of little use against the horde, but it was his only remaining weapon save for his knife. Years of hard-won survival instincts made him loathe to lose any weapon.

The utility staircase that was to have been his demise was now his only source of salvation. He bounded up the steps, his boots rattling the metal lattice. The sound of running feet filled the air around him, making the sounds of his own frantic flight seem somehow muted.

The staircase jerked as the leading edge of the surge hit the bottom of it, and he almost lost his balance and fell off. Recovering, he planted a foot on the safety rail at the top and jumped onto the highest shelf he could reach. Behind him, the staircase tipped and clattered to the floor.

Vir's heart pounded in his chest as he turned to look down. The silver-eyed dead stood shoulder to shoulder in the aisle beneath him, staring up as one. "Bloody hell," he whispered, and the sound of his own voice was a shock in the sudden silence of the warehouse.

The crowd *rippled*, and those closest to him began to attempt to climb. Their movements were awkward, and many of them fell. Those that did fall, though, became stepping stones for those who came after. Grasping hands began to draw closer.

Hesitation froze him for a heart-stopping moment, but he forced himself into action. Vir reached up, took hold of the top shelf of the racks, and pulled himself up.

There was about five feet between each shelf. This high up, the shelves weren't so packed. The top racks were empty save for a few shrink-wrapped pallets. Vir supposed they served as long-term storage, since it was higher than the staircase. For the moment, it was a moot point. He glanced down. The pile of dead had risen to just below the second shelf, perhaps fifteen feet below him. At this rate he didn't have much time at all.

He looked up to gauge the distance, and then reached out at his furthest extension to no avail. The metal support structure of the warehouse roof was ten feet above the top shelf, far out of his reach. The skylights and rippled steel surface of the roof were three feet beyond that. Short of sprouting wings, he had no escape in that direction. He turned in a desperate search, then stopped.

There was a roof-access ladder bolted to the front wall of the warehouse. The first two-thirds were simple rungs. From that point a metal safety cage encircled the ladder until it terminated at a hatch leading to the roof.

The shelving shifted under his feet with the groan of metal. The weight of the dead pushing against it was threatening to tip it over — it was now or never. Vir adjusted the sling of his shotgun so it crossed his chest in a more secure diagonal fashion. He studied the distance to the top of the next shelf over. He took a deep breath to fuel his courage, then jumped.

His primary concern had been falling short, but it shouldn't have been. He cleared the aisle with room to spare. The biggest problem was not going too far. He arched his body in a desperate attempt to slow himself without falling. Even then he came close to going over the edge.

The sounds of running feet filled the warehouse once more, and he gritted his teeth. "Hope you dead bastards are enjoying the show," Vir said. He stood on the last shelf, the one next to the warehouse wall. Any thoughts of climbing down to the ladder ended when tentacles of the dead started to flow around either end of the shelf. *This is going to be one dandy of a story to tell if I'm lucky enough to make it back.* Vir spread his arms wide and jumped again.

He fell far enough to clear the bottom of the safety cage, though it was a close thing. His *dastar* tugged on his hair as it brushed the cage on the way past.

The rungs of the ladder slammed into his chest, and he groaned as he rebounded and began to fall. With a shout, he grasped for his life — and caught himself. One hand locked onto a rung, which slowed him enough for him to get a foothold. The jerk of his stop loosened his grip, but by then his other hand had found purchase, and he was secure. Vir hung there for a moment and attempted to catch his breath.

Below him, scrabbling.

Vir glanced down. The dead were as implacable as ever, and now seemed to be rocket-propelled. Below, they were once again piling up. Vir began to climb.

He supposed theft might have been a concern, but then he remembered that Donald had said that the warehouse had been open three shifts. He crawled outside, slammed the hatch closed, and collapsed to the roof in exhaustion. He did nothing but breathe and stare at the darkening sky until his heart slowed its frantic pounding.

As his breathing calmed, he became aware of a dull sound in the air around him. *No. No, no no . . .*

Vir climbed to his feet and staggered to the edge of the warehouse roof.

Below, a mass of dead flesh filled the grounds, moving at a steady shuffle. As Vir watched, he could see streams of them pouring from each of the warehouses in the industrial park. It was almost as if they'd hidden inside of them. Was such a thing even possible?

It was as quiet an undertaking that Vir had ever seen from such a mass of bodies. There was no jostling for space, no pushing to move faster or slower. They moved, tall and short, young and old, all gray with time and decay, and poured out of the buildings. He couldn't have tallied their numbers, but it had to be an unspeakable amount. If any saw him, he did not know, for they did not react, only continued to move forward. Had the arrival of the salvage team roused them, or some other stimuli? Whatever the case, they moved as one, like army ants. The stream of animated corpses filled the gaps in the terrain as they flowed along the path of least resistance. The road fronting the warehouses snaked along the river, and the marathon mass surged along it. They had packed themselves together in such a tight formation that Vir didn't know why some of them weren't trampled. The exact route varied, as needed, but the direction in which they moved was quite clear.

The horde marched north.

Chapter 7

Halfway up the ladder to the Crow's nest, Alex made the mistake of looking down.

With a gulp, he raised his head and stared at the side of the grain bin. *You're fine, you're fine.* He still had a good grip and both feet planted on a rung.

The little voice in the back of Alex's head sneered. *Chicken! Can't even climb a ladder!*

He gritted his teeth and forced himself to look up. It wasn't all that far — he could do this. "You can do this," he repeated to himself. For a long moment, his feet refused to move, but finally, he made the rest of the ascent, hand-over-hand, up the ladder and onto the catwalk. From there it was another climb up to the Crow's nest itself. This one was a little less nerve-wracking, even though he was much higher. The ladder angled forward, and he felt much less afraid of falling. Finally, he reached the top and stuck his head through the open hatch.

A voice hailed him immediately as he climbed up onto the wooden deck. "Hey, kid, how are you? Pete Matthews." The Crow stuck out his hand. Alex stared for a moment before he reached out and shook the older man's hand. *Idiot.*

"Sir," he managed, through a tight throat.

"Well, let me give you the dime tour. You know Cara, Vinnie, and Bruce, I assume."

The older kids gave Alex looks that ranged from curiosity to outright boredom. Sure, all Miss Val's kids lived together. That didn't mean they associated with each other. The older ones especially tended to keep to themselves, and he wasn't a part of that group. Alex was on a kind of threshold; he wasn't old enough for some, and he was too old for the little kids.

"Workbench, my cot." He indicated the vista around them, which was impressive enough that Alex forgot his fear over how high they were. "And, the Wild. What do you think?"

He turned a slow circle, taking it all in. He knew the terrain from ground level, but up here he could see all the twists and turns that the creek made, and the low spots that he could never see into. The chorus of green seemed to explode, and he stared for a long moment before he realized the Crow was waiting for a response.

How long did I space out?

One of the older kids snickered.

"Wow," Alex said. Down there, he could see nothing but fields and forest, but now he could see other farms around them. The survivors had scavenged every usable scrap from the houses he could see, down to the foundations. Further out, past his point of being able to make out any detail, he saw a cluster of buildings.

"There's nothing like a bird's eye view," Pete commented. "You ready to get started?"

Alex tore his eyes away from the surrounding landscape and turned back to the Crow. "Yes," he said. "Sorry."

The Crow waved a hand, declining the apology. "Lesson number one. We're not up here to shoot. That's our action of last resort. First, we watch." Pete wheeled his chair around and indicated the county road to the west of the community. "First test — how's your eyesight, kid?"

Alex shrugged. "I don't have to squint to see." It was a good thing, too. The glasses the community had were either recycled or cobbled together. One of his roomies, Casey, had a bulky pair he was blind without. All the Coke bottles Alex had ever seen were soft plastic, so the meaning was still a mystery, but he'd heard one of the adults tell Miss Val that Casey's glasses had 'Coke bottle lenses.'

"Just to check — can you read the sign?" Pete indicated the crossroads of the western road and the road that ran through the community.

Alex squinted. He could make out a green blob on *top* of the sign, but if there were letters there, he couldn't see them. "No, sir," he said, then added, "I can see it's green, and there's some sort of orange rag tied to the top."

Pete patted him on the back. "No worries. I can't read it either. At this distance, just seeing there's a sign is good enough for me." He pulled the strap to his binoculars over his head and settled it around Alex's neck. "Look through there and tell me what you see."

Alex brought the binoculars up and the world leaped into focus. For a moment, he was so overwhelmed by the absolute *coolness* of being able to see so far away that he forgot why he was looking. When he remembered, he scanned around for a moment before finding the sign.

Two green plates topped the support pole with a long streamer of orange fabric tied just beneath them. "What's the orange for?" Alex asked.

"Windsock," Pete replied. "Depending on how the wind is blowing, it gives us an idea of the direction and strength."

Alex thought about it. For the most part, he'd figured out shooting on his own after the familiarization and safety sessions his class went through. Most of the shots he'd taken were from a short distance compared to this. "The wind moves the bullet." He drew the statement out, impressed with the concept.

"More than you'd think," Pete agreed. "We'll work on that later. Like I said, first, we watch. The signs?"

He looked again. The signs were perpendicular to one another, in line with the roads themselves. Huh. It was a concept that he imagined the adults took for granted, but Alex couldn't remember riding in a car, much less navigating a road. There was an efficient logic to it, but what did it mean now?

"The one in line with our road is 300 South," Alex announced. "The other one is Stone Creek Lane." He frowned.

Why is that familiar?

"Good," Pete agreed. "You've got sharp eyes. Congratulations, that means you passed the first test." He turned his wheelchair away and rolled over to the workbench. After a moment of rifling through drawers, he found a packet of papers.

"Here," Pete said, and handed the packet to Alex. "Your first assignment."

Alex flipped through the packet, taking the time to examine each page. It was actually printed, which was something you didn't see much of anymore. That by itself would have been enough to make him take care, but the pages were also well-thumbed and curling up at the edges. Each page had a grid filled with numbers.

He looked up, baffled. "What is this?"

"It's called a ballistic table," Pete explained. "There's one for each type of bullet we use up here." He stabbed his finger at the sheet Alex had the packet open to. "This axis is the range, this axis is the drop. Bullets don't fly in a straight line, kiddo, they curve. Study this. Memorize it. Learn it."

Alex stared at the chart and grimaced. "So I can come up when I have this memorized?"

Pete grinned. "Miles told you there was a use for math. Welcome to geometry. And no, you don't need to have it memorized. Get started. Keep working in school, and come up every other day or so."

"Every other day?" Alex echoed.

"Or so," Pete agreed. "You need to be out, I don't know. Playing in the dirt. Be a kid. You've got the rest of your life to work, don't be like these maniacs." He jerked a thumb over one shoulder. Alex thought he saw a grin flash across the face of the girl, but he could have been wrong.

"Okay," Alex said, drawing himself up. Even at his tallest he could just look Pete in the eye. "But I don't play in the dirt, sir, I'm almost thirteen."

For one heartbreaking moment, Alex thought the Crow was on the verge of tears, but the older man composed his expression and said, "Ah, forgive me. Consider yourself an . . . intern, then. Part time only, until you learn the ropes."

"What's an intern?"

"Never mind," Pete waved a hand. "Now go on, scoot. Study the tables. You can ask the others, I like to give quizzes. Come back Wednesday after school — and no more cutting class!"

Alex gave an enthusiastic nod. "Yes, sir." He folded up the charts and stepped back down into the hatch. His first visit to the Crow's nest had been a short one, but it hadn't been as scary as he'd feared.

And, for the first time in his life, he was looking *forward* to homework. Crazy.

After depositing his tray on top of the well-used table, Miles sat down in one of the cafeteria's folding chairs. He glanced at the group of people sitting at the other end and nodded to them in greeting. After returning his greeting, the group returned to their own conversation. In a way, he was grateful for that. The lights were set to dim, to conserve battery power. The entire building had a close, cozy feeling. Any conversation louder than a whisper would have seemed out of place.

There was a sudden boom of noise, and Miles turned and straightened at once. Calvin Anderson, one of the three council members, stood near a table with no occupants. A chipped and faded wooden box with a slotted lid sat on the table next to a stack of papers.

"People, I know some of you think this is funny, but we are *not* naming this community Disneyland. We've gone through the suggestions and narrowed them down to the top five. We have removed the immature names. Pick one and vote. We'll announce the winner at a later time."

Calvin turned and stormed off, chased away with a smattering of laughter and light applause. Miles grinned to himself.

Well, so much for the town meeting.

He picked up his spoon and stirred the bowl of beef stew. That, at least, was something they could make well out of their own ingredients. The ersatz dinner rolls were more akin to flatbread, but they weren't bad. Better than pancakes, to be certain.

Kitchen duty wasn't glamorous, but they didn't force anyone into it, either. The folks who gravitated to it usually did so because they enjoyed cooking and couldn't contribute in other ways. And there was always something better about dining in a group, even if Miles didn't particularly feel like socializing at the moment.

A familiar touch brushed against his shoulder and the back of his neck. He straightened in his seat. There were exceptions to every rule, of course. "Hey, you," he said with a smile.

"Hey, yourself," his wife said as she circled the end of the table and sat down across from him with her own tray. "I hear you caught the Great Cornholio."

Miles groaned. "Not you, too."

Tish giggled and began tearing her flatbread into pieces. "Sorry, I couldn't resist."

He shook his head and smirked. "I *do* have to give you points for the most creative name." He took a bite of stew. "You'd think we were running an apocalypse shelter for wayward comedians. How about you?"

"Took out Todd Jenkins' appendix this afternoon."

Miles' eyebrows went up a notch. "Nice," he said, drawing out the vowel. "Everything go okay?"

"A little nerve-wracking, but yeah, it came out okay in the end."

"Humility, Doc?" Miles teased with a wink.

She took a bite of her own stew and paused. "It's all kind of a blur now," she said. "It was terrifying at the time."

Miles nodded. "I know what you mean," he said, and then grinned. "I'd have never passed sophomore year biology if I hadn't been able to copy your lab notes."

"There's an ever-so-slight difference between a fetal pig and a grown man," Tish pointed out.

"Well, this is why you're a doctor and I'm not," Miles said. "I couldn't tell an appendix from an eardrum."

"How about you?"

"It sounds like you already know most of it. We busted Chris Naylor for property damage and theft." He thought of something and smiled. "He pissed on your dad."

Tish laughed. "That detail did *not* make it into the rumor mill. Speaking of, where is Pops?"

"Val needed something done at her place, so he and Trina are eating dinner with her and the rest of the kids."

His wife chuckled. "Well, I wondered when Dad would decide to move out of Tom's bachelor pad." She paused for a moment at Miles' quizzical expression, and her chuckle turned into a full-throated laugh. The group at the other end of the table looked up, surprised at the sudden burst of sound. Tish waved a hand in apology, and they turned away. "Are you serious?"

Miles raised his hands and shrugged. "I feel like I'm late to this party. No clue what you're talking about."

"You do realize Val has had a thing for my dad for years, right?"

"Well, yeah . . . Oh. Wait. Our six-year-old daughter is a wingman?"

"Pretty much," Tish said.

"Well," Miles began, and then fell silent. His lips compressed and he frowned as he worked over his words. "And here I missed it. That's just another example of why—"

"Hey, Marshal," a silken voice said. "Great work today." Miles and Tish turned to the newcomer. Miles, to his credit, managed to keep his features blank, but Tish had a slight smirk on her own. *And,* he mused, *given the quality of my wife's bedside manner, that expression is purposeful.*

Jaid Sims was brunette, curvy in all the right places, and had been chasing after Miles Matthews since she'd been varsity cheer captain and he'd been a starting guard on the basketball team.

In a rare moment of cruel teenage honesty, Miles had once dubbed her a small-town nine and a big city seven. By post Z-Day standards she was a supermodel. Every single guy — and a few of the married ones — in the community would have jumped at a chance with her. Despite that, Miles had never had the same interest in her that she had in him.

Pressed to answer why, Miles would always say that the treatment his best friend had gotten at the hands of Jaid and the rest of her crew was the main reason for his disinterest. The fact that Cole "Sticks" Ferguson had been one of the initial survivors along with Jaid was enduring evidence of the fact that high school never ended.

The real truth was more visceral. Jaid had a dazzling smile, and she used it to great effect. Despite that smile, there was something about her eyes that had always unnerved Miles. They didn't match the expression on the rest of her face. It was as though she was attempting to assess the impact her face was having, rather than sharing in the emotion.

"Hey, Jaid," Miles replied. "Done for the night?"

"Yes! Aasha traded shifts with me. She said her little ones were having a sleepover and she would be in the apartment alone, anyway." Jaid leaned forward and whispered. "If you ask me, I think she's hoping Buck's crew might radio in." Jaid paused for a long moment and turned to Tish. "How are you this evening, Doctor?"

"I'm well, Jaid, thanks," Tish said. "Sit down and join us."

"Oh, I'd never think of intruding! I'm going to eat dinner and then turn in early. See you tomorrow, Miles." And with that, she turned away. *Was there a bit of a strut there?* Miles made a point to look in the opposite direction. A couple of the men in the other group were admiring the view as Jaid walked over to a table on the other side of the room. *Yup.*

He turned back to his wife. "Can I take you to work with me?"

She favored him with a knowing smile and took a sip of water. "She does like her titles, doesn't she?"

"She tried laying 'Deputy' on your dad, but he stomped that one down, hard. Now it's 'Mr. Vance'." He grimaced. "So, as I was saying before I was so rudely interrupted."

"Oh, do carry on." Tish raised an eyebrow. "I've always wondered, by the way."

"Huh?"

She jerked her head sideways, in Jaid's direction. "Not that I mind, but practically every guy in this room is trying to roll his tongue back up, but you could care less."

He raised an eyebrow. "You do realize I've been pushing that away since high school, right?"

"Sure, and I'm not saying I mind. Just curious as to why."

He shrugged. "She's always pinged my radar, for some reason. There's just something off about her."

"You should have seen your face when I invited her to join us. It's fun watching you squirm."

"You need to teach me that, Obi Wan. Asking someone to do something in a way that says it's not a real invitation, I mean."

"It's an estrogen thing, you wouldn't understand."

He sighed. "Fair enough. So — I arrested a man for stealing corn today, did you know that?"

"I may have heard something," she allowed. "Sorry, I'll stop. Your turn."

"I almost feel like it was a waste. Whoever his supplier is, he's more afraid of them than he is of Larry or I. He wouldn't tell us a thing."

She thought that over for a moment. "That says a lot, doesn't it? Must be a rough bunch."

"I guess. Not like all our folks are saints. It's not exactly a small suspect pool." Miles winked at his wife. "Most of the nice guys and bleeding hearts aren't around anymore."

Tish threw a piece of bread at him. "You ain't as bad as you think, tough guy."

"Still nothing on your other patients?"

Tish grimaced. Over the last few months, they'd found three people, unconscious with drug paraphernalia. All were still in the small hospital, unconscious, and fading fast. The demand had put a huge dent in their supplies of IV fluids. The medical staff was down to boiling water for the IV and trying to spoon-feed coma patients chicken broth. Even if Buck and his team brought supplies back before they faded away, it was no sure thing that they'd wake up. If they did, it was possible they'd be able to identify their supplier. Just in case, Miles had assigned a rotation of a couple of deputies to keep an eye on the clinic and make sure unauthorized people didn't go inside. "It's not looking good," Tish admitted. "We're doing what we can, but . . . To be honest, I doubt they all make it."

"Damn." Miles shook his head. It wasn't like they had the people to spare. "So, back to corn. Naylor knew it was just as stupid as I did. It wasn't about the corn, it was about what he could get with it. And God help me, I was this close to torturing the guy to find out who he stole it for. Corn." His face twisted into a grimace. "This is what we've come to."

"There *is* more to it than that," Tish said. "It's about the drugs, right?"

He was silent for a long moment. Finally, he said, "I talked to your dad about quitting today, after we got done with Naylor. Larry told me I'm in this job because I have a different perspective, but the more I think about it, I don't think that's the best thing for a lawman." He waved a hand. "Hell, I didn't even recognize that your dad had a date tonight. I saw it and didn't think anything of it. They've been making Bambi eyes at each other for months, and I was completely oblivious.

"I'm not the right fit for this job. Ever since all this started everyone has looked to me like I have all the answers. They keep shoving me into positions of leadership, but I don't even know what I'm doing half the time.

"I told a kid today that he needed to keep going to math class. Was I full of it? Maybe I'm just kidding myself." Miles held up his glass of water and twisted it, letting the light play through it. "This is just a glass. We can't duplicate this, not in fifty years. The knowledge required to create the equipment that produced this, the skill to use the precise proportions of ingredients for something so pure, that's gone, now. Civilization ended, and we're just scratching in the dust pretending like the old rules matter." He shrugged. "We turn a blind eye to the booze and the pot because, well, it's not like any of us have anything else to blow off steam, what's the big deal? Who are we to draw a line and say that meth isn't the same thing? I'd never do it, myself, but if someone else wants to, what right do I have to stop them?"

"It's about our responsibilities," Tish said, after a moment of consideration. "Would you want me taking out an appendix drunk off my ass? Same thing goes for the drugs. What happens when one of the wall guards gets hopped up on the stuff and decides to, I don't know, start making all sorts of noise? Causes another breach?"

"You wouldn't do that because you're responsible. Same for the wall guards." Miles waved a hand. "The rest of these folks? Who knows? The people in the comas — who are they? What did they do?"

"Lizzie Johnson worked — *works* — in the kitchen. JT Kepler, ah, I don't know, I think he was a farmhand for Tom off and on." She thought for a moment. "Not sure about Bob Gentry."

Miles nodded. "See, another thing your dad and I talked about. The people stepping up, doing things around here, are the same ones that have from the get go. Everyone else is just content to slide on through life." He shook his head. "It's not going to end well."

"So you're going to quit then, and become a slider?"

He winced. "Gee, thanks." He sighed. "I don't know. Maybe it will be a shock to the system, get somebody to wake up out of their stupor and decide to do something positive."

Tish gave him a thoughtful look. Finally, Miles broke the silence.

"I know, I know, stop being a whiner. But who else do I have to whine to?"

She smiled. "Not what I was thinking, at all. I was thinking that it was a long winter. It's spring, that's liable to help right?" She reached across the table and rested her hand on top of his. "I think I'll support you in whatever you decide to do. Just don't jump off the bridge right away. Give it some time. And, finally — I think that we have the house to ourselves, tonight."

Miles raised an eyebrow. "I like that thought."

"I thought you might."

It was beef stew tonight, but Pete didn't have much of an appetite. He ate half of it, then stirred the remnants around in the Tupperware until he grew tired of looking at it. Vinnie had carried it up after the students had left for the day and headed down to dinner for themselves. Pete knew he should try and eat more, lest he crush the boy's feelings. He just couldn't summon the energy to finish. With a sigh, he pressed the top back onto the dish. Maybe he'd eat it later.

Every night, once he had the nest to himself, he'd set up his HAM unit on the workbench and let it scan through the frequencies. In the early days he'd amassed a solid list of people broadcasting. He'd even talked to a few of them, though more than a few spoke in foreign languages. As time went by, more and more of the stations dropped off-line, leaving him alone with the static.

Pete glanced at the sky as the wind turbines mounted on top of the grain bins began to spin up. The light was fading fast, but he could make out a broad bank of dark clouds to the west.

Storm coming in, he judged. *Later tonight, maybe in the morning.*

He rubbed one of his stumps. The prudent thing to do would be to don his prostheses and climb down. Maybe play with his grand-niece and curl up in a real bed for the night. He had an old Army surplus folding cot up in the nest but there was a decided lack of creature comforts like, oh, windows. In the sandbox, he'd slept outside more often than not but you could hardly compare Indiana in the spring to a Middle Eastern evening in any season. He considered the ladder, then sighed again.

Pete jerked the chair around and wheeled over to the other side of the nest. Earlier, he'd clamped a Newcon 60-power spotting scope/ range finder to the railing. He'd given his students an overview of estimating ranges based on visual cues earlier. He had a half dozen laser range finders in varying degrees of quality, but they wouldn't last forever. On the bright side, they had enough scopes with mil-dot marks for Pete to teach range estimation. He wondered what the instructors from TBS Quantico would think about him passing their wisdom on to a group of junior high kids.

On the bright side, they were good with math. A couple of the guys in his entry cohort had been hopeless. Pete chuckled and looked over the scope. Cara, bless her heart, had offered to pack it up into its padded case before she'd climbed down for the day, but Pete had declined. He lowered his head to the eyepiece and wondered how she'd react if she knew his reasoning for wanting to keep the scope up.

Given the position of the nest and the shape and size the settlement had taken, it was difficult for Pete to offer fire cover to the east wall. Any shot he took had to traverse three-quarters of the long axis. That was just too far to be effective, even with the .338. For that reason, most of their defensive firepower was in the eastern bunkers, with a small but not insignificant amount kept to the west. Generally speaking, Pete liked to keep an eye out in all directions, but his main areas of concern were with the north and south fences. Despite their height, he still regarded them as being minimal protection.

Yeah, the creeks and their banks increased the theoretical height of the barrier, but just *looking* at the chain link gave Pete the willies. More than once he'd suggested beefing up those portions of the wall in meetings, but his fellows had voted him down every time. The walls were up, there hadn't been a breach in years, and that was that. The three-person advisory council considered the issue tabled. He grimaced. *Never should have gone along with the idea of the damn 'council' in the first place. Ain't no room for democracy in a lifeboat.* Jim Piper wasn't bad, though he hemmed and hawed so much that Pete had often considered *beating* an actual position out of him.

He swiveled the spotting scope and zoomed out. After a moment, he found the crumpled corpse of the zombie that Alex had shot this morning. He zoomed in to maintain some field of view while easing the scope up. He panned across the forest that paralleled the creek on the south side of the settlement. *Oh Alex, you poor dumb kid. You'd have wet your pants this morning if you had any idea.*

He saw the motion first, a slow blur in the scope as he worked his way across, and he paused, licking his lips while he waited. *There.* In the deepening twilight shadows, he saw an emaciated figure, concealed behind one of the trees. It exposed just enough of its head that gray eyes could stare northward across the creek.

So that it could study the fence.

After a moment, other shadows began to form into recognizable shapes. A long branch moved against the wind, and become obvious as an arm. A round bulge on a tree trunk turned, and a head leaped into recognition.

In the shadows, the woods *teemed* with the dead.

Pete thumbed the range finder button on the spotting scope. 1907 yards — just over a mile. It was within the Savage's range, but this . . . this was a whole other ball of wax.

How many do you see? A hundred? Two? You don't have enough ammo, *for starters. And what happens when people start hearing gun shots in the night?* "What if *they* rush the fence when you start shooting, Marine?" he muttered to himself.

If anything, Larry or his nephew would climb up to see what the hell was going on, and then Pete would have to *explain* himself. And wouldn't *that* just go over like a lead balloon? The council was sure to love finding out that he'd been keeping things so close to the vest. Maybe Jim would back him, and maybe not, but sure as the world, Calvin and that nitwit Norma would lose their minds instead of being effective leaders.

No. It would be chaos down there. Pete knew that the others worried about him and his propensity to stay in the nest, but he knew how fragile things were down there. Before Z-Day, twenty percent of their population would have been in an institution. Many of the rest were functional, if shaky. For now, the facade had to remain, until he could either figure out what the creeps were up to or a way to get rid of them without causing a panic.

Air strike would be good. Some A-10s or maybe a Spooky. Just rain down hell fire and damnation on the dead, burn them out once and for all. "Heh. Might as well wish for an aircraft carrier to sail up the creek. It'd be just as likely."

In the west, thunder rumbled.

Chilled by the rising wind, Pete endured. Pete watched.

Captain Adam Hanratty, United States Marine Corps, rubbed the grit from his eyes and tried not to yawn. "Back it up in the barn, there, Corporal. We'll hole up here for the night."

"Aye aye, sir," responded Corporal Greg Patterson. "Backing her up." The big diesel of the LAV — light armored vehicle — whined, but the eight-wheeled personnel carrier still moved well. It was long overdue for depot-level maintenance, but Patterson's MOS had been repairing the big machines since before the ball dropped. Given the lack of opportunities for career changes, he'd gotten quite good at keeping them going with little or no logistical support over the last eight years. Although, in all honesty, the duct tape was starting to overwhelm the interior.

Once he had the vehicle centered inside of the rotting old barn, the Corporal shut down the engine. Noise discipline was a standing order these days. And more often than not, executed out of habit and reflex rather than from a superior's command. The Marines who had needed reminders hadn't survived this long.

Adam turned in his seat and looked at his four passengers. Baxter, to no one's surprise, was still racked out. The other three, also to no surprise, were completely awake. The personnel in the LAV were as jumbled as he'd ever seen. Patterson, at least, had been in Hanratty's command structure for an extended period of time. The brass had attached Baxter to their team, even if it was only for this mission. The other three? Well, in a sense, they were just like Baxter — they were from a separate unit now attached to his small team. "You guys mind checking the perimeter while we set up?"

Lieutenant Michael Ross, one of the few remaining members of US Navy SEAL Team 8, gave a silent nod. Hanratty might have outranked him, but both men knew that there was no place for rank on their current mission. On issues of the LAV, the SEAL deferred to the Marine. When it came to just about everything else, they were equals.

"Let's go, fellas," Ross said in the smooth baritone that didn't match his bushy beard and overlong hair. The Marines were scruffy, with a few days of stubble from their time inside the LAV, but the trio of SEALs took that to the next level. Back when the enemy had been muj, the relaxed standards just made sense. In certain parts of the world, clean-shaven men with close-cropped hair stood out like a sore thumb. Beards were just another form of camouflage. Despite the fact that the enemy couldn't distinguish differences in appearance, the SEALs still went around looking like a biker gang. Hanratty figured the brass was either too busy or just didn't care. Ross and his men clambered out of the vehicle through the rear hatches and secured them.

He turned back to Patterson. "Blue Force Tracker up?"

The Corporal glanced at the LCD display in the controls and nodded. "GPS signal is spotty, sir, but we should be able to get text through." The radios in the LAV were iffy at best. Even with the spectrum cleared from lack of signal activity, they couldn't reach more than a hundred miles or so. At this point, they were over twice that from base. The

GPS satellites had been failing in piecemeal fashion for years, but more often than not the remaining units were enough to use the next-gen communications and control system. As things stood now, the LAV was a lone blue dot in an empty blank sea. If they scrolled further north there'd be many other accompanying blue dots but for the moment, the LAV was alone.

We're Recon, he reminded himself. *Alone is what we do.* "How are we looking forward, Rivas?"

The LAV's gunner — and the crew's only woman — reported from her position up in the turret. "Looks clear from here, sir." The vehicle commander's normal station was up in the turret next to the gunner, but Hanratty preferred to stay down in the crew compartment.

Though the LAV only had light armor, it was impervious to the infected. Before Z-Day it had been common practice for vehicle commanders to keep their hatch open. This provided a full field of view until it was time to get to work. In urban environments, this was a suicidal tactic against the infected. The dumb things would walk right off of rooftops. The chances of them landing on top of a vehicle were low, but enough crews had taken casualties over the years that doctrine now called for secure hatches unless in a known safe zone.

To offset the inability to look outside, they'd wired small cameras into the turret to allow a supplemental field of view. The resulting images were then displayed on a flat-panel inside of the crew compartment. It was the definition of cobbled-together and never would have lasted in a fight against a modern opponent, but it was good enough for infected.

"Lock it up, Private," Hanratty ordered. "We're done for the day unless our Navy friends come scrambling back."

"Roger that, Captain," Rivas replied, and began unstrapping herself from the gunner's position. Hanratty slid over to give her more room to extricate herself. The position was far from the most comfortable in an already uncomfortable vehicle. Hanratty was just a shade over six feet and extended time in the gunner's seat usually put his legs to sleep. Rivas was maybe five feet in boots and he expected it wasn't any better for her. The short and scrawny Rivas made for an interesting contrast to the tall and chunky Patterson. Warts and all, though, he wouldn't trade either of his crew for any other Marine in the Corps. They'd been through far too much together, and he knew what they were capable of under pressure. That was more important than surface appearance.

He'd been out of the Naval Academy for six months when the outbreak hit. Since then, he'd seen too many spit-and-polish Marines crack in the face of the infected to gig Patterson for his scruffiness, or Rivas for her lack of height. Someone rapped shave-and-a-haircut on the rear hatch. Hanratty racked the camera display back into its storage slot. "You two get the drone up, I want to scope out our target before we settle in for the night." He glanced back at the figure curled up in one of the seats. Baxter was still out like a light with his uniform jacket off and over his head. "Let Prince Charming catch up on his beauty sleep. He'll just get in the way, anyhow."

Patterson grinned and Rivas rolled her eyes. The two opened the rear hatch and hopped down while he headed forward to the Blue Force Tracker. Ross clambered back up inside the vehicle as Hanratty tapped a message for headquarters.

"Hayloft is still solid, even as bad as this place looked," Ross announced. "I've got Janacek up there on over-watch. Gus is covering the back."

"Good," Hanratty said. "Big enough for everyone?"

"Should be, yeah. Ladder's loose, too. We can pull it up."

"Nice. We'll leave the top hatches unlocked," Hanratty decided. "We get swarmed in the middle of the night, we drop the ladder down onto the turret and just drive out of here."

"It's pretty clear," Ross said and settled into one of the crew seats with a heavy sigh. "Hell of a lot quieter than up north."

Hanratty stabbed the button to send the message and thought about it. "Lower population density in the immediate area, I guess. Couple of big cities around, but there are some good terrain features. Nice place to hole up and ride things out." Inside he cringed. *Better than what my folks had, for sure.* The BFT pinged. "And command acknowledges." He looked up at Ross. "You ready for tomorrow?"

The SEAL worked his mouth as though he were tasting something nasty. "Haven't fought people in a long time," he said. "Can't say I'm looking forward to it."

Hanratty grunted. "Let's get some overhead, first."

He stood and walked out of the LAV in a crouch. Ross followed, and when Hanratty was on the ground there was a thump.

A sleepy voice cried out in complaint. "Hey!"

"Sorry about that, Baxter," Ross said. "Didn't mean to wake you."

Hanratty shook his head and tried not to sigh. He understood the reason for Baxter's presence, even if the other Marine annoyed the rest of the crew.

Rivas and Patterson knelt in the driveway in front of the barn, assembling the Goshawk reconnaissance drone. It was roughly the size and shape of a manhole cover, and its four rotor housings made it look a bit like a large button. The top glittered with solar panels, and the bottom was a bluish-gray color that blended well into all sorts of skies. It was lightweight, state-of-the-art, and irreplaceable. The company that built them was just outside of Las Vegas. Even if they'd been able to reach it overland, the remaining spy satellites painted a stark picture of the state of the situation there. The infected seemed to thrive in arid environments; perhaps their decay rate slowed even further with low humidity. *Good thing we made it out of the sandbox when we did,* Hanratty mused.

"We're up, Captain," Rivas reported. "Batteries have a full charge."

"Let's do it," Hanratty ordered. Patterson and Rivas stepped back. The former drew the slim control tablet out of his rucksack and began pressing buttons. The Goshawk wasn't piloted, per se. It had a built in processor that controlled its flight functions. The operator determined its path through a GPS interface on the tablet; drawing a route for it to follow. This freed the operator up to be able to control the cameras the drone mounted and made it more robust for field use. Powered by lightweight carbon nanotube batteries and trickle-charged by the top-mounted solar panels, it could loiter in almost complete silence for up to two hours depending on wind conditions.

Of course, the Goshawk had also cost Uncle Sam a cool quarter million per unit, but you couldn't have everything. If the outbreak had never happened, something similar would have been on every kid's Christmas list right about now, and they'd be playing with even fancier toys in the field.

Patterson pressed a few buttons on the tablet and the rotors of the drone began to whir. After a moment, it built up enough lift to rise from the ground. It hesitated there as it downloaded coordinates from the tablet to determine a flight path. It began rising again, tilted and faded off to the southwest as it moved toward the objective. The camouflage was quite effective — even knowing it was there, Hanratty couldn't follow it as the drone moved off into the distance.

They crowded around Patterson as he knelt back down. If the officers peering over each shoulder unnerved him, the NCO didn't show it.

"Set up a repeating orbit," Hanratty ordered. "I'd like to focus on the perimeter fortifications."

"Aye, sir, repeating orbit," Patterson said. The farm they'd chosen to hole up for the night was five miles from the settlement, as the drone flew. The Goshawk was already halfway there. At a mere 500 feet above-ground-level, the picture quality was already better than their satellite shots.

"Huh," Hanratty grunted as the drone passed over a field outside of the settlement's walls. "They're farming the land outside of the walls." A tractor was running through the field, leaving neat lines of tilled earth behind it. "What do they farm here?" Hanratty was a city boy, and not ashamed to admit to his shortcomings.

Ross smiled a crooked smile. "Corn and soybeans, I'd guess," he murmured. "Grew up about a hundred miles east of here."

Hanratty was silent for a long moment. What *could* you say? Most everyone the surviving service members had known in the civilian world was likely to be long dead. A lot of troops hadn't been able to deal with that. The rest of them? Well, you just tucked it down and continued mission. Hanratty almost spoke, but finally decided to remain silent. He respected Ross, even liked him to some extent, but they weren't friends and he didn't know how the other man would react to any sort of personal words, particularly in front of enlisted personnel. He nodded toward the tablet. "Isn't that risky, planting outside of their walls?"

Ross whistled between his teeth as he considered his response. "It's kind of a catch-22; make the walls big enough to enclose the farm land you need to feed hundreds of people and livestock, you need thousands of people to make sure the walls are secure. If it were me, I'd grow a crop like soybeans outside the walls, and a foodstuff crop like corn inside. Given that the tractor is still moving I'd guess they're using the soybeans to make fuel. Not the most efficient use of it, but needs must."

The Goshawk was passing over the northwest corner of the encampment now, and the angle allowed for the study of the northern and western walls. The western wall was far more substantial and solid where the northern fence was chain link.

"Northern fence line runs along the creek," Hanratty noted. "Smart. Focus resources in the areas without terrain features that can act as a stop." He leaned closer to the tablet. "Patterson, can you zoom in any on the west wall?"

"The orbit is starting, let me dial it up, sir."

Hanratty let out a grunt of surprise. "Telephone poles. They planted telephone poles and used them as the frame for the fence."

"That's a hell of a lot of poles," Ross mused. "They've got houses lined up on the inside of the wall. Barracks, maybe?" He traced a pair of bigger buildings that flanked the two-lane road that ran through the settlement. "What are those? Guard posts?"

"Zooming in," Patterson said and dialed the cameras up further yet. They were HD-quality, but there was only so much you could make out from five hundred feet on a moving platform. Still, some shapes didn't need to be clear to recognize.

"Those are .50-cals," Ross said, in a surprised tone. "Ma Deuce on each of the guard posts flanking the road. Where the hell did they get those?"

"Who knows how much stuff was lying around?" Hanratty said. "Think how long it took to police up all the loose equipment at Camp Perry. All it takes is one or two National Guard units getting swallowed up, and someone to stumble upon what's left."

Patterson chimed in. "You like that, you're going to love this." He opened the field of view on the camera a little bit. In the middle of the settlement, to one side of the road, was a large graveled area. Hanratty had seen enough combines and farm tractors sitting idle on their journey from Camp Perry to recognize the group of vehicles lined up beside one another. The other vehicles in the lot needed no such familiarity.

Four Hummers and a lone deuce and a half occupied the opposite side of the parking area. Not only that, but there were several empty spaces in the neat row. Given the order with which the agricultural equipment had been set up, he didn't feel that it was a bad assumption that there were other vehicles that had once been there in those empty spaces. The uncertainty was bad enough, but what was present was still worse. He brought his finger down close to the tablet without touching the screen and made a circle.

"These Hummers still have the turret rings, that's where the guns at the guard posts came from. This one, though . . ." The fourth and final truck had a turret ring as well, but where the others were empty, a blue tarp covered the weapon mounted there. "Mark 19?" Hanratty referred to the ubiquitous, belt-fed 40mm grenade launcher that had been in US military service for decades.

"Gotta be," Ross said. "Barrel is too short for anything but that or a SAW, and there's no reason to leave a SAW in a turret. Nineteen's a hell of a lot heavier."

"Out-freaking-standing," Hanratty declared with a sigh. He studied the changing screen as the frame shifted from farmhouse to farmhouse, across barns converted into living quarters, fields and gardens, and the men, women, and children who moved around below in blissful ignorance of the observation. "Doesn't change anything," he decided. "We have our orders, and we proceed as planned. Patterson, how much time left on the drone?"

"The wind is picking up, sir, so that will cut into the endurance a bit. Call it forty-five minutes."

"A few more orbits, then, and let's bring it back and get settled in for the night. Tomorrow morning, we go in." Hanratty shared a glance with Ross. The other man was expressionless, but finally, he nodded his agreement.

In the distance, thunder rumbled.

Chapter 8

Alex usually slept great in the rain, but Casey's allergies were acting up. The snoring was doing a great job of keeping him awake.

After each snort, Alex punched the bunk above him, but Casey was out cold and didn't move.

Great. Stuck in the dark with his thoughts. Alex couldn't remember his old bedroom, but he wished he was there now, without anyone to keep him awake.

There were things you just didn't think about, now. Miss Val was an okay 'mom' to her charges, and all the other adults sorta kinda pitched in, but it was nothing like the real thing. Alex felt his throat getting tight and he swallowed. The last thing he wanted to do was start crying. If he gave into it, he wasn't liable to be able to stop, and that would just suck.

Sometimes Alex hated kids like Twigs and Vikram. Yeah, Twigs' dad had died and that stunk for him, but he still had a mom to give him a hug every night. Vikram had *both* of his parents, and his dad was cool as hell — he had a *sword*, for cripe's sake!

He sighed as a wave of shame rushed through him. *Real nice, Alex, hate a couple little kids just because they still have parents.*

No way he was going to be able to go back to sleep now. He had a wind-up flashlight he could read with. But it would be just his luck that Val or Mr. Vance would walk by and see the light under the bedroom door. Miguel and Kevin were sound asleep in the other bunk bed, and the adults wouldn't appreciate him being the only one awake. He actually understood that part, at least — it was hard enough getting Betty and the other weird adults calmed down and asleep without kids running around. So he was stuck in the bedroom, for better or worse.

Frustrated, he huffed a sigh and gave the bottom of Casey's mattress one final, sullen punch. As if in response, the other boy emitted a long snort, his loudest yet.

Alex had a moment of inspiration. He'd stashed his iPod under the bed. If he was lucky, there'd be enough of a charge that he could listen to music until he fell asleep.

He ninja-rolled onto the floor and peered into the shadows under his bed. Each of the boys in the room had a shallow box of personal items they kept under their beds. With a bunk bed on either wall, space was at a premium in the room.

Not that any of the boys had much. For the first few months after their rescue, Val's students had owned little more than the clothes on their backs. When the salvage teams had gone through the school, they'd brought back all the backpacks they'd found. It was sad, but it had been a little like Christmas, getting their own stuff back, even if the contents had been school junk for the most part.

Alex fingered the worn Spider-man logo on his backpack. He'd thrown away the papers and folders inside long ago. The bag still worked well to keep smaller things together so they didn't rattle around inside his box. He pulled the bag out of the box and unzipped it.

One of the hardest adjustments for Alex had been the loss of music. Some of the most vivid memories he had of home were of his mother dancing in the kitchen as she prepared dinner or folded laundry. The details of his mother were nothing more than a faded, faceless presence, but he remembered the music.

That first Christmas, the adults had tried to make things as normal as possible for the kids. There'd been gifts — most of them scavenged, Alex assumed, from stores around town.

As soon as Alex tore the paper off of the music player, he had a sudden, piercing insight. It would be a long time if ever, before people could ever make something like this again. It was a terrifying thought for a five-year-old, and he'd burst into tears.

As he'd gotten older Alex had realized that his sense of panic had been overblown. With any luck, there were *millions* of sealed iPods around the country. Maybe some would go bad over time, but many others would not. There was so much stuff lying around, and so few people left to use it, that he didn't need to worry. Despite that, his treatment of the small device was almost superstitious in its care.

He pulled the small box out and slid the sleeve off. The cardboard was starting to get a little rough around the edges but it still kept the two halves of the plastic clamshell together. At some point, he supposed he'd need to replace the sleeve with a rubber band or cord.

He plucked the music player out and tapped the wheel. After a moment, the screen lit up, and he smiled. He had a little over a third of a battery left. That should be enough to lull him to sleep, he judged.

Reassembling the box, he dropped it back in the bag and rooted around for his headphones. The room was dark enough that the screen served as a decent flashlight. He panned it around the inside of the bag as he searched. Where were the stupid . . . Alex froze.

The glow of the iPod had fallen across a white patch sewn into the backpack just below the zipper opening. Alex knew it was there, but he'd never *looked* at it.

Whoever had written the three lines had neat, angular handwriting — his mother's?

Alex Worthington
18701 Stone Creek Lane
Lewisville, Indiana 47235
Of course.

His search for the headphones forgotten, Alex leaned back against the bed. He pressed his hand to his mouth to hold back a shout.

Memories surfaced. His mother was still a shadow, but he remembered a voice and a hand, holding his own.

Look both ways, Alex, it's your first day of school.

Look both ways.

His hand fell away from his mouth.

"We lived across from the school," Alex whispered. "We walked every day."

Casey snored again, but Alex didn't care; his mind was a blur.

He hadn't been outside of the walls since the rescue, but he thought back to that afternoon, when he'd studied the area around them with binoculars. That cluster of buildings — was that his old school?

It was Stone Creek Elementary; he saw the words every day on a cafeteria tray, but he'd never made the connection to his address. Why would he? He only rarely got into the backpack, and it was *his* bag, he didn't need to study it.

How far is it?

Charlie regained consciousness when his wife began gnawing on his hand.

Despite the agony of his skin ripping and the warm rush of blood dripping off of his fingers, he didn't process his surroundings for a handful of breaths. His automatic reaction to the pain had pulled his hand up into his chest and smeared his shirt with blood.

He stared forward, not understanding why the world seemed sideways through the spider-webbed windshield. Then, all at once, awareness returned, and he realized. He was hanging from a seatbelt, and their Tahoe was laying on its passenger side.

A hand latched onto his right arm and pulled.

He looked down. His wife had reached up from her position in the passenger seat. She dragged his wounded arm back toward her blood-smeared mouth with a strength he'd never seen her exhibit in all their years together. "Sheila!" he screamed and tried to pull his arm back. "What the hell are you doing?" He met her eyes, but that sight was somehow worse than the knife-sharp pain in his hand and the dawning realization that his wife was trying to eat him. Her eyes, her sky-blue, soft, and caring eyes, were a flat, dull gray. They were lifeless eyes, but his wife's body still moved. A hissing moan rose out of her throat as she strained to pull him to her.

"Stop!" Charlie screamed, and yanked his arm free. Turning away from the mind-shattering sight beneath him, he scrabbled at the handle to the driver's door and tried to pull it open. It was even harder pushing against gravity, but he got it open and snaked his forearm through the gap before it slammed back down. He cried out at the

added pain. Pushing his feet against the firewall, he reached down to his waist with his maimed hand. A couple of his fingers weren't responding, and further waves of agony began to snake up his wrist. After several agonizing moments, he popped the seatbelt release and caught himself as it rewound into the door frame. A loop captured his left arm, but that was a minor concern at the moment. Beneath him, Sheila hissed again. Probing fingers brushed against his legs.

Charlie arched his body and thrust his shoulder up and out of the Tahoe's passenger compartment in one convulsive motion. The door slammed back down again, this time on his back. It knocked the wind from him for a heart-stopping moment, and when he regained it his cries of pain were weak and strained. He pulled up one leg and fumbled for a foothold. Finally, he was able to snake his shoe inside the steering wheel, and he shoved himself up again. He had both arms out now. The door rode his back for the entire motion; he hadn't pushed with enough force for it to lurch up and away from him. Charlie gasped for breath, pushed with his legs and pulled with both arms this time, and swung out from the inside of the truck. The door slammed down and latched behind him. Spent, he lay on the driver's side of the vehicle and tried to regain his breath.

As the pounding of his heart calmed he became more aware of what was going on around him. He eased his head up to assess the world he'd entered. If anything, sanity had departed even further from this reality than it had from the one inside of his truck.

Up and down the highway, vehicles had rolled over, stopped, or ended up in the ditches. Smoke trailed up into the sky from burning wrecks. Charlie didn't know how long he'd been unconscious, but the lack of emergency response was striking. What in the world had happened? The destruction stretched as far as the eye could see. There didn't seem to be any one point of origin. His head throbbed from where he'd hit it on something, but he was starting to remember. Another car had slammed into the Tahoe and the truck rolled as he tried to regain control. He stared at the rail at the side of the road for a long moment before he realized that he was on an overpass. He'd been within a few feet of hitting the side rail and going over.

Screaming, from nearby. He looked, and almost wished he hadn't. In a car just behind him, the vehicle had slammed into the guard rail and stopped. The airbags had deployed, but he was still able to see the spray of blood inside of the car as the driver turned on the female passenger.

"What in the hell . . ." Charlie whispered. This was insane. It was like one of Cooper's zombie movies . . . Cooper!

He raised himself up onto hands and knees and peered down into the back of the Tahoe. His son had been lying down on the back bench napping. Oh, Lord, had he taken his seatbelt off? He couldn't make out the third row through the window. Cringing in agony, he slid off of the Tahoe and limped around to the back of the truck and tried the handle. Locked, of course.

From further down the road, a roaring engine interrupted the intermittent screams in the silence. Charlie turned away from the back of his truck and faced the road in an attempt to see what was coming. The roof of a single vehicle was visible as it jerked back and forth across the highway, dodging wrecks. It wasn't moving all that fast, but from Charlie's perspective, it seemed like an approaching freight train. The roof shifted to the median as the driver avoided a large knot of vehicles, and then, in an instant it was upon him.

With the humming purr of knobby off-road tires, the lifted Jeep zoomed by. Charlie leaped out of the way on instinct alone, but the vehicle hadn't been all that close. The driver of the Jeep had been running on the far edge of the overpass, well away from the wreck of the Tahoe. He walked around the back of the truck and opened his mouth to call for help, but then looked down. Generous smears of blood decorated the front of his shirt. All around, survivors of wrecks were pulling themselves out, but the others were as well. The momentary silence broke with rising screams as the others fell upon their friends and families as though they were mere prey. It was as if the Jeep's passage had awoken something dormant in the wrecks on the highway.

Hell, Charlie wouldn't have stopped, either.

When the Tahoe had rolled, the rear window popped out of its frame. Charlie snaked his fingers into the seam and tugged. The safety glass was somewhat intact, but loose slivers of it dug into his palms and the bottom of his fingers. His left hand joined the right's chorus of pain.

Finally, with a protracted ripping sensation, the window came loose. He cast it to the pavement and leaned over, shoving his upper body inside of the truck. It was dim, but Charlie could make out the shadow of his son, crumpled on top of the rear passenger window. He stirred as Charlie crawled further inside. "Cooper!" Charlie shouted. "Coop, you okay?"

A hand like a vise clamped onto his wrist, and Charlie jerked backward. Cooper came with him, and as the light fell on the battered form of his only son, something snapped in Charlie's mind. Charlie would never know the extent of his son's injuries. The only answer Cooper gave him was a low hiss; his eyes the gray of a storm cloud sky. The scream started out as a cry of denial, but it became something more primal. Charlie screamed and screamed. When he ran out of breath he took another breath, only to keep screaming until the agony of his tortured throat overwhelmed the mindless shriek of terror and loss that consumed him.

Charlie jerked awake.

He lay still for a long moment and took slow, deep breaths as he tried to slow his racing heart.

The damn dream again. It had been months, and he'd allowed himself to think that maybe, just maybe, he was done with it. No such luck.

He shifted into a sitting position, more out of the desire to not tip the folding cot over than to be quiet. Across from him, Corey slept on his own folding cut, snoring. Charlie smiled. Back when electricity had been ubiquitous, he'd grown accustomed to sleeping with a fan blowing beside him for the noise. In the absence of bedside fans, Corey's buzzing snores made for an adequate replacement.

His heart had ceased its trip-hammering rhythm, but he knew from long experience that sleep would be elusive. He reached under the cot and pulled out his boots. He laced them up and tied them, and then levered himself up and out of the cot.

The interior of the bus was actually quite spacious. They'd removed the bench seats save for a couple at the front, leaving the entire interior wide open. After only a day of scavenging, full totes stacked in neat columns filled the back quarter of the bus. It wasn't the greatest haul in quantity, but they'd gotten some good, useful salvage to bring home. He tiptoed down the center aisle of the bus. The folding doors were open to allow for a bit of breeze — even in early spring the interior got a little stuffy. Dalton sat on the bottom step, carving on a shapeless chunk of wood. He glanced up at Charlie's approach.

"Bit early. Can't sleep?"

Charlie shrugged and huffed a sigh. He jerked a thumb over his shoulder and raised a questioning eyebrow.

"Yeah, sure." Dalton glanced at his watch. "Only a couple of hours early. Been quiet. Just me and the stars."

Charlie nodded. Reclaimed tin roofing material plated the sides of the bus like medieval armor. There had been enough barns in the area surrounding the community that there was plenty of it. The upper row covered up all the windows save for narrow vision and firing slits. A hinged lower row, when loosened, hung down a bare inch off of the ground. This combined to make the former school bus a mobile, anti-biter pillbox. The panels also served as an effective alarm system. Any biter that walked up and tried to claw its way in created an amazing racket. The fact that Corey was still snoring away was a testament to the fact that yes, it was a quiet night.

Dalton stepped up and out of the doorway. As Charlie stepped down he sketched a salute with one index finger and clambered inside.

Charlie was still restless, so he elected for a short stroll to stretch his legs before taking a seat. They'd dragged a rusting sheet metal fire pit from behind one of the houses and set it in front of the bus door. Many of the trees in the subdivision were non-native breeds that had died without frequent watering. This provided a more than adequate supply of firewood. The rations the supply teams carried were in cans and didn't need cooking, but there was something soothing about a fire. Fire appealed to some base instinct, recently reborn, that reveled in the capability of a dancing flame to chase away the terrors of the night. They didn't have a lot of things, but last night at least, they'd had warm Spaghetti-Os, heated over a crackling fire.

The irony there, of course, was that light attracted biters almost as well as sound. The lack of widespread man-made lighting made small light sources like campfires stand out like neon signs. But the fire was small, and the bulk of the bus served as an adequate block. By now, the fire had dwindled down to a warm, comfortable bed of embers. Charlie knelt down and press-checked his sidearm in the faint light. Brass winked at him from the loaded chamber, and he holstered it once more. He'd not been much of a pistol man before everything fell apart, but he'd been through a hard and unforgiving school these past years. This changed world was intolerant of mistakes, even if

Charlie had an advantage they had yet to see in any of the other survivors.

He flexed his fingers and watched shadows play over the twisted scarring on the back of his right hand. The motion still felt stiff and unnatural, but Tish had put his hand back together as well as she could. She was good, but she was no orthopedic surgeon. He doubted she'd have disagreed with the assessment, but he'd never be so uncouth as to say it to her. He liked Tish, but then, he liked most people. Always had. That, at least, hadn't changed.

The fire crackled, and an ember fell to the ground through one of the rusted-out spots on the bottom of the fire pit. After tonight it was bound to be useless, but they wouldn't be needing it any longer. The team had gone through eight houses that day, two-thirds of the way through the addition. Charlie didn't expect that the others would take them much past noon tomorrow. Especially given the state of the homes they'd already made their way through.

They'd been careful in scavenging through the home with the burst-open door, but it had been devoid of any living, or non-living, presence. Charlie suspected the escapee had not been human — there was too much useful equipment left behind.

What was most troublesome was not the existence of the home with the burst-open door, but the two more just like it. It was a small statistical sample, but they'd gleaned two concrete facts from the searches. The homes with broken doors or windows were empty. The homes that were intact generally had one or more biters, though they'd all been in sorry shape. As best as they could tell, the events that had precipitated the breaking of the doors and windows occurred around the same time. If it were survivors fleeing, there would be evidence of a horde large enough to force them from homes that had attics to hide in. Even if it had been a group of human raiders — rare but not unknown — there would be some evidence of their passage. And raiders wouldn't have skipped going through the other houses in the subdivision.

The three of them had grumbled over it while packing the bus and eating dinner, though none had any grand insight. What Charlie knew, though he'd not expressed it to his partners, was that something had changed. The crawling feeling at the back of his neck when he studied the broken doors and windows told him that change was unlikely to be a good one. For that reason if nothing else, he was glad for the speed with which they'd worked their way through the division. This was something that the other survivors needed to know about. Part of him considered radioing in to report, but in the end, he'd elected not to. He'd have to rely on Corey and Dalton to do the lion's share of the speaking, and he didn't know if that would convey his concern over what he'd seen.

No, he wanted to look Miles in the eye when he explained what he'd seen. Charlie smiled again, though his expression was wistful. Miles, good Miles, would understand, and would believe.

Out in the shadows, something shifted.

Charlie willed his body into stillness. *I didn't see that*, he lied to himself. Perhaps his body believed the lie and perhaps not, but he didn't flinch or react, and that was his intention. Without moving his head, he raised his eyes and waited.

Another shift, and now he knew *where* to look, on the left side of the cul de sac, near the third house they'd scavenged. It had been intact and inhabited by an elderly man. He'd died in a bathroom and spent the following years doing laps on the tile floor until it collapsed from the sheer wear and tear on its feet. Before it had fallen it had made a God-awful mess of the interior. The damage caused to the medicines and toiletries as the biter ground them underfoot rendered it all worthless.

He studied the shadows beside the front porch. He thought the noise might perhaps have been the brushing of fabric against the wooden lattice along the bottom of the porch. They'd given it a cursory glance and tap earlier that day, but nothing had reacted from within. He'd thought the lattice tight on his first inspection, but now he questioned his judgment.

The movement in the shadow this time was silent, and he studied it, without expression as it shifted. Yes, there at the back corner, he judged. He flexed his fingers and debated whether to draw his pistol. A biter would have moved in for the attack by now. With the fire before him, there was no missing Charlie, even with their reduced state of awareness. Whatever crouched at the corner of the porch was something else.

Which made it all the more dangerous, of course.

Charlie studied the shadow and mentally grumbled at the impact of the fire pit on his night vision. Details came into slow focus.

At once it hit him.

The figure in the shadows was not crouched by the porch; it stood upright. One hand rested on the corner post to the porch railing; the other cocked in mid-air as though waiting for something. Charlie's sense of danger left him, replaced by a hollow sensation in the pit of his stomach.

It was a child. Who could guess how old, given the vagaries of diet in this fallen world? Either way, frozen in fear rather than playing some deadly version of freeze tag. This was no world for a child to grow up in, especially alone. The mere fact of survival was incomprehensible.

Where are you from? Is this your neighborhood? Charlie ached to call out, but he knew how his raspy, damaged voice would come across. No. Best to back off and show a lack of interest in harming the child, lest he spook him or her into running. At once he felt a rush of fear. Had the child been watching him when he'd toyed with the biter and allowed it within a hair's breadth of biting? How that must have seemed, to someone unaware of Charlie's ability to handle himself.

He licked his lips, then made a point to turn his head and study the right side of the cul de sac as though it were the most interesting thing in the world. After a long pause he heard a slight rustling sound, and when he glanced back, the child was gone.

Charlie sighed and flexed his fingers.

Finally, he rose from the fire pit — his knees cracked like gunshots in the night — and moved back to the bus. He glanced over his shoulder, and of course saw nothing. Stepping inside, he peered into the shadowed interior. Corey snored on, and Dalton teetered on the edge of heavy breathing and outright snoring. Neither of the men was aware of what had just happened outside, and Charlie smiled at the irony. He eased into the back of the bus and studied the stack of totes. Where had they . . . Oh yes, that one. He shifted one tote out of its position at the top of a stack and opened up the one beneath it. The revealed tote held miscellaneous foodstuffs. The top layer consisted of canned goods, a case of Ramen noodles, and a sealed six-pack of Hershey bars. Glancing over his shoulder, Charlie drew out his knife and made a slit in the packaging of the pack of candy bars. Sheathing the knife, he considered the pack and extracted three bars. He set them aside for the moment and rearranged the totes. This task complete, he grabbed the candy bars and crept back out of the school bus.

At the bottom of the steps, he studied the shadows near the porch. The figure of the child was gone, and he detected no further movement. Decision made, he took slow, careful steps forward. As he went he made a fan of the candy bars and held them out with one hand to display them.

Still on the roadway, he paused at the base of the third home's driveway. He looked at the porch for a long moment and considered, then decided to not push his luck. He displayed the candy bars a final time, then closed the fan into a neat rectangle. The mailbox of the house was the shape of a miniature barn, peaked roof and all. Clamped to the pole next to it was a square receptacle for the local newspaper. He stacked the candy bars on top of the newspaper box and backed away. After taking a few steps, Charlie turned his back on the house and crept back to the bus.

This time, he took Dalton's seat on the bottom step. With a slight smile on his face, he lowered his eyes to the embers of the fire pit and listened. He didn't know if he'd hear anything, but for the first time in a long time, Charlie waited with something other than tired resignation. He listened, and he hoped.

Tom Oliver's sarcastic sense of humor was famous throughout the community. When he'd built a bar in front of his homestead and begun bartering home-brewed beer, a chalkboard on the front door had featured a series of names that elicited either guffaws or confused frowns from eager patrons. He'd finally settled on a name that tickled his fancy, and mounted a carved wooden sign over the door that read, "The Last Bar."

Maybe Tom's place was the last bar, and maybe it wasn't. It was the only bar anyone knew of, so maybe that was close enough. And while it wasn't quite last call at The Last Bar, Ronnie Cartwright decided to make it a night.

Home-brewed beer and scavenged hard alcohol made for a decent selection, though prices tended to shift some. As garden crops came in, Tom liked to trade beer for vegetables; during the winter, he traded it for know-how or labor. The vegetables ended up on The Last Bar's ever growing dinner menu along with the latest sacrificial victim from Tom's herd of beef cattle. The labor he generally used to help wrangle the cattle or do other chores around the farm. It wasn't quite the commune that Miles Matthews liked to complain about, but it wasn't a capitalist utopia, either.

Promises of "splitting a rick of wood for you in the spring" for a beer in the winter came close to Wimpy's promise of paying next week for a cheeseburger today, but it had generally worked until the mass of notes had overwhelmed Tom to the point that he'd made an executive decision to streamline things.

The salvage crews got the first choice of any alcohol as part of their pay. They drank some of it, but a lot of it got traded to Tom in exchange for drinking and eating credit. On one salvage run, Tom convinced Charlie Maddox to run by a few banks and collect all the quarters he could lay hands on.

The quarters were a relic of a nation that existed only in memory; valueless without the backing of the Federal Reserve. On the other hand, pocket change was also relatively scarce throughout the settlement. It was akin to striking gold, especially after Tom defaced each coin with a pattern he'd etched into a chisel. He split the quarters with Charlie 50-50, and hence an economy was born. It wasn't as fancy and complete as some would have liked, but it was a start.

When Charlie needed things, he swapped quarters for them and pointed out you could get a brew and a pretty decent burger (the less said about the bun the better, of course) for one. Tom still did a good business in vegetables, but the same chalkboard that he'd used for the series of changing names now listed a price list of other barter items. All at once there was a source for luxuries above and beyond the hygiene items and clothing that the settlement stored and doled out as needed.

In quick order, The Last Bar became The Last Bar, Bank, and General Store. There were complaints of course; many people in the settlement invested any and all their free time into such endeavors, but Tom pointed out that he'd accept any quarter in trade, defaced or not. The complainers just had to go out and get them.

That shut up most of the overt complaining; those who were of a sort to whine not being the sort that would go out and scavenge, especially more than once. The scavenger teams risked everything for the settlement, and part of the payoff for that risk was the ability to find a little extra funding, and the right to first dibs on any luxury items. All things considered, it wasn't that much.

A secondary benefit to Tom's quarters was the newfound ability to compensate survivors for things other than manual labor. These exchanges somehow ended up creating more paper than his ticketing system had. It wasn't long before Tom contracted with Charlie to acquire him a laptop, due to the increased complexity of the transactions.

Tom's dealings with Ronnie were a prime example. The older man's land fell outside of the boundaries of the settlement, but he'd more than compensated his fellow survivors over the years with his know-how and lifelong farming background. Looking forward to the future, Tom could see a day where they'd consume all the closest available salvage. They needed to plan ahead.

While Ronnie's farming tended toward corn and soybeans, he also was a fair hand at gardening and had grown his own potatoes ever since he'd been a youngster. You could make lots of good things from potatoes — one of which was vodka, of course. When Ronnie told Tom Oliver that he'd once made his own vodka for the fun of it, Tom recognized the opportunity at hand.

Which was how Tom Oliver ended up with a rented vodka still — acquired on a short salvage run to Ronnie's old barn — next to his beer brewing equipment. The compensation worked out well for Ronnie; there was enough to go around to maintain everyone in the basics, but a life without anything more than that is one that isn't much worth living. This, in the end, was why no one had much to say about Tom's venture. If nothing else it created something for people to *do*, and as Tom liked to point out, it wasn't like he had an exclusive license on any of the things he was doing. In all honesty, he would have welcomed competition. It would have made some of his more high-maintenance customers less difficult to deal with. Ronnie hadn't approached Tom just for the material benefits. Oh sure, he liked a beer now and then, but more than anything, just socializing with people made it worthwhile for the retired farmer. His health wasn't the greatest, he couldn't take a leak without straining fit to bust a gut, but his mind was still sharp and he still had a storyteller's wit. The vodka, beer, and burgers were just a means to an end.

Ronnie hauled his handkerchief out and covered his mouth as he began to cough. Talking seemed to make his coughing worse, but it had been worth it tonight. The entire bar had been on the edge of their seats for Ronnie's recounting of the arrest of Chris Naylor and his later urination on Larry Vance. Raucous laughter filled the place when he'd ended the story in a quiet, dry tone that would have fit right in with NPR. The laughter had been so loud that some of those in the bar had jumped in surprise at the volume, but the rest seemed to welcome it.

"Night, RC!" Tom called from behind the bar. He waved his hand in farewell, and Ronnie returned the gesture. Several others in the bar bid him farewell as well, but things were beginning to wind down.

Ronnie took the steps one at a time with an excruciating slowness that would have driven him to frustration if he hadn't long ago resigned himself to the fact of his own age. It was what it was, and there was no need to complain about it. His wife, God rest her soul, had once complained that he could have given lessons in stoicism to a Spartan. Ronnie didn't know about all that — Greta had been an honors English teacher at Lewisville High for most of their four decades together — but he did know that complaining didn't fix anything as fast as buckling down and doing something about it.

Not long after Z-Day he'd made a similar comment to that black fellow, Vance, and the retired Marine had given him a solemn nod. "Charlie Mike, Ronnie. Continue mission." Ronnie smiled at the memory. *Charlie mike. Well, it's easier to say than 'grin and bear it', isn't it?*

He step-shuffled out of Tom's driveway and onto the pavement of the county road. A couple of hundred feet down the road, walk down Martha's old driveway, and his bed would be waiting. Maybe tonight he'd be able to get some sleep without that dumb kid across the way screaming every time he had a cough.

Overhead, thunder rumbled and a light sprinkling of rain began to fall. Ronnie extended a hand, palm-up, and appreciated the feel of the drops against his skin. Right on time, the rain was. Get the fields a little wet, let the sun keep the soil temperatures up so they could start planting. This year, maybe, they could even extend them some. None of the plow teams had reported any attacks. The first few years, they'd had to use jury-rigged noise emitters as a distraction to draw the dead away from where they wanted to farm. It had been a complex dance of farm, stop and try to clear things out when the dead started trickling back in, then distract in another place. If they could increase their acreage enough this year, maybe they could start running a surplus instead of living on the knife's edge.

All in all, not a bad way to spend a retirement, Ronnie judged, and stepped off of the paved road and into Miss Martha's driveway. Well, now it was that teacher lady's house, and a bunch of the kids, but damn if he could remember her name half of the time. When in doubt, Ronnie just resorted to "ma'am," and that was just fine. He was still plenty sharp upstairs, like his dad, and his grandpa before him, but sometimes names slipped his mind. *And after what Greta went through with the Alzheimer's, I'll take a few messed up names every day of the week.*

The house was silent as he shuffled past. The teacher lady — Val, that was her name, he remembered in triumph — ran a tight ship, and her charges went to bed not long after the sun went down. Good kids, every one of them, respectful and polite whenever they had occasion to speak with him. Val and some of her helpers would shush them when they played outside, as though they might bother Ronnie or any of the other residents of the horse barn apartments, but Ronnie liked the noise just fine — it reminded him of happier times. It sounded like life.

Halfway across the back yard to the horse barn, Ronnie pulled up short and gave an annoyed grunt. He'd only had two of Tom's beers tonight, but they were already demanding release. Vance's daughter, the doctor, had laid it out for him a couple of months back. Enlarged prostate, most likely. Nothing to do, nowadays. She'd been nice enough about the diagnosis, almost apologetic in fact. He had a couple of years, maybe more. Maybe less.

Of course, all things considered, the worsening cough was more likely to be the end of him than slow-spreading cancer. Bunch of things that could be, and hard to nail down without the benefit of an x-ray. The doc had been apologetic about that, too, tip-toeing around references to pain management before it got too bad.

Hell, I'm almost eighty years old. Not like death is a foreign concept, girlie. Ronnie stepped around the windmill's holding tank and unzipped the fly of his overalls. *Charlie mike, young lady.*

He stood for a long moment and tried not to strain so hard. He was finally rewarded with a weak stream, and he tried not to tense up despite the urgency of his bladder. Patience, patience. It might take a while, but he'd get there, and then . . .

White-hot pain blossomed in his lower back. He staggered forward, and urine splashed the front of his bibs. He couldn't care about that; the pain was the center of his existence at that moment. Despite the pain, and the crippling urge to curl forward away from it, he managed to keep his feet, until a rough shove slammed him into the side of the holding tank. He fell, turning as he went, and landed face-down in the wet grass.

Ronnie got his arms under his chest and tried to push himself up, but a weight slammed into his back, above the spot of pain. He opened his mouth to cry out from the agony of it, but a hand grasped the back of his head and shoved his mouth into the grass.

A hot warmth was spreading from the point of pain in his lower back; blood, he supposed. His feet were starting to go numb, and he realized that he must be bleeding out.

The weight on his back shifted, the hand still pressing his face into the ground. More spots of pain blossomed, punctuating the harsh words whispered into his dying ears by a voice he not only knew but never would have expected.

"*You . . .*" Stab.

"*Make . . .*" Stab.

"*Too . . .*" Stab.

"*Much . . .*" Stab.

"*Noise!*"

Finally, the weight lifted from his back, but Ronnie was already beginning to drift away.

Derisive humor tinged his final thoughts. *Guess we were both wrong, weren't we, Doc? Wasn't cancer or a cough.*

The coldness of the rain on his exposed skin dueled with the spreading warmth of his wounds, but even that began to fade. By then, what he had been was gone, and he no longer cared.

Chapter 9

Miles was already half-awake when something rapped against the window across the bedroom. He levered up on one elbow and gave it a quizzical glance.

Real or not real?

In the light of day he was usually able to keep his internal freak outs to a minimum. It was worse at night, though he went through spells. Sometimes he slept with a pillow over his face, to muffle any cries he made in his dreams.

When the noise repeated after the space of a few seconds, he breathed a sigh of relief, pulled the covers aside, and stepped across the bedroom.

They'd boarded up the windows of the bedroom to the height of Miles' chin. The windows in the old farmhouse were quite tall for ventilation purposes, so there was two feet of exposure above the final barrier. When things got too stuffy in the summer, they could lower the upper sashes and allow air to circulate through the house.

He pulled the drape aside and peered out over the top board. The sky was still gray with the promise of dawn, but he could make out the figure of his father-in-law standing outside. He looked harried.

"What?" Miles yelled. Tish grumbled from the bed, but he ignored her for the moment. Larry just gave him a look and pointed to the back door. Miles gave him a thumbs-up and turned away from the window. He snagged his watch off of the bedside table on the way.

Halfway down the hall, he had the watch strapped on. Miles angled the face to read the hands. *Five thirty? What the hell* . . .

His pace quickened, and he unlocked the back door and pulled it open. "Is Trina all right?" he asked, in a rush.

Larry looked grim. "She's fine. She's still asleep. This is something else." His father in law wiped his face with his hand and was silent for a moment of consideration. "I need you and Tish both, she needs to check something."

Miles shook his head, not understanding what the other man was trying to tell him. "She's still asleep, but . . ." He looked at Larry's face and studied it for the first time. The other man seemed almost haunted. "Pops, what's going on?"

The other man frowned. "I think somebody murdered Ronnie last night."

Last night's rain had been slow and steady, and the grass stuck to Miles and Tish's shoes as they followed Larry behind Val's house. Despite the early hour, several people were milling about on the road. The presence of the graveyard shift deputies, Brett Simmons and Jenny Faqir, dissuaded them from coming any closer.

Numb, Miles thought, *we never scavenged crime scene tape. We've never* needed *it.* "Brett, Jenny," he said as they passed.

The pair nodded greetings. Brett, who was red-headed and pale at the best of times, was paler even than was normal for him. Jenny was usually upbeat enough for an entire team of high school cheerleaders. This morning she was as reticent as Miles had ever seen her.

Ahead, Larry came to a stop at the back corner of the house. "I came out to take a leak. No moon, so I had a flashlight." He swallowed. "The first thing I saw was the blood."

He stepped aside and let them take in the sight. The windmill Miles had reminisced over just yesterday was now the scene of unspeakable horror. Ronnie's overalls were so stained with blood it would have been impossible to tell the original color if he hadn't seen them before. If not for the blood Miles could almost have convinced himself that the old man was sleeping. Almost. The crumpled form at the base of the overflow tank was bad enough. What was above the body made Miles lurch to the side and vomit into the damp grass. He stood there for a long moment with his hands on his knees. A gentle hand rubbed his back, and he straightened. "Sorry," he whispered to his wife. Tish gave him a sympathetic smile, and he turned back to the horrific tableau behind Val's house.

Someone, presumably the killer, had left them a message on the water tank, written in Ronnie's blood. The lean-to they'd constructed over it to shield it from the sun and keep the water a little cooler had protected the lettering from the worst effects of the rain, although some had still slanted in under the roof line and washed into the statement. Trails of drying blood dripped down from the letters, but the intent of the message survived.

A WISE OLD OWL LIVED IN AN OAK
THE MORE HE SAW THE LESS HE SPOKE

THE LESS HE SPOKE THE MORE HE HEARD
WHY CAN'T WE ALL BE LIKE THAT WISE OLD
BIRD?

Larry broke the silence. "Tish, honey, I need you to check the body. There might be clues or something." He groaned. "Ah, I feel crazy even asking."

"I'll look," she whispered.

She stepped over to the prone figure on the ground. She pulled a pair of rubber gloves out of the pocket of her jeans and pulled them on. They were heavy-duty dishwashing gloves, but most important, they were reusable. Disposable latex surgical gloves were just one more item on their list of things to use only in time of absolute need. Ronnie, at least, didn't need to worry about the sanitary condition of the gloves. She pulled at the blood-soaked clothing, stepping to either side to adjust her point of view as she looked up and down Ronnie's motionless form.

Larry stepped closer to Miles and said, sotto voce, "Val's keeping the kids away from the back windows."

Miles looked at his father-in-law and felt a wave of relief wash over him. "Thank you," he said. "Damn, I didn't think about that." He rubbed his eyes with the palms of his hand. "Gah, what the hell are we going to do, Pops?"

"We got to figure it out, kid. This is going to send people into an uproar . . ."

A loud voice from behind them brought Larry to silence.

"What in the world is this?"

As Larry and Miles turned, Brett Simmons was already stepping forward, "Mrs. Benedict, this is a crime scene, please stay back . . ."

The subject of his entreaties blasted through them as though they weren't even there. "*Deputy* Simmons, you will address me as Councilwoman Benedict or I'll bring up a resolution to put you on the wall so fast your head will spin!"

"Oh shit," Miles said, then, with a sigh, "Here we go." He stepped forward and injected enough sweetness into his tone to cause spontaneous diabetes. "Councilwoman Benedict, as Brian said, this is an active crime scene. Please stay back while we assess the situation."

If nothing else, Norma Benedict was the prime example showing that Z-Day had selected survivors on the basis of luck rather than fitness. She hadn't been a politician before. As best as Miles could determine she'd been a receptionist for a shipping company. When the survivors had put forth the original proposal to create the council she'd not only been in the forefront cheering it on, she'd managed to wrangle enough support to nab one of the three seats on the fledgling political venture. Short, opinionated, and loud, she grated on even the most patient of nerves, but when it came time for campaigning she turned into a warm-hearted caricature of everyone's favorite grandmother. Miles knew for a fact that if the rest of the settlement could see the way she treated her "subordinates" she'd be out on her ear at the next election. He'd never been lucky enough, though, to have enough witnesses for tales of her sound and fury to spread. Larry was more phlegmatic on the issue. "There are always lousy officers," he'd proclaimed once. "We had a doozy of a Major once. Your Uncle just ignored the stupid orders and filtered the rest down to what was actually doable. Same principle here."

"I will *not* stay back, and I will be assessing the situation for myself, Marshal," Norma barked. She marched between Brian and Jenny. The latter settled for rolling his eyes; Jenny was beginning to turn a bright shade of red. Miles made eye contact with her until she read his poker face and nodded. This was neither the time nor the place for a bureaucratic pissing contest.

Miles shrugged. "Be my guest."

Norma stalked between Larry and Miles and took a long look at Ronnie's body. Tish continued her examination and ignored the other woman. Norma lifted her eyes from the ground and studied the writing on the water tank.

"And what does this mean?"

Larry's voice was droll. "Looks to be a nursery rhyme, ma'am."

She whirled on him. "And have you identified any suspects?"

"Not as such," Larry said. "Particularly considering we've just begun looking into the matter."

Miles opened his mouth to ask if Norma had anyone in mind, then decided against it. If she'd ever had a sense of humor, it was long replaced by an outrage circuit. "Well, it should be obvious," Norma said, then waved a lazy hand in the direction of Val's house. "One of Miss McKee's maniacs has finally snapped. They happened upon poor Mr. Cartwright in a rage and finger-painted one of the nursery rhymes read to the children." She sniffed. "I was against the commingling of children and those psychotic freaks from the get go. I still say we should do the merciful thing and just do away with them."

Miles frowned. "Mighty Christian of you, Councilwoman," he said. It was a well-known fact that Norma was only found in Pastor Dave's church services around election time.

She whirled back to Miles, eyes flashing. Her finger came within a hair's breadth of Miles' upper lip as she jabbed it at him to emphasize her words. "It has nothing to do with charity or kindness, Marshal. It's a simple matter of resources. They sit around consuming and consuming, yet provide nothing to the larger population. We'd be far better off if we didn't have to account for such a drain on what limited foodstuffs we're able to produce and salvage."

Miles winced. The argument came a little too close to the debate he'd shared with Larry yesterday for comfort. "Be that as it may, ma'am, I'm confident in saying that none of the *people* in Val's house were responsible for Ronnie's death. Wouldn't you agree, Larry?"

"I think that's a fair statement," Larry said. "Councilwoman, Miss Val had a movie night last evening. I stayed on to help out as a chaperone. I didn't hear much of anything outside due to the rain, but that old house creaks and moans fit to wake the dead. No one left the house until I went out this morning and found Ronnie. So you can drop your 'undesirables' from our suspect pool."

Norma pursed her lips. Larry's revelation had thrown her off track. Before she could gain her bearings, Miles chimed in. "Councilwoman, we'll have a verbal report for you by the end of the day. We'll need to retrace Ronnie's steps last evening; I imagine he was at Tom's for a while, and the murder occurred when he was nearing home." He shrugged. "To be honest, Chris Naylor was my first thought as a suspect, but I believe he's still in a cell. That's on my mental list to check, in case you were wondering. We don't have a big population, so we should be able to narrow it down soon." He paused and debated whether to continue. *What the hell.* "You and the council gave me this job for a reason. You coming down here and throwing your weight around, trying to bully my deputies, puts a bad taste in my mouth. If you, Jim, and Calvin don't like the job I'm doing, say so, and I'll hand in my resignation. But don't expect me to be quiet about your attitude if and when I do resign." He met her eyes without blinking.

"I don't appreciate threats, Marshal," she said with an icy glare.

"Not a threat at all, ma'am, just a statement of fact. The way I see it, we let the council come together to manage things because we were busy focusing on projects like the wall, or scavenging missions. Maybe it's time I take a bigger interest in domestic matters. Just say the word."

She stared at him for a long moment. "I, and the rest of the council, are completely satisfied with the work you're doing, Marshal. We'd never think of asking you to quit, and we would try to talk you out of it should you decide to do so."

Miles kept his face stony. "That's good to hear, Councilwoman. I'll look for you this evening to keep you up to date, all right?"

She nodded and turned to walk away. The group was silent until she reached the road and walked out of earshot, then Brian and Jenny started snickering. Larry looked more serious.

"Don't think you made yourself a friend there, son."

Miles shrugged. "Forget her. She drives Jim as crazy as she does us, and Calvin's from out here, he'd never back her in a serious power play." He shrugged. "I'd rather have her in her little fiefdom there than getting involved with, oh, the school, or supply management." Over by Ronnie, Tish stood. She pulled the gloves inside-out off of her hands and walked back over to Larry and Miles.

"Well, what I know about forensics you can write on a sheet of notebook paper, but as best I can tell, every wound came from the same knife. They are all about the same size." Tish blanched. "There are over twenty of them. One of them hit Ronnie's kidney. That's the source of most of the blood." She shrugged. "The grass is pretty thick, and it's matted down, but I didn't make out any footprints. Whoever did it had to get up close and personal, so that's something, at least. They had to have gotten drenched in blood."

"Just one person, you think?" Miles mused.

"Hard to say. I'd guess so since there was just one weapon involved, but they could have passed it around. I wouldn't *think* so, but I don't know enough to be able to say yes or no in any firm sense."

"We're all in the blind here," Larry said. Death was no stranger to any of them, but not like this. Death in a sick bed, or at the teeth of a zombie, sure. They'd all seen too much of that. Outside, even the scavengers had noted that other survivors they'd run into, as rare as they were, often seemed reluctant to make any sort of aggressive action toward another living person. The human race was an endangered species — murdering each other was just piling on.

Miles put his hands on his hips and said, "Anyone know how to run a murder investigation?"

Vir woke as soon as the rising sun crested the parapet of the warehouse's roof. He gasped in surprise and fumbled for his *kirpan* before he realized that all was well.

Last evening, after observing the tide of the dead for a long, stunned moment, he'd pulled back from the edge. With as many as he could see, if they tried one of those climbing maneuvers, it wouldn't have mattered how tall the building was. They'd have surmounted it in short order. So he'd taken up station atop the roof access hatch to wait for the inevitable assault from below. The entire time he sat and prayed that his weight would be enough to keep anything below from pushing it open. No such attempt ever came, and as night fell, he began to relax, until he fell asleep. All the while he maintained his position atop the hatch.

He stood with a wince and stretched his cramped limbs. It had been chilly overnight, and the morning air still held a hint of that coolness. Vir cocked his head to one side and listened to the world around him. He heard nothing out of the ordinary. The morning, in fact, held an eerie quiet other than the rush of the wind through the trees. He moved to the edge of the roof and looked down.

Countless feet had churned the grass into the ground and littered the area with bits of debris. Nothing moved, living or undead. If there had been stragglers, perhaps they'd passed him by in the night, or perhaps that great horde had absorbed them. He waited for a bit, but nothing revealed itself. That, perhaps, was more disconcerting than the alternative.

One of the problems the salvage teams encountered, Buck had explained, was the trailing tendency of the dead. Once aroused to a noise or some other form of input, they tended to follow it in single-minded fashion unless distracted by something else. Knowing that the warehouse clearance would need more than one trip, they'd mapped out several alternate routes, but they'd always known that the activity at the warehouse would draw in various biters over time, depending on their rates of speed.

With all the hubbub yesterday, there should have been *something*.

After a few minutes Vir shook his head and shrugged. He'd write it off to good luck and go with it. The trick was to not allow his good fortune to make him drop his guard. He moved back to the roof hatch and lifted it. The interior of the warehouse was dimmer than the afternoon before, but like the road outside, it was empty. He lay on his stomach and shifted forward until he could lower his head through the opening and look around inside. The floor wasn't as clean as it had been yesterday, but as with the outside, nothing moved.

Vir took his time going down the ladder, pausing every so often to listen for anything roused by the noise he was making.

The interior was as still and silent as a tomb.

At the bottom, he waited once more, but nervous energy didn't permit him to stand still for long. He unslung the shotgun and crept to the end of the aisle to peer around the corner.

The warehouse was brighter toward the loading docks. He puzzled over that for a moment then moved forward. Any other time his suspicions would have been somewhat alleviated, but after yesterday, he couldn't allow it. Buck had made plenty of noise, but somehow, an entire horde of biters had waited rather than rushing to attack. He shivered. Things were bad enough without having to worry about the dead exhibiting intelligence, even if it was just a sort of animal cunning.

Let's pray that's as far as it goes, Vir thought as he stepped up to the loading dock. If there'd been enough left of Donald and Buck to get up and walk away, they were long gone. He searched the floor. Only light smears of blood stained it, and he gave an involuntary nervous titter as he realized that hundreds of feet had wiped up most of the gore. The men who'd been about to kill him — and the rest of the team — had met their fate, and it wasn't one Vir would have wished up on his worst enemy. Joey, over all of them, had deserved better. He gave the floor a second look and shuddered.

Pull yourself together.

As he'd seen, the loading dock was well-lit. Light poured through the hole where the personnel access door had been. The more impressive sight lay next to the man-sized opening. With the bottleneck of the smaller door, the biters had spread out. There'd been enough of them to rip the first roll-up door from its track. The twisted pieces of the door had landed on the rear half of Buck's cargo truck, crushing the frame over the bed. From his position, the other truck seemed undamaged. After further study, Vir surmised that the area behind the warehouse was as deserted as the front.

Vir knelt and glanced below the desks. His pistol lay underneath with the slide locked back on an empty magazine. He fished it out and noted with surprise that it was clean. Either Donald had dropped it before being dog-piled, or it had just luckily avoided any blood spray. Despite that, he took a moment to wipe it off before reloading it with a fresh magazine.

Now what?

Vir looked around. He studied the interior of the warehouse then turned and looked at the empty roll-up door frame. There'd be no way to secure it by himself, particularly without tools or any sort of heavy equipment. He might have managed if any of the crew had survived, but he doubted it, given the size of the horde.

He needed to get what he could, as fast as possible, and get back to the other survivors. Yes, the information about the change in biter behavior was important, but biters were headed *away* from the settlement. As far as Vir knew, there were no organized communities save for lone survivors or small family groups in that direction. For the moment, the information was of secondary importance. Medical supplies were more crucial.

When Miles enlisted Vir for this assignment, he'd provided him with copies of the medical supply wish list, put together by the clinic staff.

"Look for anything out of the ordinary," the Marshal had instructed. "It's understandable if they grab stuff like booze or snacks. Candy bars are usually stale by now, but a lot of people don't care how bad they taste. Keep the list close at hand. Stuff like painkillers is on the list, but they aren't as important as say, antibiotics. You see somebody loading up on Oxy — that may be our guy. Same goes for decongestant."

Vir opened one of the cargo pockets of his khakis and withdrew the list. It was legible despite some deep creases in the paper. Ordered in priority of need, as he remembered.

So get to it, he told himself.

He turned back into the warehouse and began to search.

Chapter 10

Pete's day didn't begin well, which wasn't helpful. It had been a long night.

Larry had radioed up early to determine if he had seen anything out of the ordinary last night. Well, he had, of course, in the tree line, but he wasn't about to tell Larry that. Ronnie's death had hit Pete like a sucker-punch. He'd had a gut feeling that the old man wasn't doing well. But he'd never expected to lose him so soon. And for it to be a murder . . .

Pete cursed his lack of focus. Sure, it had rained a bit last night, but would he have seen anything if he hadn't been so intent on the fences? Larry hadn't mentioned the possibility, which meant he hadn't considered it relevant. They'd been friends too long to worry about such small things as hurt feelings. That didn't help Pete's own self-recrimination, though.

When the kids clambered up after breakfast, chattering about Ronnie's death in the strange, fascinated and non-frightened way that teenagers seemed to view such things, it was more than Pete was ready to deal with.

All things considered, he would have much rather had a quiet morning, so Pete let his kids make ammo.

The advantage to that was that it was a skill they'd already gotten down pat. So if he decided to tuck his chin into his chest and snooze for a moment, all would be well. Sleeping as needed was a skill he'd perfected to a science in the Corps, and it was something that he could still draw on as needed. After a while, the rhythmic clicking of the press and the clink of finished cartridges dropping into ammo cans lulled him into an even deeper repose. It wasn't a particularly restful sleep, as the sounds of reloading and quiet conversation tempered his dreams. Despite the soundtrack, he dreamed of the death of his friend, alone in the rain.

He came awake at once when Bruce murmured, "Vehicle coming from the east. Still too far out for any details." Pete lifted his head and looked in the indicated direction, but without the aid of the spotting scope all he could see was a small smudge on the horizon. *Good eyes,* he thought in approval.

"Is it Charlie, Captain?" Vinnie asked. They kept an up-to-date list of the teams out in the field on a white board, along with their anticipated return time.

"Charlie should be coming in from the west. One vehicle or two, Bruce?" It was too soon for Buck's group to get back, but maybe the medical warehouse had been a bust and they had returned earlier than planned.

"Can't tell yet. Still a couple of miles out."

Pete wheeled over and elbowed the youngster out of the way. "Cara, Vinny, watch north and south. Bruce, grab the walkie." He leaned over and pressed his eye to the eyepiece. Bruce had the zoom dialed to the max, and he opened it up a bit so he didn't lose sight on the approaching vehicle. He squinted, but details were murky with the sun haze. He thought that the vehicle — he could see now that it was just

188

one — might be tan or light brown, which would eliminate Buck's team as a possibility, but that could also just be dirt or mud.

Bruce pressed the walkie into his hand. Without looking away from the spotting scope Pete lifted it to his mouth and keyed the transmit button. "Gary, come in, we have incoming to the east."

"Any ID?" Gary came back almost immediately, and Pete offered a ghost of a smile. The man was as steadfast as ever.

"Nothing yet, but we have no eyes to the east at this time."

"Roger that, back in one." After a moment, Gary came back on. "West wall understands they're on their own, they're doubling eyes until we give the all clear." Generally speaking, each wall bunker had three men on duty in twelve-hour shifts. To ease the tedium and keep them fresh, observers usually rotated out often to ensure that those who were watching weren't asleep at the switch. The off-duty personnel would nap, prepare meals for the others, or tend to equipment. They'd experimented with various methods. The current method was the one that worked best given the limited number of people who were willing to take a turn at standing a watch.

Pete's brow furrowed — the vehicle was within a mile of the settlement now. A little less than a mile from the gate was a small rise, after which the road sloped down to the settlement. After the rise, vehicle identification became much simpler. His breath caught as it crested the hill and kept rolling toward them.

"Holy shit, Gary," Pete managed after several attempts to key the transmit button. "All hands on deck. Get the

Brownings up and have your guys standing by with Javelins. It's a LAV."

"Say again, Pete, what is that?"

He zoomed the spotting scope out as the vehicle kept coming. "Bruce, get the Savage and all the spare magazines and ammo out of the locker." He brought the radio back up. "Gary, it's an armored personnel carrier. Eight-wheeled, cross-country and river capable. Crew of three with room for six infantrymen. And a 25mm cannon that will make our wall look like tissue paper." Bruce slapped him several times on the bicep. "Hold on." He looked up at the teenager. "What?"

The boy pointed. "They're stopping."

Pete turned back. Sure enough, the vehicle had come to a stop at the crossroads a half-mile from the gate. It sat there, idling. Pete watched it for a long moment. The hatch above the driver's position opened up, and the driver reached up with both arms. He had a wad of fabric clutched in one hand. With slow, exaggerated motions he knotted one end around the barrel of the cannon running over the compartment. Complete, he brought his arms back down while pulling the hatch closed. The barrel of the cannon began to rise. Once it was at about a forty-five degree angle, the turret began to rotate to Pete's left — avoiding a barrel sweep of the bunkers, he noted. When the cannon was at a right angle to the body of the LAV, the motion stopped.

The long stripe of white fabric — bandages, perhaps — fluttered in the breeze.

"Pete?" Gary inquired.

"Hold your fire," Pete directed. "Keep the Brownings pointed at the sky and keep the Javelins out of sight. If we need them they'll be our best option, anyway." He released the transmit button, clicked his tongue in his mouth for a moment, and then pressed it again. "Stand by. I'm going to get Miles and Larry. Somebody needs to go out and talk with them. Keep the gate shut until I get there." He lowered the walkie and gave Bruce a baleful look. After a moment, he turned and shared the look with Cara and Vinnie. "I'm leaving the three of you up here. I don't care how interesting *that* gets, you keep eyes in every other direction, get me?" He jerked a finger over his shoulder to indicate the showdown at the wall.

The three chorused that they understood. He sat there for a moment, considering, and then said, "You radio me before you shoot. You start hearing gunfire from the wall, you get the hell down that ladder as fast as you can. This observation post is a sitting duck for that cannon down there." All three had pale faces and wide eyes.

"Yes, Captain," Vinnie said, his voice strained. "What are you going to do?"

"What else? I'm going to walk out there and talk to them."

Charlie and his team had finished their mission.

The rest of the houses had gone nice and easy, with no surprises or mysteries. They had, in fact, been devoid of life or unlife. The people who'd lived there had never made it home or had been somewhere else on Z-Day.

Dalton hauled a final storage tote into the school bus as Charlie and Corey took care of the fire pit. It shed ash and flakes of rust as the two men lifted it and dumped it without ceremony on a lawn. Task complete, Corey put his hands on his hips and waited. Charlie didn't notice; his focus was on the third house on the left.

The candy bars had been gone when the sun had come up, though he hadn't seen or heard anything more during his watch. The outcome was a disappointment, but he wasn't surprised. Charlie had once been a man of faith, but his experiences had shaken that faith to its foundations. This was no longer a world of answered prayers if it ever had been.

Back at the settlement, one of the wall guards had been an ordained pastor before Z-Day, and he held regular church services when off duty. Many of the other survivors seemed to appreciate it and had even encouraged Charlie to attend. Those entreaties usually fell on uncaring ears. Charlie had descended into himself for a time immediately after the end. He likely would have died in his catatonic state if Larry hadn't found him and brought him back. Even after the quiet patience of Miss Val had coaxed him out of the prison of his own mind, he wasn't one for exposing his soul.

He'd scavenged plenty of Bibles, to be sure, even a Koran for Hamid Faqir. Without so many of the distractions of modern life, and with existence rendered into the simple binary equation of survive or die, many of them had turned to any trappings of comfort they could.

Charlie didn't know what brought him comfort. He'd never been one for deep introspection, and his difficulty speaking made using others as sounding boards harder than it had been even when he'd been more verbose. Last night, though . . .

For a while, he thought he might have found something, but this morning, that hope seemed a childish dream. For a moment, he began to doubt himself. Had he even seen anything at all?

The chocolate is gone, whispered a small, still voice in the back of his mind.

Charlie snapped into motion, unaware of Corey's startled reaction as he went from a near statue to a blur. He stepped up into the school bus and strode past Dalton, who cocked his head and looked puzzled.

Charlie grabbed one of the empty totes and set it on the floor. None of the filled totes had labels, so he had to open several before he started to find what he needed. Satisfied, he began to transfer items from the full totes to the one at his feet.

Half a flat of bottled water. A can opener. Cans of fruit, already-cooked fare like ravioli. Corey stepped up into the bus, loud and confused. "Dalton, what the hell is . . ." The bigger man shushed him, and Corey fell silent. Charlie paid the two no mind. He found a spiral bound notebook and he tore a single sheet out of it. He laid it on top of the stack of totes and considered what to say. Finally, in neat block print, he wrote.

I saw you last night.

We have a safe place. There are other children. Mothers and fathers.

I will come back soon by myself. Stay here. The houses are all safe right now. Hide in an attic, if you can. Watch for me.

Please.

Charlie placed the note on top of the goods inside the tote and sealed it. He bent over to lift it. *Is it too heavy?* His thoughts had an almost frantic quality to them, and he shook his head as though to clear them away. Anyone who'd been able to survive on their own was smart enough to figure out how to move it if it was too heavy.

Turning, he walked past his teammates and stepped down out of the bus. Charlie marched to the head of the driveway and placed the tote at the edge of the long grass surrounding the pond in the center of the roundabout. He straightened and took a slow look around. The houses were still; he saw no curtains stir, and no signs of movement.

Finally, Charlie turned and walked back to the vehicle. They'd collected and stowed all their gear; the only thing keeping them from leaving was his sudden outbreak of eccentricity. He stepped inside and shut the bifold door with the handle.

He sat in the driver's seat of the school bus and stared forward. His hand was on the key, but he didn't turn it. Finally, Charlie raised his eyes and looked in the mirror. Dalton ran his fingers through his beard and gave him a placid look.

"Someone is here," Charlie croaked, and then he was silent once more. After a long moment, Dalton nodded. The look that passed between the two men was enough; no more needed saying.

With a final look out at the tote, Charlie cranked the bus to life. He pulled out, eyes forward and focused on the road. *A couple of days, and then I come back and wait. And then I'll see.*

Chapter 11

Pete eschewed his prostheses while in the nest. On the rare occasions when he saw fit to come down, the ladder was downright nerve-wracking without any sensation to give him feedback. On the bright side, the assembly of the nest had required the lifting and assembly of some heavy components. To get it done, they'd installed an electric winch and bracing on one of the grain bin catwalks. An L-shaped swivel arm with pulleys shifted the lift point to open air. While it had once been useful to lift decking and I-beams, it now made a serviceable elevator for Pete's personal use.

The drawback, of course, was that for the 30 seconds it took for the cable to unspool, his ass hung in the breeze for all to see. When his boots hit the ground and he began to unbuckle the chest harness, a human whirlwind was waiting for him.

"Word is, the military is outside the walls and you aren't letting them in." Norma Benedict exclaimed as she stomped up to him. "What's going on? Shouldn't we let them in?"

Pete ignored her and finished removing the harness. Looking up into the sky, he waved his arms above his head. After a moment, the kids up top threw a switch and reversed the winch. After the harness was out of standing reach, he waved again for them to cut it off. This left the harness high enough to not clothesline anyone walking by, but low enough that he could have it back on in short order if necessary. Finally, he turned to Norma. "Not right away, Norma."

A vein throbbed in her temple and she began to turn a particularly interesting shade of purple. She sputtered, "Under what authority are you basing that decision?"

Pete made it a point to study the ground. "Ma'am, my grandma raised me right, so I'll refrain from using my adult words. Last I checked, you're standing on my property. Now, I've been plenty patient and let you and yours manage the counting of the beans and bandages, so long as you've remembered the fact that me and mine are what stand between you and Hell on Earth. If you're going to forget that fact or impede my duties in any way, my patience ends." He began to stride to the east.

Gibbering in outrage, she attempted to keep up and failed. Finally, she lowered her head and surged forward. At a brisk jog, she was able to stay near his shoulder. Despite the odd gait imparted to Pete's movement by the prostheses, he moved well on level ground. The paved section of the county road was nice and flat between the grain bins and the east border.

"I'm sorry, Mister Matthews," she managed as she struggled to keep up with him. To her credit, she was only a little of breath. For all her faults, no one could say that Norma Benedict shirked on work, or took more food than was her fair share. "Could you *please* tell me what you're thinking?"

"Absolutely," Pete replied. "It's one vehicle, not 'the military.' It could just as well be a couple of scavengers out for a joyride as it is anyone representing an official body. As such, before we let them in, we need to determine their bona fides. That's my job." Without slowing his stride, he glanced down at her. "And I need you to be doing your job, not getting in the way of mine."

She gritted her teeth but said nothing. After a moment of her silence, Pete offered, "Look, we need to get everyone back into the shelter, just in case. I don't want any noncombatants anywhere near the wall if it comes to that. Can you do that for me?" After a moment, he added, "Councilwoman?"

The term of authority seemed to mollify her somewhat, and she drew to a stop. "Yes, yes, of course, you're exactly right," she said. "I'll get right on it. Do carry on, Mr. Matthews. But please — keep the council in the loop?"

Pete resisted the urge to shake his head. "Ma'am, you're going to be in the loop right quick with or without me telling you."

Gary West had been a tall and skinny man before Z-Day. The hard physical labor over the years had added a layer of lean muscle mass to his frame, but he was still a bony conglomeration of parts that seemed to move just out of rhythm with one another, like an ill-operated marionette. Despite his tendency toward awkwardness, he moved with care as he carried the olive drab Pelican case out of one of the bunkers flanking the gate.

No matter how many times Pete and Larry had assured him that the contents were safe, it just felt *wrong* to jostle an anti-tank missile launcher.

The Javelins had been in a cache of National Guard supplies they'd come upon after Z-Day. Why they'd deployed them to the roadblocks enforcing the quarantine zones was anyone's guess. It wasn't like the infected drove armored vehicles.

When the roadblocks fell, the missiles remained, along with an enormous amount of useful material. The Guardsmen had gone down hard, but not hard enough. It was impossible to tell what sort of odds they'd faced, but in the end, their jury-rigged fortifications and firepower hadn't been enough.

Most people assumed that Gary stayed on the wall out of a possessive sort of pride, having been the main driving force behind its construction. He didn't make any attempt to change those assumptions, but for Gary, the reason was far simpler. He remembered the lesson of those fallen Guardsmen, and had no desire to repeat it. To his mind, being a little OCD about the wall was reasonable given the multitude of mental disorders in their current environment.

Gary set the Pelican case on the ground in front of Dave Wesley. Dave led the community's Christian services on Sunday mornings when he wasn't standing watch. "Like Pete said, Pastor Dave — get it up and ready, but keep it out of sight unless we need it."

"You got it, Gary," the other man responded. He knelt in front of the case, opened it, and began to inspect its contents. They'd gotten some familiarization with them from the veterans in the community, but there'd never been a need to *use* the things. Gary groused mentally, kicking himself for the oversight. Finally, he gave a half-hearted shrug and stepped back up onto the ladder leading to the roof of the bunker.

"How we looking, Burke?"

The other man's voice was tight. He was kneeling behind a Browning machine gun. Other than that scant protection, he was in full view of the armored vehicle. They'd built their defenses on the assumption they'd be facing hordes of infected or raiders with guns. They'd never expected tanks. Another oversight. Gary hoped that they wouldn't prove to be fatal mistakes.

"They ain't moving, and I ain't moving, either," Graham Burke said, then gave a weak chuckle. "If my nose starts itching I may need a hand."

"Stay cool, bud, we're getting things together down here. Call out if you need relief and we'll switch off." The visitors had been considerate enough to turn the main gun turret of the armored vehicle to one side. Keeping the barrels of the Brownings up was going to get tiring, fast. *Damn it, where's the cavalry?*

"Gary!" a voice shouted behind him. He resisted the urge to sigh in relief as he turned. Pete was hobbling toward the bunker along the paved road. Almost as though they'd coordinated it, Larry and Miles were approaching from the southern side of the community. He stepped off of the ladder and went to intercept them. They formed a loose circle and stared at each other. Up until that moment, Gary hadn't considered how much their world had changed. For years now he hadn't thought much, if ever, about seeing any sort of civilization that they hadn't created on their own. It had been so long since anyone alive had shown up that the realization that they might not be alone was at once terrifying and thrilling.

Miles broke the ice. "Did I hear right on the radio? It's an armored transport?"

"Looks to be that way," Pete acknowledged.

Gary pushed his faded International Harvester baseball cap back and rubbed his forehead. "I don't like it, fellas. Not one bit. Been a long damn time without even a peep of the military; how do we know that these guys are legit, and not just some scavengers looking for an easy way in?"

"Gary, you got a better look at it than I did, but it doesn't look too messed up. If somebody salvaged it, they did one heck of a job making it look presentable." Pete shrugged. "That may not mean anything, but there really is only one proper way to sound them out."

"I'd ask what, but I have an inkling as to what you'll say," Larry remarked.

"We talk to them, of course, Top," Pete said shortly. "The LAV is, or was, Marine issue. If they're legit, you and I will know." He thought about that for a second. "Well, hopefully. I'm sure the composition of any remaining forces is going to be a bit murky by now."

Miles shook his head and barked, "No way. This isn't Star Trek, Pete, and you aren't Captain Kirk." Larry gave a short bark of laughter.

Pete wheeled on his nephew. "Now wait just one damn . . ." He began, but Gary interrupted.

"Kid's right, Pete. Right or wrong, you're too important in a number of ways to risk." The big man jerked his chin in the direction of the silos. "It's hard enough getting the council to support the manpower requirements of the wall now, with you backing me. What if something happens to you?"

"If something happens to me you'll have bigger problems to worry about," Pete snapped, waving his hand at the wall. "Like that LAV blowing holes in our security."

"They won't get too many shots off," Larry muttered. "Javelins are up, right?" Gary nodded. "Well, there you go,

Captain. Anything happens to the greeting party, our visitors are not long for this world."

"Larry and I will do it," Miles said. "Should be my job, anyway."

"No," Pete said. "I can think of a dozen arguments against it, not the least of which is the fact that you've got a little girl that needs a father."

"Oh, gee, thanks," Gary barked. "And here I thought I was in charge of security. You decide to come down from your tower and now you're running the show, Pete?"

"Come on, come on," Patterson whispered. "What's taking so damn long?" The Corporal's head was on a swivel, panning to the sides of the LAV and then back out the front. "They talk long enough, every infected in twenty miles will be coming over to see what the fuss is."

"Easy, son," Hanratty said. "Just take it easy." He had his own eyes glued to the men standing station on the heavy machine guns. Each of them looked about as nervous as the Corporal, and they made frequent adjustments to the position of their arms to ease the strain of holding the barrels vertical. A military-issue mount would have had no problem in balancing in that position. Examining the turrets the guns were sitting on, Hanratty decided they'd made their own. After a moment, he realized why. A standard mount allowed the barrel of the weapon to rise, for anti-aircraft and plunging, indirect fire. The survivors had rigged these mounts to allow the gunners to depress the barrels of the guns. This allowed them direct fire on the ground in front of the palisade. It was a hybrid of medieval fortifications with WWII-era firepower. In modern combat against an armed, living foe, dirt was life, and had been a soldier's best friend ever since artillery was first used in battle. Against the infected, though . . . Hanratty shuddered. He'd seen some terrible things in the last eight years, but nothing that would have called for fortifications like this. His estimation of the danger they faced rose a bit, but at the same time, so did his respect. These people had survived and even thrived. They were the exception to the rule. "Rivas," he murmured. "Do *not* fire if those barrels drop. They look like they're about ready to pass out from holding them up, and I don't want to start an incident over a slip-up."

"Aye, sir, check fire until I hear it pinging off the armor. Just like the Sandbox, sir." The PFC's voice held just a touch of snark. Other officers might have jumped on her with both boots, but Hanratty just grinned. He glanced back past Rivas at the SEALs. They looked placid, maybe even a little bored. Corporal Dylan Baxter, his own personal Voice of America reporter, was wide awake and looked curious. He opened his mouth to ask a question, but Ross jerked an elbow into Baxter's side, and the skinny Marine just grunted. Hanratty turned back before he let himself smile this time. They all understood the brass's reasoning behind sending Baxter — it wasn't like they had a plethora of good news. Morale was frayed, and while it might be weird to milk a community of survivors for stories, it would give the troops something to think about other than the mission and their own lost families.

That didn't mean that the entire team wasn't enjoying picking on the kid.

Someone climbed up on the palisade next to the right machine gunner, and mimed a 'time-out' signal. Hanratty nodded to himself, then raised a hand out of the open hatch above his head and gave a thumbs-up. "No rush, Corporal," he said. "We've got the air conditioning going."

The argument had ended almost as soon as it had begun.

Miles didn't know if they'd all realized they were just wasting time, or if the common arguments had finally beaten down everyone's objections.

After he'd signaled time out to the LAV, he'd gone halfway down the ladder and hooked one leg around a rung to provide a bit of support. This let him use the roof of the bunker as a shooting platform. The .308-caliber bullets out of his short-barreled rifle wouldn't do anything that the heavy machine guns couldn't do better, but they just needed enough fire volume to keep the occupants of the armored vehicle off-balance until they could hit them with a Javelin or two.

Happy thoughts — maybe it won't come to that.

Miles licked his lips and looked down. "Ready whenever you guys are."

Down below, Larry nodded, and turned and slapped Gary on the back. The other man looked a little green around the gills, but to his credit, he tightened his jaw and forced a look of determination onto his face.

Miles glanced up and met Pete's eyes. His uncle had taken up a similar position on the opposite bunker. Pete nodded and gave him a wink.

"Open the gates just enough for us to get through and leave them that way," Gary instructed one of the gate guards from the other bunker. He turned to Pastor Dave, who stood on the ground at Miles' feet. "Miles, if it comes to it, I'd appreciate if you'd get the heck out of Dave's way." Miles held back a laugh and nodded. "If it comes to it I'll be pulling him up as fast as he's climbing."

The eastern gates hung a bare inch over the highway from a welded frame of I-beams. Metal cables and pulleys allowed for the entire assembly to open with a single winch. Brackets on the inside of the wall and the gate were usually filled with heavy timbers to brace against any outward force. They'd already removed those timbers and cast them aside.

The generator inside of Miles' bunker came to life with a cough. After a moment, the winch kicked on and began drawing the cabling inward. As the door closest to Miles began to slide over, another cable ran through pulleys, over and down, and began drawing the opposite door open. At full speed, the doors could be open and closed in a total of forty seconds. It was a drawback, and a dangerous one, but they didn't have the resources for something better that would be as sturdy.

Opening for personnel access was much quicker. Almost as soon as the winch was on, the guards inside the bunker cut it off, though they left the generator running. Larry hesitated a beat, gave Miles a nod, and stepped out.

Once outside the gate, he spread his arms wide to display that his hands were empty. Gary aped the gesture as he stepped through himself; both men had left their carry pieces behind. If it came to a fight, they'd be diving in the ditch and trying to scramble inside rather than participating. Miles heard metal on metal at the back of the LAV, and he saw one of the rear hatches come open. Inside there would be as many as six troops, sitting back to back on a bench seat that ran down the center of the vehicle. He wondered if they were as nervous as he was.

A figure in Marine-pattern camouflage stepped down from the back of the vehicle and Miles relaxed, just a bit. A raider wouldn't go so far to wear a military uniform, would he? Or would that just be a prime way to put any potential marks off of their guard? Miles swallowed and adjusted his grip on his rifle. *Here we go.*

The Marine that stepped out of the back of the LAV looked a little careworn. His hair was longish, he had a decent bit of stubble on his face, and his MarPat showed some age, though it was clean. Like Larry and Gary, his hands were empty, and he kept them open and low as he walked around the armored personnel carrier and stopped near the nose.

Captain, Larry noted. He drew to a stop ten feet in front of the visitor's resting place and studied the insignia painted on the nose of the LAV. "1st Light Armored Recon, 1st Marine Division. You boys are a hell of a long way from Pendleton."

The Marine Captain's eyebrows ticked up a notch. "That we are. You serve?" He sounded surprised, but hopeful, Larry thought. *Interesting.*

"Gunnery Sergeant Larry Vance, Force Recon, 2nd of the 2nd. Retired, of course." He smirked. *Please pass the test.*

"Swift, silent, deadly."

"Oorah," Larry said. He hesitated for a long, silent moment and finally stepped forward. He extended a hand. The other Marine looked at it for a moment as though unsure how to react, then caught himself. Larry chuckled as the Marine shook his hand.

"Adam Hanratty, Captain, USMC, First of the First." He gave a faint smile. "Tip of the spear, Gunny. Although the rest of my team is a bit of a mixed bag, we're on a first contact patrol as part of Operation Atlantic Fury." He glanced at Gary and nodded. He released Larry's hand and shook Gary's. "Sir," he said.

"Gary West," he said, then grinned. "Late of AT&T; now, I guess, I'm the wall guy."

Larry laughed, and after a moment so did Hanratty. The brittle tension underlying their conversation eased somewhat, and Larry felt himself relaxing. "What can I do for you on this fine spring day, Captain?"

Hanratty scratched his chin. "Well, it may be a lost cause, Gunny, but we're looking for someone who lived in this area. Some of the surviving eggheads think they're onto something to maybe stop this thing cold, but they need some additional information that, for certain reasons, can only be, umm, accessed . . . by this person."

Larry frowned in thought. "So this person, it wouldn't be a doctor, I'm guessing, given how they don't necessarily have the information?"

"Correct. It's a long story, but suffice it to say we're just looking for someone to open some doors for us. Well," Hanratty waved a hand toward the LAV. "Some of my friends in the Navy."

"Well, that's good, because we have a decided shortage of doctors. One no-kidding dentist and my daughter, who graduated med school a few months before everything went to hell. Can't think of any locksmiths around home off the top of my head. What exactly are you looking for, Captain?" Hanratty hesitated for a long moment. "More than that, I don't feel comfortable saying, Gunny. I'm not sure what sort of leadership setup you all have, but I do have a briefing I'm allowed to offer. I'd just rather do it once to avoid miscommunication."

Larry considered that. "Fair enough. Well, you obviously have someone in mind. I can't promise I know everyone personally, but I imagine Gary or myself are liable to recognize it if it's a familiar name."

"We're looking for someone named Matthews. Miles Matthews."

To Larry's side, all Gary West could manage was a stunned, barely audible, "Huh."

Chapter 12

In the end, things went better than Miles ever would have allowed himself to hope. The man in Marine camouflage shook hands with Larry and Gary and they talked for a few minutes. Finally, the two from the community turned to face the east wall, and Gary waved his arms wide. "Open it up!" he called out. "It's all good."

On the ground, Pastor Dave let out a relieved sigh and eased the Javelin off of his shoulder. "Thank you, Lord."
The wall guard inside the bunker kicked the winch on once more, only, this time he let it run the doors all the way open. If possible, this was perhaps even more nerve-racking than the parley with the visitors. Any zombies that stumbled upon the commotion outside of the gates had a beeline straight into the heart of the community.

The trio on foot trotted forward, and the LAV rumbled in behind them. As the three stepped through, Gary motioned Larry and the Marine to one side and began making signals to the LAV to pull off the side of the road. The armored personnel carrier cleared the gate housing with ease. They'd designed the gates to allow access for the combines, which were far taller and wider than the military vehicle. As soon as the LAV was through, Gary shouted, "Reverse it!"

The winch came alive once more, but Miles didn't let himself pay attention to it. He was staring at the terrain outside of the gate. If they had any luck, it was the fact that the fields on this side of the community were already disked in preparation for planting. As far as Miles could see, the only thing moving were the weeds at the edge of the road as they rippled in the light breeze.

The gates came together with a muffled thump; thick rubber matting nailed on the inside edges reduced the contact noise. The first time they'd shut the gates the crash of collision had been audible at the other end of the community. Miles heaved a sigh of relief. The gate guards were already scrambling to maneuver the heavy timbers back into the support brackets.

Miles slung his rifle over one shoulder and clambered down the ladder off of the bunker. Larry and Gary — *Heh, gotta razz them about that* — stood near the LAV, talking to the Marine officer. The rear hatches of the vehicle opened up, and the Marine's compatriots climbed down beside him. He strolled in that direction as he studied the visitors. Pete was moving just as slow, though for a different reason — he was taking his time climbing down the ladder on the opposite bunker.

Three of the passengers, like the officer, wore faded Marine-pattern camouflage. The only woman in the group was a short, athletic Latina with close-cropped hair, and two men who were both white and of middling height. The commonality ended there. One of the male Marines was thick-waisted and solid looking while the other was skinny and didn't look old enough to shave, much less put on a uniform.

The other passengers were more interesting. The three men wore Naval woodland pattern camouflage. It took him a moment to place it, but then his old shelf-stocking memories from working in Larry's store kicked in. The Marine uniforms tended to have more browns, whereas the Naval versions were greener. Not a big deal these days. Camo was camo, and it wasn't like it distracted the zombies, but one part of the Navy, in particular, tended to use that sort of uniform. SEALs.

The men who wore it added more confirmation to the suspicion; although they had various builds, they all sported non-regulation facial hair, which was typical for Special Operations troops. The oldest of the group had a bushy beard that was particularly impressive, even being more gray than brown. Despite what Miles assumed was a long deployment, the Marines accompanying the SEALs were well-groomed, for certain values of the term. This was as typical for Marines and regular line troops as the opposite was for Special Ops.

He stepped up and joined the group with a nod. "Marshal," Larry boomed, and Miles rose a mental eyebrow at the volume and title. "Please allow me to introduce Captain Adam Hanratty of the Marines." He indicated the officer. "Your men, Captain?"

"Absolutely," Hanratty replied, and if his eyes looked tired, his smile seemed genuine. He indicated the chunky Marine. "Corporal Patterson." Toward the short Latina, "Private First Class Rivas. And this," he indicated the skinny kid, "Is Corporal Baxter."

Baxter stepped forward. "Dylan Baxter, folks, pleased to meet you. I'm attached to the Captain's unit as part of Stars & Stripes. We're pretty much the only news outfit left, anymore. Excited to talk to the people, maybe share your stories."

Larry coughed into his fist, and Miles could tell he was trying not to laugh. *The first sign of civilization in years, and of course they brought a reporter with them.*

Pete squinted his eyes and put both hands on his hips. "Ah, Corporal Baxter," Pete said. "I was under the impression that Stars & Stripes reporters tended to be senior NCOs."

Baxter gave Pete a crooked grin. "The old dudes ran slower."

"Right," Pete muttered, which elicited another spate of coughing from Larry. Miles resisted the urge to roll his eyes by looking away. Gary stood just outside of the group and to the side, and he had the same wide-eyed look of shock he'd had since Miles walked up. As Miles glanced in his direction, he noticed that the other man was staring at him for some reason. *Is my fly unzipped or something?*

Hanratty interjected. "If I may, Corporal, I'd like to allow Lieutenant Ross to introduce his party." He indicated one of the three other men. "Lieutenant?"

The most average of the remaining three stepped forward. Miles placed him in his mid-thirties. Sharp blue eyes peered out from a tanned face, and his beard was the same dusty brown as his hair. "Hello, everyone. Lieutenant Michael Ross, SEAL Team 8. This is Chief Petty Officer Gus Foraker," as he indicated the bearded older man, "and this is Gunner's Mate Brian Janacek." The youngest of the three was blond and wore a time-faded San Diego Padres baseball cap. Ross concluded his speech by saying, "If anything, I am understating things by saying we are ecstatic to meet you all."

Larry made a surprised noise in the back of his throat. "So I'm guessing these are the Navy friends you were talking about." He glanced at Miles. "Marshal, the Captain informs me that they're here looking for someone named Miles Matthews." He said it with casual disregard, as though he were reporting on an everyday occurrence outside of the front window. *Hey, look at that, the neighbors across the street got a new lawn-mower.*

Miles had the sense that he was standing on the edge of a precipice. How he reacted, at this moment, would determine the course of not only his future, but the futures of everyone around him. His eyes flickered from person to person. Hanratty bore a slight frown as though he had picked up on the undercurrent of Larry's comment, but the rest of his team didn't seem to be paying much attention. The Marines save for Baxter were looking around like tourists. The Stars & Stripes reporter had somehow glommed onto Dave Wesley and was jotting down notes in a small book he'd produced from somewhere. The SEALs stood stoic, though their eyes flickered in constant motion, as though waiting for an attack.

It was a lousy place for a shootout. Miles considered the care with which the group had approached the base, the methodical nature in which they'd moved to defuse any tension, and the situational ease they displayed in exiting their armored vehicle. Rifles were slung; pistols holstered. This wasn't a group that was looking to fight. It was a group that was hoping for something more.

"Well," Miles said finally, taking his step to a side of the precipice with all the boldness he could muster. "I hope this isn't about overdue library books, or I'm screwed." He laughed, but it came out strained. "I'm Miles Matthews."

Hanratty laughed and relaxed. Miles noted that all three SEALs focused their attention on him as one. "Nothing that bad," Lieutenant Ross said, finally, after making an assessment. Miles couldn't even tell what criteria the SEAL was judging him by, but he felt lacking, regardless. Ross glanced around the group, which seemed to be swelling by the moment. "I don't know that I feel comfortable explaining this to a crowd, but we need your assistance with something."

Gary noted Ross' discomfort and turned. Much of the crowd were wall guards who had gravitated toward the gate, though it also looked like the message had spread that the visitors were not a threat. People were starting to trickle up the road, curious as to the goings on. "Seriously, people?" he yelled. "Engine noise, gate noise, and you just abandon your posts like rookies?"

The crowd dissipated as chagrined guards sprinted back to their posts. The rest of the onlookers were too busy gawking at the newcomers to react. Gary rubbed his forehead and muttered under his breath.

"Tell you what," Larry said. "Why don't we have a quick town meeting, Captain? We'll let you introduce yourself, then you all can circulate for a bit, maybe grab some lunch. We were planning on having one tonight, anyway, but we can certainly move things up and add to the agenda. Meanwhile, Miles and your Navy friends can slip away to somewhere a little more private. We've got a real, live bar and grill, and the owner owes me a few favors. I should be able to get him to open up early."

Hanratty glanced at Ross, and the SEAL gave him an imperceptible nod. "Corporal," Hanratty ordered, "You and Private Rivas will remain behind with the LAV and assist Mister West and the other folks on the wall." He turned back to Larry. "My people have their own rations, and we don't want to impose on your town's supplies."

Larry shook his head. "No worries, Captain. Springtime can be a little lean, but we're doing all right. The kitchen crew will be glad to bring out a few extra meals for your people." He winked at Patterson and Rivas. "It may be a little bland, but I wager it'll be a darn sight better than any MREs you have left."

"Sounds good, Larry," the Captain agreed. "Lead the way."

The group coalesced into an odd-shaped formation as everyone tried to determine their place. Gary finally extricated himself and waved off the invite to join them. "Got plenty to do here," he said.

Miles and Larry ended up flanking Hanratty, with the SEALs close behind the Marine officer. Pete fell in line next to them and showed no signs of being unable to keep up, despite his odd gait. Miles could hear him quizzing the SEAL officer, though the conversation wasn't loud enough for Miles to hear. He imagined that it was some form of "What the hell do you want with my nephew?"

Kind of wondering that myself, actually, he mused. He glanced over and watched Hanratty. The Marine was studying the fields on either side of the road with interest. Larry drew away and ahead, and began waving the onlookers they were attracting back the way they'd came. A few shouted out questions, to Larry or Miles, and a few of the bolder ones even yelled out to Hanratty.

"Why are you here?"

"Larry, what's going on?"

"Miles, who's that with you?"

After a round of deflecting attention and directing people to the cafeteria for a meeting, Larry turned to

Hanratty and Miles and announced, "I'm going to run ahead and maybe collect some of this rabble before the rumor mill goes wild. You got the tour under control, son?"

"I'm good, Pops," Miles confirmed. Larry gave Hanratty a nod and turned to jog down the road.

The Marine Captain watched him go, and said, finally, "That's a formidable man, right there. So where are we heading?"

Miles glanced at him. "My Uncle Pete's old equipment barn. We moved the tractors and combines out and use it pretty much as a catch-all. It's the largest building in the community. Serves as a cafeteria, school house, meeting hall." He laughed. "And as Pastor Dave calls it, the First Church of the Time Share."

Hanratty gave him a quizzical look, and Miles explained. "Pastor Dave's one of the wall guards, he conducts a non-denominational Christian service on Sundays. We tried balancing it out between the Lutherans, Catholics, and Methodists, but it was kind of a hassle coming up with times everyone was happy with. So now they all get together at the same time and argue over points of doctrine. I tell Dave sometimes we should let him wear a referee's shirt. Umm, Fridays and Saturdays Rabbi Behrens has a dozen or so folks. We've got a couple of Hindu families and a Sikh family, but from what Vir tells me, they don't have a certain day of the week, and just get together in their homes. One of my deputies is married to a Muslim, they pretty much do the same."

"Pretty big melting pot," Hanratty noted.

"It's a good snapshot of before. There were a lot of tech firms and factories around here, so they brought in a bunch of technical and engineering folks. There's a ton of German and Irish ancestry in the region; they were the majority of the initial settlers when Indiana became a state. Lot of farming families. Not so many now."

Hanratty nodded. "Yeah," he drew out. "There is that." He indicated the fields on either side. "Mostly gardens on the inside?"

"Gardens and hay, yeah. Mostly greenhouses, we don't have the luxury of year-round growing seasons so we have to have some way of producing in winter. Tom Oliver's farm is right up here." Miles indicated the group of buildings they approached. "We've got three of them inside the walls — Tom's, what used to be Miss Martha's, and my Uncle's place. Tom runs cattle and we grow pretty much anything we can on the rest of the ground. Outside is soybeans with some corn in the rotation for cattle feed. Most of the folks live in converted buildings or in houses and bunkers on the wall. It's a bit tight but we've got one hundred ninety-eight people in here." He paused and winced. "One ninety-seven."

Hanratty glanced at him with a cocked eyebrow. "We had a murder last night. Larry and I were actually looking into it when you guys showed up."

"That's horrible."

"Yeah, you don't know the half of it." The two of them fell silent as they walked past Tom's place. Smoke was already coming out of The Last Bar's chimney as Tom fired up his grill. Miles turned back to look at Pete, but his uncle waved him off and led the SEALs into the building. Watching them go, Hanratty had a good chuckle at the sign, but it was what he saw as he turned to move back down the road that served as an icebreaker for their conversation to begin anew.

"Cattle?" The Marine gave a slow whistle of appreciation. "Man. Oh, man." He stood there and looked over the small herd that returned his own curious and excited stare with disinterested eyes. "I can't remember the last time I had a steak." He paused. "Is that all you have?" Miles laughed. "We cull down to breeding stock when it starts getting cold; it's hard to store enough feed through the winter if you can't haul it in. They're all bred, first calves should be born in the next month or so. Only takes about ten months. So if you want a steak, we should be able to arrange that. The Last Bar makes a pretty solid burger, too, though the buns suck and we don't have a whole lot of cheese that isn't freeze-dried or canned stuff."

"A burger. Man," Hanratty said and shook his head with a broad smile on his face. Still smiling, he turned and started walking again.

"I'd trade it for some bacon," Miles noted. "Haven't seen a pig in years."

As they passed Tom's farm and neared Miss Martha's place, Miles pointed out the police station and clinic, each of which were some of the only examples of new construction in the community. "Just can't give up the field space," he noted. "Though I guess we had to for the parking lot."

Miles watched Hanratty's eyes as they flickered to the lot. Was there a hint of surprise on the other man's face? Not as much as he might have expected. No, it seemed to be a wary sort of curiosity. And, to be certain, the up-armored Humvees and the battle-worn deuce-and-a-half did seem out of place next to the green and red hulks of the tractors and combines. For a moment Miles felt compelled to explain, but hesitated for fear of sounding defensive. Finally, he said, "Those Army guys, always leaving messes around for others to pick up."

Hanratty half-choked and half-laughed. "Well," he finally managed. "I'm glad you guys cleaned up the mess instead of letting it go to waste."

An hour into the drive, Charlie turned the driver's seat over to Dalton. The long night had left him exhausted, and it wasn't long until the hum of the bus's tires on the pavement lulled him into an uneasy sleep. It wasn't deep enough for him to succumb to dreams, but he had a vague, senseless sensation of motion and the noise around him. He cruised the borderland between sleep and wakefulness. When Dalton's voice rose in volume, he straightened immediately and blinked himself awake. The nap had been an unsatisfying one. There was a sour taste in his mouth and his skin was clammy with sweat despite the coolness of the air.

Another hour or two, and that won't be a problem. Get horizontal on a mattress and I'm out. Then, after sleep, he could figure out how he was going to finagle a personal vehicle. *Maybe Miles will loan me his Jeep.* Charlie smirked to himself at the thought.

"Damn it, why don't they answer?" Dalton grumbled. "West gate, this is Team Charlie. Approaching with a load of salvage. How do you read, over?"

Charlie pulled himself up and out of the seat and moved to the front of the bus. He leaned on the back of the driver's seat and peered through the window. The western border of the compound was just becoming visible on the horizon. They were only a couple of miles out, and well within CB range. *Not good.*

He glanced over at Corey. The kid's face was pale, and his hands were tight on the grips of his rifle. "Relax," Charlie rumbled. Corey gave him a tight nod.

"Come on guys, get off the pot and come back, over," Dalton barked. They drew closer and closer to the gate. Charlie squinted, but they were still too far away to make out anyone on the wall. After what felt like an eternity, the CB crackled with static.

"Ah, sorry about that, guys. Got a little bit of craziness going on right now. The generator is on and we have the gates ready for you. The field is clear, I say again, the field is clear. Maintain speed unless we call you off, over."

"Understood," Dalton replied, and threw the CB handset on the dash in obvious disgust. "What the hell is up with that, I wonder?"

Charlie shrugged and sat down on the edge of the seat behind Dalton to continue looking out the front window. Whatever it was, they'd be finding out soon enough.

The overgrown scrub and weed-choked houses on either side faded away as they entered the zone of the western farm fields. Charlie tapped Cory on the shoulder and pointed out the right side of the bus.

"Got it," Corey said and turned to study the landscape that passed by. Charlie did the same on the left, sliding further onto the bench of the seat for more comfort. The field wasn't tilled, he noted, but everything was clear as far he could see. A half-mile or so north the creek snaked through the landscape and supported a few trees. Nothing moved on two or four legs between the road and the trees.

I suppose I could have taken their word for it, Charlie mused. *But I haven't lasted this long without being sure of my own safety.*

The whine of the engine dropped a bit as Dalton slowed and downshifted. Given how many people used the highway as a walking path, roaring through the center of the settlement with the pedal to the floor was frowned upon. Charlie glanced forward. A few hundred yards ahead, the west gate was half-open. Satisfied, he turned back and continued looking to the left.

The wall blurred past, and he let out a faint sigh of relief once they were inside. Dalton slowed further as he caught sight of the crowd milling around on the road in front of the storage bins. "What in the world?" the big man wondered. The armor on the driver's side of the bus prevented him from using that window to communicate, so Dalton hauled the bi-fold doors open and slowed the bus to a crawl. He navigated a winding course through the crowd as he headed toward the grain bins. Spotting someone he recognized, Dalton yelled out the door, "Frannie!"

The nurse straightened and turned toward the bus. Dalton braked to a complete stop and she hopped on board. "Hey, boys," she chirped.

"Frannie, where's the fire?"

Out of breath, she responded, "The military is here, Dalton." She looked at Corey and Charlie. "Emergency meeting in the cafeteria in thirty minutes."

"Great," Dalton said. "Can you hop out and tell people to wake up and get out of the way? I'd rather not create any work for y'all in the clinic."

Frannie laughed and hopped out of the bus. She strode in front of it, waving her arms and generally herding the crowd out of the way as though she were wrangling cattle. The onlookers finally got the message and cleared a path for the bus to get to the bin's loading doors.

"Ain't seen that girl so chipper in years," Dalton observed. Charlie grunted and nodded.

"We're not alone," Corey blurted. "That's what this means, doesn't it?"

Charlie caught Dalton's look in the rear view mirror and shrugged.

"Looks that way, kid," Dalton said. "But keep your eyes open. Could just be a couple of guys in uniforms who've been scratching at survival. Doesn't mean the cavalry's coming to bail us out."

"Right," Corey said, his voice faint with disappointment. Charlie chuffed and reached across the aisle and tapped him on the shoulder.

"Don't need bailed out," Charlie managed. "We stand on our own."

Corey grinned. "I like the sound of that, boss."

"Amen, boss," Dalton echoed. "Let's get this crap unloaded and see what all the fuss is about."

He pulled to a stop in front of the smaller storage silo. Jim Piper, the official quartermaster and one of three council reps, was already standing outside. He'd either been watching the fuss around the cafeteria, or he'd seen them coming. Dalton gave him a wave and killed the engine.

By the time the three of them were hauling totes out of the bus, Piper had assembled a crew to bring the supplies inside the storage bin. From there, Jim's people would sort the goods to determine the best place for them.

"Mostly dry goods," Dalton informed the tall, balding man. He'd been in management at a services company before Z-Day, but he'd had the good luck to be stuck in Larry's gun shop. He'd tagged along when the other man had bugged out. Jim had a quick, easy smile, and a booming laugh. Charlie supposed that he would have been a good man to work for, before. He'd heard grumbling from others that didn't like his style of leadership on the council, which tended toward the introspective, but Charlie supposed it took all kinds. Besides, Jim was usually receptive to changes or suggestions to scouting routes. He was also one of the guys Charlie needed to convince to let him go back out so soon. Usually, they would delay repeat runs on the theory that the noise could lead groups back to the settlement, but the countryside had been almost barren this time out. Another quick run couldn't hurt. *I'll talk to Miles first,* Charlie thought. *Then we'll both see Jim together, about drawing some fuel out of stores.*

"Glad you made it back safe, fellas," Jim said, and shook each man's hand in turn as they set down their loads. Jim's crew stepped up into the bus as Jim waved them onward. "Little craziness today, so we'll speed things up a bit. How did things go?"

"Just the way we like it, nice and quiet," Dalton replied. "Charlie knows how to sniff 'em out, that addition wasn't touched. We've got a pretty extensive list of vehicles if you're looking for any parts."

"I'm *always* looking for parts," Jim said and flashed a grin. "We'll take it from here, you guys. Go get cleaned up or whatever, meeting's going down around 5 or so."

He gave them a nod of farewell, then moved onto the bus himself to assist with unloading. Charlie turned and looked toward the cafeteria. The crowd had eased a bit, and a figure waved an arm to draw his attention. Miles stood talking to an unfamiliar man in military camouflage.

Charlie raised a hand and waved in return. *How about that,* he thought. Frannie had been right. He paused, trying to decide whether to interrupt. Miles made the decision for him, breaking away from the military man and jogging over to Charlie and his crew. "Hey, guys. Everything go all right out there?"

"Smooth and easy," Dalton confirmed. "Corey's shaping up. He'll be ready to lead his own crew before we know it."

The youngest member of the crew laughed, though he looked pale at the prospect. Miles laughed along and slapped a hand on Corey's shoulder. He glanced at Charlie.

"I don't have a whole lot of time," Miles said. "I need to get back to our guest and take him into a town meeting. Dalton, Corey, if you guys haven't eaten it'd be great to see you there."

Dalton's forehead wrinkled, and he looked between Miles and Charlie. "I don't follow," the big man started, but Charlie raised a hand to quiet him. He gave Miles an intent look, indicated the scars on his hand, and then looked back up at Miles. With that, he didn't have to say a word.

"Yeah," Miles said. "Exactly. I don't want them to get too curious about you, just yet. They haven't come out and said exactly what the deal is, but they need me to help them do something." He glanced back over at the Marine and waved. "They seem nice enough, but I'm not going to risk it, buddy. I know you sure as hell don't want to spend the rest of your life getting poked and prodded."

Charlie shrugged, then waved his hand from side to side. "And miss all this?" he rumbled.

"Laugh it up all you want," Miles replied. "Just . . . Make yourself scarce for a bit, all right? Anyone asks, we'll tell them you were feeling a little under the weather and hit the sack."

Dalton nodded. Corey looked confused but he nodded, as well. The source of Charlie's scars wasn't a secret, per se, but it wasn't something that he advertised.

I'm enough of a freak already with my voice, Charlie thought. *Don't need people pointing and whispering at the only immune guy in the camp.* He glanced at Miles, then turned to Dalton. He paired his hands together, then spread them apart in a mimicry of breaking glass. This was something that called for more detail than his voice would permit.

"Some weirdness on the run, Miles," Dalton said, immediately. "The houses were all locked up tight, and most of them still had their biters in residence. A few of them, though, were empty and had doors or windows broken from inside-out. Doesn't make sense that a survivor would do something like that, to us anyway."

Miles frowned. "Doesn't make sense that a zom would do it, either," he pointed out. "It's not like they have the strength, especially if they got stuck inside. Any other theories?"

Charlie shrugged, and Dalton said, "Not a one. But we lean more toward biters than survivors. And it was recent, too, maybe in the last few weeks."

Miles scratched his head and sighed. "I'll ask around, see if any of the other crews have run into anything similar. Unfortunately with all of this, it's going to have to go on the back burner."

Charlie nodded his understanding to Miles, then said, "Tomorrow. Need favor. Something else."

Miles nodded. "I'll find you," he promised. "For now, get scarce."

Chapter 13

Alex stirred the pot roast on his plate and tried not to make a face. Beef got old, especially when you ate it at least once a day for months on end.

If I start mooing, that's it. I'm skipping beef.

Cole Ferguson, Junior — Twigs to most everyone under the age of 18 — set his tray down with a clatter across from Alex and gave him a gap-toothed grin. Alex acknowledged him with a nod, then resumed staring at his plate.

Most little kids drove Alex batty, but Twigs wasn't too bad. Though he was short and scrawny, he was sharp and mature. It helped that Miss Val had moved him up into higher grade levels of work when he breezed through the first and second-grade assignments. Alex was a little behind in math, and sometimes his friend grasped the concepts faster than he could.

"Alex, did aliens come down and steal your brain or something?"

For a moment, Alex didn't even recognize that Twigs had asked him a question. Realizing that the silence was in anticipation of his answer, he looked up from his plate and said, "Huh?"

Twigs laughed in the middle of a drink and snorted water out of his nose. This just made him laugh even harder until Lindsay, one of Miss Val's helpers, cleared her throat and gave the two of them a pointed glare.

They hunched in their seats, presenting the image that they were suitably chastened. Twigs took a bite of pot roast, chewed, and said, "What you doing after school?"

"You have pictures of your dad?" Alex blurted. He regretted the question at once and grimaced. For better or worse, he'd broached the subject.

His friend looked down at his plate, then raised his head to meet Alex's eyes. "You know I do."

Alex gave him a ghost of a smile. "I try not to think about it, but I don't have any pictures of my parents. I don't even remember what they looked like." Twigs took another bite of food and chewed it longer than was necessary. Alex was going to wait but decided that he needed to further explain his train of thought. "I was up in the nest yesterday, and I realized we're not all that far from the school."

Twigs frowned. "Okay?"

"My old house is right across the street from the school."

"So, what — you want somebody to go get you a picture? Dude, they scavenged those houses years ago."

Alex frowned. "Yeah, but, they weren't looking for photo albums, they were looking for food, stuff to live on."

Twigs straightened in his seat and set his spoon down. "You're going."

"Keep your voice down," Alex hissed.

"I wanna come!"

"Shut up!"

Their argument was moot, at that moment. A wave of murmurs broke out across the room. Alex and Twigs turned to look, but they couldn't see what the excitement was about through the wave of bodies that drifted toward the main door from the serving line.

Alex turned back to Twigs. "It's just a pipe dream, kid," he muttered. "I lost my rifle privileges after I skipped class. Miss Val locked my .22 up in the safe."

Shrug. "I got a slingshot. That's quieter, too."

Alex gave Twigs a thoughtful look before waving a hand in disapproval. "No way. I'm not dragging a seven-year-old into the Wild to get eaten."

"Seven and a half," Twigs groused. "Besides, didn't you say that there aren't as many creepers around now?"

He looked at the smaller boy. *This is nuts. Why am I even considering this?*

"Come on, Alex," Twigs whined. "We can totally do it. After school tomorrow, I'll get my slingshot and a bunch of ball bearings — you should see what these things do to a can, pow! We'll be back in time for dinner. It's not that far, right?"

Alex gritted his teeth and thought back to his time on the tower. No, it wasn't all that far. Hit Stone Creek Lane, and the cluster of buildings was two intersections down. There wasn't a thing between here and there; just fields and emptiness.

Nowhere to hide, either.

He pushed the thought away. "All right," Alex drew out. "If we do this, you have to stay cool. I know how you geek out."

Twigs looked like he was trying not to bounce in his seat. "You got it, Alex, this is going to be so awesome!"

"Shut *up*," Alex hissed again, shaking his head.

It had been a long time since Hanratty had felt so out of place. It wasn't so much the attire of the people around him. After years without resupply, many of the troops wore whatever they could lay hands on. No, if anything, it was the *attention*. On ship, or at any of the forward operating bases, he was just another troop, an officer to salute. If anything, the general mood he'd become accustomed to was one of indifference.

That was *not* the case here, and there was no middle ground. The people regarded him with either awe or outright contempt.

The large barn was clad in faded red sheet metal, and the crowd milling around it parted as Miles led him toward a personnel door in the side. This particular side of the building looked as though it had been set up to be a large sliding door at one time. The survivors had installed hardware and welded beams into place to secure that part of the building in a closed position. *This was where they stored their farming equipment before. Now, it's the — what did he call it? — The First Church of the Time Share.*

Miles opened the door for Hanratty, and he stepped through with a nod of gratitude. The interior was neat and to his surprise, well-lit. His guide must have noticed his interest in the overhead lighting and commented, "The light fixtures in here are all LED. They're not as much of a drain on the batteries. We use most of the capacity from the solar panels and wind turbines to run the refrigeration equipment in the storage silo. There's enough left over to run some lights into here and the hospital. We make do with what we can elsewhere." He shrugged. "Lanterns and candles, to be honest."

Hanratty looked at the young man and tried to keep his expression blank. *Does he understand, I wonder, how impressive this all is?*

The Marine had, in essence, circumnavigated the globe in the years since the fall. The initial infection rate in and around Al Asad Airbase in Iraq had been low. Much lower, in fact, than what the United States and Western Europe had experienced. If the surviving CDC guys knew the reason for this, they weren't sharing it. Not at Hanratty's level, anyway.

When the second stage infection had kicked in, the number of cases were small enough that the situation should have been recoverable. The response that any society was capable of was often only as good as the level of cooperation inherent in said society. In Iraq, that level of cooperation was right at zero. Sunni and Shia took the opportunity presented by the chaos to kick off another round of sectarian violence. This negated any possibility of an effective quarantine. American troops that could have assisted in securing pockets of infection had instead fallen back to their own positions. Iraq had carried on with admirable determination after the first round of infection, but the eruption of tribal warfare doomed it. When the infected rose up amid the intermittent fighting, the chaos redoubled.

When the evacuation flights ended not long thereafter, Hanratty and thousands of American military personnel were a long, lonely five hundred miles from their secondary extraction point of Umm Qasr on the Persian Gulf.

They'd fought hard and gone down harder, but by the time they reached Iraq's lone deep water port, thousands were hundreds. At the end, Hanratty had been the most senior surviving officer. He'd led his troops through an unending hell that left many of them wide-eyed and shaking, even once they were out to sea and away from danger.

"Butter bar" Second Lieutenant Hanratty burned away in the fires of that chaos. He'd seen the worst humanity had to offer, led troops against both infected and uninfected, and lived to tell the tale. The Colonel who'd debriefed him had given him a fierce hug, then pinned the silver bars of a first lieutenant on Hanratty's shoulders.

He'd done nothing but distinguish his reputation since. Much of his success — and survival — built off of two key lessons he'd learned on the retreat to Umm Qasr. First and foremost — always keep your hatch dogged.

Second, the infected were not as dangerous as the uninfected. The infected were predictable. You couldn't trust the uninfected to act in a rational manner.

Nothing he'd seen in the years after had disabused him of either notion. But now . . . he wondered about his second lesson.

The crowd inside of the building was still light as word of their arrival trickled out. This gave Hanratty time to give the interior a quick assessment. The section to his left featured what looked to be an added-on kitchen and serving line. Near that, the survivors had lined up picnic tables and battered folding tables in neat rows. A few steps away from the last row of tables sat a wooden podium — for the meeting, Hanratty assumed. Low shelving units cordoned off the other half of the building. The contents inside that area proclaimed it to be some sort of classroom setup. Colorful mats covered the floor, and white boards and posters covered the blank spaces in the walls that weren't filled with shelves. The warm scent of cooking meat and baking bread filled the air, and Hanratty's mouth began to water. Miles and his people might have considered it bland, but it smelled damn good to him.

The gentle hum of curious conversation fell dead silent as a shriek filled the air. Hanratty turned, seeking the source of the noise, as a figure sprinted toward him.

Instinct screamed at him to draw his weapon and defend himself. He pushed it away with titanic effort. The figure sprinting toward him continued to scream as she came. The woman looked to be in her mid to late 40's and wore shabby, shapeless clothes. As she drew to a stop in front of him her screaming died out and she brought her hands down on his shoulders. Rather than being an assault, the motion was loving. As she brought one hand up to cup his cheek, she began to babble.

"Tommy, oh Tommy, why didn't you come sooner? We needed you, Tommy. They hurt your father and your sister — *where were you!?*" The last came out as a high-pitched shriek, and the loving hands clutched at his uniform with sudden desperation.

Miles stepped forward and wrapped his arms around the screaming woman. As he pulled her away, she began kicking and screaming even more. A second woman, tall and slender, with long, ink-black hair, ran up and grabbed her as well. Despite the combined strength of the two of them, she still bucked and flailed.

"No! I want my Tommy to take me home! Let me go!"

A pretty black woman with close-cropped hair stepped in to aid the town marshal and first woman. "Calm down, Betty," she said, "Just calm down, hon, it's going to be all right." She raised her head. "Somebody give me a hand, damn it!"

A big man, easily one of the biggest Hanratty had ever seen, stepped forward and pushed Miles and the slim woman to one side. "I've got you, Betty," the big man said, and he picked her up as though she weighed nothing. Once her feet were off of the ground, the shrieking woman collapsed into sobs and buried her face in the big man's broad chest.

"Thanks, Dalton," the black woman said. She turned to Hanratty. "Are you all right, Captain?"

"I'm fine," he assured her. "No harm done."

At that, she swiveled toward Miles and said, "We're going to give her something to help her rest. Be back as soon as we can." She gave Hanratty another look. He couldn't tell if the expression was one of veiled disgust or pity, but she didn't elaborate as she and the big man headed for the door.

"All right, Tish," Miles said and ran a hand through his hair. The conversation around them bubbled up even higher as the people inside the building began chattering about what they'd just seen. Miles looked at Hanratty. "Shit, Captain, I'm sorry that happened. Betty, she's, well, she's been pretty much out of it for a long time now. Her son was overseas when it happened, and the rest of her family . . ."

"Yeah," Hanratty said quietly as he tried to hold back his own tears. "Yeah, I think I got that part."

Someone approached from Hanratty's side, and Miles' faced flickered through several emotions. He wouldn't have noticed it if he hadn't been reading the facial expressions of enlisted men for years. The small-town sheriff — marshal, rather, he corrected himself — looked not too different than some of the troops when notorious, annoying staff officers approached. Hanratty turned.

The woman looked about as unimposing as they came; short and slender. She'd pulled her medium-length gray hair into a tight ponytail, and a pair of half-framed reading glasses perched on the end of her nose. The ratty sweater she wore over a button-up blouse only made her look more like a stern librarian. She beamed as she stepped up to Miles and Hanratty and extended her hand.

"Norma Benedict. Let me say how ecstatic we all are to have an official government representative here, after all this time."

"Happy to oblige, ma'am," he said politely. "Captain Adam Hanratty, United States Marine Corps."

She kept hold of his hand and began patting his forearm with her other. "Oh splendid, splendid, a Captain! I myself am the head of the small town council here, in case you didn't know. We're all excited to hear what you have to say and offer any help you might need." She beamed. "Oh, but I'm being a terrible host! Please, sit and eat with us, and then you can discuss what you've come all this way to say."

"Thank you, I'll do that," Hanratty said. She gave him a nod and Miles a thin smile, then turned away. Stepping toward the rows of cafeteria tables, she raised her hands and spoke in a commanding tone.

"Ladies and gentlemen! We have a special guest this evening, but of course, you all know that. Captain Hanratty will be joining us for dinner, then we'll have a meeting to hear what he has to say and open the floor for any questions." A few in the crowd clapped, a few directed curious looks in Hanratty's direction, but the majority of the body began queuing up in the cafeteria line. The buzz of conversation was suddenly interspersed with the clinking of serving utensils and tableware.

Miles clapped him on the shoulder. "Good luck," he said. "I'm headed over to sit down with the three amigos."

Hanratty glanced at him. "Right. Dumb question here, now, and I hate to ask it, but do you have any idea which way you're leaning?"

The other man grimaced. "Yeah, I mean, I know none of the particulars other than it sounds like a *super awesome* field trip."

"Had to ask," he replied, evenly.

"Oh, granted," Miles said with an easy grin. "Allow me to return the favor. Is any help you and your superiors offer contingent on me saying yes?"

Hanratty's initial reaction to the question was anger. Just asking it was an insult to everything he stood for. Before he could reply, he realized that the question wasn't intended that way at all. Miles delivered the question without animus; he simply wanted to know where he stood.

This is the world now, for them. We've kept it all together because of The Mission and the command structure, but these people haven't had that. We weren't here to protect them and we took our sweet time to get here. Why should they trust us?

"No," Hanratty said. "It's not." He shrugged. "I'm sure Ross would prefer I not reveal the nature of his mission in a non-secure setting, but I think you'll laugh about your question, later. Whatever your answer, Atlantic Command is intent on creating forward-operating bases to use as sally points for recovery operations. Piggy-backing off of existing communities of survivors is easier than putting together our own setups. I wasn't briefed on that aspect of the mission, as it's more a strategic focus than tactical, but from what I've gleaned, they're planning on enhancing fortifications, opening up the service to new recruits, but also helping out in any way we can." Hanratty shrugged. "Combat occupations took the biggest hit, after the fall. More than half of us are Fobbits and admin pogues, but we're all hard-core infected killers, now. We've had to be. But there are engineers, medical staff, and the like, who'd be glad to step aside and offer local support if we can add some fresh blood."

"Volunteer, not a draft? We're not exactly brimming with excess manpower."

"Volunteer only. We discussed a draft but rejected the idea for pretty much that reason."

"Engineers and medical, huh. Any psychologists?"

"Some, not many, I guess. I'd have to check to be sure."

Miles nodded. "Well, part of the reason we're so upside down on manpower is the psych cases. We had, uh, a lot of people who never did track right after everything that happened. We've been taking care of them as best we can, but it's not like we're professionals or anything."

Hanratty smiled. "That's one of the reasons why I'm excited to help, Mister Matthews. Far too many places we've come across went a . . . different direction, with those sort of survivors."

Miles gave him a hard look. "I won't say it hasn't come up. And it would be downright insubordinate of me to mention that my quote unquote boss is one of the people who keeps pushing for it, so I'll avoid that."

He nodded sagely. "It's important to keep discipline in the chain of command."

Miles laughed. "All right. I'm out of here. Enjoy dinner."

He watched the other man go as he left the building. Most of the crowd reacted well to Miles, reaching out to shake his hand, exchanging high-fives, or simply giving friendly waves.

Wonder why he's not in charge instead of Conan the Librarian?

Hanratty shrugged and stepped up to the end of the serving line. He picked up one of the well-worn serving trays and studied it for a long moment. Though scratched and faded, he could make out the remnants of a stylized cartoon bulldog painted on the tray. He chuckled to himself and mused, "It looks a bit like Chesty."

From his left: "Chesty?" Hanratty raised his head and turned. The tall, slender woman who'd helped out with Betty stood there with a bemused expression on her face.

"The bulldog, ma'am."

She smiled, though there was a tinge of sadness to it. "Ah. That's Benny the Bulldog. There is — was — a K-6 school a couple of miles north of here, Stone Creek Elementary.

"Believe we saw it, ma'am," Hanratty said with a nod. "We drove by when we came into the area." He paused. "If I'm not being too intrusive, there was quite a bit of battle damage to the building."

She smiled again, though this one was more legitimate. "You can blame that on the Gunny and a few of the other boys. They saw us barricaded in my classroom — some of the students and me — and stopped and got us out of there. It made quite an impression."

"Marines have a way of doing that, ma'am," Hanratty agreed and returned the smile with one of his own. "Particularly Recon Marines, like the Gunny. So, the trays?"

She shrugged. "If we didn't have it, we needed to get it somehow. The school was an amazing resource for us. Books, supplies, furniture . . . Once it was clear, of course."

Hanratty winced. Kids were the worst; more than a few of the troops he'd served with had eaten a bullet after actions with infected children. Such reactions were almost nonexistent, now, of course — years of constant fighting had hardened the soft edges. Sometimes he wondered if that was a good thing.

"So — Chesty?"

"Ah," Hanratty nodded. "Marine Corps tradition. Our mascot has been an English bulldog for a while. They're always named after Chesty Puller, the most decorated Marine, well, ever."

"I see." She stuck out her hand. "Valerie — Val — McKee. I'm a teacher."

Hanratty shifted the tray to one hand and returned the gesture. "Captain Adam Hanratty. Call me Adam, please." The line shifted a bit, and he grabbed a plate, knife, and fork out of a bin in front of him.

"Pleasure to meet you, Adam," she said. "I'm sorry about what happened with Betty. She's been improving a bit here, lately, but I guess it was just too much of a shock to the system."

"No apologies necessary," he said. "I should have been ready for it. Guess I was just so overwhelmed with how . . . how . . ." He searched for the words. "You realize how *special* this place is, don't you?"

She frowned. "I don't follow."

The line advanced and Hanratty studied the contents of the first serving pan. It looked to be actual, no kidding, pot roast — big chunks of beef swam in the broth with healthy pieces of carrot and potato. Here and there he even saw bits of onion. His mouth began to water.

"Well," he said, as he grabbed the serving spoon and doled some out onto his plate. "This right here is a great object example. We do have some farming, at certain bases we've reclaimed. Believe it or not, the military does have things like veterinary specialties, and you can be damn sure we've been cross-training as much as possible. But for the most part, if it's not a prepackaged meal, it's something simple like a rabbit or a deer, or something a scavenging party dug up. Now sure, part of that is economies of scale; we've got . . ." He bit back the hard number; safe as it felt here, it wouldn't do to breach OpSec, "a lot more people, and it takes a great deal more effort to keep them fed. And we've had other priorities, if I'm being honest."

Her tone betrayed her amusement. "I follow. I've had to do my share of farming these past few years. It's definitely labor-intensive, and that's with plenty of equipment available to us. Fuel and the zombies are our big obstacle there."

"Sure," Hanratty said. Chunks of what looked like cornbread filled the next pan. He offered a piece to Val before putting one onto his plate with a pair of tongs. She declined, wrinkling her nose in mild disgust.

"Sore subject," she said. "Cornbread kept us fed for a long time, but it gets old."

"Understood, there have been times where I thought I might cry if I had to eat another MRE. Okay, so, let me ask you this — what sort of experience have you all had with other survivors?"

Val shrugged. "Not much, myself, but word gets around, of course. There were a couple of smaller families around, in the beginning. We offered to have them come in and join us, but they held out on their own for various reasons. They, well, aren't around any longer. There was some funny guy they called the Tinker who used to travel around and try to trade for supplies, but no one has seen him for years. Other than that, not much. Some of the salvage crews have some pretty hair-raising stories, but we've never had barbarians at the gate, or anything like that."

Hanratty studied the last pan and tried to decide if he was seeing things or not. It looked like some sort of pastry, but flecks of bright red and larger, pale chunks shot through the crust. It looked almost like . . . He licked his lips. "Is that *fruit?*"

Val glanced down. "Yeah, apple turnovers. We don't have a ton of sugar, so they're not super sweet, but they're not horrible. There are a couple trees behind my house."

Hanratty grinned and put one on his plate. "Yeah. Haven't seen fresh fruit in a long time. Reason number six hundred and twelve why this place is special."

"Well, I'm glad you think so," Val laughed. They collected their trays and walked to one of the tables. A few folks were already sitting there, but there was plenty of room. Hanratty nodded to the people already sitting and took his own seat. Val sat across from him, and he began to tuck in, in earnest.

The hardest part was not wolfing it down; he'd been eating just for fuel for so long that any variance in flavor and texture was pure ambrosia. Not to mention that the fighting conditions of the past few years had not been conducive to drawn out, relaxed meals.

He'd made a good dent in the pot roast when Gunny Vance walked up with his own tray. The older man sat down next to Val with a slight smile on his face as he took in Hanratty. The captain took note of the glance that passed between the teacher and the retired Marine and thought, *Ah.* Well, that helped categorize Val's friendliness and willingness to speak. Fair enough. He needed to focus on the mission before everything else, even though the circumstances in this community were idyllic compared to the rest of the world.

"Well, I believe I've rounded up everyone there is to be had," the Gunny said after he'd taken a few bites of his own meal. "So you should have a fairly representative audience. Course, the rumor mill being what it is, the rest of the town will know everything in due course."

Hanratty laughed and broke his cornbread in half. The texture was a bit rough, but he was in no position to complain. "Just like the old sergeant's network, eh, Gunny? Whenever I need to know the real scuttlebutt I just hit up the First Sergeant."

The other man chuckled. "Guess some things never change." The Gunny reached out and squeezed Val's hand. "I worried you might not be too impressed by the soup of the day, but I guess I forgot how old MRE's get."

"Amen to that," Hanratty said. He was just reaching out to take a bite of the turnover when Norma Benedict called out from the podium. "Captain Hanratty? Would you like to say a few words?"

He sighed mentally and lowered the lump of dough and fruit back onto the tray. Standing, Hanratty moved to the podium and shook the woman's hand. "Thank you, ma'am," he said and looked out over the crowd. He knew what he needed to say, and perhaps more important, what he *wanted* to say, but he didn't have it mentally composed into any logical order. Finally, he began, "Ladies and gentlemen, fellow Americans, my name is Adam Hanratty. I'm a captain in the Marine Corps and let me say to you, kudos for what you've accomplished. It's impressive, given the challenges I know you've faced." He paused for a moment and studied the crowd. There were more than a few hard faces out there, but some looked hopeful, as well.

"My Marines and I came to you for a couple of reasons. First, on behalf of the command staff of the United States Armed Forces — we're back."

"Took you long enough," a voice accused from the audience.

Hanratty looked down at the surface of the podium for a long moment and tried to compose his thoughts. Finally, he raised his head and looked out to the part of the audience where the accusation had come from.

"You're right. It did. But I'm just a captain. Not too long ago, I was a lieutenant, and on the day of the fall I was what senior enlisted men like to call an F-U-N." A chortle of laughter rippled through the audience from those who understood the reference. "Spoiler alert for those who've never served, it doesn't spell 'fun', and it's an acronym that ends in 'useless newbie'. You can fill in the blank, I'm sure.

"I follow orders unless I believe them to be illegal. In my case following orders meant remaining on base not too long ago when I was less than thirty miles from my parents' house. I grew up in Toledo. Air reconnaissance determined that infected density remains too high there for recovery operations." Hanratty fell silent again. His throat was thickening with emotion. He attempted to regain his composure, then decided it wasn't worth it. He raised his head back up. "We've all lost people. And we're not serving under emotionless robots. My commanding officer sat with me as we watched the drone feed over my neighborhood." Hanratty shrugged. "The cameras in them are pretty good, but we try to stay high enough to stay out of sight. Even without a clear picture, I got my closure. Took us long enough? You don't know the half of it, pal.

"We presume that members of the military within the continental United States were either killed in action or infected. The surviving element consists of those members who were in overseas stations, and those we've managed to recruit to our cause.

"In the past eight years, we faced many of our own struggles. The second wave hit the Navy hard, and we lost a lot of ships. But we were also able to hold quite a few. All in all, we have a not-insignificant amount of sea lift power. You'll forgive me if I don't go into specifics; it's moot for the purposes of this discussion as well as classified.

"A modern military runs on its logistical support. Fuel, food, fresh water. The fall cut us off from our normal resources. Before we could be of any help to anyone, we had to secure lines of supply for ourselves. With the reduction in the size of the military, existing stockpiles of rations were sufficient, but getting to them was a problem. We had to develop new skills to fight the infected. I'm sure you went through something similar. Fuel was more problematic. I'm happy to say that, for the most part, those issues are gone. One of the things we're happy to offer down the road is a steady supply of fresh diesel fuel in exchange for surplus food. If you're interested, of course."

The crowd began to buzz with excitement. He saw motion out of the corner of his eye, and turned to look. A pale, dark-haired brunette in medical scrubs had stood up to speak. Hanratty gave her the once-over despite himself. He'd never thought much of the nurse look, but she pulled it off, in spades. "What about medical supplies? Any chance of getting anything there?"

Hanratty nodded. "I can't promise much, but we've been producing as well as scavenging, so there's a bit of surplus. When the time comes, I'll have our corpsmen meet with you, Miss . . . ?"

"Ferguson. Frannie Ferguson." She nodded her thanks and retook her seat.

Medical supplies must have been an issue because the room buzzed with conversation. Hanratty let them talk until the discussion died down a bit, then resumed his speech. "I understand you've been growing a lot of soybeans. Well, perhaps with a better fuel supply, you can switch over to something more fit for human consumption. I'm not speaking only for myself when I say that it's been too damn long since I've had a hamburger. You may just become my General's favorite people in the world once he hears about your cattle herd."

A ripple of laughter went through the crowd.

"As part of Operation Atlantic Fury, my unit has the task of establishing secure bases within the eastern half of the country. From these bases we will begin clearance of the infected population and return this land to the living once more. We transited the St. Lawrence Seaway and have secured Camp Perry, Ohio, as the first of these bases. With the blessing of this community, and on behalf of my commanding officer, General Dennis Vincent, we'd like to offer to make this the second base in that effort."

This time, when the crowd fell silent, you could have heard a pin drop.

Chapter 14

When Tom Oliver decided to build the town's first pub, he'd reasoned that having a meeting room with more privacy would be a good thing to have. Since then, it had become an impromptu conference room for anyone who needed to meet without having the entire cafeteria around. When Miles had recruited Vir, they'd met here and hashed out the details over Tom's ubiquitous burgers and hand-cut French fries.

By the time Miles pulled back the curtain that partitioned the meeting room from the rest of the bar, Pete and the SEALs already sat around the room's lone table. The finish of the huge circular table bore the scars of wear and tear, but the wood was well-polished and sanded smooth as silk. Furniture was never a high priority for salvage crews. If the rumors held any truth, Tom had made it more than worth Charlie's while.

Miles pulled the curtain closed as he stepped through, then turned and mock-sang. "We're Knights of the Round Table, we dance whenever we're able. We do routines and chorus scenes . . ." He trailed off; his audience consisted of four blank faces.

"All right, then, tough room," he said, and pulled out a chair and sat down. The Navy guys had clustered together on the opposite side of the room from the entrance. Watching the door, Miles guessed. His own chosen seat was opposite the lieutenant, and Pete was a couple of seats away to his right.

"My nephew thinks he's funny," Pete remarked, "but he's not entirely useless in a fight."

Lieutenant Ross eyed Pete with a frown. "I'm prepared to give your nephew a bit more detail than we're sharing with the general population. But it would be a waste of time asking you to step out, wouldn't it?"

Pete's eyes twinkled. "You're pretty sharp, for a swabbie."

The burly old chief chuckled, and the lieutenant just shook his head.

"Fine," Ross said, "we'll begin. Just to confirm, you *are* Miles Matthews, once employed by GenPharm BioMedical as an IT administrator?"

"Uh, yeah," Miles said. "If you don't mind me asking, how did you come by that information?"

The SEALs laughed. After it died down, the lieutenant said, with a wry grin, "IRS database."

Miles crossed his arms in front of his chest. "Yeah, it figures *that* part of the government would keep functioning."

Ross shrugged. "National crisis contingency; all electronic government assets go into secure mode and are accessible only via a rotating encrypted cipher installed on strategically important military assets. Thankfully, that includes automatic data backups to certain key satellites; running an op in downtown DC would be a cluster of epic proportions. As it is, we just had to park a ship with the necessary communications equipment long enough to pull the relevant data down. NSA, IRS, CDC. Which is what brings us to you." He fell silent as footsteps approached.

Tom Oliver stuck his head through the curtain. "Gentlemen, I don't have any menus — did Pete or Miles give you the gist of things?"

"Not just yet, Tom, but let's get it over with." Pete turned to the SEALs. "Easy as it gets. The only choice you get is how well you want it cooked, cheese or not — I'd pass myself, it came out of a can — and vegetables on the side."

After the SEALs put in their orders, he and Pete put in theirs. Miles couldn't help but notice a similar look of wonder on their faces to what Hanratty had possessed when he'd seen the herd of cattle. As Tom turned to leave, Pete concluded, "And bring us a round of beers and plenty of ketchup." He winked at Miles. "I'm sure Councilwoman Benedict will be glad to cover the cost."

Miles ignored the jibe and said to Ross, "All right, you've got me and I'm listening. How can I help you, Lieutenant?"

"We have a not-insignificant number of medical staff still around — doctors and corpsmen, that sort of thing. In the beginning of the fall, key members of particular agencies evacuated, albeit in a haphazard manner, to various offshore elements. Which is how we've come to be babysitting quite a few virologists and research scientists who were former employees of the Centers for Disease Control and the US Army Medical Research Institute for Infectious Diseases — USAMRIID. Until recently they haven't had the opportunity to devote much time to their actual profession; we've been too busy trying to find ways to feed ourselves and find secure places to live.

"That situation is no longer a problem, which has given the eggheads time to dig through the data dump we pulled out of the CDC. There were quite a few e-mails in that data, and a few of them refer to a promising experimental treatment that had shown lab success in vaccinating against the Brazilian flu. Revolutionary stuff, apparently, out of a nondescript bio-tech."

"I'm starting to see where this is going," Miles said.

Ross gave him a thin smile. "Problem, of course, was that this particular bio-tech was in the Midwestern United States. We've lost most of our fixed-wing fleet. But even if we parachuted people in, we'd have no good way to extract them."

"Done crazier stuff, of course," Chief Foraker offered. "I put my foot down on that one."

Ross smiled. "Indeed, he did. So it comes down to a question of geography. Command was planning the operation to begin retaking the country, anyway, so we suggested some modifications to the op order." He glanced over at Pete and said, "The Marine contingent was voting for us to land at Parris Island and make MCAS Beaufort our first waypoint, but we couldn't pass up this opportunity. So approximately two months ago we made landfall and began the process of retaking Camp Perry."

Miles blanched. "You came in through the Great Lakes?" He tried to visualize the route in his head and failed. "How?"

"There are canals, of course." Ross sounded tired. "The width of the canals limited which ships we could use, which made things a little dicey. We had to use submarines to scout the way; who knew what sort of sediment had built up over the years and changed the depth of the rivers." He rubbed the back of his head. "We had a crew of engineers with us, and we had to rig each lock to be remote-operated. Some places, that wasn't such a big deal; they were pretty much abandoned . . . Others, not so much. We lost a few men."

"I'm sorry," Miles said, and Ross nodded.

"Thanks. We pushed through, though. Once we rigged the locks it wasn't so bad, and we could begin ferrying supplies and troops. Secured a portion of Camp Perry, and then began pushing out patrols to the south.

"We've got enough functional satellite recon left that we could do a pretty good assessment of the area leading to and around the GenPharm complex. And it became obvious pretty fast that going in on the ground was a bad, bad idea."

"I can imagine," Miles said. "Most of my recurring nightmares involve being in the city on Z-Day."

The Lieutenant chuckled. "Z-Day; that's a good one. The brass has been resistant to any zombie or undead-related terms for the enemy. They're infected with a pathogen, end of story." Pete snorted and shook his head. Ross glanced at him and smiled. "Well, on the bright side, Captain Matthews, most of the PowerPoint Rangers got munched.

"GenPharm is a bit over two hundred air miles from Camp Perry, well within round trip range of a chopper. So, a couple weeks back, we inserted onto the roof. We attempted to find the research, but it's behind a security door with some pretty serious biometric controls on top of the card access. Rather than blow it and damage the research, we regrouped. So — still got your badge?"

Miles blanched. "Yeah, I'm pretty sure I do. If it even works for this door you're talking about; it doesn't sound like anything I ever accessed."

Ross shrugged. "We'll cross that bridge when we come to it. We're going to take some more exotic explosives in with us this time around that won't be as destructive if we need them. The ideal situation, of course, is to have you badge us in."

Miles shook his head as he realized the level of forlorn hope the SEALs were talking about. "You hacked government databases to find somebody with a swipe card?"

"IRS, anyway, yeah. We started going through everyone who'd received payment from GenPharm's tax ID number. Most of them we could eliminate based on where they lived. If there are any survivors in Cincinnati, we haven't been able to spot them. But lo and behold, the search program some of our tech guys whipped up found something interesting." He glanced at Pete, then back to Miles. "Not only was there a Miles Matthews with a rural address listed as GenPharm IT; NSA radio intercepts had marked a possible survivor in the same area who, son of a gun, had the same last name and address. So maybe, just maybe, there was a good chance the first Matthews survived."

Miles frowned and looked at Pete who was beginning to turn red. "NSA, Pete? What the hell is he talking about?"

His uncle just shook his head. Finally, he said, "Nights I can't sleep and get to feeling down, I get on the CB and just . . . talk. Haven't heard a soul in years, but sometimes I think I hear something out there." He glared at Ross. "So what, NSA was just sniffing through the spectrum and recording everything?"

"Apocalypse protocol, 'Uncle Pete'," Ross said. "All the systems went into automatic. It's amazing how well you can catalog survivors given radio traffic."

"So we're not alone?" Miles said.

"Not by a long shot, but there are no major settlements close enough to be of interest. They tended to be in the less densely populated areas up north and out west, for example." Ross shrugged. "Of course, we're just basing that on satellite pictures and radio intercepts; smaller settlements pass under the radar. But either way, it's thin."

"Ah," Miles said. He fell silent as he considered what to say next. The appearance of Tom Oliver, bearing a load of plates and bottles, rescued him from further conversation. The faces of the SEALs brightened at the sight of the food, and for the moment, everyone turned their attention to the serious business of lunch.

"I shouldn't let you boys drink on duty," Ross said to Foraker and Janacek. "But I find myself unwilling to cast any shadows on such a fine occasion."

Foraker grinned and said, "Much obliged, Lieutenant." Janacek just grunted and kept eating.

"So," Pete said, putting his burger down for the moment. "What's your story, Ross?"

Ross chewed his bite for a long, uncomfortable moment, then said, "You want to know where we were on Z-Day, is that it?"

Pete shrugged. "I was home, myself. Didn't have much to worry about till friends and family started pouring in, telling crazy stories. Course, the zombies started trickling in not too long after, so I started believing pretty quickly." He grinned and jerked a thumb at Miles. "Raised this one since he wasn't much more than a pup, so I saw my share of monster movies. Kid ate 'em up. So I don't have any aversion to calling them what they look like. I never was the best officer as far as the politically correct admin crap."

Ross took a sip of beer. "There were sixteen of us in all. I was second in command behind Commander Mike

Jameson, who was, if I dare say it, one of the finest men I've had the honor to serve with. I fall short of his example every day."

"I'd object to that notion, sir," Foraker interjected. "You do just fine."

"So you say," Ross said. "We'll agree to disagree. Anyway, we were doing deep recon in Ukraine. Russians were getting a little frisky, and there was a concern they might make some sort of move to take advantage of the first wave of the outbreak.

"Z-Day," he nodded to Miles, "comes, and things went to hell in a hand basket. Exfil was a cruiser just off of Sevastopol. Thankfully the Russians were too damn busy to care much about us. It took some of the heat off of us with the infected, but not enough." Ross raised his beer and toasted the table. "Absent companions."

"Absent companions," Pete echoed, and drank as well.

Sevastopol? Memories of his college literature classes bubbled up, and Miles murmured, "'into the valley of death, rode the six hundred.'"

Foraker half-smirked and half-grimaced. "'All that was left of them, left of six hundred.' Horses would have been nice; we walked and did our best 'Ten Little Indians' impression."

"Sixteen of us were in on the initial helo insertion. Nine made it to the ship." Ross stared at the table, though Miles doubted he saw it — his voice came from somewhere far away. "If there's any consolation, we made sure they wouldn't succumb to the infection. We couldn't pull their bodies out, but we could do that little thing for them. After that? It's all kind of a blur. We spent the last few years re-consolidating our assets. Loss rates for the Army, particularly in CONUS, were near total as best we can tell."

Ross took another sip of his drink and kept staring at the table. His voice held an uncertain tone. Miles wondered if he'd ever tried to string the entire story together before. "Same for the bases in Europe. The population density was just too high. Any organized resistance went under less than a month after the second stage of the infection kicked in.

"Middle Eastern units got out as long as the air support and evac kept coming, but the draw on the Air Force was too much. They started losing refueling flights to pilot error, I suppose from fatigue, which spread things even thinner. The last flight out of Bagram had dozens of infected clinging to the landing gear as it took off. Hanratty's got stories that'll turn your hair white."

"All things considered being in the Ukraine wasn't so bad," Chief Foraker offered with a dark laugh.

"Right. So the naval forces made out better than ground-based ones, for obvious reasons. We still lost quite a few ships to out of control infections. We fell back on Diego Garcia at first and tried to figure out mission protocols. We never got any consistent orders out of civilian leadership; the failsafe plans and fall backs didn't work out. As best we can tell, the bunkers intended to ensure continuity of government were all compromised. We've been doing the best we can, clearing islands here and there to get a foothold established."

"Well," Pete said. "Regardless of how long it took, I'm glad y'all made it."

"Same," Miles agreed. "It may not look it, but a lot of folks here were just barely clinging on. This . . . This gives them *something*, at least. Something bigger than walls and farming, and sleeping in rooms with boarded up windows."

"So, let's cut to the chase," Ross said. "Will you help us?"

The answer was obvious, but for some reason Miles had trouble putting it to words. Tish would be furious, of course, but this was about more than his own self-interest; it was about the potential survival of the human race. If the infection was no longer a concern, things would just be so much *easier*. A scratch or a bite wound would no longer be a death sentence. They could concern themselves with living and not just surviving.

"Yes," he said. "I'm in."

Chapter 15

The morning was crisp and cool as Pete made his slow ascent up the ladder to the Crow's nest.

A few hours into Miles' planning session with the SEALs, he'd sent a runner to tell the kids to call it a day. With all the hubbub in the settlement, he doubted they'd have paid much attention, anyway. On any other day, he would have been frantic with the post unmanned, but the presence of their new arrivals had eased that worry. He'd spent the rest of the afternoon and evening with his family — and with his feet on the ground, for a change.

His grand-niece's excitement at his presence had left Pete feeling ill at ease. More often than not, he was a couple of hundred feet away from her, but there was a palpable difference to being close at work and just plain being close. The bed had been a nice change, as well. As he stepped up to the observation platform he gave the woods to the south a sour glance. Maybe now that they had external support, he could figure out a casual way to mention that there was a horde of zombies loitering in the tree line.

Dear US Marines, please carpet bomb my dark forest. Thanks, Pete Matthews.

He snorted to himself as he plopped down into the wheelchair. No, this wasn't the sort of thing you could just tell someone about. It was so far beyond the level of their experiences since Z-Day that few would take him at his word without seeing for themselves. Hell, he saw it every night and he still half-doubted it in the light of day.

Pete stared south and thought about digging out the spotting scope. *Heck with it, I'm doing it*, he thought and began to roll toward the footlocker where he stored the Newcon. As he stopped, he realized the nest was vibrating — someone was climbing up the ladder. It was too early for his charges to be showing up, so it was someone else. He rotated the chair and faced the hatch. "Now I thought for sure people were exaggerating," Hanratty said, "but this is a pretty nice observation post. Morning, Captain. Mind if I join you?"

Pete waved a hand in acceptance and the young officer clambered up. He was of only average height, but he still had to stoop. Finally, he settled for taking a knee and extended a hand.

"Adam Hanratty," he said. "Since we haven't had a formal introduction. From what I hear, Lieutenant Ross was pretty impressed with your boy last night."

"Pete Matthews," he replied, shaking firm and fast. "He's my nephew, and he's a damn good kid. Don't go and get him killed, all right?"

"He'll be in the best of hands," Hanratty assured him, and Pete snorted.

"That may well be, but no plan survives contact with the enemy. Otherwise, they wouldn't be the enemy." He cocked his head to one side. "Got a lot of professional respect for SEALs. Participated in quite a bit of inter-service rivalry, as well, of course. All things considered, I'd rather him accompanied by a platoon of Recon Marines, but beggars can't be choosers. Particularly nowadays." Pete fell silent and glanced to the south. Maybe Hanratty would be receptive to what he had to say. The problem, of course, was the approach. "Tell me, Captain Hanratty," he said. "What kind of hardware y'all got back up? I know Camp Perry wasn't big as far as heavy equipment goes, but you've got the LAV running still. Anything heavier?"

The other man hesitated, and Pete could tell he was trying to decide how much to say. Good; it meant he wasn't so naive to completely trust them. Pete had never had the honor to serve under him, but General James Mattis, former commander of the 1st Marine Division, had once commented, "Be polite, be professional, but have a plan to kill everybody you meet." Hanratty had learned that lesson, even if from organizational osmosis.

"Nothing too heavy. We got a few Abrams tanks back up and running, but they're resource pigs and over-armored for the task. There aren't a ton of surviving fixed wing pilots, so the majority of our air consists of helicopters." Hanratty gave Pete an even stare, and he could tell the other man was trying to discern the reason for his interest. "It's sufficient for our needs, Standard clearance doctrine is to use noisemakers to bunch up a herd, then make sweeps with gunships to reduce their numbers. That usually creates a big enough time window to throw up field expedient fortifications. CONEX containers, usually, on top of raised berms. Engineers whipped up some with access doors in the side, we usually pack them full of ammo. Once the attack helicopters are out of ordnance, we start ringing the dinner bell at our fort and draw the rest in." He shrugged. "If we need to ammo up, we've got a few helicopters with those big psyops speakers on the side. Play anything loud enough and it will draw them away."

Pete blanched. "Gah, that's . . . Oof." He was silent as he tried to find the most diplomatic term for what he thought of the tactic. "Inefficient as hell. Hasn't anyone done the math?"

Hanratty cocked his head to one side. "How so?"

"Well, sure, it's a lot of sound and fury, and ooh-rah gung-ho bullshit. But how about just digging some angled trenches and fill them up with half the fuel you're using to run the choppers. Then sound your dinner bell from a device inside the trench lines and light 'em up when they start falling in. No fuss, no muss. How many times have you guys done this?"

Hanratty sighed and began rubbing his forehead. "We've been doing it for years, getting supplies from islands and the coast. You have to understand, on islands especially, thorough sweeps are the name of the game. All it takes is one infected to start a new outbreak."

"Well," Pete said, and thought about it for a moment. "I imagine it's good for morale. But bullets don't grow on trees, Marine."

The younger man looked unconvinced. "It would surprise you what Uncle Sammy stashed away for a rainy day." He shrugged. "Fuel isn't a problem, and we've got ordnance for an army a hundred times larger than what we currently have."

"Still. Hundreds of millions of them — how many thousands of us?" Pete shook his head. "Hell, we've been making pistol bullets out of reclaimed lead for a few years now. I still get nervous whenever I hear about any gun play out beyond the walls."

Hanratty shook his head and smiled. "Maybe you're right. Keep talking this way, Pete, and they'll be bringing you back in and putting you in planning."

"Good luck with that," Pete snorted. "I'm too old and two legs short." He rapped on one of the prostheses for emphasis.

Hanratty's eyes twinkled. "You seem to get around all right to me. And unless I miss my guess, you've been staying active. We drove by your neighborhood school on our way in. Don't tell me you didn't participate."

Pete crossed his arms over his chest and scowled. "Eight years ago, kid. I'm a lot creakier than I used to be."

"Call me Adam, I get 'kid' enough from my First Sergeant," Hanratty suggested. "I'm not talking about a front-line position. But if we designate this as a forward-operating base, there's no reason why we can't cycle troops through here for training. You've not only got combat experience, you've got experience surviving, as well. I've had boots on the ground for less than three months and I can already tell that there's a world of difference here from what we had to face."

"That's up for debate," Pete hedged. "Your Navy buddies have some pretty hairy stories to tell."

"True enough, and I'm not saying we're not hardcore, but I'd be stupid to pass up the opportunity to widen my knowledge base. There's a difference between raiding islands and coastal warehouses for supplies and holding a position for years."

"I'll mull it over," Pete said. "Can't be much different than teaching marksmanship to a bunch of teenagers." He waved his hand and indicated the workbench and cot. "Maybe with tactics I can spend a little more time with my feet on the ground."

"Good, glad to hear it." Hanratty glanced at his watch. "Don't mean to rush, but I need to get moving. We're rolling out in thirty."

"Ross said you're just dropping them off, last night. What time you think you and your troops will be back?"

The younger man shrugged. "We prepositioned some fuel about a hundred miles north of here for the helicopter. Figure six hours round trip, if all goes well. Be back in the afternoon."

Pete looked at him in mute assessment. Finally, he said, "After dinner tonight, climb back on up. There's something I need to show you."

His eyes were heavy and his stomach was growling, but Vir was almost home.

The rumble of the big truck's engine was almost *too* soothing. He'd lowered the driver's window halfway and turned the heat off to try and channel a bit of cold air into his face.

It had taken him longer than he'd expected to search the warehouse for the items on the list. By the time he packed the back of the truck and the cab with as much as he could manage, the sun was down. Not trusting his own recall of the route back home without daylight, he'd spent another chilly night huddled on the roof of the warehouse. At first light, he'd fired up the truck and pulled out. To his amazement, he was still on track to return in the planned time frame.

Of course, as luck would have it, the falling roll-up door had landed on the truck with the radio. Vir spent an hour transferring the CB to the other truck before finding that the door had not only crushed the bed, it had damaged the whip antenna. Perhaps there were others about who could fix it, but Vir knew his limitations — he was a structural engineer. The vagaries of electronics were, more often than not, above his head.

He hoped the terrain outside of the walls was clear of biters because he wasn't going to be able to let the guards know he was coming. If the walls weren't clear — well, things might get a little sporty. His pistol and shotgun lay in the passenger seat, and his *kirpan* was in its sheath under his arm. One way or another, he had prepared for the worst.

He crested the last shallow rise and the eastern wall came into view. *Here we go.*

Vir kept the wheel straight and glanced to either side. The fields in front of the wall looked clear, for the moment. Nervous, he pressed the accelerator down a bit, and the truck surged forward. The stick figures on the walls began to resolve themselves into more recognizable shapes, and he saw them scrambling around. The covers came off of the Brownings on either side of the gate and the gunners raised the barrels to point at the approaching vehicle. So far so good, just the way Gary had trained them.

"Stay chill, gents," Vir whispered. "Say to yourself, hey, that truck looks bloody familiar, don't it?"

He eased off the accelerator. Instinct made him keep his head on a swivel, checking either side of the road even as he drew closer to the gate. A couple hundred yards out now, and he squinted. The man on the right Browning looked like Graham Burke. As soon as sunlight glinted off of the round spectacles worn by the man on the right, he smiled to himself. Ivan Dantzler was the man on the other gun. He knew and had worked with each man, but better than that, he knew them both to be solid. Neither was the sort of rookie who might riddle a vehicle with bullets on accident. Of course, if it was going to happen, it was going to happen at any moment. He lifted his foot completely off of the accelerator and let the truck coast forward.

At once, Burke lowered the barrel of his Browning. He turned and began shouting with cupped hands. Vir was close enough to see Dantzler squint, and mouth a "What the hell?" before lowering his own gun.

Burke turned to Vir and waved him forward. Below him, the gates began to open. He let out the breath he hadn't realized he'd been holding, and put his foot back on the pedal. The truck had almost come to a stop by now, and it surged forward through the gates. He'd made it.

Vir slowed to a stop and rolled his window down the rest of the way. The guards from the gate bunkers were milling around, and he put the vehicle in park as Dantzler leaped off of his bunker and sprinted over. The other man climbed up on the running board and proclaimed, "Damn, old boy, what the hell's going on?" Dantzler was a slight, wiry man with receding curly brown hair. He wore a pair of old-fashioned round, wire-frame glasses, and looked like an accountant or lawyer. Despite his Germanic last name, his accent was pure Louisiana. Vir had always liked him, Dantzler was quick with a joke and quicker with a grin, but he had the capacity to speak well on a variety of topics. All too often, wall duty consisted of groaning about what one missed more, professional football or college basketball.

Vir was about to answer, but the hulking shape parked near the wall just past the gate bunker stunned him to silence. *When did we get a bloody tank?*

Dantzler followed his eyes and turned back with a laugh. "The Marines have landed, my man. Looks like civilization might just be coming back to us. Had a nice little speech yesterday. This whole place is giddier than a school girl on prom night."

"Right," Vir said and shook his head to regain his train of thought. "Buck and the others didn't make it. There was a bloody damn horde inside the warehouse. They got overrun and the other truck got damaged. It may be salvageable, but it was more than I could do on my own." He shrugged. "I loaded up as much as I could find, all the critical stuff, anyway."

Dantzler stared at him. "Well, damn. You are a bona fide, a-number-one hero, ain't you?"

Vir grimaced. "Just doing my part, Ivan. You mind radioing ahead for me? I'm going to pull right up to the clinic and start offloading this stuff. I imagine good Doctor Matthews will be happy to have it."

"Right," Dantzler said and hopped down. "You got it, superhero." He made a joking salute and flashed a grin at Vir. "Don't let me keep you."

Vir returned the nod and dropped the vehicle back into drive. Despite his fatigue, a buzz of adrenaline was running through him. Hopefully, his report to Miles would be fast and he could get home to Aasha and the boys. It wasn't like his undercover work had been a smashing success. Sure, he'd established who'd been getting some of the ingredients into the community. But he was nowhere near helping find out who was actually making the stuff.

Of course, he reflected with a small, satisfied grin, without a ready supply of ingredients, it was going to be hard for their mystery man to continue his illicit work.

Chapter 16

It wasn't as though he'd sprung forth fully-formed from the forehead of a criminal mastermind. He'd never made it his goal in life to be a drug dealer, either. Ivan Dantzler's childhood had been pedestrian and, if he were being honest, not a little pampered. An only child, his parents provided him with love, affection, a roof over his head, and three squares a day.

It had been so *tedious*.

The level of his annoyance with his own life hadn't hit him until one summer day during his junior high years. He was riding his bike, without a care in the world, when he drove past an empty lot in an ordinary — and *tedious* — residential neighborhood in his hometown of Luling, Louisiana. A couple of the bigger kids, renowned in the neighborhoods and in school as being bullies, were kicking around one of the other kids, who was also well-known, though for different reasons. For a moment, young Dantzler paused, one foot on the sidewalk, still perched on his bike, and considered the tableau. He almost pedaled off. But something inside him saw what was happening, assessed the probabilities, and saw an opportunity.

He was on the first bully's back before his bike clattered to the ground, and the boy didn't know what hit him. Ivan Dantzler was only of middling height and weight, and even then near-sighted enough to need glasses, but he was not, by any stretch of the imagination, weak. He was fast, wiry-strong, and relentless.

Each of those qualities combined into one as he rode the first bully to the ground and slammed him face-first into the crumbled asphalt of the empty lot. The larger boy's nose went with a wet splat, and he gave a high-pitched squeal as blood began to course down over his lips.

For a moment, the entire scene seemed to freeze. Victim and aggressors stared at Dantzler as though unsure how to proceed. At once, time reasserted itself, and the second bully surged toward Ivan with an articulate roar.

It was painful — one could almost say tedious — how easy it was. Ivan slid to one side and offered a helpful foot. When the second bully tripped and landed on top of his companion with a huff of expelled air, Ivan jumped up and planted both feet in the center of the boy's back, driving the air even further from his chest. So quick was the strike that the second bully couldn't even *breathe*, but Ivan didn't let up. He stepped off, oriented himself, and placed a quick snap-kick between the second boy's legs. He'd gotten a little breath back, but the extent of what he could manage was a low wheezing sound. Ivan waited a moment, and then gave him another shot in the balls for good measure.

Both lay there almost motionless. The boy on top wept and clutched his aching crotch. The first boy still struggled to get out from under his friend and stem the flow of blood from his nose. Ivan noted, with not a little satisfaction, that it lay over to one side.

"Get on," Ivan whispered, as though he were making an observation about the weather. The two larger boys scrambled to their feet and looked as though they were preparing to wade into the fray once more. Something in Ivan's carriage or expression dissuaded them of that notion. They took up their own bikes and pedaled away as fast as they could.

Dantzler turned and looked down on the kid who they'd been beating on. Dust smeared his face from the ground of the lot, though blood from one nostril and tears from both eyes had cut clean tracks through the mess. "What'd they want?" Dantzler said, in a kind tone.

"Last year I started giving them my lunch money twice a week. I was playing here and they rode by . . . They wanted me to keep paying them this summer, too."

Ivan knelt down and made eye contact with the other boy. "You don't have to worry about them any longer. Not this summer, and not when school starts back up. I just need one thing from you."

"What's that?" the other boy asked, eager.

"I want your lunch money *once* a week. Just when school's in, too. Vacation time, it's all yours." He clapped the other boy on the shoulder and put a broad grin on his face. "Sound fair?"

The sheer *gratitude* the little loser exhibited was almost embarrassing. But it taught Dantzler a key lesson of human nature. So long as you make things hurt less than the alternative, and put a happy face on it, why, folks will *hop* to pay up.

Oh, he was smart about it, of course. He never took more than a taste, and he never spread his net wide enough to attract attention. By the time he graduated from high school — with honors, of course — Ivan Dantzler had become friends with some interesting people. That made life so much less tedious. They encouraged him on to college but kept him in mind when they had jobs that needed to be done.

Four years later, as his fellow graduates scrambled for jobs, Ivan Dantzler already had one. His infrequent jobs had turned into a position as the Dixie Mafia's newest — and most charming — enforcer.

They didn't send Dantzler to do anything so mundane as breaking fingers or kneecaps. No, the pleasant-looking young man with old-fashioned round spectacles was something of a specialist. More often than not, a pleasant conversation with the curly-haired young man ended well. Accounts that had been in arrears were all at once paid up. The alternative was coming home to discover your toddler had disappeared, or your house had burned to the ground while your wife napped on the couch.

Time passed, and as with any organization, performance and success on Dantzler's part meant promotion. And so, on one otherwise ordinary Wednesday, with a cooling, tarp-wrapped corpse in the trunk of his sedan, a traffic jam became ground zero for the feasting of crazed, silver-eyed cannibals.

The turn of events didn't stun him as it did so many others. No, Dantzler's reaction was best summed up as curiosity. It had been self-evident after his college psychology classes that he was a particularly nasty form of sociopath. Sitting in his car amidst sudden onset cannibalism, he couldn't help but wonder. Had he finally gone off of his rocker?

A screaming woman pounded on the driver's window of his car, begging for him to let her in. He watched, expression blank, as a dozen of the rough beasts the denizens of this particular slice of Middle America had become pulled her away.

At that moment, Dantzler realized that he was *free*. The old, binding rules no longer applied, and the name of the game was mere survival. In a world remade for ruthless men, Ivan Dantzler fit the bill.

That dream ended in short order, of course. He learned that murder and mayhem were only fun when you could kowtow potential victims into terrified acquiescence of their fate. The beasts that ruled the new world feared nothing and often gathered in numbers that presented Dantzler with more of a challenge than he desired.

For the sake of his own survival, Ivan put on his old, friendly mask. He found a community where he was not only trusted but secure.

But . . . something was missing. For a while, he contented himself with standing watches on the wall and indulging in the occasional supply run to pad his small cache of luxuries. The days began to drag, and the people surrounding him became inane. They were so *earnest*. A good chunk of the population were mental cases, but at least *they* weren't boring.

People like him always attracted like-minded fellows, as though there was some sort of subconscious radar that homed in on the lust and greed like flies seeking out rotten meat. The capacity for personal profit had always been there, but the icons of the community held sway on any thoughts he might have entertained of going off of the reservation. Dantzler was cunning enough to know that Larry Vance or the Matthews boys would destroy him if he gave them the excuse. Get drunk and smack around a lady friend once, and you could bank on a weekend drying out and a little social awkwardness. Repeat it, and the hammer of doom was likely to fall on you.

So for a time, Ivan watched and waited. He considered the angles and the opportunities, and when it came to him, he wondered why he hadn't thought of it sooner.

Coffee and tea were still available, although not in the instant-gratification quantities people had once been accustomed to. On top of that, many of the members of the community still weren't acclimated to the sort of long-term, low-grade physical labor that subsistence farming required, even after they were able to produce enough biodiesel to use machinery for some of the work. A morning pick-me-up had been a long-term habit for so many of the survivors that the absence of plentiful caffeine was jarring. Some overcame, but for others, it was still a struggle. Abuse of prescription painkillers had been the drug of choice for middle America in the years before the end. A few of the survivors had the habit, but fentanyl and hydrocodone were, if possible, in shorter supply than coffee. The addicted survivors had either kicked the habit or died trying.

Ivan himself had never cooked, but he was familiar enough with the requirements. A few of his people *did* know the methods, and a few more were on the salvage crews. It was simple enough to entice the latter into collecting the necessary supplies. Dantzler's moves were so slow and methodical, the straight-laced dupes running the show hadn't even noticed what was happening until the operation had been up and running for almost a year.

Finding somewhere to conduct the illicit manufacture was another issue. The fumes the process gave off were not only nasty, they were obvious, even in the middle of a camp lousy with open cooking fires. In an ironic twist, the wall that kept them safe was the eventual solution to that dilemma.

The crew building the wall placed the southeastern corner in deference to the run of Stone Creek across the southern border of the community. Before Z-Day, the county highway department had just completed repaving the road and installing larger storm drains. The output for one of those drains emerged right under the southeastern corner of the wall. At this point, the wall was closest to the creek — a mere six feet from the edge of the bank. The culvert dog-legged from its straight path from the road to come out at an angle in the creek. Were it laid at much more of an angle, it would have required a shift in the placement of the wall. As it was, the last section of the culvert was only a few feet in front of the southeastern corner.

The six-foot diameter corrugated pipe wasn't visible from atop the wall, but as soon as Dantzler had seen the top curve of it sticking out from the bank, he'd known the solution to his troubles.

The bunker at the southeast corner helped reinforce the shift from chain link to board. It had taken some patience, but over time, Dantzler had orchestrated enough personnel switches that the three men in that bunker worked for him. After that, it was easy. Dantzler and his three buddies built their small, adjoining sleeping quarters next to the southeastern bunker. He'd worried at first that someone would have objected to the siting of the shack along the southern fence, rather than against the more solid eastern wall, but if anyone noticed or cared, they never made mention of it. The wall of the shack had a concealed half door that opened up beside one of the southern fence's support poles. They'd replaced the wire securing the fence to the pole at the lower corner with several twist-on pieces rather than the heavy-duty crimps used on the rest of the fence. It weakened the structure at that point, but Dantzler and his friends weren't suicidal. With the wall of the shack abutting the fence it was still plenty strong.

Such an arrangement would never have worked in the early days. As the population of the cannibals fell, there was no longer a constant presence at the wall. The short walk to the mouth of the culvert could be nerve-racking, though Dantzler chafed at the notion that he'd grown accustomed to the security of the walls.

They'd installed a heavy gate of heavy iron bars a few steps inside of the culvert. It was solid enough to secure against cannibals or unauthorized inspections, but open enough for water to drain through. The interior got a bit damp at times, but anything left in there long term stayed up high on shelving they'd rigged, or wrapped in plastic.

This was all becoming moot in short order, of course, given what he'd just heard from that goody two-shoes Vir. Ivan Dantzler sighed as he mentally calculated the extent of the supplies he'd been able to sock away versus what he'd wanted to have.

All things considered, perhaps it's time for a reduction in headcount. He grinned as he approached the southeastern bunker, raising a hand in greeting. His facial expression betrayed nothing of his thoughts.

Ben Carlyle was the man on duty at the moment. He noted Dantzler's approach, returned the gesture, and turned back to survey the area outside of the fence.

Ol' Ben's a big guy, and handy in a fight. None too bright, but that's okay. Course, he also eats a hell of a lot and snores. His smile broadened. *Sorry Big Ben, looks like you're the first pink slip.*

He pulled open the door and stepped inside the bunker. The remaining men on the crew, Victor Kerr and Lloyd

Granger, sat at a small table playing a card game. When they saw him enter, both looked up in greeting but waited to see if he was alone before speaking further. Canny, both of them. Victor Kerr had been a diesel engine mechanic before the Day, and Lloyd a line worker in one of the factories. There wasn't much work for Victor these days, but he supplemented his duties on the wall by assisting in the ongoing maintenance of the community's vehicle fleet. Lloyd was just a cog, simple labor.

Sorry, Lloyd. Looks like you're on the chopping block.

"Bad news, fellas," Dantzler said as he dropped into an empty chair. "Buck and most of his crew got wiped out."

"Shit," Lloyd hissed. "What happened?"

"I couldn't get the full story just yet, but it doesn't matter. The only survivor was that Singh cat. He looks to have brought back plenty of medical supplies. It's up in the air if any of our stuff is on the truck." And, he didn't say, with a replenished supply of IV fluids, the laid-up customers were now more likely to wake up and recover. Would they be eager to rat out their dealers after almost dying from the product? Dantzler thought there was a pretty good chance of that.

"Damn," Victor commented. "We're just shy of tapped out on pseudo and the customers have been getting antsy wanting to know when we'll have more for them. What's our move? Do you think Buck and the boys had time to get it out before it hit the bricks?"

Dantzler shrugged. "No way to tell until we check. In the meantime, I think this calls for a tweak in our timetable. How much diesel do we have stored?" Most of their 'customers' pilfered anything that wasn't nailed down to get their fix, but Dantzler had a standing arrangement with Buck to cut some of his fuel allotment off of the top. They traded diesel and precursors in exchange for some of the finished product and a percentage of what the customers paid. You wouldn't think that someone on a salvage crew would have much of a need for anything else, given the free pass they got on a lot of what they brought in. Then again, Dantzler had never seen a man exhibit such raw avarice as Buck Buckner. Well, had exhibited. *Vaya con Dios,* buddy.

"Just shy of ten gallons. It should be enough, but it doesn't leave much of a safety margin," Lloyd noted. About five miles south, in a garage already salvaged and marked as empty — courtesy of Buckner's crew — sat a diesel Chevy Suburban. Victor and Dantzler had spent several long nights going over the truck with a fine-toothed comb and transferring supplies. The Suburban was in as good running order as they could make it, but it needed fuel.

The germ of Dantzler's bug-out plan began when one of their customers made an interesting offer in the form of payment. He offered a bright-yellow float on a ring of keys and asked if they'd take a boat in trade. The owner had parked his boat a week before Z-Day at a marina seventy miles south, on the Ohio River. It was debatable whether it would still be there after all this time. He'd spent many a night kicking himself for jumping at such a forlorn hope. Despite that, there was a little itch in the back of his mind that whispered that this deal might just pay out. The arrival of the Marines had only affirmed to him that it was time to get steppin'.

In theory, they'd be able to get the Suburban down to the dock on five gallons. This left the other half to get the boat started and down the river until they could get the sails up. It was, as Lloyd noted, a thin margin.

"We're not using more than five gallons in the Suburban," Dantzler announced. "We'll bring the bikes and kiddie trailers. If we come up short, Lloyd and I can ferry the supplies to the boat while you get the engine up, Victor. Ben can cover your back." They had a pair of Trek mountain bikes with trailers tucked into the culvert. They'd need no more than two trips to empty the Suburban if they came up short, Dantzler judged.

Both men blanched. He could tell they didn't like the idea, but they'd been with him long enough that they knew Dantzler's first rule. If you didn't like the way he ran the show, you were free to leave. That departure wouldn't be on your own terms, nor would it include walking, but it was always an option.

"Penny for your thoughts, Lloyd?" The man looked particularly doubtful about the plan.

"Just thinking, boss. Now that the Marines are here, doesn't that make things more stable? Couldn't we stay, instead?"

Dantzler could fly off the handle. *Hell, I'm intending to cut Lloyd loose as it is.* But he was also astute enough to know that he couldn't just do it front of Victor. It had to be organic, deniable. Acting like a tyrant showed a lack of confidence in self. He needed to save those times for when he truly needed them.

"Lloyd," Ivan said, with exaggerated patience. "They're already putting undercover cops on salvage crews to try and track us down. That's when no one has gotten hurt. What happens when one of those overdose cases dies? Do you think that will make them more or less inclined to go easy on us if they find out what we've been doing? Besides, laying out on deck and fishing sounds a heck of a lot better than being drafted, to me. How about you?" Dantzler could see the wheels working in the other man's head, but after a long pause, Lloyd nodded.

"I'm with you, boss."

"All right," Victor said, drawing out the sound in the silence. "What do you want to do in the meantime, boss?"

Dantzler thought about it for a moment, then said, "I'll see if I can't finagle some more diesel. If nothing else, that's more range on the boat or more distance we can take the Suburban if the roads are too hairy. When it gets dark, I'll cross my fingers and hope Buck got his job done before he got munched. We'll have Ben make up one last batch with what we got left, see if we can't round out our provisions a tad. Either way, we're out of here after sundown, the day after tomorrow."

Silent, they watched. They waited.

The Flesh had barricaded themselves behind walls where They could not reach. Sometimes those walls opened, and the machines of the Flesh left, but still They waited. Propagation was their primary driving directive, but as They had become more aware of their world They had also become more patient. Someday, the Flesh would be quiet, and satisfy the directive. There was no emotional attachment to this notion; it was the way of things. It would be so.

The terrain outside where so many of the Flesh had gathered was not conducive to stealth, and the Flesh were watchful. Every so often They would send less-capable or damaged members of Their society forward, to gauge the response of the Flesh.

Many of their number had gathered inside of the forest, concealing themselves away from where the Flesh might be able to see them. Some watched, and some waited, but some also prepared. Alone, with only hands for defense, the Flesh were weak, but the Flesh that remained almost never had empty hands. They could not match the tools of the Flesh, and They did not have the intellect to master those tools themselves, but there were other, simpler tools which They might use.

They had no real concept of linear time, but somehow They knew that an opportunity would soon come. Once it did, the Flesh would be one with Them. They would satisfy the directive.

Until then, They watched. They waited.

Chapter 17

They'd argued last night, and even as she'd stated her case she'd known that the fight was one she wasn't going to win. This wasn't a night out with the boys or missing an in-law holiday. If ever there could be a legitimate excuse for what Miles had to do, he had it here, in spades, and she felt small and a not little guilty for her fear and selfishness. Reason didn't enter into it; this was pure emotion. *Why does it have to be* my *family that risks everything? Haven't we done enough already?*

She'd never say those things out loud, but of course Miles understood. More than likely, he felt the same way. The measure of a person's worth wasn't their emotional reaction to hardship, it was their *actual* reaction. Any number of other people in the community would have wilted in the face of this challenge. Miles just shrugged and said, "I have to."

It wouldn't have been so bad if that meddling twit Norma hadn't come sniffing around their house after the meetings died down. She'd gotten wind of what the SEALs needed, and despite assurances that future support wasn't predicated on Miles' assistance, she made her expectations clear.

Miles' polite refusals to speak with her on the topic had left Norma red-faced. In a way, it was a good thing he'd intercepted the councilwoman at the door before Tish had been able to speak with her. *I was ready to strangle the conniving twit just overhearing what she had to say.*

Now, after a restless night, Tish didn't know what to feel, or how to act. She settled for silence punctuated with calm looks as she watched her husband dress to venture outside the wall.

It was nothing she hadn't seen before, of course. Before he'd become Marshal, Miles and her father had been on a scavenging team, in between other tasks such as marksmanship and self-defense training. Hell, they'd been the *first* team, and they'd figured out the best techniques to stay safe — much of which had been, ironically, provided by Miles' now nonexistent passion for zombie movies — and passed those skills along to men like Charlie and Buck. They were the men who took over the reins so that her family could be safe. So that her husband didn't have to go out into the Wild.

The hollow feeling in the pit of her stomach was like an old friend that visited when you had plans to relax or clean house, and least desired company.

Miles pulled on an often-mended load bearing vest. He tugged at the straps in an attempt to adjust the fit and hissed in frustration at their recalcitrance. After a moment, Tish sighed and stood. She crossed the room and whispered, "Let me."

"Thanks," he said, his tone subdued. She straightened the straps with quick, efficient tugs until the vest lay properly across the shoulders of the long-sleeved BDU shirt he wore beneath it. He nodded in satisfaction at the fit and began securing a pair of pouches to the vest using the

MOLLE straps. Tish hadn't spent as much time in her dad's store as Miles had, but she recognized it and knew the terminology. It was hard not to; there'd been times when overflow inventory had collected in their living room. Miles' upper body was outfitted in gear that could have — and most likely had — occupied the shelves of her father's store. Miles wore a pair of heavy Carhartt carpenter pants and a pair of high-ankle Merrill hiking boots. He noticed her study and winked. "If I had *too* much surplus gear on I'd feel like a poser."

"The Carhartts are a bit harder to bite through than BDUs," she commented and cocked an eyebrow.

"That, too," Miles admitted. He opened an ammo box filled with loaded rifle magazines and began transferring them into the pouches. He took a moment to examine each and remove the dust covers before sliding them home.

Once he'd filled up with rifle magazines, he retrieved another, smaller pouch and slid loaded pistol magazines into it. He centered that one on his chest, between the first two. "It's a lot," Tish said. He rewarded her with a faint smile, and for a moment she saw a flash of the gangly-limbed boy she'd played with when they still lived on base. Outside of the service their friendship would have been even more unlikely. Her father had often said, with quiet pride, that the only color that Marines saw was green. That attitude had extended, for the most part, to the families in the on-base housing. Black girl and white boy; in the end, all that mattered was that their daddies were fighting together Somewhere Else. Her father had always called it the Sandbox. To a kid, a sandbox was a pretty fine thing. Miles, Tish, and the other Lejeune children had always called it something else. "You're going Away."

He looked at her and his face fell. "Oh, babe," he whispered. "It's not that bad, is it?"

"Miles, I worried and worried every time you and dad went out the gates, but this . . . This is different. We've been on our own for so long, but the military comes back into our life and we start jumping on cue, again?"

"I know. I do. They weren't here when we needed them most, so what do we owe them, really?" He shrugged. "If it were for any other reason I'd turn them down, believe me, I would. This is a game changer, though."

"I know. But I've been unselfish for over eight years. Give me a pass on this one."

Miles grinned. "Hey, this is a lot better than I was expecting."

He snaked his way into a lightweight leather jacket that had been hanging in his closet for years. Despite the layers beneath it, Tish noted that it was actually a bit baggy. "Our daughter's sitting on the floor outside the door. I think how bad it gets is still up in the air."

He grimaced and pulled on the pouches one last time to ensure they weren't loose. "Well," he said with a sigh. He picked up his rucksack and threw one of the straps over a shoulder. "I guess it's time to find out, isn't it?"

The last time he'd walked outside of the walls, his daughter was too young to know the difference. As he opened the bedroom door, Miles reflected that the weight of her awareness was heavier than the equipment he carried.

Trina's bedroom was across the hall from the master, and his daughter sat cross-legged in her own open doorway.

Her head hung low, following her fingers as they traced patterns in the carpet. He came down on both knees in front of her, but she didn't look up.

Miles put a gentle finger under her chin and raised her face up so he could look into her eyes. Her cheeks were wet with tears and she sniffled as she saw his clothing.

"Alex says it's dangerous out there," she whispered.

"He's right," Miles agreed. "But only if you're not ready for it. Look." He grabbed hold of his pants at the thigh and tugged on the fabric. "Nice and thick. Can't bite through it. Same for my jacket."

"But your *hands*," she said, and the plea in her voice almost broke him, right there.

He reached into the pockets of his jacket and pulled out the motorcycle gloves. If they'd had these in the beginning, maybe a few more people who'd succumbed to bites would still be around. The stock from Larry's store had given them a leg up in so many ways, but it had been lacking in others. But those were things that his daughter didn't need to hear, so he put one of the gloves in her hands and showed it to her.

"See these? These are Kevlar-reinforced; that means they're *bulletproof,* what are some piddly old teeth going to do to me? And see how the knuckles have armor? I can punch one of them right across the face — pow! — and I won't feel a thing. I went outside all the time when it was a lot more dangerous than it is now." He ruffled her hair, and she ducked away instinctively. "Where do you think Mr. Bunny came from, goofball?"

She gave him a skeptical look. "Serious?"

"Scout's honor. Ask your grandpa if you don't believe me, he was with me." He thought back and added, "It's not a fun story, but it's a true one. Maybe one day when you're older I'll tell you about it. Your friend Cole? It's a story about *his* daddy."

"Only adults call him Cole, daddy," Trina said with an exasperated look on her face. "His *name* is Twigs," she corrected him. Miles couldn't help but grin. For a moment, she'd looked like a miniature version of her mother.

"You're right, and maybe we should call him Twigs, but it reminds us — me, especially — of his dad. And that still hurts a little. You'll understand someday."

"All right," she said on a down note, and then perked up. "So will you bring me something this time?"

Miles forced himself not to give her a visible reaction. It wasn't like there were going to be shopping opportunities. "I'll see what I can come up with, you little con artist." He gave her another ruffle of the hair, and this time, she didn't duck it.

He got to his feet with a grunt; there was a tendency to forget how heavy all the stuff was when you weren't carrying it every day. For the most part, he was running light compared to what he'd carried back in the early scavenging days, but it was still an adjustment. Miles gave himself one final mental once-over to ensure he hadn't forgotten anything, then turned to walk out of the house.
It won't be the last time.

When he opened the door and led his family out onto the porch, someone he'd never have expected was waiting for them. His uncle had come down from the observation post to see him off, and in an even bigger shock, he stepped forward and wrapped his arms around Miles. "Stay safe, boy," Pete whispered in his ear and clutched him for a long moment. "Your parents would be proud as hell to see what kind of man you've become."

Miles was so overcome by the uncharacteristic show of emotion that he didn't know what to say. Pete's style of parenting had ranged from unamused grunts to middling heaps of praise. Finally, he managed, "You all right, you old coot?"

"Shaddup," Pete said and shoved him away with a joking slap to the chest. "I may be old but I can still take down your scrawny ass."

Miles grinned. This was more like it. "Keep an eye on them for me," he said. "Larry's liable to have his hands full while I'm gone."

Pete nodded. "Course." He glanced over at Tish and Trina and sighed. "Keep your head on a swivel. Don't take anything for granted, you hear me?" He looked Miles hard in the eyes until he nodded, then said, "Good. When you get back, we need to talk. Maybe should have said something earlier, but there's no time now. I . . ."

"Tish!" someone shouted from down the road, and the group turned to see. Frannie Ferguson was sprinting down the highway and waving both arms over her head. "Medical supplies are here!"

"Sh . . . crap," Tish corrected herself. "I need to get down there and help sort. Trina, why don't you hang out with your uncle for a while?"

Miles handed off his rifle to Pete and knelt before his daughter. "I'll be back before you know it, kiddo," he promised and hugged her one last time.

"Daddy, you're squeezing me too hard," she complained. He relaxed his grip and pulled back. He hoped she didn't see the beginnings of the tears welling up in his eyes.

"Sorry. Be good, all right?" He ruffled her hair as he stood and she ducked away with a grin. Miles took his rifle back from Pete, gave his uncle a final nod, and then turned to his wife. "I'm walking that way. Want some company?"

"You bet," she said, and they began to cut across the lawn in the direction of the highway. "What's Pete talking about, you think?"

"I have no idea," Miles confessed. "But I figure anything pressing enough to make him come down off of his perch is worth listening to."

"Can you trust them? The soldiers, I mean."

Miles shrugged. "Don't know. They seem to be all right guys, but who knows? The military going off the reservation is a time-honored cliché in apocalypse films." He chuckled. "Which, if anything, makes me tend to trust them. God knows the movies got it wrong more than they got it right."

"Until, you know, zombies started walking around and trying to eat people," Tish offered.

"Right. Of course, you could look at that as a chicken versus egg scenario." He glanced over at her, noted the frown, and explained, "None of them came out and said it, but I got the strong sense that they have a pretty good idea where this epidemic came from, and that it wasn't natural. Comments they walked back, or corrected themselves. Starting to say things like 'the people who did this' — then realizing who they're talking to. I don't think they're used to having to keep that so close to the vest. I think it's common knowledge in their circle so they're having a hard time getting back to the concept of 'need to know.'"

"Ah, yes," Tish said. "Lord knows I've heard that phrase a time or two. 'Dad, why won't they tell you when and where you're deploying?' 'Need to know information, and I don't need to know.'"

"Right," Miles agreed. "So yeah, mystery person or people that did this say hey, boy, there sure are a ton of zombie movies and TV shows out there, what if that were real? Wouldn't that be a great way to kick off the end? Chicken, egg."

"So you think TV made them do it?" Tish scoffed. "Did you get a personality transplant when I wasn't looking because that sounds nothing like something my husband would say." She elbowed him in the side.

"Hah," he said. "No, I'm not saying it's cause of the TV; I'm saying that some scientist who already has a mad on for the world says, boy, that looks like an interesting way to do it. And it would tie into people's assumptions based on what they've seen. If anything, think about how the news media scoffed at first. They thought it was a hoax. How different would things be if the press hadn't made a joke out of it, in the beginning?" He snorted. "Hell, if they'd been able to do it when *Twilight* was popular they might have engineered a vampire virus."

"Something like that," Tish mused, "an angry person couldn't manage it. The emotion would get the better of them and they wouldn't be able to complete the task. You need a true believer or a group of them. Fanatics. People who think they're doing something for the greater good."

"Maybe. Maybe so." He fell silent and squinted. They were approaching the clinic, but there was only one truck parked in front of it. Many figures were moving in and around it, bearing arm loads of material into the clinic.

"Where's the other truck?" Tish said.

"We'll find out soon enough, but I bet we're not going to like the answer." Miles' initial concern eased as soon as he saw Vir marching toward the clinic with his own load. A pair of excited children orbited him as he moved; Miles could hear the happy chatter from where he stood. Vikram, who was around Trina's age, was trying to help with his own load of supplies. Anoop, who was just shy of his fourth birthday, was too busy dancing around his father to be of much help. "Half the school is going to be late to class this morning," Miles noted. Inside, he was less collected. *Okay, good, so Vir made it. But where's everyone else?*

By the time they walked up to the clinic doors Vir had dropped off his load of supplies and was coming back out for more. As he saw them he stopped and raised a hand in greeting.

"Miles, my friend, good to see you." Vir shook his hand and clapped him on the shoulder. "Ran into some difficulties, but I got one vehicle back with as many of the critical need items as I could fit."

Miles glanced sidelong at Tish. "Everyone's going to be finding out pretty soon, anyway, Vir. You can speak openly."

Tish gave him a curious stare in return but said nothing. Vir grinned. "Well, I have to confess, we were both wrong. I don't believe Joey had anything to do with it." He sighed. "In point of fact, I caught Donald and Buck in the act of loading up a goodly number of precursors."

Miles groaned. "Oh, this week just keeps getting better. So, did you arrest them, ah, *Deputy?*" Tish's look shifted from confusion to surprise. She turned on him, her tone annoyed.

"Seriously? You have someone undercover and you don't bother to tell your own wife? Don't trust me?"

"Larry and I knew, that was it. I kept my mouth shut out of general principle, don't take it that way. I didn't want anyone overhearing."

She rolled her eyes and crossed her arms. This was going to be a bone of contention at some point in the future, Miles judged, but for the moment, there were matters too pressing for her to go down the road. He turned back to Vir and said, "Sorry, you were saying?"

The other man winced. "I didn't have the opportunity to. That's one of the things we need to talk about. There was a horde of biters cozied up inside the warehouse, but they weren't acting right."

Miles frowned. "How so?"

Vir shook his head and looked at the ground as he attempted to compose his thoughts. "They didn't react as usual; at first, we didn't even realize they were there. We made a bloody racket coming into the place, and *nothing*. As far as what set them off, I can only guess, but we split up and I suppose the other group stumbled over them. But that's not the worst part. They overran the entire team. I made for high ground — but they started dog-piling to come after me."

Miles rocked back on his heels. "They *climbed?*"

"Right. So I made it to the roof, and outside, what do I see but just literal streams of them coming out of the buildings in the industrial park. Like bleeding army ants."

"How did you make it out?" Tish wondered.

Vir shook his head. "They ignored me. Couldn't have cared less. I camped out on the roof overnight, and in the morning, they were all gone. They dropped a garage door on the truck with the radio in the process, or I would have called in. Thankfully they were all heading north, so I had the time to fill a large chunk of your wish list, Doctor, as I said."

Miles frowned. "North?" He rubbed his chin in thought. "How sure are you about that?"

"Yeah, well, I didn't check them with my compass, but it was northward for the most part. Barmiest thing I ever saw."

"Right," Miles said. "Look, I'm kind of on a schedule, Vir, so I'll make it quick. Great job, talk to Larry if you want to stick around. If you want to go back to the wall, I'll understand, but there's some stuff going on that could use your assistance." He stuck out his hand. "Thanks for everything, really."

The other man gave him a puzzled look but returned the handshake with vigor. "If you'll have me, I'll be glad to stay on. But what's the big rush?"

Miles began walking backward and pushed down the urge to outright sprint. "I'll be gone for a couple of days. Larry can fill you in, but I have to go."

Tish hesitated for a moment near the clinic. "Be right back," she said to Vir, and then trotted after Miles. He hesitated to let her catch up, and then turned and began striding toward the east gate and the men waiting on him. "Damn it, Miles, what's the rush?" she said as she quickened her own pace to match his.

"What's north of Cincinnati, Tish?"

"Dayton," she said with a frown. "Toledo, and . . ."

"Camp Perry," he finished.

Chapter 18

"Yeah," Hanratty said. "That doesn't sound good."

Miles gasped. "That's it?" the other man said. "Doesn't sound good?" He seemed surprised that Hanratty hadn't laughed in his face at the revelation.

Hanratty shrugged. "To be honest, it's not the weirdest thing I've heard this week. I'll radio ahead and let command know, they can push out some drones and try to locate their track. How long ago did you say he spotted them?"

"Late Monday."

"So forty-eight hours, give or take. Add another twelve for Monday evening and early this morning. Typical walking pace of an infected over open ground is around two miles per hour. That's approximately a hundred and twenty miles. They're still a good 80, 90 miles short of the camp, most likely. ETA tomorrow, if that is where they're headed." Hanratty nodded. "No worries, Mister Matthews, let's saddle up and get this wagon train rolling."

He turned to leave the civilian to say his goodbyes to his wife and stepped up inside of the LAV. Ross and the other SEALs were already assembled in the crew compartment. He gave Ross a wordless glance, and the other man nodded. He'd heard the brief conversation.

288

Hanratty squeezed past Rivas toward the front of the LAV. All in all, it rubbed him the wrong way to play things so close to the vest, but he had his orders. The burgeoning relationship with the people in the community had gotten off to a rough start, but he'd done his best to smooth things over during the town hall. Inciting a panic was hardly the best method to instill trust. On the other hand, failing to disclose the nature of the changing threat wasn't good diplomacy, either. He hoped it wouldn't matter. The area surrounding the settlement was as sparsely populated as any he'd seen in a long time. If they were all streaming northward, well, that was why.

"Fire it up, Corporal," he said. "As soon as our passenger is on board, we're rolling out."

"Yes, sir," Patterson said. The LAV rumbled to life as Hanratty started tapping into the blue force tracker.

BEGINNING MISSION PHASE TWO, he typed. FIRST-HAND HUMAN INTELLIGENCE REPORTS LARGE HORDE HEADED DIRECTION OF CAMP PERRY. ESTIMATE APPROX 80 MILES AWAY BASED ON TIMING OF SIGHTING.

He pressed the transmit key and waited. The GPS network must have been feeling benevolent this morning because he got a receipt notification in quick order. Shortly thereafter, command's response came through.

ACKNOWLEDGED. BE ADVISED DUST OFF DELAYED DUE TO MAINTENANCE ISSUES. ESTIMATE 12-18 HOURS. RECOMMEND ALTERNATE RENDEZVOUS.

Hanratty cursed. Well, it figured. They'd run half the helicopters in the fleet almost literally into the ground over the past eight years. The other half had been sitting in various stateside hangars during that same time. It was inevitable that those sort of issues would crop up, particularly when the airframe mechanics began digging into maintenance now that they had the benefit of a secure base and spares. He tapped a quick response.

STAND BY, CONFERRING WITH GROUND TEAM COMMANDER.

Hanratty pulled a marked-up map out of a storage pouch and turned to Ross. Matthews was just climbing aboard, and Chief Foraker closed and secured the rear hatches as he stepped inside.

"They've delayed pickup," Hanratty informed Ross. "You want to wait here, or do you want to divert?"

The lieutenant thought about it. "Let's head for alternate Delta. We can hole up in that farmhouse overnight again, and I like being that much closer to HQ if something happens to the chopper." Delta was just shy of 80 miles north of the settlement. The home Ross referred to had a large front yard, clear of electrical wires or other aerial obstacles, and they'd secreted one of their refueling blivets on the property to support future aerial operations. "We top off the chopper in the morning. That gives them enough range to swing down to the objective and return to base with a good reserve."

Hanratty scanned the map and identified the mark location. They'd crisscrossed their way south in search for places to cache fuel supplies for the helicopters. The irregular pattern was intended to throw off any infected that pursued their noise signature. They'd overnighted at Delta over a week ago, so any stragglers should — theoretically, of course — have moved on. He turned back to Patterson and displayed the map. "Delta, Corporal. How we looking for fuel?"

Patterson eyed the map, then glanced at the LAV's fuel gauge. "Should have plenty of a safety margin for a return, but I hope this works out as our new base, because we won't have enough to get back to Camp Perry."

Hanratty chuckled. "I don't think that will be a problem. Let's start heading that way, see if we can get back before dark, all right?"

"You said the magic words, Captain," Patterson replied, and dropped the LAV into drive. As the gates opened and he drove forward, Hanratty composed his response to command.

Enough hands made all the difference in the world, and the survivors unloaded the truck in a fraction of the time it had taken Vir. Of course, in addition to working alone he'd been trying to arrange the contents in some semblance of order — keeping the more fragile materials in padded areas, or upright as needed.

While the speed of the unloading was hardly a shock, one thing that did surprise was the presence of his wife at the clinic when he pulled up.

Aasha had been a chemical engineer before Z-Day. She had worked for a company that made chemicals for circuit board manufacturing. It had always struck Vir as interesting work despite his own background in mechanical engineering. Where the structures he worked on depended on strength and robustness, his wife's own work was neat, almost delicate, the balancing of various chemicals to develop compounds for specific purposes.

Circuit board manufacturing, of course, was a far-lower priority than it had once been. Where Vir had been able to lend a hand to the community in design and construction, Aasha had in a sense been adrift. She'd found things to occupy her as well as giving her some sense of purpose, but he'd always had the sense she wasn't satisfied with their situation. But what did you say? It was hard to express complaints with the state of your life when so many had died and you were still alive.

But there was a change to her demeanor when he'd arrived at the clinic that his presence alone couldn't explain. Oh, she'd been happy to see him, as had his boys, but there'd been more to it, a sparkle in her eyes and an uprightness of her carriage that he hadn't seen in years.

They hugged, and he whispered, "I thought I might not see you again."

"Me, too," Aasha said. "Will they allow you to stay on as a deputy?"

"It seems that they will," he assured her. "With any luck, I'll not have to make many more trips outside of the walls. But forget me; you are beaming. What is happening with you?"

Her smile broadened. "There were some discussions about the shortages of antibiotics while you were gone, and that moved over into chemistry. I pointed out that the manufacture of them was simple, from a technological standpoint. One thing led to another, and Doctor Scott and I have been coming up with a list of the materials we'll need to begin wholesale production." She favored him with a proud smile. "So you may need to go outside the walls at least one more time."

Vir laughed. "For such a cause as this, I will be more than happy to. I'm surprised that this has never come up, before."

She shrugged. "They always had sufficient stocks on hand. One never values something as much as when it is no longer there." She squeezed his hand. "But for now, I need to get the boys off to school, we are running late."

His sons overheard this edict and groaned aloud. "Do we have to?" Vikram asked. "Can't we stay with daddy, just for today?"

He shooed the boys away and said, not unkindly, "I will see you tonight, I promise. For now, get to school and apologize for your lateness."

Vikram frowned and said, his face serious, "We were helping, not playing."

"Yes, you were," Vir agreed. "But you also owe respect to your teachers, and need to show that even when other things happen, yes?"

His oldest son considered, and nodded. "Yes, sir." He grabbed his brother's hand and pulled him away. "Come *on*, Anoop." Smiling, Aasha followed and shepherded the boys in the proper direction. Vikram's initial vector would have taken them into one of the fields and nowhere near the school.

"Bye, Daddy!" Anoop called, waving as his brother dragged him backward. "I missed you!"

Vir smiled and returned the wave. "I missed you too, little one." He turned back to Tish Matthews. The doctor stood with her hands in the pockets of her light jacket and a sad smile on her face.

"They grow up too fast," she observed. "I don't think I was ever that serious."

Vir sighed. "It's our lot in life, unfortunately. Hopefully this generation will be the one that allows children to be children once again." He cocked his head and gave her an appraising look. "But you don't want to talk about philosophy, I'm sure. What did I miss?"

Tish shrugged. "Oh, nothing much. Just the return of the Marines and their demand for Miles' assistance." She hesitated. "Well, it wasn't a demand, I guess, but it was one of those offers you can't refuse." She noted his blank look. "Godfather? Never mind."

"It doesn't behoove them to *not* bring him back if they expect ongoing cooperation," Vir pointed out. "I'm sure it's difficult, knowing your loved one is in harm's way."

"It's too many things at once. First, there's the weirdness that Charlie's team spotted, the horde behavior *you* saw, and the Marines showing up. Sorry, things have been too static for too long for all that to be coincidental."

Vir frowned. "What happened to Charlie's team?"

"Nothing as bad as what you saw, but they found several houses on their last scouting expedition where something had broken out rather than staying inside. Assumption being that something was zombies."

"But biters—" Even now, after all these years, her term rankled him, and he refused to use it. His refusal changed nothing, but there were certain places that he refused to go to. Zombies conjured up thoughts of the metaphysical; Waheguru didn't *do* cannibalistic walking corpses. This was something man had wrought upon himself, with some perversion of science. "Are not strong enough to do something like that, particularly now." He finished and considered his own words. "Of course, I'd have said they weren't strong enough to climb or knock down a roll-up door, either."

"Right," Tish said. "Something has changed. And, on top of everything else, someone murdered Ronnie Cartwright Tuesday night." She shook her head. "It's enough weirdness that the council came out after the town hall last night and said they want to lock the community down until Miles gets back. Guess they're afraid salvage teams might decide things are getting too sporty and decide not to return."

"No," Vir exclaimed. "Do you have any idea who killed Ronnie?"

Tish gave him a cool look and said, "I think that's your job to help figure out, isn't it, Deputy?"

He chuckled. "I suppose it is. If you're squared away here, I suppose I'll park the truck and see what my new coworkers have to say." She turned and regarded the piles of supplies filling the clinic's front room and smiled.

"It's not everything I wanted and more, but it's better than nothing." She turned back and looked him in the eyes. "Thank you, Vir, truly. You have no idea what this represents."

He smiled and shrugged. "I do the best I can, Doctor. If you'll excuse me?"

She waved her hand. "Go. I've got plenty to do here without babysitting you. My dad should be at the station."

Chapter 19

The seats of the armored personnel carrier were even more uncomfortable than he'd imagined they'd be. To add insult to injury, despite the relatively good condition of the road, every little bump hit like a ton of bricks. Something inside of the vehicle rattled. Miles stayed silent, but dubiously eyed the strips of duct tape holding various panels in place.

"What ya packing, nugget?" Janacek, the SEAL in the Padres cap said. His tone was anything but friendly. Lieutenant Ross had tucked his chin into his chest and appeared to be sleeping. His two subordinates were wide awake and seemed to be in the mood to chat.

Miles bristled, but he forced himself to push the reaction down. These guys didn't know him from Adam. Yeah, sure, they knew he was the town marshal of a group of survivors, but what did that mean? For all he knew, they figured he only got the job because of his family connections, not because he was actually capable of taking care of himself.

Second, and perhaps most important, he had nothing to prove to these guys, any of them. Yeah, sure, they were Navy SEALs, baddest of the bad even before Z-Day, but he'd survived just as long as they had. The world didn't offer much slack for the incapable, these days. If they didn't recognize that, then tough. He'd show them by doing, one way or another.

Miles forced a cheery smile onto his face. "Custom-made short-barreled 300 Blackout upper with an EOTech holographic sight. Troy free-float rail with a Surefire tactical light, AAC compact suppressor, and a MagPul vertical grip and adjustable stock. I swapped the lower out with one from an M4A1 we salvaged right after the day so I can go full-auto if need be." He patted the rifle that lay across his lap. "It's a bit of a mutt, but I built it and it's saved my ass more times than I can count."

Janacek grunted. "Yeah, well, if you burn through all your magazines in 'fun mode' don't look to us; we're using 7.62 and 5.56." He jerked a thumb over at his own rifle, an immaculate-looking FN SCAR 17. It was either brand new or the SEAL treated it like a vintage car. Miles leaned toward the latter.

"Don't mind the Gun Monkey," Foraker interjected with a grin. "He's got a quartermaster's heart; mismatched parts give him the willies." Janacek looked away and scratched his nose with a middle finger. The Chief chuckled and turned back to Miles. "You give up a lot of range with that round, don't you?"

Miles smiled. This, at least, was something he could roll with. If not for the environment it was not unlike working in Larry's shop, shooting the breeze and debating the merits and ballistic properties of various loads. "Sure," he said. "If I was shooting supers I wouldn't have any benefit — I'd be better off with a 7.62 like Janacek. But at short range, the heavy subsonics perform like a .45. And instead of having thirteen in a mag —" Miles patted his holstered Springfield.

"I've got thirty. I've made head shots on zombies as much as a hundred yards out. Any further than that it's a waste; the round starts dropping like a rock." Miles fell silent as he reflected back on more dangerous and chaotic days. "When we used to go out, we'd alternate weapons systems on our teams. My father-in-law and, ah, Derek, usually handled the long range stuff. Sticks and I were more up close and personal." He raised his head and met the Chief's eyes. "Absent companions," he said, in echo of their meal the night before.

The Chief nodded and Janacek frowned. Miles couldn't read the underlying intent behind the expression. The guy looked like a stereotypical surfer dude but he had an amazing poker face.

"What happened to them?" Janacek said, finally. "Your friends."

Miles paused for a moment. It wasn't something that he talked much about; everyone he might have discussed it with already knew the story. It was something that just was, and any discussion of it had been long ago. *Where to begin?*

"You guys cross over many bridges on your way down here?" His tone was mild, but there an enough of an undercurrent in it that Janacek and Foraker glanced at one another. Finally, the Chief took the ball.

"No, we didn't. Seems like most of them got blown up." He patted the side of the LAV. "Slowed us down a bit, but it takes more than a creek to slow this baby down."

Miles smiled, but the expression didn't touch his eyes. "First week or so, we just holed up. I don't remember who suggested the wall at first, but just like that, we were figuring it out. The first thing we did was block off traffic from the east and west. North and south we at least had the creek and the river to slow the things down, so it wasn't as bad.

We used cars, farm equipment, even school buses as temporary walls." He looked up. "Pretty common job for farmers, in case you didn't know, driving school buses. Gave them a steady income, and kept them busy in the winter months. Insurance, too, I guess. Anyway, as we got more and more secure we realized that while we did have a lot of what we needed, there was plenty of stuff that we had little or no supply of. Early on we realized there were some kids surviving in the school, so we went and got them, but they didn't have *anything*. They were from all over, so it wasn't like we could go to their houses and pack them a bag, you know? Some of these kids barely had clothing to wear, they'd gotten bloody, or ripped up, you have it.

"We got thirteen kids and one teacher out. I don't know how many kids were in school that day. Surely there were a bunch at home sick, or whatever. A hundred, maybe?" Miles shivered. "I try not to think about it too much."

"Been there," the Chief echoed.

"So anyway, we had a secure position, so we figured no better time than any to start scavenging." Miles snorted. "We had it all figured out. Even went pretty smooth, at first. Sticks was my best friend from high school. Big into off-roading, that sort of thing. He had a dune buggy he'd put together with his dad as a project car. We armored that thing up nice and tight, covered it up with chain link and sheet metal. He'd run interference for us. Run up and down the roads with his stereo blaring, get the zombies chasing after him. Worked like a champ.

"We went into Lewisville because it's smaller; we figured it wouldn't be as dangerous as Cincinnati. The town is this huge triangle in the junction of a couple of rivers, so you cross a bridge coming from any direction.

"When the National Guard got called up, they set up blockades on some of the bridges. As best we can tell they got overrun, because they left behind all their equipment and weapons. We had to unload to clear a path for the salvage vehicles, and we took that time to grab what we could." He patted his rifle. "That's where I got the more legally dubious parts of my gun, along with the Humvees and the bigger cargo vehicles. So that part went pretty smooth, all things considered, so we kept moving forward.

"The plan was to use three school buses to block off the entrance to the local Target, then go through the place at our leisure. We stripped most of the seats out of the buses to make room. And, it worked great. Sticks cleared out the parking lot, we parked a bus on either side of the doors, then capped it off with the third bus. Ended up spending the night and packed those buses up to the *roof.*" Miles shook his head at the memory. "Place was abandoned. Any survivors were chased out by anyone who turned, and the ones that hadn't wandered out were easy pickings.

"Honestly, if we'd had the room we would have kept at it; there was still plenty of stuff in the Target, and there were several other stores in the strip mall next door. Of course, it was a good thing we didn't stay longer. Hindsight, and all that.

"We were getting close to the bridge out of town when the ground started shaking. At first, we didn't realize what it was, then we saw the fireball to the north. The Air Force had come to save the day," Miles spat. "And they were blowing the bridges for us. The first two buses made it over the line, and I don't know what the hell the pilots were thinking. I *know* they were low enough to see the school bus, they were in A-10s, for God's sake, but they fired anyway. The bridge went up when Derek's bus was halfway across. It just, I don't know, disintegrated. You look at a school bus and think hey, that's big, and it's solid, but it's nothing." Miles reached up and rubbed the back of his neck. "We knew it was pointless, but Larry and I were in the second bus, and we stopped and got out. We had to make sure, you know? If there was some chance that Derek and the guy who was with him—" Miles voice trailed off. "Huh. Can't remember his name for the life of me. How horrible is that? Tommy? Bobby?" He shrugged. "Too many people over the years, I guess. But, yeah. They did a good job. Took the bridge out and dropped the entire span into the river. We got down there and started looking, just hoping, I guess. By the time we got down onto the bank the zombies were starting to lemming off the other side. Nice big boom on the outskirts of town — it drew them out like somebody kicked an ant hill. We never did find anything; there wasn't any time. Made it back up the far bank and back onto to the bus. Back behind our wall." He stared at Janacek and Foraker in turn. "So, sure, call me nugget all you want, guys. Make your jokes. I don't have your skills in any way, shape, or form. But I survived eight years, on the ground, when people who should have been doing something to help were stabbing us in the back." His voice was starting to rise in anger, and he forced it back down. "You know how much harder it got to do supply runs when we were exposing ourselves every couple of miles, trying to find crossings or fords where there used to be a bridge? How do you put in a new bridge *quietly?*" He stared at Janacek. "You know how to do that?"

The other man regarded him for a moment, then gave a shallow shrug.

"Yeah, didn't think so." He settled back into the seat and tried to get comfortable. Finally he gave up and mimicked Ross' position by tucking his chin into his chest. At this rate, the trip was liable to take at least another couple of hours, and all things considered he'd rather spend them sleeping than in uncomfortable silence.

He hadn't realized the depth of his anger. Once the initial shock and surprise of the last few days had worn off, once he'd started thinking about those old memories, the rush of emotion that had coursed through him had been overwhelming. And while he himself had good reasons to feel the way he did, he was hardly the only survivor that had a bone to pick. He'd told Tish that the concept of an 'evil military' was a silly trope of apocalyptic fiction, but the truth they'd experienced was perhaps more pitiful. The survivors didn't trust the military, and by extension, any remnants of government, because when the chips had been on the table they had exhibited little more than sheer incompetence from the top down.

Was that broken trust irreparable? He didn't know. There were others, maybe, who hadn't lost as much, or hadn't been so directly impacted by what had gone down, but he'd heard about the undercurrent in the town hall. For every person who was happy to see some semblance of the old government, there was someone else enraged by the reminder. *Nothing to do, now — I need to keep my focus on the now and not worry about what comes next.*

And then the drone of the engine and the sense of movement did something he never would have expected — they lulled Miles into a light, but dreamless sleep.

Charlie's awakening came as a shock.

It wasn't the result of any external factor. No, his shock stemmed from the fact that his return to consciousness was slow and natural, prompted by the slow-building pressure in his bladder. As Charlie lay there and composed his thoughts, he realized the reason for the abnormal morning was that he hadn't dreamed. He'd slept well for the first time in a long time.

He opened his eyes and studied the wall next to his bed. Ever since Z-Day, he'd preferred his bed to be in the corner. On the nights when he did sleep he'd often thrash himself away from a nightmare only to find himself wedged against the wall. Even in the depths of sleep he sought the security that the wall seemed to provide. He'd tried sleeping with the headboard against the wall, only to wake and find himself curled into a ball at the headboard. So, he slept with the mattress paralleling the wall to satisfy his own unconscious desires. Even though the rough-hewn timbers of the cabin left scrapes and scratches on his back, more often than not he'd find himself wedged up against it.

This morning, though — he'd not only slept well, he'd done so in the center of the bed. Odd, that. He ruminated over it only shortly before the insistence of his bladder drove him to throw the covers off and rise.

The light was blinding as he opened the door to step outside. He glanced at the position of the sun and judged that it was almost noon; he'd been more tired than he'd thought. Small wonder Dalton was nowhere around. This time of day, he was liable to be horse-trading their share of the salvage for things that were more useful to them than booze or Spaghetti O's.

I hope he took Corey along, Charlie thought with a grunt. He had things he needed to get done, and the boy was liable to get in the way. Especially if he had to spend all day dodging the military as Miles had asked.

Inside, Charlie wet a towel from a pitcher of water and rinsed the night sweat from his face, torso, and crotch. *I need to talk someone into going in with me to build a bathhouse or something.* There were a few showers set up, but they were cold due to the logistical difficulty of heating intermittent amounts of water. If it were centralized, though . . .

Put in a wood furnace of some sort, have a hot tub for soaking, and rig up some showers. He sighed at the thought. Maybe the Carpenters would have an interest in expanding their laundry and incorporating some of his ideas. He'd have to check with them later. If nothing else, it would give him some sort of avenue to put his savings to use. For the most part, he just accumulated trade credit through Jim Piper and only rarely used it for the few personal items he needed. *Have to do something about the soap; the home-brew wood ash lye soap the Carpenters used to launder clothes would never do.*

Charlie paused. Another oddity — here he was, thinking about the future, with himself as something other than an inactive observer. He couldn't remember the last time that had happened. He looked at his reflection in the mirror hung over the sink and studied the planes of his own face.

Don't get your hopes too high, he thought to his reflection. *Who's to say the kid will stick around? They could make a break for it instead of waiting.*

He stared at himself for a long moment, until he finally smiled at himself in the mirror. *At least I know I'm not around the bend, I didn't start talking to myself.* He huffed laughter at his own expense. *If the kid's there, or not, it doesn't matter. It's a leap of faith, but it's also time for me to live again. There's nothing* wrong *with wanting to do that.*

The old sore spot deep inside of him ached at the thought, but he knew that was just an emotional reaction. Sheila and Cooper were dead and had been for a long time. They weren't coming back, and short of killing himself, he wasn't liable to see them again, if at all.

Charlie had never been a churchgoing type. He'd gone, mainly for his wife at first, and later for his son. After Z-Day, any interest he'd had in attendance had been burned away. If there was a God, He was obviously an uncaring one, to leave a doubter like Charlie alive and immune through all this, while letting two who'd so fervently believed in Him to be reduced to monstrosities.

Despite Charlie's antipathy, the community wasn't large enough to entirely avoid the concept. While their doctrine was different, the one thing that both Pastor Dave and Rabbi Behrens had spoken on was the subject of suicide. They'd both observed that while they couldn't understand the reason for the end, they could understand the way they needed to react to it.

"Lift each other up," Pastor Dave had proclaimed one Sunday where Charlie had found himself close enough to overhear. At the time, he'd listened just long enough to get angry and make his way out of the building, but now, the words resonated with him. "Life is a precious gift, and not ours to lose for our own sake. If you must die, die well, as our Lord did, and as he said in the book of John — 'there is no greater love than to lay down one's life for one's friends.'"

Charlie flexed his fingers and studied the scars on the back of his hands. Of course, he'd never *really* tried to commit suicide. For whatever reason, the infection would not take hold in him as it had so many others. Testing the possibility was perhaps toeing the line, but short of being completely consumed, biters posed little threat.

But there was a difference between living to live and just existing. Charlie could not in good faith declare that he'd been doing more than treading water for a while now. Well. No longer, it was time to put away the shell and see what kind of life he could build if he was actually trying to build one, instead of just sleepwalking through his days.

He dabbed himself dry and put on a fresh undershirt and a button down that was still on the clean side. He considered for a moment, and then grabbed the small backpack he carried on runs. There were sufficient supplies stocked in the buses before every run, but he still preferred to carry something portable just in case. The backpack held a change of socks and underwear, some bottled water, a bit of food, and several loaded magazines and some boxed ammunition for his pistol. He balanced the pistol on his left hip with the scabbard for his Bowie knife on the right and shrugged into his leather jacket despite the relative warmth of the day. If all went well, he wouldn't be wearing it for long, anyway.

He considered his M-1 Carbine for a moment but decided to leave it hanging from the hook where he'd left it. If it came to it, the pistol and knife should be enough, even if the noise they'd made leaving the subdivision had attracted more biters.

Be less intimidating without it, he judged. *Don't want to spook the kid.*

Satisfied with his load-out, Charlie shouldered the backpack and stepped out of the cabin. They'd built it on the southern half of the western wall for the proximity to the storage bins, so it was a short walk from his home to the bins.

Jim Piper's office was on the first floor of the refrigerated bin. The wiring for the cooling equipment provided power to run a few laptops and a printer to keep everything organized. At some point, it was going to become impossible to find ink, never mind printers, and they'd have to figure out something else to produce the paperwork that ran the administrative side of the community. It wasn't a huge concern for Charlie. He knew for a fact that Jim had at least a half-dozen printers in their original packaging just waiting for use. Charlie himself had hidden several of them inside one of the office supply stores in Lewisville. The toilet paper and paper towels were long gone, but there were still plenty of electronics.

He stepped inside and looked around. Dantzler, one of the wall guards, was in quiet conversation with one of Piper's assistants, Foster. It looked a bit heated, so he chose not to interrupt and looked around the office area on his own. It was a simple layout. Banker's boxes full of paper sat in piles here and there, with folding tables supporting other paperwork or computers. After a quick survey, he saw Jim. He leaned over a stack of filing boxes piled underneath the staircase to the second floor. The look on his face was so intense that the file he sought might have contained a map to buried treasure.

Charlie stepped over beside Jim and waited a moment. When the other man failed to notice his presence, he cleared his throat. Jim jumped and looked over his shoulder. "Shit, Charlie, you a freaking ninja, or what?"

Charlie just shrugged.

"What can I do for you?"

"Need to make a run," Charlie said. "Quick, few hours."

Jim grimaced. "Ah, I don't know if I can swing that right now. Did you go to the town meeting yesterday?"

Silent, Charlie shook his head and cocked an eyebrow.

"After that Marine got done speaking, Norma proposed a motion that we keep everyone inside for the time being until Miles gets back."

He frowned. "Gets back from where?"

"I don't know, it's all hush hush. He lit out this morning in the tank. The tank and the soldiers should be back later on this afternoon, but Miles may be gone for a few days they said. We voted, and we're keeping things close to the vest for the next few days."

Damn it, Charlie said to himself. He didn't know what bug had gotten up Norma's butt, but she wasn't exactly the type you could talk out of a decision, even if Charlie had glib verbal skills. *Should have gotten up earlier.* Maybe Miles had gotten occupied with other things, or maybe he'd thought Charlie had forgotten about him. On the bright side, if the Marines weren't around, he didn't have to keep under cover, he could actually get out and about.

"Fine," he said finally. "Later?"

Jim nodded. "I can swing it once Miles is back. The military is going to start trading fuel for food, so we might be able to free up more frequent runs. Know anywhere where you can find some ballpoint pens? We're running low."

Charlie did, as a matter of fact, but there was no benefit to coming out and telling Jim that. Something was only as valuable as it was scarce. "Maybe," he said. "Get quick solo, might have for you."

Jim gave him a sour look and shook his head. "Fair enough," he said. "I'd be plenty willing to let you have a set of keys for a bit if not for Norma's proposal. You don't have to rake me over the coals to pay for them."

Charlie shrugged. "Welcome to get yourself." He *liked* Jim, the man was affable, but to Charlie there were two sorts of people in this world — those who were willing to go outside of the wall, and those who weren't. As far as he knew, the last time Jim had been outside was when Larry had brought him home like a lost puppy. And he wasn't in the mood to take crap from someone who lived in relative comfort on the efforts of braver men.

Jim glowered over the top of his reading glasses. "You don't have to be such an asshole about it."

"Asshole with *pens*," Charlie pointed out. "Later."

He adjusted the pack on his shoulder and walked out. It looked like he'd geared up for nothing. He sighed and looked at the clear, blue sky. All in all, it was looking to be a fine day. His stomach gurgled and reminded him that he hadn't eaten since the day before. He turned and headed for the cafeteria. Maybe the day's luck would change, and there'd still be some food left.

Chapter 20

He'd slept over bumps and shakes, and even managed to hang onto a fitful sleep as the LAV climbed in and out of a creek bed or two, but when it came to a halt, Miles woke.

The three SEALs were already in motion, up and out of their seats and moving to the rear hatch. Up front, Hanratty leaned around and shouted to the other men. "Coast is clear, and dust off will be here at 0900. Good hunting, boys."

Ross gave him a thumbs up and slapped Miles on the back as he walked past. "Time to earn the paycheck, champ," the officer said with a wink as he hopped out of the LAV's rear hatch.

Miles gathered up his backpack and rifle and followed, trying not to trip and fall as he arranged his gear on the fly. Down on the ground, he took a moment to sling both straps of the pack on, then clipped the locking disconnect on the single-point sling to his rifle. Behind them, the LAV accelerated away. He assumed they'd loop around a bit further down the road. This tended to draw any roamers past the drop-off point, so long as those dropped off kept quiet as they went about their business. They'd used similar methods in the past when scavenging locations that they knew would take time to go through.

Miles shifted his focus away from the LAV and to his environment. There were no landmarks in sight; he could have been standing on any standard-issue Midwestern country road. There was a large field off to one side, spotted here and there with trees. It had lain fallow for so long that the weeds had taken over. Freed from the winter snows, they stood waist-high and waved languidly in the breeze. Shifting his grip on his rifle, Miles pivoted and continued to scan his surroundings. Yeah, he had three of the best the military had to offer with him, but that didn't mean he was going to take it as an excuse to play dumb. A decaying farm sat across from the field. A couple of the barns had already collapsed and another looked close. The old farmhouse still stood strong, but the paint was peeling from the clapboard siding. None of the ground floor windows remained intact. Much of the yard in front of the farmhouse was gravel, but there were also a few patches of tall weeds present. He studied them for a moment, then pivoted again. At the moment, the field was the greatest danger. Both ends of the road were as clear as far as he could see, and there were enough open lanes in the front of the farmhouse that he'd either see company coming or hear them stumble over the gravel.

To one side, Ross glanced at him as he began sharing hand signals with the other SEALs. "Stay close," the lieutenant murmured. Miles nodded but didn't take his eyes off of the field.

"How clear is this?" Miles said in a low tone. He glanced over at Ross, who shrugged.

"We holed up here a little over a week ago, I guess. Clear-ish. But not so clear that I want to stick around out here talking about it if you know what I mean."

Miles nodded. "Don't like the weeds — crawlers," he said.

Ross nodded, his face somber. "Thought about burning them off when we left but we didn't want to draw attention to this place. No worries. The phone and electrical service are underground, so the chopper can land right on the road." He put a hand on Miles' shoulder and gave him a gentle shove in the direction of the house. "Go, I've got rear guard. Stay behind Foraker and Janacek."

Keeping his rifle at the low ready, Miles stepped onto the gravel and followed the other two SEALs. Each man would lead in turn, kneeling or pausing behind cover, and then wave the other man forward. At each interval, they'd pause for a few moments and scan the area around them. As he came up behind them, Miles noted a few crumpled forms in the weeds. The accelerated decay that came on after the second death had rendered them little more than bones and leathery skin. He could tell from the way they had crushed the weeds down, rather than being overgrown by them, that they'd not been here long. If these had been here the first time the SEALs visited, it stood to reason more might show up. He licked his lips.

Janacek bounded forward, but rather than stepping up onto the front porch, he followed his way around it to the side of the house. After a moment, Foraker followed, and Miles heard a subtle, "Come on," from one of the two after the older SEAL reached Janacek's position. He mimicked their motion and came around to the side of the house.

The two men were arranging an extension ladder under an open second-floor window. The growth near the foundation was flat, matted by the pressure of the ladder. Miles nodded in approval. They'd stashed the ladder where they could easily get to it, and if someone moved it they would be able to tell. Finally, with a light thump, they arranged the ladder to their liking. Janacek slung his rifle over his back and scrambled up the steps. He glanced inside of the window for thirty seconds or so, then reached out and lifted the sash so he could climb inside.

"You next," Foraker said to Miles. He gave the big man a thumbs up. It took him a bit more time to arrange his rifle since the sling was under the straps of his backpack, but once he set it so it wouldn't run into the ladder, he followed the first SEAL up and inside of the old farmhouse.

The gable window opened up into a bedroom that had likely belonged to a teenage boy before Z-Day. Superhero and comic book posters plastered the walls along with pennants for sports teams. Everything had a sun-faded and worn look, and the room smelled of dust. The twin-sized bed, for some reason, had no mattress.

He cleared out of the way as Foraker followed him up the ladder and inside. Shortly thereafter, Ross brought up the rear. Once he reached the top, he reached down and took hold of the sides of the ladder. With a grunt, the SEAL lifted the ladder off of the ground and inside of the window. When he levered it on the bottom of the window sill it made a harsh grinding sound, but Janacek and Foraker stepped forward and supported the sides as Ross backed further into the room. As soon as the collapsing locks were inside the window, the SEALs on the sides of the ladder opened them up and slid the extension back into place. As they did that, the feet of the ladder just cleared the window before Ross backed into the wall opposite the window. The men set the ladder down, and Foraker closed the sash with a grunt.

"Let's go," Ross said to Miles. "We'll crash in one of the other rooms."

He led Miles into a short hallway that overlooked the ground floor of the farmhouse. As they came around, Miles looked down. He made a surprised grunt as he saw the stairs — or what remained of them.

Some survivor had removed the bottom half of the stair treads. This left only the stringers, which were climbable if one were careful. At the point where the steps ended, the survivor had constructed a vertical wall that ran to the ceiling of the second floor. Angled four by fours descended from the top corners of the barricade and anchored to the top of the staircase for support. Even if someone were able to climb to the uppermost exposed stringer, the wall blocked off any access to the second floor. It would take dexterity beyond zombies as well as most humans.

"Damn nice work," he commented and glanced up at Ross. "You guys?"

The lieutenant shook his head. "This is the way we found it. One of the reasons we holed up here. All the broken windows expose the first floor, but we checked it out on the chance of finding some supplies. You never know. Saw the modifications to the staircase and figured, why not?"

Miles ran his fingers over the wood. The two-by-fours used in the construction of the wall had been mechanically sawed. The nails holding everything together had the tool marks of a framing nailer. This was either put together before the power grid failed, or the builders had possessed some form of electricity to run their tools. He glanced up at Ross. "No survivors?"

The SEAL shrugged. "Feel free to look around; the place even *feels* abandoned. The downstairs is a wreck. Upstairs, not so much. It's weird."

Miles followed the lieutenant into a room at the opposite end of the hallway from where they'd entered the second floor. Given the size, this looked to be the master. It took up what appeared to be a full quarter of the upper story and had an en-suite bathroom. The SEALs had pushed all the furniture over to one side and placed several mattresses on the floor. The ones from the other bedrooms, he reasoned. A heavy quilt hung from the wall, pinned in place in front of a window by a pair of nails.

Janacek and Foraker were already dropping their packs onto respective mattresses. Miles chose one for himself that wasn't claimed and set his own bag down. Free of that, he divested himself of the single-point sling and lay his rifle on the mattress next to the pack.

Ross spoke from the other side of the room as he fiddled with a radio. "You know the drill, people. Keep it quiet, keep it dark. Janacek, you've got first watch. I'll take mid-watch, and Foraker is after me." He glanced over at Miles. "You good, Mr. Matthews?"

Miles stepped aside to let Janacek leave the room. "All set. Might take a look around."

Ross waved a hand, intent on tuning his communication device. "Knock yourself out. I assume I'm not telling you anything when I say be quiet?"

"This isn't my first salvage run," Miles replied. He leaned over and released the Surefire from the side of his rifle. The interior of the house wasn't too dim in the second-floor hallway due to the windows below, but the rooms were all pitch black save for the room through which they'd entered the house. He nodded to Ross and Foraker, but neither man seemed to notice his presence. The lieutenant whispered into the mouthpiece of the radio while looking at a folded map. The big Chief was lying down on his mattress with his head resting on a folded-up poncho liner. He'd left enough of the liner unfolded to flip the flap over his head to cover his eyes.

He'd seen the rooms at either end of the hall, but there were several other doors he wanted to check. Miles was confident the SEALs had cleared them their last time in here. If any zombies had somehow climbed up and hidden in the interim, the noise of their presence would have alerted them to the house guests. Vir's experience in the warehouse, notwithstanding, he felt pretty confident that nothing had scaled that staircase barricade.

Miles was curious for a few reasons — first because you never ignored the opportunity to scrounge these days. Perhaps just as important, he was curious about the fate of the people who'd lived here. Had they abandoned the house for some reason? There was no blood or evidence of foul play anywhere that he'd seen, so where were they?

The former owners had decorated the room closest to the master in pink and yellow. Stuffed animals lined shelves along with picture books. The four-poster bed, like the other bedrooms, lacked only its mattress. Other than a few knick-knacks that would have appealed to a preteen girl, there was little of interest in the bedroom. A light patina of dust covered everything. He studied the stuffed animals for a moment and considered grabbing one for Trina, but refrained. It just felt wrong — salvage should be about need, though he would readily admit that not everyone shared that position with him.

The second door opened up into a family room. Bookshelves lined the side walls, and a large flat-screen TV sat on the wall opposite the entry. A leather couch divided the room between the door and television. This room felt even more unused than the previous bedroom — the bookshelves contained photo albums, Blu-rays, and video games. There was a definite lack of actual books, and without power, the television, disk player, and game console were worthless.

He panned his flashlight around and studied the movie and game collection, but nothing jumped out at him that they didn't already have. Miles smiled. During their ill-fated run to Target, his friend Sticks had gone through the electronics section with dogged determination. He ensured that he procured at least two copies of almost every disk in the store. When Miles questioned him, Sticks had responded, "The people of the future are going to *need* Friends and Seinfeld, Miles. I'm relegating Gossip Girl to the dustbin of history, though. Nobody needs that crap."

Damn, I miss you, buddy.

The collection had only grown in the years since. And yes, there had been plenty a night when the community sat together to watch a slice of what they'd once had. To remember, to laugh, and maybe even to cry a little bit.

He closed the door behind him and checked the last door. This room looked to be a small laundry room. A stackable washer and dryer set, sorting hampers for whites and darks, and a folding table took up one side of the room. Shelves lined the other walls, though they weren't as dusty as the rest of the house, despite being empty. He panned the flashlight around and noted an object back in the corner of a bottom shelf. Miles knelt and fished it out. It was a dented can of Vienna sausages, and he grimaced. This room, presumably, had served as a pantry. Whoever cleaned it out had missed this one can. *Or just didn't care for the nasty things.*

He stood, and was ready to leave the room until he panned the flashlight across the ceiling. In the center of the ceiling was a rectangular piece of wood, painted white to match the ceiling and framed in mitered trim. A hole at one end of the rectangle supported a short string with a plastic ball on the end. It was an attic hatch, Miles realized, and he frowned. Had the SEALs missed this? He supposed anything was possible. They were likely more attuned to fighting the dead, which didn't use human tactics of hiding and high ground. Maybe the family cowered up there now, worried about the visitors that had returned to their home. He reached up to grasp the plastic ball.

Despite his care, the springs rattled as he brought the hatch down to its open position and locked it there. There was an aluminum folding ladder bolted on the inside surface, ready to deploy as needed.

Miles reached up and pulled the attic ladder open. He unfolded the steps until they locked into place and rested on the floor. Clicking the flashlight back on, he ascended the steps while listening for any hint of movement. The attic was as still as the rest of the house, though a wave of heat and a musky smell washed down over him as warmer air flowed out of the opening.

Wisps of blown-in insulation wafted through the beam of his flashlight as he panned it around. The smell gave him an inkling of the story, but for some reason, he needed to know for certain.

The attic was only partially finished. A good number of the beams were open, and drifts of insulation overflowed the troughs formed between the joists. In other places, someone had nailed plywood paneling on top of the joists.

Cardboard boxes and totes sat on these platforms. Broad marker strokes on the sides boasted of 'Fall Decor' and 'Christmas Decorations'.

He had no way of telling why the family had retreated up to the attic. Their haven on the second floor remained impenetrable, as far as he could tell. Had the first floor been so packed with the dead that they'd been unable to stand to be so close to them?

Had these people faced the same threat as Vir? Had the temporary security of their exposed staircase shattered when those seeking them climbed ever closer? He panned his flashlight across a heap of aluminum cans and empty water bottles. Dark urine filled several of the water bottles. Questing fingers and starving lips had polished the interior of the cans to a mirror shine.

There were fewer cans and bottles than he would have expected for the number of bodies he saw up here. However long they'd been up here, they hadn't had enough food and water to sustain them.

Their story would remain untold because all that remained were bones wrapped in worn fabric. Two adults and two children. One of the children was about the same size as Trina, and a sharp pain hit him in the throat as he made that connection. The smaller skeletons lay still and unbroken. The female adult skeleton was crumpled to one side, the skull shattered in multiple places. Entry and exit wounds?

The larger, and final skeleton sat leaning against the pitch of the roof, knees drawn up. Desiccated finger bones still cradled the pistol, and a small shaft of light illuminated the entire display from the hole in the roof the final shot had wrought. Their story was untold, but Miles had a pretty good idea as to the structure of it.

You came up here to what, wait them out? But they didn't go away, because all they have is time. You were out of food and water. So the desperation built and built until you couldn't handle it anymore. Did you wait until the children were asleep to smother them? That would have been the kindest way of doing it, I suppose. Your wife was next, but I imagine you had to work your way up to yourself. Maybe that wasn't the easy way to do it, though, because the longer you waited the worse the feeling got until finally, you reached your breaking point and just pulled the trigger.

Who knew when the dead had cleared out of the first floor, but it wouldn't have been anytime soon after the suicides; the noise, if nothing else, would have had them in a frenzy, albeit an aimless one. *Eventually even they can tell that a house just feels empty, I suppose, and they moved on. And here we are.*

Miles stared into the eye sockets of the skeletal husband. "I'm not you," he whispered. "I never would have stopped fighting for my family. You took the coward's way out." Maybe that was true, and maybe it wasn't, but Miles had to believe it. He was in this place, at this moment, not because he'd given up, but because he had to believe that there was promise for the future. This family hadn't had that opportunity. God willing, it was a choice that Miles and his family, and every other family left out there, would never have to face.

Beef again. This time, stew, which was just pot roast in water, right? Couldn't the kitchen come up with something different? Alex let congealed gravy drip off of his spoon and tried to hide his distaste. He didn't need a lecture about being grateful for what they had. The adults *loved* that one. Then they'd turn around and gripe about Starbucks, or air conditioning, or one of a dozen things Alex couldn't remember. Phonies.

A tray clattered onto the table in front of him and Twigs slid into the seat opposite Alex. To his credit, the kid wasn't bouncing up and down in his seat as much as he had the day before. "I got all my stuff together," he muttered. "We still on?"

"That's the plan," Alex said under his breath. "After school, we go over the wall, then . . ."

"Over the wall?"

Alex cringed and looked up. Not only had he been overheard, he'd been overheard by Trina freaking Matthews. Awesome.

"What'd you say?" Alex replied, trying to keep his face blank. The little girl wasn't buying it because Trina plopped down in a seat near them and gave Alex, then Twigs, a derisive look. The other boy's face turned red and he stared at Alex with wide eyes.

"You said something about going over the wall. What were you talking about?"

"Nothing!" Twigs managed, and Alex held back the urge to groan. *Way to keep it cool, buddy.*

This could go one of two ways. Either Trina would rat them out, or she wouldn't. Alex studied her. She was one of the few kids who'd been born after Z-Day, and most of the older ones ignored her more than anything. She didn't seem to have a lot of friends, and if anything was more comfortable around the mental cases.

"Just what it sounded like," Alex said, ignoring Twigs' dropped jaw. "Why do you ask?"

Trina and Alex eyed one another for a moment. He could almost feel the moment when she broke. He tried to keep the smirk off of his face when she leaned over and whispered, "Why? I wanna go."

Twigs just stared. Alex waited another moment to turn the tension up, then replied, "I figured out my house is close to here. I want some pictures of my parents. I don't remember them." He shrugged. "No big deal." Inside, he marveled. *Holy crap, I can't believe that worked.*

Trina grinned. "I'll help."

Twigs snorted in disdain, but Alex held a hand out to shut him up. *Don't blow this, kid.* "What can you do?" Alex said.

Trina straightened in her seat and an unchildlike expression crossed her face. For a long moment, she looked just like her mom had when Alex broke his arm jumping off the roof a few years back. "What do you need?"

He thought about it for a moment. "We've got Twigs' slingshot, but that's it. Can you get us a gun?" *Lay something big like that on her, and if she can't come up with it, she can't complain.*

"No problem," she said immediately, and Alex raised an eyebrow. "I'll get one of my dad's house guns," she explained. "It's got a suppressor and everything."

Twigs looked impressed and Alex thought about it. "All right," he said, drawing out his words. "But if you rat us out, you'll be sorry."

Trina shrugged. "You take me with you, I won't rat you out."

"Alex," another voice interjected, and the three of them jumped. When Alex turned, Cara from the Crow's nest stood there with her own tray in her hands.

"Yeah," he said, hoping his voice didn't sound as strained as he thought it did.

"Captain Matthews wants you up in the nest this afternoon. Got it?"

"Right," Alex said. Cara nodded, turned on one heel, and walked toward another table. When she was out of earshot, he muttered, "Crap, how long was she there?"

"She just walked up," Twigs said. "It's not like she was standing there. Do you think she heard?"

Alex watched her go and thought about it for a moment. "No. No way. If she had, she would have said something to shut us down." He sighed. "Crap. So there goes today. We'll try for tomorrow."

"You better not back out," Trina whispered, and Twigs snorted a giggle. Alex couldn't help himself; he laughed too.

"You're in, kid," Alex said. "Just play it cool."

Chapter 21

Larry, sure enough, was at the small police station. As he stepped inside, Vir realized that it was the first time he'd actually been in the place. When Miles had begun the process of his recruitment, he'd kept things as low-key as possible. Talking to him in his 'office' might have elicited too much attention. Vir couldn't help but wonder now if that decision hadn't saved his life.

There wasn't much to the place; it was a square, rough-framed building of perhaps four hundred square feet. A pair of counters sat on either side wall, and Vir smiled as he studied the spring-loaded half door someone had installed to bridge the gap between them. From a distance, it looked like a prop from any of a dozen police procedurals. As he got closer, he could see the slight variations in fit and finish that proclaimed that the builder had assembled the door without the benefit of luxuries such as power tools. He reached out and swung it, watching the slight play as it moved back and forth.

"Can I help you?"

Vir glanced up. A few folding tables were set up behind the counters to serve as desks. When he'd entered they'd been empty, but now a young brunette stood beside one with a look of curiosity on her face. He couldn't help himself. He smiled, though not out of any desire to enhance his greeting. He was recalling Miles' visible consternation when the topic of the station's secretary had come up.

"Ah, you must be Jaid," he said and extended a hand across the half-door. "Vir Singh. I'm here to see Larry."

Her face flickered from bland curiosity into warmth. "Of course, Deputy, come in, come in."

Vir shook his head. "You're the second person that's called me that. I'm not sure I'm accustomed to the title."

"Well, no worries, I'm sure you'll be fine in no time." She stepped closer and returned his handshake. "Come on back, Larry's doing some work in Miles' office." She indicated one of a pair of doors set into the back wall of the station. The door stood ajar enough to conceal much of the room beyond. Once Vir stepped behind the counter, the angle of his perspective changed. He could now see Larry sitting behind another folding table that had been shoe-horned into the small space. He glanced left at the other door, and raised an inquisitive eyebrow at Jaid. She dimpled.

"That's the holding cell. Currently, we have a party of one in the house. Did you hear the story?" For the last part, her tone turned almost conspiratorial, and her eyes danced with hidden mirth.

"That'll be enough, Jaid," Larry said from his position in the doorway. "Hey, Vir." He stepped over and shook the other man's hand with a strong grip. "I'm a tad put out that this the first time we've met, but I understand why Miles did it the way he did." He glanced at Jaid. "You get Chris his lunch?"

She nodded. "Just now."

"All right. Vir and I are heading over to grab a bite ourselves, then we'll be out for a bit. Send a runner or hit me up on the radio if anything comes up."

"Will do," she replied. She smiled at Vir. "Enjoy, Deputy."

Larry led the way out of the office, and as the door closed behind them and he stomped down the steps, the older man shook his head and sighed.

"I swear the only reason that woman even has her job is so she can keep Norma in the loop on what we're up to." As Vir drew up to his side, he gave him a sidelong glance. "Miles mention her at all?"

"He did," Vir nodded. "I've never spent much time in her company, but, well, I respect Miles' opinion. I'll watch how I conduct myself around her."

"She's an insufferable gossip and an irredeemable pain in my ass, but on the bright side, I'm not the man in charge. Miles gets to deal with her more than I do. I just try to stay out of the office as much as possible. Given that my son-in-law has decided to take an impromptu vacation, I no longer have that luxury." He heaved another sigh. "Don't get me wrong, she's not a *bad* person, it's just that there's no there, there. She's got the conversational depth of a golden retriever. She's not stupid, she'd just rather talk about, I don't know, yoga classes or the latest thing that happened to so-and-so."

Vir wanted to ask if they still had yoga classes, but he sensed his best choice for avoiding a lengthy rant was to steer the conversation in a new direction. "So, before Miles left he told me that someone murdered Ronnie Cartwright. What's our investigative priority, the murder, or the drug issues?"

Larry sighed. "In case anyone asks, Ronnie's murder, but I'll be honest with you — we've got nothing. No witnesses, no suspects, no clues except for that stupid poem. According to Val, there are at least half a dozen books of nursery rhymes that have it in there. Our killer may not have even gotten it from one of those."

"Poem?" Vir said, puzzled. "I'm sorry, Miles didn't have time to go into much detail."

Larry waved a hand. "I'll explain later. Let's grab some grub and I'll fill you in on the details as we go. I've been going over reports and lists all morning and I'm starving. Let me get some sustenance before you start giving me the third degree."

"Fair enough," Vir agreed, and he followed the other man into the cafeteria and through the serving line. The women dishing up lunch were apologetic. The stew was last night's leftovers spruced up with some filler. The nice thing about stew, Vir reflected, you could just keep throwing stuff in it and warming it up. At some point, you could even argue it wasn't the same stew it had been before, especially if the pot was never completely emptied. He assured the harried-looking woman working the serving line that he'd not been there for dinner the night before, and it looked just fine to him. When they got out of the line and headed for an empty table in the corner of the cafeteria, Larry had a smirk on his face.

"The famed British politeness. That stick around on the subcontinent?"

Vir chuckled. "In some regard, but I also spent much of my childhood in the UK."

"Worked with a few Sikhs over in the Gulf. Good people. Good troops."

"I never served," Vir said. "I hope that isn't a problem."

Larry laughed. "No worries. These days, it doesn't matter. Everyone knows you can take care of yourself. I got no issue with you, trust me on that." He settled into silence and made a considerable dent in the food on his plate.

Vir took a few bites of his own stew and decided enough time had passed to comment. "So. You want to prioritize the drug case if I'm not mistaken. We have a dearth of suspects in Ronnie's murder, whereas, with our meth problem, we've at least identified one leg of the stool."

"Right. I've got Jenny and Brian watching Buck's place now. We'll toss it here in a bit to see if we can find anything. We already did a discrete check of Joey's apartment while you were gone." Larry shrugged. "Didn't find anything, of course. Which makes all the more sense given that he wasn't involved."

"Buck doesn't strike me as the type to leave things lying around, but I could be wrong. It's not like there's anywhere else he could keep any proceeds. Wealth is not exactly portable, these days."

Larry nodded. "Still got to check. One thing you'll learn, people will do a lot of stupid-ass things when they think they can get away with it. Assuming someone will or won't do something because it's reasonable or logical will trip you up, every time."

"Perhaps so. I guess in the end I don't understand the . . ." Vir trailed off, searching for the right word. "The *logistics* of it. It's a complicated chemical process, yes? Not something that one could do in the close proximities we live in."

"So I'm given to understand," Larry agreed.

"So they have to have enough stock to sell, or trade, or whatever. So what do they do with it?"

"Miles and I have been bouncing that back and forth for a while now. As best we figure, they've got to have a place outside of the wall where they're cooking and stashing their loot. It's not like we're conducting door to door searches or anything nutty like that, but like you said, it's close quarters, and people notice stuff." He stirred his stew, then commented, "You've seen it from both sides. On the wall and outside the wall. How would you do it?"

Vir worked it over in his head for a bit then said, "They could not ditch it outside to retrieve it later, even if they're cooking it out there."

"Why not?"

"Well, look at Buck's crew. For sure Donny and Buck were in on it, but not Joey. Would they risk someone not in the know seeing something they shouldn't if they threw a bag in a ditch before coming back in through the gates?" He paused, remembering the way the two men had spoken to him in the warehouse, before. *Damn shame, he missed one step and fell the whole way down.* "What was the turnover on Buck's team? Any accidents?"

Larry thought about it, then shook his head. "Tim Halverson quit because he wanted to farm instead. That's the spot Joey took. Harry Nevins started working with Jim in the warehouse, which was your slot. Buck was one of the best." His voice got bitter. "Hell, I trained him."

"You should *not* blame yourself for that." Vir shuddered as he recalled the flat look on Buck's face as he'd discussed Vir's impending accident. "There was just something lacking in the man's spirit. To be honest, when I confronted him it sounded like he was doing it out of boredom."

Larry nodded and took a drink of water. "Lot of that going around. You'll see, the longer you work with us. Petty theft, fighting in the bar. I don't know, maybe we got stuck in survival mode for so long we don't know what to do when we're faced with the future."

"There is nothing more terrifying than the unknown," Vir thought aloud. "Even biters can seem ordinary when you're expecting them. In the small, still moments, we create our own demons." He drummed his fingers on the table and shrugged.

"Poetic. But I can see where you're coming from. We've got a couple hundred people accustomed to their own private space, their own recreation, living in packed quarters for damn near a decade. Bound to be some friction there."

"No turnover means they're not particularly worried about uninvolved members of their crew picking up on anything untoward. What's the standard process for returning salvage crews?"

Larry finished the bite he was working on and said, "Easy enough. Vehicles drive in, go to the warehouse, and unload. Haggle over their share and complain, usually."

"Any chance Buck involved someone in the warehouse?"

"Piper's a pain in the ass, but he's not that type of pain if you follow me. He runs a tight ship."

"We're missing something," Vir said. "I don't have the basis of understanding. Is there anything from when you were doing runs you can think of that would be a possibility?"

"How well do you know Charlie Maddox?" Larry asked suddenly.

"Just in passing," Vir said. "Why?"

Larry nodded across the cafeteria. "He's eating by himself. Let's pick his brain."

Bemused by the proceedings, Vir followed Larry as the other man returned his used utensils and tray to the

330

dishwashing station and moved to the table where Charlie Maddox sat. He was an average-sized man, clean-shaven with plenty of white in his otherwise dark hair. He sat hunched over his tray of food and the intensity he exuded in this relatively mundane task was striking. Vir wasn't the only one who felt it; the table was almost entirely empty, and the people who sat there had moved as far away from Charlie as possible.

Foregoing a greeting, Larry sat down opposite Charlie. Vir paused to see if the other Deputy would introduce him. When no introduction was forthcoming, he followed suit and sat down, leaving a single seat between Larry and himself. The three men described an almost perfect equilateral triangle over the surface of the table.

Charlie lifted his eyes and glanced at Vir and Larry in turn, but kept chewing. After he swallowed, he said, "Help you?"

Vir knew at some level that many of the survivors referred to the man in front of him as Quiet Charlie. He'd always assumed it was because he preferred not to speak. When Vir heard the tortured, rasping whisper his throat produced, he understood that it was not a preference but an adherence to the reality of the situation. Vir considered the worst sore throats he'd ever experienced and imagined that they paled in comparison.

"Charlie, meet Vir. Miles recruited him in as an undercover deputy."

Charlie's eyes flickered over to Vir with an almost audible click, and for the first time, Vir felt that the man was *looking* at him. "Pleasure," Vir said. "Don't believe we've met."

The other man grunted and took another bite of stew. He gave Larry a thoughtful look, then cocked his head to one side.

Larry must have been around him long enough to pick up on his nonverbal shorthand, because he said, "Got a bit of a situation. Maybe you've heard."

Chew. Chew. Chew. Swallow. "Lockdown. Panic attack." Annoyance flashed over Charlie's features. "Needed to go somewhere." He frowned as he looked at Larry. "What *you* need?"

"Information," Larry said. "You've heard about the meth problem?"

Charlie shrugged. "Some."

"We have at least part of the structure. We know who was bringing the ingredients in for the processing. What we can't figure out is how they did it with no one noticing."

"Who?"

"Buck and his team."

Charlie grunted, and Vir sensed it was out of surprise more than anything else. *Perhaps that makes the betrayal all the more stinging, knowing that he was so respected.*

"Jim?"

"He's clean, he runs a tight ship." Larry's voice turned accusatory. "You *know* this."

Charlie shrugged, then grimaced. "Yeah." He sighed and stared down at his plate. Finally, he looked back up at Larry. "Need a vehicle for half a day. No questions asked."

"Charlie, for God's sake, this isn't a negotiation. I was hoping you'd give us some information out of the kindness of your heart. There are three people in the clinic right now cause of this crap. We need to put a stake in it, once and for all."

"It's *important,*" Charlie said, wincing as he put too much emphasis on his reply. "Wouldn't ask, otherwise."

Larry stared at him for a long moment then sighed. "Fine, I'll see what I can do."

Charlie seemed satisfied with the answer. "Hidden lockers. All trucks got 'em." He shrugged. "Extra space, at first. Jim got pushy on salvage cut. Start hiding best stuff." He took a long drink. "Show you?"

Larry's voice was furious. "You bet your ass you're showing me."

It took him a moment of searching with his cheek pressed up against the fender, but Charlie found it.

He pulled away from the truck and let the concealed panel fall via gravity. The knobby, off-road tire interrupted the short arc of its travel. Larry didn't quite shove him aside as he moved in to look, but he was none to gentle about it, either.

On a general level, Charlie got it. All the salvage teams had sort of a Three Musketeer credo. They did what they did for the good of the community. But in a world without paychecks or Christmas bonuses, sometimes a man needed a little more motivation to get up and get going in the morning than three hots and a cot.

When it came to his own crew, Charlie was actually quite strict about the whole thing. If they found a nice bottle of scotch, for example, it didn't go in their compartment unless it was already open. Intact seals were for the community. And while he had a strict 'no guns' policy, he didn't care much if his guys topped off their own personal supplies of ammunition while searching. Hell, they'd most likely be drawing them out of stores, anyway, so it wasn't shorting the community. When it came to guns, though? Firepower was too narrow a line to cross. Despite what they'd scrounged over the years and what Larry and Pete had seeded the community with, there'd never been enough to go around. Springs and firing pins broke, pieces wore out, and — although rare — things were even lost from time to time. New acquisitions provided spare parts or even full replacements for weaponry that was wearing out without the benefit of a robust, modern supply chain. *Maybe that's something the return of the Army will alleviate in the future.* For now, though, the point was moot. They made do with what they had or could find.

Charlie backed away from the truck and pulled a green canvas duffel bag with him. He cocked an eyebrow and handed it to Larry.

The bag clanked and rattled as he set it on the ground beside the truck. "Anyone take an interest in what we're doing, yet?"

Vir had his back to the entire proceedings, keeping a look out. He turned. "None that I can see," he replied. "You should be good if you make it quick."

Larry unzipped the bag and threw it wide. A broad assortment of goods filled the bag, all in high demand.

Vir made an amused sound in his throat. "They must have raided the house we holed up in while I was upstairs doing recon. Ballsy of the buggers. Surprised they didn't nick Grandma's bloody silverware."

Charlie grunted his own laugh and studied the contents of the duffel. There were a few full — and sealed — bottles of Jack Daniels, a carton of cigarettes, lighters, a shiny revolver of some sort with requisite boxes of ammo, and an odd-looking black monstrosity that Larry teased out of the bag with a low whistle. "Damn," he said in admiration.

Charlie frowned as he studied the gun. It was bigger than a pistol, with a short barrel that just jutted past the short, black hand guard rail that surrounded it. A massive, curved magazine jutted from the receiver, while a collapsed stock lay against one side of the weapon's frame. Charlie revised his estimation of the weapon's size as he mentally added the stock to its length and saw its evident mass as Larry turned it over in his hands and gave it a quick inspection. The bore of the barrel, he noted, was bigger around than his thumb.

"What in the bloody hell is *that?*" Vir exclaimed.

"This, my friend, is a VEPR-12, but it looks like somebody had some nice work done before Z-Day and had the barrel shortened a tad. It's a design off of the AK platform, but it's chambered in 12-gauge instead of the regular Russian calibers." Larry dug through the duffel a bit more and came up with several more magazines. "Twelve shells per mag, semi-auto." He grinned. "Kind of wanted one of these since I ordered one for a guy back when I had my shop. Shame I have to turn it into the warehouse."

"You shouldn't do that at all," Vir mused.

Larry turned and gave Vir a confused glance. "Why is that, exactly?"

"The moment we turn any of this into the warehouse, you know the rumor mill is going to go into overload. Our dealers will hear about it and realize that you found their hidden stash. They'll be in the wind."

"Maybe."

"This calls for some sort of stakeout, right? As far as they know, Buck and his boys filled a supply order before things went to hell."

"How could they not? With the rumor mill around here, it would surprise me if your miraculous tale of survival isn't the highlight of the day." Larry snorted.

"I haven't told anyone other than Miles and yourself the complete story of what went down. No one *knows* that Donnie and Buck didn't load any pseudo-ephedrine into the truck before they met their fate. I shouldn't know anything about it, anyway, so why would I even be talking about it?" Charlie studied Vir; the man was almost bouncing in place with the thought of his nascent plan. He turned to Larry. The other man was frowning, but there was a thoughtful cast to it.

"Vir's right," Charlie added, and the other two men both turned to look at him with evident surprise. He shrugged. "Buck makes us look bad. I'll help."

"Just the three of us, then, eh, Larry? Keep everything hush, hush. Find a few convenient places to hide after it turns dark, and see who shows up."

Larry nodded, finally. "All right." He lifted the shotgun, then patted it on the side with a grin. "But I'm keeping this. I'm not keen on having it turned on me."

Chapter 22

After the exhausting trip back to the survivors'
compound, Hanratty debated long and hard on how he
wanted to spend his evening. Rolling out his bedroll and
curling up on the grass under the LAV was mighty
tempting, but it didn't coincide with his orders regarding
diplomacy and relationship building with the civilian
survivors. So, once they parked the LAV, he made a
demonstrative display of trust and ordered Patterson and
Rivas to accompany him to the dining facility. As he led his
small procession away from the wall, he winked at one of
the guards and said, "No joyriding, now. I know every
scratch on her."

The guard laughed and flashed him a thumbs-up. Poor
reactions last night to the contrary, *some* of the population
seemed to be coming around. If they weren't friendly they
at least held an air of acceptance. He'd take that over
outright hostility any day of the week.

The meal was simple, but filling, another variation on
meat and vegetables, but well-made. Perhaps it got old for
the people here, but to Hanratty, it was *haute* cuisine. Meal,
Ready to Eat was three lies for the price of one.

He sprung it on the enlisted toward the end of the meal. As close as he was, he had no real excuse to bow out of his meeting with Pete, and he didn't see the need to drag either of them along. In a lull in the conversation, he glanced at Rivas and Patterson and said, "Take the night. I hear there's a halfway decent pub here."

Rivas smirked, and Patterson blinked in surprise. "You sure, sir?"

Hanratty halfway shrugged. "It's a secure area, Corporal. Don't go crazy, and don't start any trouble with the locals." He favored them with a wicked grin. "I may consider calling for PT in the morning, mind you, so don't overindulge."

Rivas plucked at Patterson's sleeve. "This is where you say 'thank you, sir' and stand up to leave. Thank you, sir. If I may?"

"Have at it," Hanratty confirmed with a wave of his hand.

Neither needed him to tell them again; they collected their trays and made their way out of the building. He smiled as he watched them go. He had the sense that neither would have to figure out a way to pay for their own drinks this evening. He also felt confident that neither would be paying for it in the morning. Lack of self-control was a decided disadvantage these days. The harsh truth of the new world had eliminated that trait from the surviving remnants of the military in short order. That wasn't to say that there hadn't been opportunities for extracurricular shenanigans over the years. It was also more restrained than what he'd once feared based on the horror stories the instructors at the Academy had regaled the midshipmen with. Patterson would keep a lid on Rivas. *I hope.* There was a reason she was only a PFC, though she'd been on good behavior for the last couple of years. She only seemed to lose her mind after she got bumped up to E3 — Hanratty had heard some of the other Marines refer to her as 'Terminal Lance.' If this weren't the end of the world, she'd have been urged to move on after her first handful of non-judicial punishments.

He decided he'd eaten his fill, and rose and cleared his own utensils. Between handshakes and intermittent greetings, it took him ten minutes to make his way outside. Once he was out, his progress toward the observation post smoothed, and he clambered up the ladder and onto the platform.

Pete glanced over as he stepped up and nodded in his direction. "How was your day, Captain?" He hesitated and corrected himself, "Adam."

"Long," Hanratty said. "My ass hurts. Somebody's been slacking on road repairs for the last decade or so."

"A wise guy, eh," Pete chuckled and wheeled over to the cot in the center of the observation post. He pulled a battered and faded .50-cal ammo can from underneath and rummaged through it for a moment. With a cry of discovery, he turned around with a bottle of Johnny Walker Black label and a pair of chipped glass tumblers. "Here, you're going to need a snootful before you take a look at what I need you to see."

Hanratty raised an eyebrow in surprise. In all honesty, he should decline. *Someone* on the crew needed to be ready to stand watch. *Hell. One drink can't hurt, right?*

He pulled up a folding chair and had a seat after accepting one of the tumblers. Pete poured a generous splash into Hanratty's glass and a similar amount into his own. He raised it and intoned, "Here's health to you and to our Corps." He tossed back the whiskey in one gulp.

"The Corps," Hanratty echoed, hesitated for a fraction of a second, and tossed back his drink in the same manner. *And that's* it, *buddy*.

Pete reached over with the bottle, but Hanratty capped his fingers over the top of the glass. "I just unleashed two Marines on your local pub; I don't know if the only officer should be partaking as well."

"Fair enough. I can drink yours just as well as I drink mine."

"So, you had something you needed to tell me about?"

Pete eyed the sky and replied, "We've got a bit, yet. You need to see to understand, and that won't work until it's a bit darker. I'm guessing your drop-off was smooth. Your man Baxter has been making his rounds."

Hanratty made a show of glancing around. "What, you have this thing wired for sound?"

Pete laughed and topped off his drink. "Nope. Just a couple of smart kids who know how to listen and fill in an old man with nothing better to do than listen to gossip and worry."

"I hope he's not overstepping his bounds."

Pete shrugged. "The ones who'll talk to him are fine with what's done and gone or else they wouldn't be *able* to talk to him. The ones it really hit wouldn't even notice him standing there."

Hanratty thought back to the meal the other night and winced. "I guess I met someone like that the other night."

"Yeah, I guess you did. Betty should be fine, for her own values of fine, of course. She had it worse than most."

"What happened?"

Pete shrugged. "Don't know. What I do know is, if we had let her, I believe she would have just, I don't know, sacrificed herself. She was the only person I ever rescued who fought more to get away from us than she did the zombies."

"Damn," Hanratty managed. He shook his head. "So you go with 'zombies', too, huh?"

Pete laughed. "I blame Miles for that. I know we watched enough of those dumb movies when he was a kid. Seems like the only thing that fits, though I know I'm not the majority opinion, there." He offered the bottle again, and Hanratty shook his head. He shrugged. "Suit yourself."

"Troops are the same way, I guess. Brass insists on 'infected.'"

Pete chuckled. "Brass is as brass does. Infected implies that there's some sort of possible fix for the ailment. That ain't happening. It's a dumb word, but zombie is accurate. There's not enough left to heal. It's just dried out meat."

"You spent a lot of time with Miles, then, growing up? I mean, he's your nephew, not your son, correct?"

Pete nodded slowly and glanced toward the south edge of the observation platform. "Adopted him when he was eight years old or so and raised him pretty much alone." He winked at Hanratty. "I'm a whiz with the ladies, don't get me wrong. Just never found one that had any interest in a disabled vet with a kid."

Hanratty raised his eyebrows. "Didn't mean to touch on a sore point. We can talk about something else."

"Might as well talk about it, it's not like it's any big secret or something. Miles didn't have the best father, growing up. His daddy was a Marine as well. A middling one, to be sure, but my sister loved him. Thought she could fix him, I suppose." Pete took a slow sip of his drink. He'd made a decided dent in the Johnny Walker, but there was no trace of a slur in his words. *Should have taken him up on that drink. My luck, he'll finish off the bottle and pass out before he tells me what's got him so fired up.* "He was in supply and not a combat unit like mine; I don't know how well he'd have done on deployment. Anyway, I was home on leave, and my sister talked me into a double date one night. Long story short, my brother-in-law had a few too many and ran his car into a utility pole. I was the only one that made it, although," he rapped his knuckles on a prosthetic. "I was not entirely unscathed."

Hanratty was unable to hide his surprise. "I guess I figured you got wounded over there."

Pete laughed. "You'd think, wouldn't you? No, I had all the dumb luck a man could ever want. Didn't get so much as a scratch. Never even lost a man over the course of three tours. Had to come home to lose my legs." He shook his head and finished off his drink. "Cruel joke, isn't it?"

Hanratty shifted in his seat. "I can't empathize, I haven't been lucky enough in either way." *Never gotten bit, but I've had some damn close calls.* He shivered.

"Aw, hell, kid," Pete said. "I'm sorry. Didn't mean anything by it."

He waved a hand at the older man. "No worries, I didn't take it personally."

"Yeah," Pete scowled at his empty glass for a moment, and then set it down. "God's honest truth, Adam, I'd take jihadis with AKs every day of the week compared to what we have now. At least the damn hajjis just kill you and that's that." He nodded in Hanratty's direction. "That you and your boys have kept it together this long is a testament to good leadership."

"It's not always been wine and roses."

"Oh, I understand that. For every few people we've got that are capable of supporting themselves, there's another who just went into brain lock. Couldn't deal with what they were seeing, I guess. You ever play role-playing games, like Dungeons and Dragons?"

Hanratty laughed. "Sorry, I was a jock in high school."

"Yeah, yeah, laugh it up. Yet another thing I picked up from Miles. I was a farm kid, myself. Anyway, one of the games he and his friends played was this ancient aliens at the bottom of the sea thing. When they ran into one of the monsters it would look so, I don't know, horrible and outside the realm of their experience that they'd have to do a 'sanity check.' Roll their dice against some number, if they didn't beat it, their character would just snap, mentally." Pete glanced up at the darkening sky. "Been thinking about that a lot, recently. Sanity checks." He lifted a pair of binoculars and gestured toward Hanratty. "Have a good look at the tree line. If it gets much darker I'll have to break out the night vision."

Puzzled, Hanratty moved over to accept the binoculars. He knelt down at the rail on the southern side of the observation post and brought them to his eyes. "What am I looking for, exactly?"

"You'll know it when you see it," Pete said. There was a deep fatigue in his voice, like that of a man resigned to some terrible fate.

With a frown, he panned the binoculars across the line of trees across the creek on the south side of the compound. From what he remembered from the drone overflight, the ground was uneven and shot through with gullies. The forest continued for several hundred yards before the ground flattened out into another field.

At first, he didn't see it. The shadows underneath the trees were heavy in the fading light. Despite this, he could make out quite a bit of detail — fallen branches, bushes struggling for their share of sunlight, and narrow trails where small game such as rabbits presumably cut through. The infected was motionless and back far enough out of the light that it was just visible. Once his eyes made out the slight oddity in the shape of the tree it crouched behind, more and more of them popped into sight. He cursed under his breath as he swept the trees again. Everywhere he looked, he could see them waiting.

The presence was disconcerting not only because of the actual presence of literal scores of infected but their uncharacteristic behavior. The community was quiet, but not to an absurd degree. The slightest noise drew them out to hunt. The infected inside of the tree line *should* have been clawing at the fences in an attempt to gain access, but they weren't.

"This doesn't make any sense," Hanratty said. "They see or hear signs of life, they come to investigate. That's what they do. That's *all* they do."

"You think they're stupid? You're wrong. There's a good two hundred of them out there. They stick outside of what they've learned is my effective range. A few times a week they'll send a lucky winner in my direction, I guess to see if we're still paying attention. But for the most part, they just wait."

"What are they waiting for?" Hanratty wondered aloud. He did another scan of the tree line; if anything Pete's count was *low*.

How far back do they go?

"Damned if I know. Maybe they're like us, just waiting for the other side to drop dead so they can have the world to themselves. Maybe they're waiting to see if we screw up. So I wait. I watch."

"So why all the secrecy; why the urgency?"

Pete sighed. "I haven't told anyone else. Didn't want to cause a panic at first, then, as time went on, it just didn't feel right, you know? Something's going on, and I didn't want to upset the equilibrium of the situation by reacting without knowing everything. I've been screaming for years that we need to beef up the fences. Everyone is just too damn complacent to listen." He laughed. "Hell, the night before you guys showed up I was wishing I could call in an air strike. So what do you say?"

"Be a shame to ruin all those trees. That wood might come in handy someday." Hanratty lowered the binoculars and massaged his forehead. "But you're right, we need to do something. Maybe draw them out with the LAV and have a gunship or two on station to shred them. That field to the south is overgrown, right?"

"Yeah. There's enough ground around here that's easier to get to, so we let it lay fallow. Good call, at this point, I guess." Pete grimaced. "Hate to think what would have happened if we'd sent a crew out there to plow."

"Let me shoot it up to command and see what they think. This is definitely weird enough I think they'll want to know about it. If they're getting smarter . . ." He trailed off as he considered a comment Ross had made when they'd been loading up for the mission. What had it been, something about new developments? He frowned as he tried to remember the conversation. He hadn't paid much attention; the main focus of his mission had been actually *getting* them here and making peaceful contact. The infected were something omnipresent you accounted for in planning, like IEDs or roadblocks.

There'd been rumors going around for years that some of the surviving scientists and medical staff in the fleet were researching infected specimens. They'd been so commonplace and pervasive that Hanratty had always assumed there was some kernel of truth to it, just expanded and spun out of control by the rumor mill. Now, though, he wondered if his initial doubts weren't misplaced.

It's not like there's a shortage of available space on one of the carriers, or even a hospital ship, where they could conduct research in relative secrecy. Is *something up?* If this change in behavior was a concern, he needed to know sooner rather than later; Pete was right on the money about the threat this posed. Based on the numbers he could see, the fence wasn't enough. If there were more infected out there, the fences were sure to fail if they woke from their hibernation, or whatever the hell it was.

"Keep this under your hat for now," Hanratty decided. "Just for another day or so. I'll see what the brass have to say about it."

He was dreaming of shapeless terrors when the hand clamped over his mouth and jerked him out of sleep.

Miles flailed his arms in an attempt to push his attacker away, but an iron grip held him still. "Easy, son, easy," came a deep-voiced whisper, so close that the other man's beard tickled his cheek and aided in recognition — Foraker. Miles relaxed, and the arms holding him down eased the pressure. "You were talking in your sleep. We need you quiet — we've got a situation here."

Miles tensed. "What's going on?"

Foraker's mouth was still close enough that he could hear the big man swallow. "Best take a look for yourself, I still don't believe my own eyes."

Miles sat up. As his eyes adjusted to the darkness, he realized that Ross crouched on his left, opposite Foraker. The lieutenant gave him a quiet nod, but there was a wild look in the other man's eyes. He would have labeled it as panic if Ross's voice hadn't been so calm.

"Move slowly," Ross whispered. "The floor doesn't creak up here, thank God, but we don't need any noise right now."

He nodded toward the opposite side of the room, at the quilt hanging over the window. A glowing LCD screen sat below the window. A green shade tinted the picture, but the screen was so small that Miles could just make out blurs of motion from across the room.

He mimicked the slow, cautious movements of Ross and Foraker as he rose to his feet and padded across the carpet. At the window, he knelt down and studied the screen. Now that he was closer to the device, he could see that it was some sort of ruggedized tablet. A black, semi-rigid cable stuck up from one side of the device and traced up the wall and underneath the quilt. *Fiber-optic camera, cool.*

The coolness factor dissipated as he studied the screen. The light-amplification rendered the image in shades of black and green and gave it an otherworldly cast. After he studied it for a moment and realized what he was looking at, Miles whispered a curse.

A slow-marching horde of zombies filled the county road in front of the farmhouse. They spilled a bit over the edges and into the ditches on either side, but for the most part, they walked directly on the blacktop. Miles' study of the movement left him with a vague sense of unease. There was a strange, almost synchronized air to their movements — not unlike a flock of birds. There was no jostling for position, nor was there any collision or ripple effect from slow-moving members impeding the progress of the group. They moved at a slow, consistent speed all were capable of, unerringly in the same direction — north.

Miles licked his lips. The camera had a limited field of view, but the line stretched across the entire piece of road that was visible on the screen. "How long has this been going on?"

"About five minutes now," Ross replied. "They just came out of nowhere."

It was impossible to calculate how many were on the screen at a given time, but it had to number in the hundreds. While they were moving at relative turtle speed, he didn't want to think how many could have progressed by in five minutes. The number would without a doubt be too horrific to contemplate. Miles settled for waiting, and prayed the tide wouldn't turn in their direction.

He didn't know how long they watched the procession in silence before Foraker spoke. "What's our move if they head this way, Mikey?"

Ross was silent for a long moment before he replied, "We don't have anywhere close to the amount of ammo we'd need to hold them off. They'll tear this place out from under us through sheer weight of numbers if we try to shelter in place." He shook his head. "They so much as look this way, we bail out the back and evade them until we can redirect dust off."

Miles winced. Hiding from what looked to be thousands upon thousands of zombies, in the dark, in unknown terrain? *Not exactly what I'd call a comforting thought.*

Ross stood and said, "I'm going to relieve Janacek so he can get some sleep. Mister Matthews, you're free to try to do the same if you can. Just . . . No more talking, huh?"

Eyes fixed on the screen, Miles nodded.

Chapter 23

Dantzler grinned in the dark.

Like a dope, he'd forgotten that the moon was in its first quarter; it had been *damn* bright the last couple of nights. A well-timed thunderstorm had rolled through right around dinner. The remnant clouds concealed much of the moonlight and created enough shadow for him to conduct his business.

If you're not good, it's always nice to be lucky. Like earlier today, when he'd braced Foster for some more diesel. Usually, it was like pulling teeth trying to finagle extra supplies. Knowing who to approach was the key, and Foster was one of his go-to guys. As far as Dantzler could tell, the man had *zero* scruples about profiting from his position in the warehouse. But, at the same time, he was canny enough to not only hide what he was doing but never take enough to stick out. Dantzler had once considered offering him a spot on his crew before dismissing the idea. The guy was too smooth and conniving. He'd find some angle to exploit and try to sweeten any deal he got with an eye toward taking over down the road. Ivan preferred his subordinates moderately-capable and satisfied with their lot in life.

If he was being honest, he didn't need to be out here. He'd gotten enough diesel from Foster to give them a healthy reserve on top of what they'd need to get the truck to the docks. What he didn't have, though, were any trade goods. The haggling had cleaned him out. If he wasn't in such a time crunch Foster's attitude in their dealings might have offended him, but it didn't matter.

When it came down to it, he was just hedging his bets. Maybe there'd be an island in the river with some survivors, or maybe he'd run into other boats. It was always good to come bearing gifts, at least at the start, until you could determine how best to take advantage of a situation. And if not, it was always good to have a little top shelf booze tucked away for a rainy day.

He'd cut through the array of greenhouses and fields and came up on the southern side of the vehicle lot. It was standard procedure to leave the vehicles unlocked and unattended. With the push-button start military vehicles, they removed the batteries and kept them topped off in the warehouse. Dantzler could have gotten a spare battery had he needed one — there were several among the supplies he'd held back for the trip — but he didn't have a need or desire to drive away. This was a quick check to see what Buck and the boys had stashed in the storage bin.

Dantzler knelt down in the grass at the edge of the graveled lot. Up to this point, he'd been able to move in relative quiet; he couldn't say the same for when he moved out onto the rocks. He listened hard for a moment. As was typical after dark, silence reigned throughout the community. They'd learned light and sound discipline early, and those behaviors were the rule rather than the exception. The lack of widespread electricity also meant that most people tended to sleep and wake with dawn and dusk instead of an artificial schedule.

Keeping low, Dantzler crept around the southern side of the lot and moved north in parallel to the eastern border. Vir had parked the truck in its usual spot, against the eastern edge of the lot, right about dead center. The gap where the third of the trio normally rested was glaring, and he considered its absence for a moment.

Wonder if there are any goodies left at the warehouse that might be worth a detour before heading south? That truck should still be full of fuel, and we can fill it up with medical supplies after clearing the door off. He thought it over for a second, then grinned to himself and shook his head. *Best not get too greedy. Let's do this, and get it over with.*

Dantzler licked his lips and stepped out onto the gravel.

Carter Drake's boots scuffed on the pavement as he staggered away from The Last Bar and in the general direction of the clinic. He was no stranger to Tom's establishment, though he usually cut things short early. Too much drinking made him dream, and dreaming usually led to thinking about the past. He'd worked long and hard to try and forget what had gone before, but he'd been swept up and carried along by the festive atmosphere in the bar. Several of the Marines had joined the usual crew, and things had gotten raucous. Not *too* over the top — Tom had a zero tolerance policy for fighting in and around the bar. You fought, you were out, for a long time.

Carter had faint memories of chasing down bottles of Tom's home brew with shots someone had ordered in honor of the Marines. *Beer before liquor, in the clear, right? Or do I have that backward?*

Either way, the point was moot — during the celebration, Carter stumbled and cracked his head on a tabletop. He hadn't felt much, if any pain, while his buzz was still going, but as it faded, his head throbbed in time with his heart. The goose egg on his forehead felt hot, wet, and almost the same size as the rest of his head.

"Good grief, Carter," Tom exclaimed as he'd held the door for his patrons after the last call and seen the results of the man's spill. "Get down and get yourself checked out by the docs, I don't need you getting a concussion on my watch."

It was hard to think straight with the throbbing agony, but Carter had to grant Tom the point. He had duty tomorrow, and he didn't know how well he was going to be able to stand his watch if he didn't do something about this, and quick.

And so, he bobbed and weaved in the semi-darkness. The county road was beginning to buckle in places from lack of maintenance. This made it treacherous footing for someone not quite in possession of his full faculties, but Carter managed to get to the clinic without toppling over. He took a moment to steady himself with one arm before pounding on the closed and locked doors with his free hand. Even when the lights were out, someone staffed the clinic at all hours.

If he hadn't been so focused on the pain in his head and his battle to remain upright, he might have noticed the figure that stepped from the shadows behind him and approached.

Larry glanced at the vague green glow of his watch and tried not to sigh. They'd set up just before dark when they'd been certain that no one had them in sight. That had been six hours ago, and all he had to show for it was a sore ass from sitting in the rear cargo compartment of a Hummer. Despite the discomfort and his desire to stay awake, Larry had nodded off more than a few times, though he'd jerked awake in short order each time. He'd equipped Charlie and Vir with two-way radios and earpieces and wore a matching set himself. If they needed to communicate with each other it was a simple matter of pressing a transmit button in-line with the earpiece cable. The other men were close; Vir lay on top of one of the parked combines, while Charlie sat in the cargo bed of the remaining deuce-and-a-half. If he needed support, Charlie was closest, but Vir had a better field of view. As for Larry, he'd chosen his position for one reason — the Humvee was next to the truck Vir had driven back. Larry had an unobstructed view of the wheel well with the hidden cargo compartment.

He rubbed his face with the palms of his hands. *This is something Miles should be doing. A man my age should be in bed asleep right about now.* Larry chuckled and whispered to himself. "Quit grousing, Marine."

He glanced around the visible area of the parking lot, then adjusted his position. The trick to setting up an observation like this was pretty simple. You didn't look at any one thing in particular; you just kind of zoned out and let your eyes go out of focus. Look for the thing that changes, not for any one thing in particular. Wait for the motion, and then focus.

His earpiece clicked. Larry reached up and pressed it deeper into his ear. Vir's voice was quiet but audible. "Someone at the east side of the lot. Right between you and the truck, Larry."

Not wanting to risk speaking, Larry pressed the push to talk button twice, sending a pair of clicks over the radio.

Vir hesitated for a second; they'd established the simple one click no, two clicks yes system before separating, but it was a bit different in this context. "We're waiting for you, is that what you're saying?"

Two clicks.

"Understood. Charlie?"

Two more clicks and Larry smiled. *Good troops.*

"Headed inside now," Vir whispered, and now Larry saw the figure slinking across the gravel and angling for the deuce-and-a-half. This was it. He reached down and ensured his pistol was still holstered at his side. He'd brought the VEPR along, just in case there was more than one person to deal with, but this looked like a solo act.

Wait for it.

The man was of average height and clothed all in black. It was too dark for Larry to make a guess as to his identity. He could have been any one of fifty members of the community, based on a possible height range. The weight was no help — pretty much everyone tended toward the bonier end of the scale these days.

Soft light flared as the man in black knelt next to the wheel well and played a flashlight around inside. *Here we go.*

Larry kept his movements slow so as not to shake the Humvee's suspension. With the pins and needles in the back of his legs and buttocks, it was easier said than done. After several nerve-racking moments, he ended up in one of the rear passenger seats with a minimum of noise. Over at the truck, the man in black had the cargo compartment open and was pulling out the bag.

Wincing, Larry pulled on the door latch and swung the back door open. Preparation saved him, though he hadn't even considered it before making the move. The hinges didn't utter even the slightest squeak as he swung the door wide. They couldn't do much about engine noise. But it made sense to limit noise emissions after stopping. It was easier for the dead to home in on a constant source of noise rather than something intermittent. For that reason, the survivors in charge of the motor pool doused each vehicle's door hinges, shocks, and other possible noise sources with oil when the vehicles returned from the Wild.

Larry brought his feet down and stood at what seemed a glacial pace. Glass clinked as the man in front of him began to dig through the bag. That seemed as much of an opportunity as any. He stepped forward and raised his pistol.

As he clicked the flashlight on and shouted for the figure beside the truck to freeze, a blood-curdling scream came from the north. He instinctively began to turn in that direction. As he caught himself and corrected the maneuver, the figure beside the truck bolted straight at him. His teeth slammed together from the impact and he saw stars as the back of his head slammed into the side of the Humvee.

Blinking, Larry realized he was lying on the ground and the flashlight was lying next to him. Gravel crunched to his right as the figure who'd bowled him over sprinted away.

"Shit!" Larry hissed as he fumbled with the button on his headset. "Charlie, Vir, he's bolting!"

Everything seemed to happen at once — the scream, the light cutting into his eyes, and the cry for him to freeze. Dantzler reacted without hesitation. His eyes followed the flashlight beam to the man holding it — it sounded like Vance, which figured. He dropped the bottle he'd pulled out of the cargo compartment and sprang that way. That, he reasoned in one instant, was his only chance. Knock the other man over before he exchanged his flashlight for something deadlier and put a bullet or six into his back.

Vance had three or four inches and maybe forty pounds of muscle on Dantzler, but he caught him just right, square in the breadbasket. The bigger man slammed into the Humvee with a thump. Dantzler didn't even bother to check on his handiwork — he took off running. Neither Vance or the kid marshal were dumb enough to try something like this alone — a freaking stakeout, part of him marveled — and he wasn't going to stand and fight. That was a losing proposition, no matter what. Running, he stood a chance to get away. It was dark, he doubted anyone had seen his face, and he didn't have to worry about any of the crazy CSI crap with DNA and fingerprints like the old days. *Make a break for it and you're home free, boyo.*

The gravel was loose under his feet, but he was nimble enough that it didn't slow him down, much. He hit the pavement just as he heard more yelling from behind. From the sounds of it, there were maybe two or three other people back there. Running had definitely been the best—

Dantzler slammed into someone and tripped, flopping to the ground on top of a soft, screaming mass. *What the hell?* He rolled over onto his back and tried to make out what was going on.

A man lay in the road at his feet, clutching his stomach and screaming between gasps for air. A figure in a long, hooded coat — some sort of rain gear? — stood over them. Despite the concealing bulk of the coat, the rounded swell of her chest proclaimed her gender, and Dantzler got a flash of pale skin and dark hair beneath the hood. Before he could make a more intent study, a beam of light shot around the corner of the clinic. He flinched in panic and rolled onto his stomach to hide his own face. The sound of Larry's running footsteps paused as he took in the strange tableau, then Dantzler heard another scuffle and the sound of someone falling down. The light blinked away as the flashlight spun on the ground, and he risked a glance back as he scrambled to his feet.

Larry was on the ground by the first victim, and as the flashlight beam swept across him, Dantzler could make out the knife stuck into his left leg. *Girlfriend's got a nasty bite.* He glanced around and saw the woman sprinting north in pursuit of her own cover. That snapped him into action himself, and he began jogging to the east. Past the clinic, he ducked into the gap between it and the police station. From the cries and shouts behind him, it didn't sound like pursuit would be forthcoming. He could take the time to be stealthier and not worry about someone spotting him in a frantic rush to make it back to his quarters.

For a moment, Dantzler considered going back to retrieve the bag of goodies from the truck. He dismissed it almost as soon as the thought occurred to him. Far be it for him to spit in the face of such luck. He'd tempted fate once already in coming out tonight, and he was reluctant to do so again.

As he slipped through the shadows, a broad smile crossed Dantzler's face. When he'd heard there'd been a murder, he'd assumed it was one of the rowdies that frequented Tom's bar, or some spat over supplies. He'd never have believed who the killer actually was. Maybe she'd recognized him as he had her, but maybe not.

Either way, we're out of here tomorrow night. "And I've got a secret," he whispered, sing-song.

The son of a bitch was *fast.*

Larry almost lost his footing a handful of times as he sprinted after the fleeing figure. The beam of his flashlight wobbled as he ran, but he was still able to make out the runner as he left the gravel and angled right on the pavement.

He picked up speed on the solid surface, but Larry was able to close ground when he was going sideways. He hoped that Charlie and Vir were following. If this went on much longer, he didn't know if he could handle it. *Can't recall the last time I was in a full-out sprint — it's a damn sight easier closer to twenty than sixty.*

The runner left his line of sight as he cut east around the front of the clinic. Larry heard another scream, a heavy sound of impact, and the ringing sound of metal on the pavement.

He forced himself to slow as he rounded the corner of the clinic. His heart hammered in his chest, and he panted for breath. He swept the beam of his flashlight across the road before him.

The screaming figure was a man in normal clothing — one of the wall guards, Larry thought. A widening pool of blood surrounded his crumpled form. The runner was scrambling to his feet just past the guard — he'd tripped over him, maybe? Light glinted off of the shiny blade of a Bowie knife lying on the pavement between the two. Confusion reigned for a moment as he tried to grasp the meaning of the knife, but as soon as he reached a logical conclusion, a bolt of pain hit him in the thigh. For the second time in as many minutes, his head slammed into something hard. This time, his forehead met the road as he toppled over. The flashlight clattered to the ground, spinning and giving the entire scene a macabre air. He shook his head in an attempt to clear his vision. All he caught was a glimpse of long, black fabric whipping away as the second attacker sprinted into the maze of greenhouses and fields to the north.

For a moment, Larry tried to rise to his feet, but his leg crumpled under him as he put weight on it. He slapped a hand down and interrupted the slowing spin of the flashlight. When he shone it on his leg, he understood the reason for his temporary paralysis.

The attacker had jammed another knife into the side of his leg. This one was much smaller than the Bowie, some sort of folding pocket knife with a textured, composite plastic handle. It wiggled in time to the motions of his leg muscles, and he fought down the urge to vomit from the waves of pain that washed over him.

The light over the clinic doors came on as Vir and Charlie ran up to him. "Bloody hell!" Vir exclaimed, and knelt down to check on Larry.

"Forget me," Larry raged. "Go after him!" He raised his hand to point, but the runner from the motor pool had taken advantage of the confusion and was nowhere to be found. He resisted the urge to slam his fist into the pavement. "Damn it!"

The clinic door came open and Grady Scott came out. The dentist rubbed his eyes and yelled, "What the hell's going on out here?"

"Wounded," Charlie growled, and Grady took in the tableau and seemed to jolt awake.

"Holy shit," he exclaimed. "Hang on." He disappeared back into the clinic. Larry watched him go with a sigh, then relaxed. With the back of his head on the pavement, he could almost forget the throb of agony in his leg, the headache that promised to be a whopper, and the thudding of his overtaxed heart.

Vir's head hovered over him, and Larry tried not to laugh. He didn't know if it would shake the knife or not. "It's a cliché, Vir, but I am getting too old for this."

The other man frowned. "Stay awake, Larry. Come on now, don't close your eyes."

"I'm fine," Larry slurred. "How's the other guy."

"Charlie's helping him. No worries, guv, looks like he's just got a couple of stab wounds, shouldn't be too big a deal."

"No," Larry said. "*Who's* the other guy?"

"It's Carter, Carter Burke. Come on, Larry, keep your eyes open." Vir tapped him on the cheek, but even that didn't hurt as bad as his headache had promised it would. He tried to smile, tried to tell Vir that he was just fine, but consciousness slipped away before he could form the words.

Chapter 24

In contrast to the rough awakening he'd suffered the night before, Miles woke Friday morning at a comfortable pace. The only thing that sped him along toward consciousness were the quiet movements of the other men. He rubbed at the crustiness in his eyes and wished for some warm water and a washcloth to kick-start his morning. There were advantages to even the small level of modern conveniences they'd maintained. No worries; he'd manage. He had some caffeinated drink mix in his pack; it wasn't Starbucks, but it would suffice.

The room was dim, but vague lines of sunlight peeked out from behind the blanket covering the window. Ross sat with his back against the wall, and the tablet at his side. The SEAL nodded in greeting, then said, "Bathroom's open. Pipes are long dry but feel free to use the john. Best case scenario we won't be back here, ever." He half-shrugged. "Just in case, dig a cat hole out back if you have to do anything more than piss."

"I'm good," Miles promised him and made his way into the master bath. Before the end, it had been a work of art. The flooring consisted of large, cream-colored ceramic tiles. That same color pattern extended to the broad counter with twin sinks and the Jacuzzi tub in the immediate center of the room. A glass shower stall sat in one corner. After sitting idle for so long, the entire room was grubby with dust.

The bowl of the john was dry, but he detected a vague scent of urine as he lifted the lid and went about his business. Without water to flush, it would evaporate like the water in the bowl and tank had, long ago. In the meantime, though . . . *I hope Ross is right. This could get a little rank if we have to hole up here for any amount of time.*

When he returned to the bedroom, Ross wore a headset and listened with an intent expression. After a moment, he pressed a button on a unit clipped to his load-bearing harness and said, "Copy that, Whiskey 3, we'll see you in ten. Hatchet out." He glanced up at Miles and shot him a thumbs-up. "Our chariot awaits." He followed the other man's look to his radio and said, "MBITR; multiband inter slash intra team radio. Not too long of a range, maybe twenty miles or so, but works nice to keep the boys and I coordinated in the field." He winked. "Plus calling in choppers."

"We're still going to be a long way from your base, do you have any way to contact them?"

"Satellite gear has been getting flaky for the past few years; we've got a boosted antenna setup that we can hit a hundred miles or so. Almost need to bounce the signal off of an intermediate receiver for it to work well." Ross shrugged. "It is what it is."

He blanched. "Welcome back to the stone age, huh?"

"Not quite that bad yet, but getting there."

Miles knelt down, unclipped the canteen from his pack and took a long drink. Rummaging around, he pulled out a granola bar that was only about a kindergartner past its expiration date. "Chocolate chip?"

Ross raised an eyebrow. "How do they taste?"

He grimaced. "Like chocolate-flavored sawdust. But it's calories, and I didn't get up in time for anything more extensive."

Ross began securing the tablet. "No worries, kid. We split up the watch shifts so everyone got plenty of sleep. No offense, but we don't give trust easy. I'd rather you get more sleep than give you a watch."

Miles didn't know how to respond to that, so he donned his pack and tore open the granola bar. He could understand the sentiment, at least, and he wasn't going to complain about getting extra sleep.

Ross had everything collected and stowed in his own pack, and Miles followed him as the other man slung it over one shoulder and headed toward the back bedroom. When they got there, the window was already open. Foraker crouched on the floor next to it, scanning their surroundings.

"Dust off in ten," Ross announced. "How's it looking outside, Chief?"

"Clear so far," the older man reported. "Janacek is down at the bottom, ready to cover."

"Outstanding," Ross proclaimed. "All right, Mr. Matthews, after you. We're right behind."

Miles slung his rifle and finagled his way out the window and onto the ladder. Getting out was a bit trickier than climbing inside. He was glad to see Janacek standing on the bottom rung to stabilize it even as he scanned the backyard for any signs of movement.

Miles hit the ground and stepped aside. Janacek ignored him, so he took the opportunity to bring his rifle forward.

He arranged the loop of the single-point sling across his chest and over one shoulder and checked that the chamber was still loaded. He left his rifle on safe, but shouldered it at the low ready and studied the backyard on his own as Foraker began his own climb down the ladder.

The knee-high grass rippled in the breeze as his eyes flickered from spot to spot. The granola bar had settled into his stomach like a rock and Miles licked his lips as he tried to discern what was natural movement and what might be an unseen danger crawling toward them.

Foraker hit the ground with a thump, and equipment rattled as he took his own position to the side of the ladder. "All clear over here, kids," the big Chief said.

"I don't like this," Janacek said, but his tone was so mild that he might have been commenting on the weather. A vague thumping sound started to the north.

Ross hit the ground. "Damn," he said. "Chopper's early. Bust a move, we need to get the fuel line ready for the crew chief. Matthews, stick close to me. Janacek, you've got point. Forget the ladder."

Janacek trotted forward, and Miles formed up just behind and to the right of the lieutenant. Foraker swept into place behind them and periodically turned to scan the rear. The grass in the front yard stood tall, though the passage of countless feet had flattened it close to the road. Without stopping, Janacek marched into the center of the growth. A few feet in, he knelt and swept his arm to the side. Grass scattered, and Miles realized that the SEALS had used it to camouflage something. Ross stopped and turned to Janacek's left. Miles imitated the maneuver and faced the opposite direction.

"We stashed a fuel blivet here on our way down. Huge pain in the ass, believe you me," Ross commented. Janacek emerged from the hiding spot with an unreeled hose.

Foraker stepped forward with a canister in one hand. He pulled the pin out of the top of it and bowled it toward the road. A moment after it struck the ground, it began emitting a bright orange smoke that angled to one side in the breeze.

"Whiskey 3, this is Hatchet 6, LZ is marked. There are no clearance issues, over."

Miles studied the field on the other side of the road. The thumping from the north grew more pronounced.

Ross came over to Miles and grabbed him by the shoulder. "Listen up. When the chopper lands, the crew chief is going to top off the tanks. He'll handle that evolution solo. We'll need to provide security. If there are any infected that weren't drawn away by that horde, we need to keep them off of us until we're gassed up. You with me so far?"

He nodded. "Got it."

"I want you to go to the nose of the chopper and cover front, the copilot is going to get out and do the same, so you won't be by yourself. We'll have the other three sides of the chopper. All right?"

Miles made an 'o' with his thumb and his forefinger and said, "I'm good. Let's do this."

Ross made eye contact for a long moment and seemed satisfied with what he saw there. He gave Miles a short nod and turned back to face the road. He made a motion with his hand, and the SEAL's knelt to the ground as one in a triangular formation, each oriented out. A moment later, Miles moved inside of their perimeter and knelt, as well.

With all the approaches covered, he scanned the sky for the approaching helicopter.

He didn't have to wait long. It came in low over the road, just a handful of feet over the trees that stood at the edge of the farm fields. At first, it was small, almost toy-like in proportion, but the Black Hawk's velocity was deceptively fast. In moments, it loomed in front of them and settled onto its wheels in front of the house. The rotors slowed as the engine dropped in pitch, but it was still loud. The whirring of the blades swept dust and grit out at Miles, and whipped the plume of orange smoke into nothingness. All at once, he realized it had been over eight years since he'd seen a helicopter in the air.

Ross leaned over and shouted into Miles' ear over the racket. "This is it! Keep your eyes out, they're running the engine hard enough to keep her light on her wheels. If we need to bug out in a hurry, we can, but it's going to be dicey if we don't top off the tanks. Got it?"

"Got it!" Miles shouted. The SEALs rose and rapid-stepped to the road in half-crouches. Foraker grabbed the sliding door on the side and helped the crew chief slide it open. Janacek handed off the fuel hose, then hopped into the body of the chopper. He slid open the opposite door, then hopped back onto the ground on the opposite side. As the crew chief began making arrangements to connect the fuel blivet, Foraker and Ross assumed their own positions, and Miles realized he was a step behind.

The co-pilot climbed out of the door on the farmhouse side. Miles moved around him and knelt on the pavement in front of the pilot's seat. The copilot came around and crouched in the opposite lane of the road, in front of his own seat. Miles couldn't make out much of the man's appearance; he was of average height and stocky. Shiny aviator shades hid his eyes and he still wore a bulky helmet. He cradled a Heckler & Koch MP-5 submachine gun with an integral suppressor. The tactical vest he wore over his one-piece flight suit bulged with spare magazines. Miles eyed the gun with interest. It was one of those ubiquitous guns that always ended up in movies or TV shows back in the day, because of its unique look. He'd handled some interesting gear working in his father-in-law's shop, but he'd never had the opportunity to check out one of these.

The copilot noticed his study and grinned. "Name's Hickson," he shouted as he pointed to the name tape on his flight suit. "Got this toy off of one of your buddies a while back." He glanced at Miles' rifle and raised his eyebrows in appreciation. "Nice!"

Miles gave him a thumbs-up and waved his hand outward at the road in front of them. The crew chief nodded, and Miles turned away and scanned the surrounding territory. Maybe the noise of the passing herd had drawn out any stragglers roaming the countryside.

But how did the herd get that big to begin with?

He shook his head to chase off the thought. It didn't matter — what did matter was he couldn't remember the last time he'd been near something so damn *loud*. Yeah, the big diesel engines in their combines and tractors were pretty noisy, but they'd done everything they could figure out to reduce the noise signature. It was doubtful that the same methods would work with a helicopter.

How did they manage this? In a way maybe the undead chorus line last night had been a *good* thing — if it had thinned the area out a bit, all for the better. This was sure to be audible for miles.

There was a slight thump, and he stiffened. Miles glanced over his shoulder and saw Janacek standing at the side with his rifle up. Again, the thump, and brass spat from Janacek's SCAR.

He looked out into the field across from the house in time to see the zombie's head shatter before it collapsed into the weeds. It was a good hundred and fifty yards away from where the SEAL had taken the shot, but the fact that he needed to shoot so early was ominous. Maybe the herd hadn't been as noisy as he'd thought. Miles turned back to his own vector and scanned the road in front of him and the field to his left. He squinted. There. Was that . . .?

Times like this, he wished he'd slapped a magnifier on his rifle behind the holosight, but he'd make do. He reached up and pressed the button to switch it on. The batteries had a full charge and the red dot was visible, even in the raising daylight. He shouldered his rifle and grinned at a sudden memory. The first time Tish had tried it, she'd proclaimed it cheating. Miles didn't believe that was possible, especially now.

She'd had grown up shooting with her dad, but Larry was old school. He didn't like anything fancier than an ordinary scope. That sentiment must have been hereditary because Tish was much the same. Miles had more of a tech-geek philosophy. The EOTech didn't do all the work for you, but it simplified things. Setting it up took some skill, but once you had it dialed in, you put the dot on what you wanted to hit, pulled the trigger, and voila.

The horde must not have made as much noise as he'd thought because there were more than a few stragglers. The road wasn't filled, but at least a dozen figures stumbled in their direction. *Slow ones?* Beside him, Hickson let off an extended burst from his MP-5. At this range, Miles couldn't tell if he hit anything. He leaned toward not, at this range.

That's okay, it's not like I can fly a helicopter, right?

He waved his palm at the ground in a motion for the copilot to stand by, and the other man nodded. Maybe the SEALs hadn't had time to train him, or maybe the guy just wasn't accustomed to being on the ground. God knew Miles would much rather be looking down on this road from a hundred feet up.

He forced himself to be patient. The stumbling figures on the road were the main danger, but the high growth on either side of the road made him nervous. The rotors made things a little better; the air they moved flattened the weeds out to some extent. Zombies didn't have guile, but their stupidity could be an asset, too. Attracted by such a loud target, they'd head straight for it, crawling over any obstacles they met with mindless dedication. So, while the road was a threat, the bigger threat was off to either side, because they could be right on top of Miles and Hickson before they could do anything about it. For now, the coast seemed clear. He judged the range, then lifted his rifle and began to take slow, measured shots.

The zombies made it easy, of course. They were slow, they didn't dodge, and they just kept coming. A human charge would have scattered when its component parts began falling to the ground. The approaching undead just didn't have the capacity to care.

The perceived ease of it was dangerous, of course. Becoming nonchalant about fighting them *was* the greatest danger in fighting them. Because if you focused too much on what was in front of you . . .

Miles grabbed Hickson's flight vest and yanked him backward. The man almost stumbled to the ground, but the zombie creeping up the ditch on his side face planted as its quarry disappeared. Miles finished the job with a double-tap to the head. He conducted another quick scan of the area in front of the chopper's nose. Another group had stumbled onto the road perhaps fifty yards away. Keeping one eye on them, Miles dropped his partial magazine and replaced it with a fresh one. He stashed the partial in the empty space in the pouch to reload later or use in case of emergency. He frowned at the brass littering the pavement, but there was nothing to do about it. Pete would have kittens at the waste of resources, but if this thing went smooth, maybe they'd have a little better access to ammo in the future.

Miles took a drink from his canteen before he realized that the copilot was shouting at him. "Are you crazy?"

He leaned over and put his mouth next to Hickson's ear. "They aren't going anywhere, champ. Stay cool and keep your heart rate down, it makes you more accurate. You watch the sides of the road, the range will be shorter and your weapon will be more effective. I'll thin them out from further away." The copilot shook his head, but finally gave Miles a thumbs-up to signal his understanding.

Miles glanced back up at the zombies. One was less torn up than the others and had pulled away from the pack. He raised his carbine and fired once. The leader collapsed to the pavement, and as an added bonus entangled the feet of two of the followers. He jerked his chin in their direction and shouted, "They have one speed, and we're not here long, right? This is a cakewalk. Try clearing out a Wal-Mart sometime."

This time, Hickson just stared. He opened his mouth to say something, paused, and then raised a hand to the side of his helmet. He turned around and nodded at the pilot. "We're full up," he yelled to Miles. "Get on!"

Miles put his rifle on safe and stepped around the nose of the Black Hawk to the side access door. Foraker and the crew chief were already inside. The big SEAL offered him a hand, and almost lifted Miles off of his feet and up into the cabin of the chopper. Miles selected a seat on the starboard side of the chopper and fussed with the seatbelt harness for a few moments before he figured it out. As he strapped in, the crew chief slammed the side door shut, and the roar of the Black Hawk's turbines intensified. Miles' stomach lurched as they lifted off the ground and rotated.

As he looked out the window, he saw staggering figures still coming on, oblivious that their quarry had left. His mouth went dry. There were hundreds of them out there. Another ten or fifteen minutes and they might have been overrun. It was a close-run thing, but these days, that knife's edge was often the difference between survival and death. For now, they'd survived. As the chopper banked forward and surged toward their final destination, he uttered a silent prayer that the rest of the mission would go as well.

Chapter 25

The clinic's small office sat in front of the entrance doors. This divided the floor space in two and gave the staff a central location to make notes on patients, store supplies, and relax. The disadvantage of the arrangement was that at a certain time in the morning, the rays of the rising sun slanted right through the front doors and made it uncomfortable for anyone sitting in there.

Tish had fallen asleep at one of the desks with her head on crossed arms. The sudden bright light landed right on her face, and she woke with an annoyed groan. It had been a long night. She'd worked the afternoon and early evening until Grady took over. With the hubbub in front of the clinic that morning, it had been all hands on deck for a while. She'd slouched in on only a few hours of sleep. *Just like being a resident again, except I'm not as bright-eyed and bushy-tailed as I was back then.* She took a sip of lukewarm tea from the mug on her desk and grimaced. If Grady or Frannie didn't have a fresh pot going, she was going to have to prop her eyelids open with toothpicks.

She rubbed her eyes with the balls of her hands as she stood and snaked around the side of the desk. There was a well-worn couch on the back wall of the office, and Grady

Scott snored on it with his back to the front doors. That was a new addition; he must have laid down at some point after Tish had nodded off. Well, no one had cried out in the interim, so Frannie must have kept things under control. Tish glanced over to the left. That side of the building had paired beds on the north and south walls, with curtains dividing them. Todd Jenkins and the three long-term patients rested in there. The opposite side of the building had been set up with their primitive surgical suite and an exam room. The chaos earlier that morning had forced them to put beds for Carter and her dad in the space.

The wall guard's injuries were much more life-threatening than those of her father. Carter's attacker had left him with a pair of deep stab wounds in his back. If the suspect had been aiming for his kidneys, they'd missed, though Tish was still concerned about peritonitis. Probing the wounds and stitching them closed had been a nerve-racking process that had taken most of the early morning hours to complete. She didn't think there'd been any damage to the digestive tract, but they had no way of knowing. Carter's cot was in the exam room, and a precious IV of painkillers, saline, and antibiotics hung on a stand beside him. If it wasn't for the supplies that Vir had brought back, they couldn't have done much more than stitch him up and pray. She hoped the medicine would make the difference.

Tish stifled a yawn as she walked into the surgery suite. Her dad's injuries weren't too bad — bumps and bruises, and the single stab wound to his left thigh. The blade had missed anything vital, and had even gone in parallel to the muscle fibers, so he was likely to recover. The limp should fade in time with physical therapy. What concerned Tish most was the possibility of a concussion. They'd tried to keep him awake to check him for symptoms, but he kept falling asleep. Even though he displayed confusion, he wasn't slurring his words, which was something, at least. Now more than ever, Tish felt a pang at all they'd lost. In the old days, they'd have been able to run a CAT scan, see if there was any internal damage, and correct it. They had so much *knowledge*, but no real way to act on most of it. It was so frustrating that she could barely resist the urge to scream. Tish stepped into the surgery suite and realized that her father wasn't alone. Frannie stood at the end of the cot, just looking at him. She cleared her throat, and the other woman jumped in surprise. Frannie turned, and Tish frowned at the odd look on her face.

"Everything all right?"

Frannie didn't speak for a moment but finally nodded. "Yeah. I guess it just hit me, looking at him. Time passes for all of us." She shook her head.

Tish looked at her father. He seemed to be comfortable, though his face was pale and drawn. Lord, Frannie was right. Right now, her dad looked every one of his fifty-five years. Somehow she always thought of him as this rock, this ever-present figure. That wasn't always going to be the case, was it? It was stupid, given all the death that had surrounded them for so long, but she'd never thought about losing her dad. Even with the risks he took on behalf of the community, the times he deployed overseas, she'd always felt that he would come back.

"He's going to be all right," Tish promised her friend, though she only half-believed it herself. "He's too mean to die. He's liable to wake up any minute and start barking orders from the bed."

Frannie gave her a wan smile. Tish reached out and took her by the arm. "You look like a hot mess, girl. It's your turn to get some shut eye. You got any coffee brewing?"

He was eight years late for work, but Miles doubted there was anyone left to mind.

Cartwright, the pilot in command, banked the Black Hawk as they crossed over the Ohio River. The man had given Miles a few choice words about the action in front of the canopy after they'd gotten underway. No one tried to speak after that. Maybe the view was just too depressing.

The vista outside of the window was as faded and worn as the countryside was green and blooming. The shattered, broken-off stumps of the I-71 and I-471 bridges hung over the sluggish river. The wreckage of the bridge deck and the cars that had rested upon it had created a partial dam. The chunks of concrete and steel had captured limbs and other floating debris.

The helicopter slashed between Paul Brown Stadium and the Great American Ball Park. In another time, this might have been a pregame flyby. Miles was on the wrong side of the helicopter to see the football field, but the home of the Reds was a wreck; blackened and scarred by fire. The tailgating lots were full of abandoned ambulances, FEMA trailers, and military vehicles. Shreds of tents rippled in the wind. They angled further northwest as Cartwright took the helicopter across downtown.

He leaned closer to the door and stared out. Miles frowned. He pulled away from the window and leaned closer to Ross. "Where are they?" he yelled over the noise of the chopper.

Ross gave him a look and put his mouth close to Miles' ear. "Hell if I know, brother. If your deputy is right, heading north, I guess."

Miles gave him a hard look, then yelled back, "Our welcoming party this morning didn't seem to be in a hurry to get anywhere."

Ross held both hands up and shrugged. Miles sighed and leaned back over to look out the window of the chopper again. Downtown flowed by beneath, but after a while, he had to turn away. He couldn't stand to look at the burned-down buildings, snarls of traffic jams, or the vague lines that could only be the skeletal remnants of the city's population. Shattered windows in skyscrapers testified to the final, desperate acts of people fleeing their certain doom. Faced with reanimated, carnivorous dead, leaping to your death seemed almost peaceful in comparison.

The reprieve didn't last long; Ross nudged him and nodded out the opposite window. Miles' first, and hopefully last, airborne commute was nearing its end.

The GenPharm office park sat near the Cincinnati Children's Hospital research tower. Though he hadn't worked on that side of the business, Miles had read enough e-mailed press releases to know that his former company had sponsored research projects into various childhood illnesses alongside the staff of CCH. Maybe it was more for PR purposes than actual altruism, but he'd never been in a position to judge one way or another. The entirety of his career there revolved around the networks and computers. And keeping his head down to avoid the chopping block after the downsizing and restructuring, of course.

Funny how different my priorities used to be, Miles mused. *I spent so much time in the car driving back and forth, and for what?*

Of course, if not for the reduction in hours and alteration of his schedule, Miles wouldn't have been so close to home on Z-Day. When everything fell apart, he would have been in the same tower the helicopter now approached — the twenty-story admin building.

This building, or the parking lot below, would have been his final resting place. At the motel, he hadn't cared enough about his job to obey the weapons at work policy; here, he'd always locked his carry gun in the car. The metal detectors at the entrance had made that decision an easy one.

All the buildings in the complex were structures of stainless steel and glass. Before, on a clear day they'd have sparkled in the sunshine. To some extent they still did, though the effect was much reduced. Broken windows dotted the complex, and dust and smoke stains smeared most of the intact ones.

The administration building — his old stomping grounds — was the tallest of the three main buildings of the office park. It loomed over the squat, warehouse-shaped form of the research and production facility. The final tower, the executive office building, was only two-thirds as tall as Miles' building, but it was more exotic in appearance. Where admin was all straight lines and right angles, the executive office building swooped and arched, from the decorative fountains in front — now overgrown with algae — to the CEO's helipad on the roof. Miles smirked and recalled how he used to look down at the top of the EOB as the old man came and went in his private helicopter. It was gone now, and he supposed that maybe the boss had made it out. *Wonder if he took anyone with him?*

It could have gone either way; Miles' only personal experience with the man had been from a single visit to his office to fix an issue on his assistant's computer. Miles might have been a potted plant or a painting on the wall for as much attention as the head of the company gave him. At the time, Miles had wondered if that wasn't worse than a dressing down.

The pitch of the Black Hawk's engines shifted as Cartwright slowed and began an orbit of the building. Solar panels lined the south and west side of the roof. Miles had always regarded them as a *definite* PR stunt. The power generated wasn't enough to run the server room, much less offset the electrical needs of the entire building.

As the rest of the roof came into view, Miles shifted, uneasy. Blocky air conditioning units sprouted from the graveled surface. The squared-off building that housed the elevator mechanicals and fire stairs sprouted on the north wall. Unlike the EOB, the admin building did not have a helipad, and it didn't look like there was enough open space for an impromptu replacement. He turned and looked at Lieutenant Ross. The SEAL caught the glance and smirked.

"Nowhere to land, right?" Ross yelled. Miles frowned and said nothing. The other man grinned. "No worries; Cartwright's a pro. He pulls into a hover over the elevator shack and you just hop on out. Easy peasy lemon squeezy."

"Yeah," Miles drew the word out. "Sounds like fun."

Ross clapped him on the back. Across the compartment, Foraker showed a broad mouthful of white teeth in the forest of his beard. Janacek didn't react at all. The intense young SEAL had his head leaned back against the bulkhead with the bill of his Padres cap tugged down over his eyes.

Is he sleeping?

The helicopter came to a stop. For a moment, the transition from airborne motion to airborne hovering created a queasy feeling in the pit of his stomach. The crew chief, Castillo, left his post near the cockpit and moved over to Miles' side of the chopper. "Here we go," he yelled out, giving Miles and the SEALs a thumbs-up. He slid open the side door of the chopper. The interior was immediately filled with the roar of the rotor blades and the wind effect off of the roof.

Castillo clipped a safety line to the interior of the helicopter and to his load-bearing harness in turn, then leaned out of the chopper. Using hand signals, he began guiding the chopper down. After a long moment of slow-motion falling, the helicopter drew into a hover again. Castillo drew back into the crew compartment and clapped Ross on the shoulder. "You're clear, Lieutenant."

Ross nodded and rose to a half-crouch. He leaned closer to Miles and shouted into his ear over the roar of the wind. "I'll lead the way. You come next, if you stumble or lose your footing, I'll be there to catch you, all right?"

Miles swallowed, and nodded. Foraker and Janacek collected their gear, including a massive duffel bag that took both of them to move. As Ross stepped into the doorway of the helicopter, Miles patted down his own equipment to ensure that everything was secure. When Ross jumped, Miles tugged on the sling of his rifle one more time, just to reassure himself that it wasn't going anywhere. Castillo beckoned, and Miles stepped forward.

Just focus on Ross, he told himself. *Don't look at what's around him. Ross, and the roof. That's your world now.*

In the end, it wasn't bad at all — Ross was right; Cartwright was a wizard with the helicopter. The right wheel was hovering a bare three feet over the roof of the elevator shack. Miles stumbled forward a bit as he landed, but he was able to steady himself and regain his balance on his own.

"Keep going," Ross said. "But wait on the roof!"

Miles nodded and bent over as he scrambled to the edge of the elevator shack's roof. Under the swirling rotors, the buffeting of the wind was tremendous; smaller bits of gravel flew around and smacked into his legs. He squinted and wished that he'd worn sunglasses or goggles of some sort to protect his eyes.

The architects who'd designed the admin building hadn't intended for frequent access to the top of the shack. There was no ladder. Miles dropped to his stomach and mentally estimated the drop. It wasn't bad, perhaps ten feet. The interior roof of the smaller building was likely to be low, but that at least meant the drop was manageable. He gripped the edge with both hands and rolled away. He grunted as his weight hit and let go after he'd slowed his fall. With the combination of his outstretched arms and height, the drop was next to nothing.

Particularly compared to jumping out of a helicopter.

There was a thump from the shack as Janacek and Foraker pitched the duffel out. Two smaller thumps in quick procession indicated the presence of the other two SEALs. The scream of the helicopter's engine pitched higher in volume. Miles crouched down and shielded his face as the gale-force winds atop the roof increased. There was a dull roar that fell off to near absolute silence as the helicopter banked away and headed north.

The storm of grit and debris died down, and Miles straightened. Without the need to shield his eyes, he was able to survey the rooftop. A low wall, about waist height, surrounded the entire perimeter. Scuppers perforated it here and there, for drainage. As he'd seen from the helicopter, the southern and western sides mounted aluminum frameworks with angled solar panels. The frames looked not unlike bleachers with the seats removed. If they had to camp out up here for a bit, Miles judged, the solar panels would make for a decent windbreak and shield them from rain if necessary.

The outbuilding housing the fire stairs and the elevator lift equipment was the only other notable structure atop the roof. Miles took a moment to study it as the SEALs lowered themselves off the top and brought the duffel down.

The heavy metal door to the fire stairs opened outward. There was a rusting metal coffee can to the side of the door that Miles assumed was full of cigarette butts. What was most interesting about the door were the newer-looking additions. A welding bead traced the seam between the door and its frame. Additionally, a thick steel bar hung across the door, supported by a pair of brackets fastened to the block walls of the shack. Coming up beside him, Ross noticed Miles' study and indicated the door with a jerk of his chin.

"First time in, we weren't sure how clear the building was. Standard procedure — stay up high and secure any points of access. The elevator car is at the bottom of the shaft, so the only way up from the ground floor is the stairway."

Miles nodded. "Hear any knocking?"

Ross chuckled, though Miles thought he detected a hint of unease to it. "Not yet. Haven't spent a ton of time up here, though. Long enough to weld and secure the door, access the server room, and determine we had no way in." He pointed at the other notable feature in the shack's wall — a set of metal double doors. "That's our way in."

Miles looked at the doors and then back to Ross. "I thought you said the elevator car was at the bottom."

Ross winked, and said, "Trust me." He turned to Foraker and Janacek as they came down off of the roof after the duffel. "Chief, I want you up on comms. Report in on our current status, to Hanratty as well as General Vincent. I'm sure Mr. Matthews will appreciate putting his people at ease. Brian, you're on overwatch. No engagements without clearance, we don't want a horde coming down on us."

"Hooyah, L-T," Janacek said. He shucked out of the straps of his rucksack and carried his rifle over to the roof's edge to set up shop.

"Highlander Six, this is Hatchet, how copy, over," Foraker intoned into the headset attached to his MBITR. "We are at the objective, over." He waited for a long moment, then shook his head at Ross. "No signal with Camp Perry, Mikey. May need to relay through Cartwright."

"Go ahead," Ross nodded. He knelt down at the duffel bag and unzipped it. "I'm going to take Mister Matthews on a tour." The lieutenant pulled a coil of heavy black rope out of the bag. "Ready?"

Miles nodded and stepped aside to let the SEAL lead the way. Ross moved to the double doors and pushed one open. At his nod, Miles stepped inside and let his eyes adjust to the dimness. It wasn't as bright as outside, but it also wasn't completely dark. As he adjusted to the difference, he saw why.

The interior of the elevator shack was clean and laid out in a well-ordered fashion. The concrete floor of the room was smooth and glossy, coated in an off-white paint. At the room's center, metal railings sprouted from the floor and surrounded the elevator shaft itself. In case the rails weren't noticeable enough, they were painted bright yellow with black bands winding around the horizontal members.

To one side, a pair of vertical I-beams sprouted from the concrete. Horizontal beams from the walls intercepted the vertical beams and supported a large assembly. Miles assumed this was the elevator lift motor itself; the cables from the shaft rolled up into a capstan on one side of it. Metal cabinets with high-voltage warning stickers lined the same wall. Thick power cables connected the cabinets to the motor and a conduit in the floor that must have led to the building's electrical system.

Light shone from the shaft. As Miles stepped forward, he noted that the topmost elevator exit doors were open. The light originated from there. *Huh.*

He turned to Ross. "We always figured the solar panels fed back into the building grid, but there must be some sort of cutoff that keeps this running." He stepped closer and leaned over the railing. The light didn't carry far enough to illuminate the bottom, so he could pretend that the shaft wasn't as tall as he knew it actually was.

The top floor of the admin building had been the employee cafeteria — so Miles had thought. He couldn't see much of the room beyond the elevator door, but he could see enough to note that it ended at a solid-looking security door with a card-reader installed in the wall next to it.

A hidden server room, running on its own auxiliary power, with no posted access from the building's lone elevator. *What in the world is going on here?* Miles found his voice. "You do realize there's a chance that I may not be able to open it."

Ross shrugged when Miles glanced at him. "Cross that bridge when we come to it," the other man said. "Let's take a look."

Miles looked back down the shaft. "Uh, well . . ."

"Ever rappel before?" Ross said.

"Yeah, no. Not my thing."

Ross chuckled. "All right, we'll do it a little different then. There's a ladder molded into this side of the shaft." He slapped the floor where they stood, across from the opening. "We run lines from the railing across there, climb down just a bit, and swing inside. I'll lead and grab you as you come in."

Miles frowned. "Sure," he said. "Sounds like an absolute blast. Glad I survived the end of the world to revisit high school gym class."

Ross shook his head and said, "Let's saddle up." The bundle of rope from the duffel turned out to be several coils. Ross secured a pair of doubled-over lines from the rail above the open door, knotting the ends into a complex arrangement with heavy-duty carabiners. He clucked over Miles' vest for a long moment before returning to the duffel and retrieving a new load-bearing harness. "Here, put this on. No offense, but I don't want to trust your life to that thing."

Miles joked, "What, adding eight years of hard use to something that was surplus to begin with isn't a good prescription for durability?" He adjusted the fit of the new harness and slung it over his existing one. He hefted his rifle and looked at Ross with a cocked eyebrow.

"I'm not leaving mine. You do what you gotta do." Ross clipped the first carabiner onto the rear of Miles' harness, then did the same for his own. He fussed over the arrangement of the lines for a few moments then finally nodded to himself. Ross threw one leg over the top railing, flashed a grin at Miles, and started his climb down the ladder.

"About ten steps, I'd guess," Ross murmured. His voice echoed a bit in the shaft, and the hair on the back of Miles' neck stood up. There was just something eerie about the sound — he hoped it didn't carry far. Failing that, maybe the building was empty. "And here we go."

Ross reached up to grab his ropes, pulled down on them, and kicked off from the wall. He swung surprisingly fast — to Miles, at least — and landed just inside the opening in the shaft. Ross' arms wheeled, and he reached on and grabbed the wall to steady himself as he attempted to catch his balance.

He was in.

The SEAL turned and gave Miles a thumbs up. "Let's do it."

Miles took a breath, gave the ropes a final tug to assure himself they were secure and threw his own leg over the top rail. When he got his second leg over, he froze on the edge with one foot on and the other seeking the top rung of the service ladder. He supposed this would have been less nerve-racking if the elevator car had been right below him. What he was about to do had to violate some sort of work safety practice. What would the signs say, after all? 'It has been 90 days since our last worker turned himself into a pancake'? Not likely.

Miles found the rung. Taking his time, he brought his other foot down to find the next one. His knuckles were white on the rail, but as he lowered himself the angle of his grip changed, and he had to shift to the middle rail. Down four steps, then five, and he had to shift from the rail and now he perched just on the rungs, who knew how many hundreds of feet in the air . . .

Seven down, then eight. On the bright side, the rungs were wide enough for him to have both feet on one at a time. Across the shaft, Ross murmured, "That's good. Keep one foot in place and turn."

Miles did as instructed. It didn't *look* like a long way to jump, but it sure felt like it. He licked his lips and looked back up. He imitated Ross' tug of the ropes, then went one better — he looped his forearm around them several times then grabbed hold. *Here goes nothing.*

He pushed off with his free-hanging leg. For a moment that felt like an eternity he hung in midair, and panic swept through him, but then gravity asserted itself. The ropes pulled tight around his forearm and he swung forward. It didn't feel as fast as it had looked for Ross, but he was sure that was just a matter of perspective. Before he was even aware of moving, he was inside the opening. His feet scrabbled for traction, and he felt the sensation of falling backward.

Ross clamped two hands on his harness, arresting his rearward motion. Momentum thus spent, Miles stood and took a deep, shuddering breath. He was in.

"Not so bad, right?" Ross said. Miles gave him what felt like a weak smile as he tried to stop the shaking that threatened to overwhelm his limbs.

"Right."

Miles uncoiled the rope from around his arm and rubbed it as Ross unclipped the rope from his own harness, then released Miles. In retrospect, wrapping it around his forearm hadn't been such a great idea. His long sleeve had protected him from rope burn, but his arm felt at once crushed and stretched. It throbbed in time with his heart.

Miles looked at the heavy metal door in the opening. The entranceway off of the elevator was no more than ten feet deep and just a bit wider than the elevator opening itself. The door sat in the exact center of the short corridor and was a flat, neutral gray.

Almost like a zombie's eyes, huh?

It could have been the twin of the server room entrance three stories down, right down to the label pasted on the outside of the door.

"Moment of truth," he said to Ross. He unbuckled the breast pocket of his shirt where he'd secured his GenPharm badge and drew it out. The plastic was starting to yellow and the picture had faded even though the card had sat in the darkness of his dresser drawer for years. If the card had used a magnetic strip, Miles doubted it would have continued to work after so long. GenPharm had switched to a combination thumbprint and embedded microchip system not long after Miles started. During that entire time, he'd never had to have the card replaced for a chip issue, only for annual picture updates. He slid the card into the slot and waited. *Work, work, work.*

The reader considered the chip, then the thumbprint scanner molded into it lit up. "So far, so good," Miles said and placed his thumb on the cutout. The activity light in the reader flashed as it considered the loops and whorls of his print and measured the temperature of his thumb.

The lock indicator on the reader changed from red to green, and with a solid thunk of disengaging solenoids, the door unlocked.

He reached out to open the door but Ross intercepted his arm before he could complete the motion. "Stand aside, please," the SEAL said. Miles nodded and moved into the far corner. Ross took a position just beside the door handle and pressed a button on his MBITR. "Chief, Brian, stand by. The door is open and I'm preparing to sweep." He released the button and listened for a moment. "Miles, how fast does that door lock?"

"It should auto-lock as soon as it swings back."

"Good. I need you to hold it open until I give the all-clear. If I come backing out, let me get out and then push it closed as fast as you can. I hope this room is clear, but you never know."

"You got it," Miles said and switched corners so that he was standing on the hinge side of the door. Ross waited until he'd completed the move, lifted his SCAR into firing position, and pulled the door open.

There was a slight hiss of air as the door seal broke; had the room been under negative pressure? Ross slid inside, and Miles stepped forward to hold the door open. He placed his foot between the jamb and the door and kept one hand on the knob.

From what he could see of the inside, the room was dim and clean, much like the opening off of the elevator. The floor consisted of suspended tiles, though there were gaps here and there to route data and power cables. Server racks lined the entire back wall, though most of the blade slots were empty. All the racks were lit up, and Miles winced. He hoped that the years had been kind, and no drives or fans had seized up. He didn't hear any noises — maybe the systems were good. If they weren't this was all for naught. Ross disappeared around a corner and returned a moment later. "Clear," he said. "Find something to prop the door open and come inside."

Miles searched the floor for a doorstop. In his server room, they used a triangular rubber door wedge one of the other IT guys had snagged from some mid-level manager's office. The petty act of inter-office thievery had been born more out of immature petulance than any real revolt. If they wanted their own, all they had to do was order it through the office supply portal. The manager was the kind of guy that looked down on anyone working on his systems, so a couple of the IT crew had decided to teach him an important lesson. Never mess with anyone who prepares your food or fixes your computers. The doorstop was level one; if the manager kept to his ways, the pranks ramped up. Passive aggressive? Oh, yeah. Tricksters or not, Miles missed those guys.

The personnel assigned to this room had no such accessories. Either propping the door open was against some security policy, or they didn't stay long enough to need it. It wasn't like there was a bathroom in the hall, after all.

He pulled a pistol magazine out of one of his pouches and laid it on the floor. It was just thick enough to keep the door from engaging the switch that activated the locking mechanism.

He stepped inside with one hand on his rifle. Ross had said it was clear, but he was well aware of how much vertical space there was between the floor tiles and the foundation below. It was more than enough room for someone to hide.

Miles stomped on one of the tiles as he moved through, then hesitated to listen. The room was as silent as a tomb save for the slow whir of a cooling fan drawing air up and out of the ceiling.

Ross gave him a puzzled look, and Miles jerked a thumb down at the floor. "There's usually a good two feet of space below these floor tiles. It gives plenty of room for cable runs and ventilation for cooling."

The SEAL blanched and shook his head. "Damn. Bad slip up." He sighed. "I need a vacation. So — what do you think?"

Miles looked around. The room curled into an abbreviated L-shape off of the entrance. It looked, as best as he could tell, as though it occupied one whole corner of the building, although none of the walls had any windows. He studied them for a moment, noting the thick conduits that passed through each of the exterior walls, before realizing where they stood. "Of course. The company signage is on those walls there. There would never have been offices here anyway, the logo would have gotten in the way. The ceiling in the cafeteria is so high that you don't pay attention to the actual dimensions. This part is right above the kitchen, and there's a faux wall over the serving line so you'd never even pick up that there's this much dead space between the roof and the next open floor." He studied the rest of the room.

The server racks extended across just the one wall, and all the remaining walls were plain unadorned concrete. In the leg of the L-shape, a workstation sat in the center of the space along with a single chair. On top of the workstation sat a large, wide-aspect flat panel monitor and a keyboard and mouse. One side of the keyboard supported an auxiliary card reader, piggybacking off a built-in USB port. The rest of the room's interior was devoid of, well, *anything*. No posters, long-dead houseplants, or family pictures that would signify in any small way that this was a place of work. Miles moved over to the computer and noted the slim bundle of Cat6 and power cabling wire-tied to one of the workstation's legs. The end near the floor descended into a small port, heading to parts unknown. The rest provided power to the monitor and a small NUC unit just a bit larger than a regulation hockey puck bolted to the VESA plate on the back of the screen. Miles pointed it out to Ross.

"Next unit of computing, we switched over to them a few years before Z-Day. Neat little systems, solid state, they can do pretty much anything a bigger PC can do without the wasted desk space." Miles rubbed his chin. "I don't get it, though. You said your source told you this was where GenPharm did the vaccine research. This looks like some sort of massive data backup setup."

Ross looked at him and worked his mouth as though he were chewing on a particularly tough piece of meat. "This is the right place, based on the information we obtained."

"And you know this guy wasn't shining you on, because . . . ?"

"I can assure you of his veracity. More than that, I can't say. Compartmentalized, need-to-know information."

Miles looked at the other man for a long, uncomfortable moment. Finally, he sighed and said, "Shit. Whatever. Let's see what we can get out of this thing."

He pulled the chair out and sat down in front of the workstation. After hunting around for a moment, he found the power button for the NUC, and the screen came to life as the little computer booted into the operating system.

"So far, so good," Miles said as the multicolored logo faded into a login screen. He slid his badge into the reader.

When the indicator light turned green, he thought for a moment. *Bad time to forget your password. No pressure, now.*

He tapped in what he thought was the password, crossed mental fingers, and hit enter. The system considered the password for a moment, then flashed a rectangular error message on the screen. "Shit," Miles hissed, and then shook his head. He cleared the error message out and tried one more time. Again, error. He read it twice to make sure he wasn't entering a wrong password. No such luck.

"It won't let you in?"

"The genius," Miles made air quotes with his fingers, "who put this setup together didn't realize that the authentication servers are down on the 9th floor. And they never ran power from the solar panels down there. So all this stuff is just sitting here twiddling its thumbs and the gatekeeper isn't even powered up." He rested his elbows on the desk and dropped his head into his hands. "We're going to have to go down there."

Chapter 26

"Twelve freaking stories," Janacek grunted. "I wouldn't recommend it." He shot Miles a look. "Not with a rookie climber. We don't have enough rope for a safety margin, either."

They'd regrouped at the top of the elevator shaft in the maintenance shack. The SEALs were in the midst of a hushed, fiercely worded debate over how to get down to the ninth floor. Miles had little to offer on the subject and listened with one ear as he made a slow circuit around the interior. Poking his nose into the various toolboxes and collections of electronics was far more interesting than the conversation raging over their latest obstacle.

"I could belay him down," the Chief offered.

"Maybe," Ross said. "That's a hell of a long way to lower him, though, Chief, and we don't have any equipment to arrest the line if you lose your grip."

"We don't have enough *rope*, Lieutenant," Janacek said. "But I'm repeating myself. Even if the Chief lowers our consultant, we have to assemble down there one at a time if you want to forget safety lines. We could do short lines and just carabiner to each rung in turn, but that's a lot of repetition and a lot of chances to slip up."

"We could pop the weld and take the stairs," Foraker offered.

"It would be too loud without the welder," Ross mused. "But the building seems unoccupied."

"Yeah, we think the building is clear, but what if it's not? Say we crack open the door and there's a herd of stiffs stumbling around down there. Backup's one hell of a long way off, Mikey."

Ross growled in annoyance. "Okay, fine, so we don't go down at all. Miles, can you go through the drives and figure out which ones have the relevant data?"

Miles shrugged and turned to face the other men. "Doubt it. More likely than not, they're RAIDed in some fashion, so if we pull one drive out of an array it's not going to be able to have access to all the information. The data will read like junk." He chewed on his lower lip and tried to think of another option, but failed. "No, our best bet is to grab the server blade from downstairs and install it in these racks. Then I can authenticate and we're in." *I hope.* Given that someone had put the entire system together without his former department's knowledge or input, would it even accept his administrator credentials? *One problem at a time.*

"So we're back to square one, then," Ross said. "Suggestions?"

"Could set up the hi-frequency transmitter. Radio back to base, see if they can top off the Black Hawk, and send us some more climbing gear." Janacek offered.

"Possible," Ross said. "Chief?"

The other man just grunted. That must have been Chief-speak for 'give me a minute', because the other two SEALs fell silent.

Miles turned back to the wall of electronics in the back of the room and tried not to think about the topic of conversation. The thought of hanging hundreds of feet in the air left him cold with a tight feeling in the pit of his stomach. But what other choice did they have?

The builder of this room had run and labeled the conduits and equipment with a precision that warmed him to the depths of his obsessive-compulsive heart. There was just something satisfying about neatly-arranged cabling. When he'd first started, the server rooms had been a mess with bundles of cable going every which way without rhyme or reason. Over time, as they replaced or upgraded equipment, they'd arranged the cabling throughout the building in a more orderly fashion. Maybe it hadn't made things work any better, but it gave him a subtle sense of satisfaction every time he badged his way through the door.

He hadn't had anything to do with the layout of the elevator shack, of course, but whoever had been in charge must have shared some of the same sympathies. The wire feeds from the solar panels came into the room inside of a series of labeled PVC conduits, which terminated inside a cabinet full of equipment marked 'inverters'. More conduits fed into a series of PowerWall units further down the chain. The conduit containing the combined, regulated output of the panels traced over to the corner nearest the server room, then went down through the floor and into the room below. Miles followed that conduit around in a slow stroll. A workbench and pair of rolling tool cabinets divided the solar power equipment from the elevator motor. The arrangement didn't look so much purposeful as it did an efficient use of coincidental space. A wire shelving unit to one side of the workbench held lengths of heavy electrical cable. *Replacement parts, I guess.*

Miles stopped pacing. He looked at the lengths of cable on the shelves, then at the outputs. "Guys," he announced. "I've got a better idea."

Getting down to ground level was becoming a habit.

Pete frowned as he pulled open the door and stepped inside the clinic. He'd never liked hospitals, much. Their smell became unbearable after his accident. On the bright side, the commercial cleansers that lent that particular nasty scent were not present here. They didn't have any. There was the slight scent of sickness in the air, but it wasn't overpowering. There was enough ventilation built in that fresh air carried most of the smell away. If he closed his eyes, Pete could almost pretend that this *wasn't* a hospital. Almost.

In the office, a curly-haired brunette raised her head and blinked bleary eyes at him. He smiled. "Hey, Frannie. Where's Larry?"

She pointed to his right and laid her head down on her crossed arms. *Poor kid.* He was feeling exhausted himself, but at least he was acclimated to it. Up until recently, the clinic had been a pretty slow building. Now, unless he missed his guess, the place was almost overflowing.

He stepped into the right half of the clinic. He was most familiar with the exam room, but he'd never seen a patient on a cot in there. They *were* overflowing. Pete studied an oblivious Carter Burke for a moment, then shrugged. He hoped the other man pulled through — maybe he'd seen something that Pete hadn't been able to.

Last night's events had left him frantic. He'd kept an eye on the motor pool as best as he could while trying to maintain observation of the woods. When everything went to hell, he froze with indecision. Should he keep watch inside the community, in case he saw something that Larry and his boys didn't, or should he make sure that Murphy's Law didn't choose that moment to kick them in the teeth? In the end, he'd settled for switching back and forth as fast as he could. Amazingly enough, the zombies outside of the wire hadn't even seemed to *notice* the hubbub going on. They'd been as still as statues every time Pete flicked the night-vision back over to them.

As far as what had gone down in the motor pool and in front of the clinic, he'd seen a bit of the action, but not enough to identify anyone. The blaze of Larry's flashlight whited out the night-vision. By the time he'd been able to adjust the intensity, the attacker who'd stabbed Larry and Carter was long gone, as was the visitor to the motor pool. *Damn comedy of errors.*

"Pete," Tish said from behind him, and he turned. A wan-looking man in a flannel shirt and blue jeans stood next to her. "I'm discharging Todd, here. Larry's in the surgery suite."

He gave her a nod and turned away as she began to issue instructions. From the sound of the conditions she was laying out, Todd shouldn't be released. But, as he'd noticed before, they needed the bed space.

He stepped into the next room. A lone cot sat in the far corner. From the collection of equipment and rolling cabinets around it, he guessed the bed had made a severe impact on the normal flow of the room. Pete steeled his nerves and forced himself to look at his friend.

He'd never seen Larry look so drawn; he looked like a literal shell of his former self. The weight of their combined years hit him all at once. With a muttered curse, Pete allowed himself to fall into the chair sitting beside the folding cot.

"We've seen a lot of hard miles, Top," he managed. "I daresay we're closer to the end than the beginning."

"Speak for yourself," Larry whispered, and opened his eyes. "I'm too damn pretty to die." He looked at Pete for a long moment, then closed his eyes and groaned.

Pete sighed and shook his head. "She didn't tell me you were awake. You did a piss-poor job of instilling proper manners into that girl."

Larry grinned. "I guess I'm a bad influence." He tried to sit up, but grimaced and relaxed. "Damn. I feel like I went ten rounds with Rousey."

"Rousey's zombie chow, but yeah, she'd still kick your ass," Pete said agreeably.

"Just because you're an officer doesn't mean I have to put up with your mouth. Make yourself useful and bring that water over here."

A plastic glass with a bending straw sat on one of the carts near the bed, and Pete held it while Larry took a few sips. "I hope you got a good look at the train that hit you, bud, because I couldn't see shit."

The other man sighed and said, "Nope. Pretty sure the visitor to the motor pool was a dude. Our little poetry killer, I'm not so sure. Kind of on the short side."

"A dude, and a short man or woman. That's something, at least. You sure the person who got you and Carter was the same one who killed Ronnie?"

"Couple of knives got left behind. The one in my leg was nothing special, but Tish says the one that stuck Carter was a match for the one used to kill Ronnie."

"She told you all that, huh?"

"I may have badgered her a bit," Larry allowed. "Now that I'm awake she keeps coming back in here to keep me that way. I told her she might as well give me something to work over in my head." He cracked an eyelid and stared Pete down. "I got something for you, Cap. Hang onto it so it doesn't end up in the back of a locker in the warehouse." He jerked a thumb toward the floor. Pete stooped down and looked under the bed. A shallow plastic pan held what seemed to be Larry's personal effects. There were no pants; he supposed they'd cut them off to get to the wound. What there was, though . . . he raised an eyebrow.

"Is that a VEPR?"

"Oh, yeah," Larry said. Pete hefted the super-sized shotgun and grunted at the weight. "Should be a few spare magazines in my duffel, too." He paused for a moment, then said, "But you came here for a reason, looks like. What's up?"

Pete slung the VEPR and crossed his arms over his chest. He hadn't worked out in his head how we wanted to spill the beans. He'd been expecting that Larry would be out for a bit, and give him some time to collect his thoughts. Now, though . . .

Don't wuss out on him. You've held out long enough — he needs to know.

Pete nodded to himself. "You're right, I need to fill you in on something."

Larry caught the tone of his voice and cracked an eye to study his face. "What, is Miles okay? Is my leg worse than Tish is letting on?"

"Last I heard, Miles is fine, and you'll be dancing in no time."

"Couldn't dance before."

"Whatever," he grumbled. "I should have told you this a while back, but to be honest with you, I wasn't sure if I was going off of my rocker or not. And yeah, I know y'all have been whispering about me spending so much time up in the observation post. Well, I've got a damn good reason for it."

"I'm telling you, it's going to work," Miles argued. "Look, the elevator motor has some pretty heavy duty capacitors. That way, if the power goes out, there's still enough juice to run the elevators to the ground floor and let everyone out. Disaster recovery 101. We temporarily disconnect the server room and run a new cable to the inputs on the elevator motor. With me so far?"

"What happens to the servers when they lose power?" Ross asked. "Do we need to worry about losing data?"

Miles shook his head. "No, no, it's fine. The rack units have uninterruptible power supplies built in; when they detect a power loss they shut down the systems if the batteries drop below a certain level. Plus the drives in there are all solid-state — no moving parts. It's redundant six ways from Sunday. Trust me on that, I checked." He shrugged. "Depending on how long it takes us to get what we need the room may not even shut down."

"Fair enough," Ross said. "I'm listening."

"All right, so depending on the voltage output of the battery packs we wait until the elevator capacitor charges.

Once it's ready, we run it up from the ground floor to the server room using the maintenance controls up here. We get in and take it down to the ninth floor. We get to the server room and get out with the right blade. Ride back up here in style and disconnect the elevator. It drops back down to the first floor on emergency power, and we boot the server room back up. Only this time the authentication server is powered-up on the local network, and I can log in." *I hope.*

"Two shooters in the elevator, one up top in reserve," the Chief mused. "I like the sound of that better than one at a time down a ladder."

"Building off of that," Janacek interjected, "what's the top of the elevator car look like? It would be a hell of a lot safer to not jump down into a potential kill box until we're sure that we're not ringing a dinner bell when the doors open up."

"No idea," Miles admitted. "But we don't *have* to open the doors; the controls have numbers for each floor and another pair of toggles for opening and closing the doors. Once it's charged, we can run it up and check it out from above."

"I like that better," Ross mused. "Who knows if the elevator is empty right now?"

"Cheery as always, Mikey," grinned the Chief. "What do you need to get started, Mr. Matthews?"

Miles shrugged. "There are plenty of tools. Maybe another set of hands?"

"Sounds right up your alley, Janacek," Ross ordered. "I'm going to see if I can get Cartwright or Camp Perry on the horn, keep them in the loop."

Janacek slapped Miles on the shoulder. "Let's do it, nugget."

Chapter 27

Dantzler was too short on sleep to put up with Lloyd's grumbling.

Just before noon, he lost his patience for the passive-aggressive remarks that the other man seemed to view as both biting and clever when they were nothing of the sort. He lowered his binoculars and turned away from his study of the Wild as he casually remarked, "Lloyd, if you're unhappy with the terms of your position, we can discuss your exit from this venture." He stopped speaking until the silence became uncomfortable, then added, "You can stay behind. We'll rough you up a bit, tie you up and throw you under one of the beds. When you're found, no one will believe you were ever involved. But trust me — this will be your last chance to blow this Popsicle joint on your own terms. When the military shows up in force, that's all she wrote. You can say bye-bye to your little taste off the top. Uncle Sam don't go in for graft and corruption unless it's *his* skim. Hell, for that matter, they may even draft your ass and send you off to rid the world of cannibals. But I need to know, right now. And if you're in, shut the fuck up." By now Ben and Victor had drifted out of the cabin to see what all the fuss was about. No one else was in earshot;

Dantzler wasn't stupid enough to spout off in front of witnesses. "And the same goes for you two," he added as he stared them down. Both men broke eye contact and looked as though they'd rather be somewhere else.

Lloyd held out both hands. "I'm cool, boss, I'm cool. You just got me out of sorts over last night."

"You the boss, Lloyd? You expect me to clear everything with you before I do it?"

"No sir, not at all."

Sir. Dantzler liked that, and for a moment, he entertained the notion of not dumping Lloyd's corpse in the river when they got to the boat. Just for a moment, though. "Well, let me lay it out for you boys, then. Just this one time. We're golden for fuel. You would know that if you listened to anything I said yesterday. But it came at a price. Now, I don't know about y'all, but I kind of feel like there's more to life than MREs and boiled river water. So here I am last night thinking to myself, hey, since Buck didn't make it back, his stash should still be intact. Booze, guns, ammo, who the hell knows what he wanted to hide away from Piper and the boys. Should have been a milk run to check his cubbyhole. Yeah, in the end, it wasn't. But I ain't taking any shit over it, either. It's just bad luck, is all."

"It's all anyone is talking about in the cafeteria," Victor observed. "Sounds like Carter Burke got messed up pretty good, and Larry, too, but he's awake, I guess." He gave Lloyd an accusing glare. "And like you said, he didn't see your face, else the rest of the law dogs would be all over us. They're not even talking about you — everyone is talking about the killer."

"All the better," Dantzler declared. "Let them chase their tails trying to hunt down their little knife murderer.

After last night, I reckon they got about zero chance of figuring out who it is unless they catch her in the act."

"Her? A chick killed Ronnie and gutted Carter?" In point of fact, the attacker stabbed him in the back, but Dantzler didn't feel the need to correct the rumor mill. It made his getaway look that much better.

"Yup. I don't know how good a look she got at me, but I got a good glimpse at her."

Lloyd chimed in. "Hell, boss, who is it?"

Dantzler waved the question off. "Doesn't matter, we're out of here tonight. Ben, your last batch still on track to load up after dark?"

"Should be."

Good. Contrary to his explanation, Dantzler wasn't planning on using the meth as trade goods, no matter who they ran into. He figured he was going to need it to stay sharp when he was by himself out in the Wild. The one drawback to this entire plan was the loss of being secure in a good night's sleep, but the military showing up was all the hint he needed. It had been a good run, but he needed to get out of here. Even the neighborhood watch supervision of the council had been annoying at times. He'd lose his damn mind under military governance, or God forbid if he himself got drafted. Ivan Dantzler risked his ass for no man without adequate compensation.

"All right. So, the plan is we roll out right around midnight. I want everyone sharp, so rotate shifts and catch as many Z's as you can. One person on watch at a time. Anyone asks, we're sharing a stomach bug. That will keep 'em all out of our hair." He tossed his binoculars to Lloyd. "You're up, buddy."

Dantzler clambered down the ladder on the side of the cabin to the ground. As he pulled open the door, a final thought occurred to him. "And just in case — if a good-looking brunette comes around looking for me, I ain't here."

The job went more smoothly than Miles had any right to expect. The PowerWall units were daisy-chained together in a neat row. The last unit in the line connected to the electrical conduit that led into the server room below them. The difficult part was splicing compatible ends on either side of an electrical cable that was long enough to reach the elevator motor inputs while still being of a heavy enough gauge to handle the current. What they ended up with was a hybrid monstrosity that looked like an engorged python in the middle where the union was. Miles and Janacek had hand-spliced the cables together, wrapped electrical tape around the splices, and then shielded each connection even more with rags and duct tape. It was redneck as hell, but the only thing that mattered was whether it worked. They strung the cable across the workbench and connected the cable ends to the appropriate ports.

Miles' hand hovered over the switch on the PowerWall module that enabled the output. "Moment of truth, fellas," he said to Janacek and Foraker. "Cross your fingers and toes." He pushed the button, and a small green LED lit above the output port.

The three of them turned and looked at the motor housing in expectation. After a few moments of silence, Miles cursed and said, "Maybe there's not enough current. It should still charge the capacitor, but maybe . . ." Before he could finish his thought, the small, square LCD screen mounted on the motor housing lit up. "Hot damn," Miles whispered. "It worked."

He rushed over to the motor, followed by the other men. Readouts flickered on the small screen as the controller went through its diagnostic boot-up. He found that he was holding his breath in anticipation, and he forced himself to let it out. If it didn't work, they'd cross that bridge when they came to it. Adapt, react, overcome; Charlie Mike; all the old catch-phrases Pete had hammered into his head when he was growing up, except now it wasn't a failed math test or a bad date. This was for *all* the marbles. The controller completed its cycle, and reported, in bold black lettering, SYSTEM READY. Miles couldn't help himself, he grinned like a fool as he tested the controls. There wasn't much to them; the touch membrane had a four-button directional pad with a button labeled SELECT/ENTER in the center. Below the down arrow was another button, this one bereft of decoration save for a stylized back arrow; technological hieroglyphics.

Miles paged through the menus a few times until he was certain of the options available to him. Satisfied, he began to select buttons in earnest. Step one — put the elevator into diagnostic mode, which locked out the panel inside the car. This would prevent the car from returning to the ground floor in a set time frame after the doors opened and closed. It made things more difficult if they had to move fast, but with someone up top running the show, he hoped that it wasn't a huge risk on their part.

Though there was no button for the topmost floor inside of the elevator, the display listing the floors programmed into the elevator did have the extra floor, though without numeral designation. It was simply labeled "T". Assuming this was the server room, he highlighted it and pressed the enter button. Almost immediately, the motor whined to life and began to pull up cabling. The hum of the electrical housing and the whir of the cables was surprisingly quiet, though the sudden noise still startled him. At the bottom of the shaft, the elevator car rose after years of inactivity. They moved to the railing and looked down. At first, there wasn't much to see. Foraker clicked on his rifle-mounted light and trained it down into the shaft. For a time they could see little, but as the car rose shapes came into slow focus.

With a whir, the car came to a stop just below them at the entrance to the server room. There was no arrival bell or sound of the doors opening; in the independent operation mode, that required another command in the menu. None of them moved from where they stood to attempt that action; the three men stared at the top of the car, frozen. "Oh," Miles whispered. "Oh, man."

The top of the elevator was nice and flat, and as he looked at it Miles noted that it was liable to serve them just fine to travel down to the 9th floor. A system of pulleys and guides distributed the cables across the top and along a pair of metal beams that also served to support the weight of the car. Wheels and guides on the ends of the beams kept the car centered and riding on rails inset to the concrete of the elevator shaft. Electrical cabling from the center beams terminated in electrical junction boxes and provided power to the interior lights and controls. A metal hatch perhaps two feet square sat on one side of the central beams.

On top of that hatch, curled up as though sleeping, lay the dead woman.

It was impossible to tell much about her; after so many years she was little more than bones in a business suit. The cut and style of it made Miles think that she was on the younger side. One of the sales representatives, perhaps. She was barefoot, and while it was impossible to say for certain, Miles didn't think she'd been bit or injured. There were no telltale bloodstains on the elevator's roof. She looked for all the world as though she'd climbed up and out, closed the hatch, and laid down to sleep.

"How?" Miles managed.

None of the SEALs answered for a long moment, but when Foraker finally spoke there was a hitch in his voice. "Maybe she held out for a while after Z-Day. At some point she ran out of break room food or vending machine snacks, I guess. Didn't take the stairs, for whatever reason. Lights still had to be on, for the elevator to work. She rides down, but there's a welcoming crew for her in the lobby. Maybe she's unlucky and that's the moment the power goes out, or maybe it *was* out all along, and her trip was all the juice the elevator had left. The natural instinct in a time like that is to climb, get up and away. I imagine that's in our genes from the caveman days, run from the lions, and tigers, and bears. But now she's on top, danger on the bottom, no way out going up, and no food and water." He studied the ladder inset into the wall of the elevator shaft. "If she had a cell phone or some other source of light, she might have seen the ladder. She could have taken it up to the top and . . . I don't know. She may have just given up, in the end. Dehydration would have killed her."

"How long does something like that take?" Miles asked.

"Three or four days, maybe. It wasn't quick." Foraker grimaced. "Come on, let's find a blanket or something. We can do that much for her."

Chapter 28

Two days of peace and quiet were already grating on Hanratty's nerves.

It wasn't that he *wanted* some excitement. For almost a decade he'd trained himself not to trust any perceived safety unless he was at sea. Staying in one spot this far from a body of water made him jittery.

It didn't help that he felt like a third wheel. He'd led the troops in PT first thing in the morning, and after that, it had been a whole lot of nothing. Baxter, at least, had found enough people to interview that he was out of Hanratty's hair. How long that would last was an open question. As for his team, they were doing a detail clean and inspection of the LAV's weaponry. They'd been running and gunning for far too long, and he was taking the opportunity presented by their surroundings to ensure everything was in tip-top shape. The fact that sitting on top of the LAV on a sunny spring day was rather pleasant made the chore of disassembling the pintle-mounted machine gun seem not much of a chore at all.

The outright hostility of the community had dissipated since his speech. He'd tried not to oversell the possibilities — plans often changed, these days, in accordance with reality on the ground, but he'd been unable to push down the swell of hope that crested in him as he considered what these survivors had built on their own. One of the first missions the military remnant had undertaken was to determine where to obtain sources of fuel. That was easier said than done. The US Strategic Petroleum Reserve sat on the coast of the Gulf of Mexico. This reduced the risk in accessing it, but much of the stores were crude, unrefined oil. This was unsuitable for use in the destroyers, hospital ships, and various civilian craft that had attached themselves to the fleet of Navy ships. As fuel supplies dwindled, they stripped the smallest ships of anything useful and scuttled them. The crews transferred to the larger vessels. In some cases, they were useful, and could augment the surviving personnel. More often than not, they were just extra mouths to feed.

Even with the reduction it was still a close run thing. The surviving military and civilians were treated to the incongruous sight of nuclear-powered submarines and an aircraft carrier taking smaller, conventional-fueled vessels under tow.

In the Caribbean, the Hovensa refinery on the island of St. Croix had, at one time, been one of the largest in the world. Inefficient and polluting, the refinery passed through multiple hands and states of shutdown and renewal in the years before Z-Day. The final iteration of the refinery was a conversion to an oil storage terminal.

When much of the workforce succumbed to the outbreak, the refinery sat idle. When the Navy reached St. Croix, the equipment was somewhat worse for wear from the maintenance-free period in the tropical weather. Despite that, a team of Navy engineering mates and civilian volunteers got it up and running on a limited basis. At full capacity, the refinery was capable of producing half-a-million barrels of refined product each day. Given the reduction in fuel needs, they needed but a fraction of the refinery's total capacity. The overage gave them a slow-building surplus. It was that surplus with which command hoped to begin the recovery of the American mainland. The island hadn't come cheaply; the infected had fought them tooth and nail for it. Before Z-Day, St. Croix's population had numbered over 50,000 souls, and vast numbers of them had succumbed to the Brazilian flu.

Hanratty and the Marines cleared St. Croix in slow and methodical fashion. The fighting was almost as intense as the retreat from Iraq, but the hard lessons of the retreat were as ingrained into the Marines as their very names. They fought from behind prepared positions, from within armored fighting vehicles, and did their level best to keep the infected at arm's length. Casualties were minimal.

Rebuilding on St. Croix had begun, and the island now supported overflow from the fleet and experimental farming efforts. In the end, though, there just wasn't enough landmass to feed the survivors, and so Hanratty's long road had moved on from the Caribbean idyll, up the eastern seaboard, to here.

Ironic, of course, given that he'd ended up so close to home. If St. Croix had been rough, Toledo was liable to be hell on earth. Part of him held out hope that his family had made it to a place of safety. The more logical part just hoped that their deaths had been quick.

He'd reached down to begin the process of reassembling the M-240 when a frantic voice cried out from inside the LAV's crew compartment.

"Captain, the BFT is going crazy! Something's up!"

411

Hanratty abandoned the pile of machine gun parts and slid down the side of the LAV. When he hit the ground he was up and inside in only a few steps. He waved Patterson to the side and took his position in front of the BFT screen.

FLASH FLASH ALL STATIONS BE ADVISED WE ARE UNDER ATTACK UNKNOWN NUMBERS OF INFECTED HAVE BREACHED THE PERIMETER.

"What the hell?" Hanratty managed. He'd given them the head's up with plenty of time to spare. How in the world had they missed a horde large enough to get through the active and passive defenses? He narrowed the channel down to his immediate command and tapped a short message.

HIGHLANDER 5 HERE, PLEASE CONFIRM RECEIPT OF PRIOR INTEL REGARDING APPROACHING HORDE.

He didn't have to wait long; things must have been hopping in the communication shack.

INTEL RECEIVED BUT NOT CONFIRMED BY RECON. THEY JUST CAME OUT OF NOWHERE. STAND BY FOR COMM HAND OFF.

Hanratty frowned but waited.

THIS IS HIGHLANDER 6 ACTUAL, ARE YOU THERE CAPTAIN?

"Holy shit," Hanratty breathed. That was General Vincent himself. Things must be going to hell in a hand basket if the old man was taking personal charge.
YES SIR, STANDING BY.

The reply came almost immediately. IS YOUR SITUATION SECURE?

AYE SIR, WALLS ARE SOLID, CIVILIANS ARE WELL EQUIPPED AND WELL TRAINED.

The General and his team stewed over that a little bit longer this time. WE MAY LOSE COMMS SHORTLY, FALLING BACK TO SECONDARY LINES DUE TO PERIMETER BREACH. REMAIN IN YOUR CURRENT POSITION AS YOU MAY BE NEEDED TO EVAC HATCHET. AIRFIELD CURRENTLY UNSECURE AND UNABLE TO EFFECT PICKUP. DIVERTING WHISKEY TO SECONDARY LZ FOR REFUEL.

Hanratty swallowed. "Hell," he said and tried to visualize the layout of the camp. If they had already lost the airfield and were close to losing the comms shack, over half of the base was overrun already. Then the insinuation behind the General's words hit him. Ross and his team had just been stranded in the middle of a city that had at one time boasted a population of over 300,000. If the helicopter made it to the backup airfield and was able to refuel, they'd still be short of fuel and have to land somewhere between here and Cincinnati. He grabbed a map and began measuring off distances. The LAV was almost bingo fuel as it was; would the community be able to spare any? It would have been an easier sell with the promise of rapid resupply via helicopter, but given the current situation of his fellow troops he could hardly promise that.

Hanratty rubbed his chin and realized the General was still waiting for a response. UNDERSTOOD SIR. WILL STAND BY AND BE READY TO MOVE AS NEEDED.

One way or another, they'd figure it out. The military hadn't been in the business of leaving troops on the battlefield *before* the end. Now, if possible, that practice was even more paramount — the living were far too vital a resource to squander.

He'd stashed his Spider-man backpack outside before heading to school that morning. He figured it would be easier to get up early and avoid any of the other kids rather than having to make the run after school. Most of his housemates tended to play or hang out outside after class was over, but quite a few congregated in the house. Even with a couple of bottles of water, some venison jerky, and an aluminum baseball bat, the bag hung slack on his shoulders as they reached the south fence.

Twigs carried a light load. He'd tucked the arm brace of his slingshot into the waistband of an old fanny pack. The pouch hung low on his hip, heavy with ball bearings. Despite the weight, the smaller boy moved with quick, jerky motions.

Nervous, Alex judged. Hell, so was he.

Trina waited for them at the base of the apple tree behind Miss Val's house. As they approached, she looked around and stood. She reached behind her back and pulled a wrapped bundle from beneath her shirt. "I got it, no sweat." She handled the bundle to Alex and stood with an expectant look on her face. "Hey, Twigs."

"Hey, Trina!" Twigs chirped.

He knelt down and unfolded the rag to reveal a black pistol and a pair of spare magazines. He hefted the pistol to get a good sense of its weight. It wasn't as heavy as his rifle, but it was sturdy. Alex ensured the safety was on before inspecting it. He ejected the magazine and fingered the slide. The metal on one side had the name 'Mosquito' on it. "It's empty," he commented.

"I've got two boxes of bullets and the silencer over here." She turned to point at the base of the tree when a fourth voice intruded into their conversation.

"Field trip day, kids?"

Alex froze, then turned slowly. The voice had surprised him, but as he turned to consider Cara's smirk, he kicked himself for not expecting it. Of *course* she'd overheard them at lunch. Why wouldn't she?

"Jeez, Alex, does everybody know about this?" Twigs complained.

"I didn't tell her," Alex replied. "She heard us talking." He looked at Cara with a raised eyebrow and the smirk turned into a grin.

"Pro tip. When planning nefarious deeds, use your inside voices," Cara pronounced as she marched in their direction. "Good news is, I didn't rat you guys out."

"Wait, what?" Twigs said.

"What he said," Alex added.

Cara settled to the ground and crossed her legs in a single, graceful motion that momentarily overwhelmed Alex's focus. "I'm going with you guys." She shrugged. "What the hey. Sounds fun." She jabbed a forefinger at Alex. "So what's the plan?"

Flabbergasted, he opened and closed his mouth a few times before his brain kicked back into gear. "Umm, well, we're going to head down that way and climb the fence. There are a couple of trees down there that we figure will keep the guys on the west wall from seeing us."

"That's a terrible place to go over," Cara said, and Alex shook his head in surprise. She explained. "The best place is right here. The apple tree covers most of the view of the fence from the Crow's nest *and* either wall. Once we're over, we get down to the creek and follow it. Here." She pulled a folded up piece of paper out of her pocket. She laid it out on the ground and smoothed the creases out. "This is rough, but it's a decent map of the surrounding area. See the creek, here? It goes right behind the school. We can follow the creek the whole way." She looked up and grinned. The splash of freckles across her cheeks and the bright white of her teeth once again derailed his train of thought. "What, were you just going to walk on the road?"

A flush rose in Alex's cheeks, and it was only partly out of embarrassment. "Okay," he managed. "Maybe I didn't think this through all the way."

"Very possible," she said, dryly. "There's one other thing." Cara turned and looked at Trina. "You're staying behind, kid. We're just orphans. If you disappear, the entire place will be in an uproar."

Alex could tell Trina was more than a little offended by the remark. She puffed her chest up and opened her mouth to respond. Cara's point, though, gave him the opportunity to amend something that had bothered him since he'd agreed to let her go.

"She's right, Trina," Alex interjected. The look she gave him was full of hurt and perhaps a little betrayal, so he added, quickly, "Besides, you can cover for us. If anyone starts looking for us, you can say you saw us somewhere on the other side of the compound." He glanced at the sky and crossed his fingers. "It's maybe four hours until sunset. We should be back before then."

Trina crossed her arms and frowned. "This isn't fair, Alex."

He tried and was mostly successful in keeping a grimace off of his face. "Yeah, I know. It sucks that you have parents who would flip out if you up and vanished."

"That's stupid."

"Yeah, maybe so. I know I promised, but Cara's right. I didn't think about it when I promised. If I had, I wouldn't have told you that you could come." She wasn't buying it. "I'm trying to keep you safe, here," he said in exasperation. "If I had anything to give you, I would. But I don't have anything."

She straightened. "Eat lunch with me."

"Wait, what?"

"Eat lunch with me every day. All three of you."

Twigs sounded as though he was over the entire situation. "Fine, we'll even *feed* you lunch, can we get going?"

Alex said nothing. He studied Trina for a long moment. *She's lonely*, he realized. *The closest thing she has to a friend is Crazy Betty*. Without looking at Cara, he replied, "You got it."

Trina beamed. "Then get going."

Ross shimmied up onto the top of the maintenance building with the MBITR in an attempt to get a better signal. No dice; Camp Perry *still* wasn't answering. He frowned and gave it one more shot. "Highlander 6, this is Hatchet 6, how copy, over."

The digital radios had eliminated the concept of 'static' over the open channel. Despite that, the static-free silence was one of the most ominous things he'd ever heard. He checked his watch. It been right at an hour since they'd inserted, so the Black Hawk should be back at the base by now. Still, the long-range aerials at Camp Perry should be capable of picking up their signal, particularly from the top of an office building. Their last time up here, it had been spotty, but it had worked.

He played a hunch and adjusted the MBITR's frequency setting. "Whiskey 3, this is Hatchet 6, how copy, over."

He got a response almost immediately. "Read you clear and slightly garbled, Hatchet, over."

Ross frowned. "What's happening, Cartwright? I can't get command on the horn, over."

"Long range comms are down. I couldn't raise command until we got into closer range, and they waved us off." Cartwright paused, and when he spoke again, the pilot's voice was tight with stress. "Looks like that horde your civilian told you about ran right into the base defenses. They overran the airfield before we got consolidated. Sounds like we're missing one hell of a fight, over."

"Damn it!" Ross cursed with his thumb off of the transmit key. "What are your orders, Cartwright? Over."

"They're clearing the airspace so they can bring mortars and the cannon from the ships to bear. I don't particularly like the idea of flying through an artillery barrage, so I didn't raise much of a fuss. We're diverting to one of the secondary LZs for fuel and then we'll be heading your way. Figure that helipad across the way is better than camping out on the ground, over."

Ross did the math in his head. They'd topped off the chopper before pickup, but a round trip to Camp Perry and back was right at 400 miles, even accounting for the dogleg to the secondary. A fully-fueled Black Hawk had a range around 500 miles. In this case, the chopper's current lack of heavy cargo would help some in that regard.

"You going to make it to the gas station, Caleb?" Ross said, his tone mild. The other man took a moment before responding.

"It might get exciting, but we'll be good. Don't you worry about me, we'll be there in time to pick up the mail."

"I'm going to hold you to that," Ross promised. "I hope you won't have to wait too long, we're preparing to retrieve the intel now."

"Be advised, closest LZ shows as having been tapped by another recon flight. There should be some fuel left, but I'm not sure how far it will carry us after we extract you." He made a face and keyed the radio. "Copy."

"Just between you and me, I'm not too keen on having to ditch this bad boy in the boondocks after the sun goes down. Take all the time you need and we'll plan on a lift-off at first light. Give us a better chance to find a place to hole up in."

"Roger that. Keep me advised. Over and out."

Below him, the doors thumped as someone stepped out of the elevator room. He stepped over to the edge of the roof and looked down. Foraker walked out into the light and paused. His head panned across the roof until he settled on a far corner, toward the beginning of the solar panel installation. He cradled something in his arms. Even though the shape was wrapped in a poncho liner, Ross could tell what it was from the contours and length of it.

"We good, Chief?" He called out. Foraker settled the shrouded form on the rocks, just under the angled protection of one of the panels, and turned. The older man nodded.

"Aye aye, sir. Whiz kid got the elevator up and we're waiting for your orders on deployment."

Ross looked up and eyed the sun. It was well after midday and the sun had begun to creep toward the western horizon. Three-thirty or so, he judged. *Time flies when you're having fun.* He grunted a chuckle to himself. "Be right there."

419

Chapter 29

Vir didn't have much experience with hospitals, but the community's small one seemed to be bursting at the seams. The problem was only heightened after he and Charlie set chairs on either side of Larry's bed and brought him up to date.

Despite his color looking more than a bit off, the other man focused on the conversation, even as he winced when he tugged at a sore spot or moved the wrong way. Vir fell silent and turned as brisk footsteps pounded into the small room.

"This is *not* conducive to bed rest, gentlemen!" Tish barked as she fixed Vir and Charlie in turn with a fierce stare. The latter just shrugged, and before Vir could speak, Larry grumbled his reply.

"I'm resting just fine, kid. If anything I'm having a hard time not nodding off from the silence. You want to let me sleep, or do you want me to stay awake?"
She hissed frustration through clenched teeth. "Fine. Just keep it to a dull roar."

Larry cracked an eye open long enough to verify that she had walked away. He whispered, "I'd say I taught her everything she knows, but that there is all on her mama."

"I heard that!"

Larry laughed, then winced. "Ugh, head's still sore. Okay, so you guys went through Buck's place again. What did you find?"

Charlie shrugged, realized that Larry had closed his eyes, and waved his hand at Vir. The other man nodded and spoke.

"Charlie spotted it, actually. All the other cabins have a window in the back wall. At some point, Buck took his out and boarded it up, but the patch on the inside was a lot better done than the job on the outside. One of his neighbors remembered him saying something about not sleeping well with the sunlight coming in. Anyway, Charlie realized they'd thickened the wall. The room is just a bit narrower than the blueprints. Never would have noticed it myself; we've been living in one of the converted barn apartments."

"So what'd you find when you got it open?"

"Well, nothing contraband, per se, but it was pretty obvious that Buck was skimming off the top of his runs. There was quite a bit of high-end liquor, bottled water, lots of canned food, that sort of thing. Found a few guns. Pete examined them and said they were Class 3 items, and that you'd know what that meant."

Larry put a hand on his forehead and sighed. "Fully automatic. He could have gotten them from a police armory or even someone's gun safe, it's hard to tell. Buck, Buck, Buck," he sighed. "Why did you have to go and turn out to be such an asshole?" He frowned. "Pete was with you?"

Vir shrugged. "He kind of glommed onto us. Didn't seem to appreciate someone sticking a shiv in you." He winced and waited for the other man to rage at him. Pete had mentioned some sort of verbal altercation between them when they'd last spoken.

"*Now* he starts feeling the urge to give back to the community," Larry mumbled. "That's fine, though. If he's with you, you're less liable to get static from Norma and the others. I'm surprised she hasn't barged in here demanding a status report."

"She very well could have," Vir pointed out. "I'm sure your daughter would have dissuaded her of the notion."

Larry began to laugh, then winced. "Right. All right. So here's what I want you to do. Track down Pete and tell him what I told you about sticking with you guys. He can help you avoid any administrative land mines. The only reason I can figure why the shit hasn't hit the fan yet is because Miles is gone. Norma doesn't know squat about police work, but she's got her mind set on results, and she can't be happy with what happened last night."

"*I'm* not happy," Vir pointed out. "We had him."

"Couldn't avoid it," Larry shrugged. "In all honesty, we needed more people. The problem there is how wide do you go before there's a possibility of tipping off our guy? I trust Miles and *maybe* the other four deputies, but that's it." He sighed. "And our wannabe serial killer threw a wrench in the works, lest we forget. No, in the end, we did as well as we could with what we had."

"What you think?" Charlie rumbled.

Larry lifted his hand and rubbed his forehead. "Head's starting to hurt a bit. Our cook has got to be on the defensive now. If nothing else, maybe last night rattled him. He's going to be off his game. Do a walk through the community with Pete, talk folks up. Go with your gut. See if somebody mentions someone, I don't know, taking the day, for whatever reason. I doubt either of our culprits got any sleep last night."

"See who's yawning," Vir said. *This is the best we can do?* He hadn't done well enough to get the disappointment out of his tone; the other man reacted immediately.

"It's all I've got, pal," Larry insisted. "It's not like I had a master's class in this shit. I'm flying just as blind as you are here."

Frustrated, Vir spread his arms wide. "Look, I understand you're not a professional; neither am I. I'm a hell of a lot more comfortable standing on the wall or building something than I am with this Barney Fife act . . ."

"You're free to go back on that wall," Larry interjected. "I didn't pick you, remember. That was Miles' call, but if I tell him you need to go, how do you think he's going to jump?"

"So what, you don't know me, so I'm not good enough?" Vir stood up. The legs of his chair squawked against the linoleum as his motion shoved them back. "If you don't want my help, that's great. Say the word."

Charlie stood as well and put a hand on Vir's chest to cut him off. He turned to glance at Larry, and the man was sitting halfway up in his bed now, cords standing out on his neck. "That's not what I'm saying," Larry managed, his face going pale from the pain of his efforts. "But don't come down on me because you don't agree with my calls. Charlie, don't waste your time playing peacekeeper, let him . . ."

"*Shut . . . up.*"

The group fell silent. The voice was weak and raspy. It was easily audible, though, because it belonged to a person a few feet to Vir's right, in one of the other hospital beds.

Lizzie Johnson was well known around the community as the lady with a brilliant smile and great dimples. She was solidly-built — not overweight, but more muscular and athletic than curvaceous. She'd worked her way through college as a sous chef, and so working in the cafeteria came as a natural progression for her. When one of the deputies had found her unconscious with a pipe of meth in her hand, the fact that it was *Lizzie* was a shock. She didn't fit the drug user stereotype, and she'd never been able to answer the most important question of all — why? — because she'd been unresponsive for so long.

She'd rebounded somewhat with the renewed supplies of IV fluids but still looked drawn and pale compared to her once vivacious self. Lizzie returned the stares of the three men from her own hospital bed and whispered, "Thanks. Can I get some . . . water?"

"Charlie," Larry barked. "Get Tish. And get Lizzie some water."

Charlie nodded and disappeared. Larry tried to keep holding himself up, but his arms were already shaking from that minimal effort. He settled back down into his own bed and kept looking at Lizzie. "Miss Johnson, how you feeling?"

She groaned. "Like hammered dog crap." She raised a hand and rubbed at her eyes, then noticed the emaciated appearance of her hand and forearm. Lizzie choked. "God, how long have I been out?"

"It's been a while," Larry said. He glanced at Vir. "Have a seat, Vir," he murmured. "My apologies."

Nothing like a chiding from a coma patient to settle you down, Vir reflected. He nodded and retrieved his chair. As he sat, Tish hurried into the room and fussed over her patient with a stethoscope and a blood pressure monitor. Charlie followed right behind with a pair of water bottles.

Vir turned to Lizzie. "And I'm sorry to you, as well. Things have gotten a little crazy here, and I let my temper get the best of me."

"I heard a bit," she said. She accepted a bottle of water from Charlie and took a long swallow before speaking. "Shit. I should never have tried that stuff. It wasn't like I did it all the time, somebody said it was a nice pick-me-up, and I figured, what the hell?" She gave a nervous laugh before taking another drink of water.

"Lizzie," Vir said. "We've stopped several of the people involved in the production of the drugs. We also believe there are still a few people left in the community we need to locate and deal with. Could you, I don't know, tell us who got you the stuff, so we could speak with them?"

"Sure," Lizzie rasped before guzzling the last of her water. "Ah, that's so good. I *thought* she was a friend, but I don't see any cards or flowers, so I guess she wasn't. I got it from Melanie Clement."

Larry cursed and Vir's heart sank. Melanie had been one of Buck's crew in the warehouse, so it made sense that she'd be in the pipeline. "Well," he said. "She has a good excuse to not be here. Melanie died earlier this week."

"Oh, Lord," Lizzie said. "I always wondered why she still went on salvage runs. I guess . . . it caught up with her?"

"In a way," Vir admitted. He turned back to Larry. "I guess we need to do as you suggested."

"No," Charlie grumbled. Vir turned to him, confused. Charlie favored him with a crooked smile and said, "Boyfriend."

A smile dawned across Larry's face as he got it. "Well, well, well. What do you think, Vir? Still got better things to do?"

Vir stared at him. *The man's got a point. If I walk away now, how can I look myself in the mirror if I didn't take the opportunity to make a difference?* "No, I don't. I'd like to see this through if that's all right with you."

"So get to it."

It had been his own home for as long as he could remember, and part of his family for generations, but Pete still felt awkward coming into the house that Miles and Tish had made their own. It wasn't anything they had done; rather, it was his own perception that he himself no longer fit here. But once again he found himself abandoning the Crow's nest in favor of the ground.

Pete's old bedroom was largely unchanged from the time when he'd been medically discharged, right down to the gun safe that occupied the entire breadth of one side of the closet. The room was dim, but he'd set up a few battery powered lanterns in the closet and on the bed.

The cache of weapons Vir and Charlie had discovered was laid out in a neat row on his bed. Even as he studied them, he debated his decision to not turn them over to Jim Piper for storage in the central armory.

In the end, it came down to trust.

There'd been too much stashed in Buck's cabin. Yeah, maybe he'd been packing it away for years or buying it with other things he'd concealed from the community. The fact remained that Jim and the rest of the people working in the warehouse should have picked up on the fact that Buck's crew was shorting them. For it to have gone unnoticed for so long meant that not only had Buck's entire team been complicit in the pilfering — Pete was willing to extend the benefit of the doubt that their involvement in the drug ring hadn't been widespread until facts showed him otherwise — but it also meant that the warehouse people were either involved or inept. Pete wasn't about to hand over this type of firepower to see it turned against his friends if the investigation bore fruit.

It was treacherous ground. For all the respect he carried in the community, his position wasn't even as official as, say, Charlie's. But with Larry laid up and Miles gone, there was no one left with any experience. Vir was a solid dude, but he wasn't ready to handle this on his own.

He put his hands on his hips and sighed as he studied Buck's arsenal. It was enough of a mixed bag that Pete felt certain that it came from multiple sources, though he could guess what those might have been. The trio of M4 variants had likely come from a SWAT armory. They showed none of the signs of exposure to the elements, as they would have had they been the former arms of lost Guardsmen. Same went for the pair of collapsible-stock MP5s. Pete hated the things with a passion. The design was over-engineered and the trigger sucked, but police departments seemed to love the things.

More interesting was the WWII-era M1 Thompson. He'd thought most of the collectors in the area had been through Larry's shop from time to time, but he couldn't remember hearing about anyone owning one in the local area. He grinned. Maybe Grandpa had stashed it up in the attic for the last 80 years or so.

Of course, the entire collection just emphasized again that Buck had been an idiot. Not one of the weapons had suppressors, and for that matter alone Pete was stashing them. He could make use of the cans of ammunition and magazines, but no way was he going to start handing out unsuppressed fully-automatic weapons. It would be like ringing a dinner bell. He thought about their friends to the south and shuddered.

Get to it, he told himself. Pete started transferring the weapons from the bed to his safe. He'd been woolgathering for far too long — he needed to find Charlie and Vir. They didn't know it yet, but they had a new partner.

Cara was full of surprises.

If Alex had any doubts that she'd planned to go with them all along, they ended when she shouldered a backpack lying on the ground at the base of the fence. "Let's get moving," she barked as she climbed the chain link.

He shared a glance with Twigs. A grin flashed across the face of the younger boy, and he said, "Race you to the other side!"

Alex growled in frustration as Twigs sprinted toward the fence before he could react. The little twerp was short and scrawny, but he climbed like a freaking monkey. By the time Alex was halfway up, Twigs had already dropped to the ground on the other side. He beamed. Alex just shook his head and kept climbing.

As Alex crested the top, he heard a light smack of impact. He forced himself to focus on the climb. When he landed lightly on the ground, he turned to see Twigs rubbing his arm while Cara shook her finger under his nose.

"Keep quiet," she muttered. "If you can't get that through your head, climb back on over."

"All right, all right," Twigs whined. "You don't have to hit me."

"Suck it up, buttercup," Cara hissed. "Let's move!" She stepped to the edge of the creek and urged them over.

Twigs moved right over, but Alex hesitated at the fence. The other two turned and looked at him with quizzical expressions. "We sure about this, guys?" Alex said finally.

"Aw, man, don't get cold feet now," Twigs whispered. Cara stuck an elbow into his side and he clenched his lips.

"What are you thinking, Alex?"

"I just . . . I don't want you guys to get hurt or worse because of me wanting a stupid picture. I don't know."

"It's all right to be scared," Cara said. She met his eyes and didn't look away. "I'm scared. But at some point, we've got to do this, right? This will be our world someday. Are we just going to hide behind the fences the adults put up for the rest of our lives, or are we going to take it back?"

Alex considered her words. "If they didn't want us to do it, why teach us how to fight? Why teach us how to stay safe, how to avoid getting infected?"

"Exactly. If not now, when?"

"Now," Alex nodded, and she smiled. He joined them at the edge and began the climb down. The mud of the bank wasn't too wet, but clods still stuck to Alex's boots and stained his jeans.

The creek was running low despite the rains they'd had that week. A mixture of sand and mud formed a strip as wide as Alex was tall from the base of the bank to the edge of the sluggish water. Cara unslung her backpack and knelt there. Before she could say anything, Alex elbowed Twigs and whispered, "Keep an eye out." He followed his own instructions and stared in the opposite direction. After a moment of hesitation, he pulled the baseball bat out of his backpack. It was more awkward to carry it, but it was also better to have it close at hand.

Metal clicked and Cara announced, "Done." Alex turned and blinked at the sight of the suppressed carbine she cradled in her arms. "It's just a .22," she explained with a sigh. "Any loners, you take them with the bat, okay, Alex?"

What was he supposed to say? *No, you go ahead and shoot them?* Alex swallowed and said, "Sure."

Cara turned to Twigs and said, "You see more than one, you try the slingshot. You any good with it?"

Twigs stiffened and grumbled, "I bullseye cans all day long."

Cara glanced at Alex, who shrugged. "He's fine," he promised her. Twigs glanced at Alex with something akin to relief on his face.

"Fair enough," she said. "This thing is quiet, but it's not that quiet. I'd like to keep from using it unless it's an emergency." She pointed the barrel to the west. "Let's get going."

They walked, three abreast in the sand. Here and there the strip narrowed to the point that one of them had to fall behind. In others the mud became so thick that they had to move in single-file, close to the bank, to avoid the slurping mess.

Their passage wasn't entirely silent, but Alex judged that it might not matter. Despite the distance from the settlement, they could still hear the sounds of society now and again. The distance muted the sound of raised voices and running footsteps on the paved road. The realization that the survivors weren't as quiet as they believed was disconcerting to Alex, and he licked his lips up and raised his head to look over the top edge of the bank. He could just see the top of the fence, and he couldn't help but wonder if it was truly enough.

They're clumsy, he reminded himself. *Pay attention.*

Twigs cried out abruptly. He restrained the sound, but it was a laugh of wonder and joy. "Look guys! A turtle!"

Alex followed his friend's pointing finger, and sure enough, a small box turtle had plopped off of a high spot and paddled through the water. He'd seen frogs and snakes before, and deer, but never a turtle.

I haven't been outside for a long time. The fact that the realization hit him so hard was strange in one aspect; it was such a fact of life that he shouldn't have given it a second thought. At the same time, though, he looked back over what his life had been and wondered what he'd missed. What had kids his age *done* back before Z-Day?

Cara drew to a halt, and Twigs and Alex followed suit. They turned to her in expectation, and she said, "Okay, the creek forks here and heads northwest, to the school."

Alex followed eyes and looked further down their path. A few yards ahead, the bank gave away to a shadowed alcove supported by concrete pillars. Piles of branches and other debris had collected around the pillars, several feet deep in some places.

Twigs made a face. "We gotta walk through that?"

Cara shrugged. "You can always head home, short stuff."

Alex grinned. He knew he should have been just a little mad that his expedition had been co-opted, but he found that he was enjoying the experience. Maybe it was the fact that he wasn't the oldest. The burden of responsibility for Twigs still fell upon his shoulders, but it was one that he shared with someone close to his own age. "Let's go," he said and continued down the bank. He thought he heard

Twigs curse under his breath, but the others caught up with him quickly.

Holding the baseball bat out to his front with one hand, Alex leaned forward and tried to make sense out of the shadows under the bridge. It was low; he and Cara would likely have to stoop over to pass through. The bed of sticks must have collected over years of runoff. The area under the bridge was full of all sorts of junk, from plastic, scraps of cloth, and . . .

He flinched backward, raising the bat higher as he went.

"Hey, watch out," Twigs complained, then caught sight of the look on Alex's face. "What?"

He couldn't speak. Alex raised a trembling finger and indicated the mess of debris under the bridge.

It was easy to identify the exact moment that Twigs and Cara understood what had shaken him so; Cara took a deep breath and straightened, and Twigs emitted a string of curses that would have put any of the adults in the compound to shame.

Nestled in the collection of debris under the bridge were countless numbers of creeps. Alex could tell they were still . . . well, not alive, because dozens of pairs of eyes stared out at him from their homes in the mess.

In the shadows, details were difficult to make out, but the fact that none of them moved toward the children was easily understood. Most lay under or within their cocoons of trash, but those who weren't all shared the same characteristic — none had arms or legs. Despite that, the creeps arched their necks, trying to bring their heads close enough to bite.

"Screw this," Twigs whispered. "I ain't walking through that. No way."

"Wait," Alex drew out. He stepped sideways and cocked his head to one side. "We can make it through."

Twigs snorted in disdain, but Cara just said, "How?"

"They must have washed up over the years when the creek was high. None of them are close to where the water's running now. We'll get wet, but we can just walk through the creek."

Cara stepped closer to Alex, and he gulped as she steadied her balance with a hand on his arm to make the same study. "Maybe so," she thought out loud. "What if we have Twigs take them out?"

Alex shook his head even before she'd finished asking the question. "No way. We're too close to the gate, and those bearings make a hell of a racket. It'll echo like crazy under there." He fingered his belt and winced. "You have a knife?" He'd neglected to bring one of his own.

She reached down and slide a blackened knife out from a sheath inside her knee-high boots. Alex laughed nervously as she handed it over. *Of* course *she has a knife. She's making me look like a little kid.*

He slid the baseball bat into his backpack and stepped into the water. Coldness rushed in over the tops of his boots, and he wished he'd brought some spare socks. The current pushed at the backs of his calves and threatened to topple him. Somehow, he kept his balance.

The first creep was just at arm's length from the bank of the creek. As he stepped inside, Alex leaned over and considered it. A blanket of debris held it tight, but he wasn't taking any chances. He leaned forward and stabbed the knife through the thing's eye socket. The wet environment had saturated its flesh, and it made a liquid squelch as the blade punched through into the brain.

He drew the blade back and took a ragged breath. Alex looked to the opposite end of the bridge and counted the creeps closest to the edge.

Six more to go.

"Here's how it's going to go," Ross said, after studying the top of the elevator car. "Janacek and myself on either side of the hatch. Mr. Matthews, you'll be on the opposite side of the main support. You will keep your rifle slung. I don't feel comfortable disarming you, particularly given our lack of intelligence. But I also haven't worked with you as often as I have the Chief and Guns. I trust them not to shoot me in the ass. You, not so much." The lieutenant smiled, though it didn't touch his eyes. "No offense."

Miles shook his head and laughed. "None taken." This was neither the place nor the time for a chest-beating contest, but . . . "You guys have much experience in building clearance?"

Janacek made a sour face and the Chief frowned. Ross' face remained placid, but his tone was a bit chilly. "How do you mean, Mr. Matthews?"

Miles held up both hands to placate them. "I'm just trying to figure out if you grasp the lay of the land. The 9th floor is a freaking rat maze. They kept shoving cubicles into it until any reasonable person would have lost their damn mind and quit. Our 'paperless office' concept never took off, but they still reduced filing capacity. Half of the cubicle walkways are overflowing with banker boxes full of files. People made forts out of them to get a little more privacy. IT headcount was nil on Wednesdays, but the rest of the floor was Human Resources and customer service. Lots of phone drones. Maybe they're still there and maybe they aren't. But tight quarters are *not* your friend when it comes to fighting these things." He crossed his arms on his chest. "I know. I lost a couple of friends in a warehouse that wasn't half as cramped as that."

Ross looked at him for a long moment as he worked out his understanding that Miles wasn't bashing their skills. He nodded. "I get you. We cleared a couple of carriers and some hospital ships. And yeah, we lost some people doing it. All things considered, I'd rather be fighting from behind a wall."

"You and me both," Miles agreed. "So how do we do this?"

"Janacek, you're on point. Mr. Matthews, you keep close to him to help navigate. I'll take up the rear. We get into a firefight, do *not* engage unless asked to do so or if you have one right on top of you."

"I can handle that," Miles agreed. What else was he going to do? If he made a fuss, the SEALs were likely to disarm him. The last thing he wanted to do was be unarmed in the Wild.

The Chief didn't like it, of course. "All due respect, sir, I'd prefer you stay up here." Ross began shaking his head in the negative before the argument began.

"Sorry, Chief, not going to happen. Close quarters, right? Remember the *Ford*?" He patted the Chief on one broad shoulder and remarked, "Hell, if the aisles are too narrow you might have to slide through sideways, Gus."

Foraker considered the order for a moment and nodded. "Aye, aye, sir." The expression on his face said that he didn't like it much, but he heard the order.

"Chief, do you feel comfortable with the elevator controls?"

"They're simple enough."

"Well, then, let's get to it, gentlemen."

The climb down into the shaft shouldn't have been as nerve-wracking with the elevator right below them to offer a place to land if they lost their footing. Perhaps it was what the elevator represented that left Miles clammy with sweat. He hadn't survived for so long making moves without knowing exactly what he was walking into. In this case, he had no chance for that. He knelt down and grasped the support beam spanning the center of the elevator cab's roof. Miles closed his eyes.

Lord, if it be Your will, please keep these men and myself safe.

Ross and Janacek arranged themselves, and once the other two men were in position, the lieutenant murmured into the headset of his MBITR. "Go, Chief."

The elevator lurched into motion and Miles gulped. *Don't throw up, don't throw up.*

He tried to tell himself that this was much safer than riding in a helicopter, but was it? The helicopter was presumably maintained by trained personnel invested in it staying up in the air. The elevator had just been *sitting* here for almost a decade. One bit of rust in a cable and boom, they'd be shooting toward the ground floor. His stomach lurched again as the cab slowed and finally came to a stop. He forced himself to relax his death grip on the support beam. *Halfway there.*

"Doors, Chief," Ross ordered. Below them, the cab shifted as the elevator doors eased open. They'd opened and closed them several times up above to ensure they were moving well. The doors had wanted to stick at first, but after a few iterations, they operated normally.

Crouched on the roof of the elevator cab, the three men held their breath and strained to listen. The floor below them was as still and silent as a tomb.

Finally, Ross made a slight hand signal to Janacek. The younger SEAL reached down and lifted the hatch open. They'd debated whether to use lights but accepted the risk. Windows surrounded the entire floor, anyway. The only areas they might need them would be the lanes between the cubicles. A flashlight beam wouldn't be the beacon in that environment as it would be in pitch darkness. Janacek crouched next to the opening and craned his neck as he shone the light down inside the cab and as far out in front of the open doors as he could. "Going in," he whispered, and slid through the opening. He'd slowed his descent with one arm on the edge of the hatch, but the cab still jostled from the shift in his weight.

Ross stared down for a moment, waiting until Janacek cleared the area on either side of the elevator. When the younger SEAL held up just inside the elevator doors, the lieutenant whispered to Miles, "You're up."

Miles was no slouch in terms of upper body strength, but he knew he couldn't duplicate the feat that Janacek had just displayed. He slung his rifle over one shoulder, put both legs through the hatch, and lowered himself using *both* arms.

On the bright side, the maneuver created less noise than the one the SEAL had performed, but he'd have been reluctant to do it if Janacek weren't covering him at the open elevator doors. Miles stepped up to the corner opposite Janacek. He itched to drop his rifle off of his shoulder, but he'd made a promise. He settled for resting a hand on his holstered pistol and stared out into the ninth floor.

It didn't look much different than the last time he'd been there, though he couldn't recall if he'd ever been there when the lights were out. Despite the light coming in from the exterior windows, shadows cloaked large swathes of the floor. Particles of dust danced in the air, stirred by their encroachment into this still domain.

Ross dropped to the floor and whispered. "We're down, Chief." He stepped up behind Miles and clasped him by one shoulder. "Move out, Brian."

Janacek nodded and slid out of the elevator, hugging the wall as he moved. Ross gave him a gentle push, and Miles mimicked the careful motions of the man in front of him.

The entrances to the restrooms sat across from the elevator. At either end lay a cubicle farm in the open area surrounding the load-bearing walls in the center of the floor. The office remained open in line with the central corridor, allowing for a freer flow of natural light. Depending on the time of day the sun would slant in one side or the other. This time of the day, it came in at their backs, from the west side of the building.

Each corner of the floor boasted a walled-in office, but save for those, the only true doors were the ones in the janitorial closet on the opposite side of the restrooms, and the server room, on the back side of the elevator shaft. Janacek slid forward and paused at the four-way intersection formed by the two sets of cubicles on either side of the opening.

Miles glanced back at Ross. The other man still had one hand on his shoulder, but he'd turned sideways so that he could watch their backs.

"Moving," Janacek murmured. He slid around the corner. Ross turned his head, met Miles' eyes, and nodded.

They followed Janacek around the corner. This corridor, walled on one side by the elevator shaft and the other by cubicle walls, was much more shadowed than the initial corridor had been. The cubicles were just over six feet high. Every few feet he found himself glancing over the tops as though he expected one of his former coworkers to lunge at them. *Jumping at shadows.*

Other than the soft scuffing sound of their feet on the carpet, the ninth floor was completely silent. Halfway down, the cubicle wall opened up into an aisle-way that led into the heart of the cube farm. Janacek panned his rifle light into the aisle. Here and there, chairs sat rolled away from desks. One even lay on its side, just inside the interior of its owner's cube. The cardboard boxes of files that Miles had mentioned rose head-high in some spots, but in others boxes had been roughly pushed over, spilling their contents out into the floor. The dark stains splashed across the piles of paper and manila folders weren't immediately identifiable by color, but Miles felt confident that he knew what they were.

Nothing responded to the light — silence still reigned. They slid past the opening, and a few moments later Janacek made the second corner. It was a bit brighter here; the corner offices had large windows out into the office floor. The blinds in the office to the northeast were open. This reduced the shadows somewhat in comparison to the area they'd just passed through.

"Moving," Janacek said once more, and they slid along the light. The heavy wooden door to the server room, marked with an identical warning sign to the one upstairs, was the first one on their left. Miles couldn't help his slow sigh of relief. Janacek glanced over his shoulder at him and nodded when Miles gave him a thumbs up.

Ross slid past Miles and took a position on the hinge side of the door. Janacek stood on the opposite side. Ross made a silent countdown on his fingers — three, two, one — and then reached out and twisted the handle. The card reader above the door lock was long-dead, and the door opened without resistance. The magnetic door locks, as designed, opened in the absence of power. *Score one for the fire marshal.*

Janacek scanned the room with his rifle, made an "OK" sign with thumb and forefinger, and then slid inside. Miles followed, and Ross was right on his heels. The lieutenant eased the door shut behind them.

The darkness, cut only by Janacek's weapon light, was palpable at first. Once Ross clicked his own light on it was dim but workable.

Miles moved over to the server racks on the back wall and ran his finger down the labeled blades. Ross stepped over to shine his light on the subject, but Miles had already found what he needed. He disconnected the cables and slid the component out of the rack. *No pressure, but if you drop this, our little venture was a massive waste of time.*

He supported it with both hands and pivoted. He was halfway across the room to his desk before he realized what he was doing, and he shook his head at the oddness of it all. If someone had told him that one day he'd be in his office with a pair of Navy SEALs on a mission to save the tattered remnants of mankind, he'd have backed away and looked for the exit. But here it was.

Miles set the blade down on the desk and removed his backpack. The blade was almost too wide to fit inside, but he'd loosened the straps enough so that it just slid in. Closing the top flap of the main pouch was out of the question, but he'd brought a length of paracord. He wrapped it around the blade and backpack, then tugged on it. The arrangement seemed solid enough. It would be anything but comfortable on his back, but he'd have his hands free. As he finished he glanced down at his desk and smiled. Post-It notes, trouble tickets, and writing utensils littered his workspace in defiance of GenPharm's clean desk policy. A squat plastic Funko action figure hung awkwardly from a corner of his monitor. The last vestiges of the double-sided tape he'd used to secure it in place were slowly drying and giving way. Impulsively, he pulled it free and shoved it in the side pocket of his backpack. He shouldered the pack, then realized Ross was looking at him with a curious expression on his face.

Miles shrugged it off. "Told my daughter I'd bring her something. Didn't figure you guys would let me stop off at the local Toys R Us."

Janacek huffed a chuckle, while Ross looked at the floor and shook his head. "Do you have everything?" The lieutenant said, finally.

"I'm good to go."

"Then let's do this. By the numbers, just as we came in." Ross waited until the other two were in position, and opened the door once again.

Janacek reversed his prior course and hugged the wall with his right shoulder this time. Despite the initial success of their foray, he did not vary his tempo one whit. The floor seemed to be clear, but the operator was taking no chances. He measured each step, pausing to listen for any sound after he moved. Miles understood that sentiment. Things always went to hell when you thought they were looking up and weren't prepared for everything to fall apart.

Just before the SEAL reached the corner of the first turn, a short, muted squeak sounded from somewhere ahead of them. All three men froze stock still and waited for the sound to repeat or shift into something more ominous. Miles licked his lips and lowered his hand to the pistol in the holster at his hip. As he pushed the retention strap forward to release the gun, the sound came again — still muted, but longer this time. Squeeeeeak.

"Mouse?" Ross whispered.

Janacek shook his head but didn't shift his position to look at either of the two standing behind him. "Too loud. Rats, maybe." He sounded unsure of his own assessment.

Miles shuddered. Unbidden, the memory of one of the zombie books he'd read before reality had made them unappealing surfaced. In that book, the zombie plague had jumped species and swarms of undead rats had pursued the hero to his mountaintop retreat for one final, grisly confrontation. The imagery of the tidal wave of undead rats had been scarier than the book's zombies and had made for particularly grueling nightmare fodder.

They'd never had to deal with that particular fiction come to life, and as the noise repeated for the third time Miles cocked his head to one side and realized that they still didn't. *Thank God.*

"It's a chair," he whispered. "An office chair." As though affirming his statement, the noise came again, and in context, it was identifiable as the complaint of metal rubbing on metal.

"Office," Janacek noted. He shifted the angle of his rifle to point at the corner office. The incoming sunshine washed out the beam of his weapon light, but it was still noticeable. Nothing moved in response, and the sound did not recur.

"Check it," Ross said, finally.

Janacek kept straight at the corner, and their route was now defined by partition walls on either side. He paused every few steps to scan the cubicle openings, but they were all empty and neat compared to the chaos they'd seen further down. The cubes closest to the actual offices, Miles mused, were the territory of admin assistants or mid-level management. They were also more likely on salary, and less liable to live in fear of losing their job over taking too many sick days. The hourly staff didn't have that advantage, and they'd paid a far greater price than just their jobs on Z-Day. He hadn't known many of the cube people — they'd mixed with IT a bit like oil and water despite the proximity — but his gut told him that he was right.

His hunch stood up as they neared the corner office and the cubes continued to prove unoccupied. That situation changed as Janacek stacked up near the door to the corner office and took a quick glance inside. This time, he looked back at Ross and Miles, and his face had broken from its normal expression of nonchalance to one of absolute confusion.

"Clear?" Ross said.

"I . . . guess?" Janacek said. His mouth worked as he searched for something to say, then finally admitted, "I have no words, sir."

Miles glanced at Ross, and the other man shrugged. They stepped forward together, and Miles' jaw dropped as they rounded the corner and looked into the office.

Real — though I wish it wasn't.

The squeaking office chair sat in the outer corner of the office at the junction of the two large exterior windows. The zombie strapped into it was intact, albeit emaciated. It had once been a man of indeterminate height and had made the transition from life to undeath while garbed in a zip-up hoodie and running shorts. The sweatshirt had once been a bright crimson but was now fading to yellow from what must have been months if not years of exposure to the sun. Its height was indeterminate for the simple fact that it had no legs; the method of removal was unclear, but it sat erect on its hips, held upright to the chair back by a series of what looked like knotted-together neckties.

As Miles and Ross stared in stunned silence, the zombie studied them as well. After a moment of study, it extended an arm — secured to the chair rest at the elbow — and pushed against the window. The chair squealed once more, and the legless observer rotated a few degrees. It repeated the motion, the chair squealed, and as the two men watched, it turned its back on them and lowered its leprous head.

It's watching the street below. Miles realized, and his mouth went dry with terror.

"What. The actual. *Fuck?*" Ross whispered.

Miles had raised his Springfield and centered the sights on the zombie sentry's head before he was conscious that he'd grasped the pistol's grips. "They don't do this," he said. His voice was calm, though his train of thought was gibbering and close to going off the rails. "They don't act like this," he concluded.

He jumped as Ross placed a hand on his forearm. "No shooting," the lieutenant said. "Not here. It could go through the window. Too much noise."

Miles stared at him, then nodded. "Okay. Okay." Ross squeezed his arm and pushed past. The sentry didn't react as the SEAL drew closer. With a quick, well-practiced motion the lieutenant drew his fighting knife, stabilized the zombie's head with his off hand, and drove the blade into the thin bone at the temple. Infernal life departed, and the creature sagged into the restraints like the lifeless thing it should have been long before.

Ross wiped congealed fluids off of his knife with the hoodie, then turned back to Miles and Janacek. "Let's get the hell out of here."

Chapter 30

The Flesh had invaded their domain.

They had no emotions, per se, but the sudden realization of the presence of their adversary roused something that one could almost call curiosity. The earlier passage of one of the Flesh's sky machines had not gone unnoticed, but the machine had moved on, and with it any interest They might have had for it.

Their Eyes were no longer in that tower, but that was of little importance. There were other Eyes. They were legion, after all.

When Pete entered the clinic, Vir and Charlie were getting ready to leave to search him out. It was a nice bit of synchronicity, as it gave them a few moments to figure out their plan of attack after filling Pete in on what they'd learned from Lizzie. Vir had been chomping at the bit, ready to kick down doors, but Pete had a different idea.

"We don't *know* if the boyfriend is actually involved. For all we know, he has lousy taste in girls. So we take a soft approach, see if we can hit him up for info. Charlie, you stay outside at the back window. If he rabbits, you're waiting on him and none of us have to get pissed on."

Pete could tell Larry wasn't anywhere close to the top of his game; the joke didn't even get a rise out of him. *We nail this drug thing down, I'm going to find our murderer and skin him alive.*

The converted barn on the back of Tom's farm wasn't the most popular living place in the community. Proximity to the cattle herd made for an interesting nasal experience. It wasn't like the entire community smelled of wine and roses, of course, but there were spots where things were more tolerable.

Pete didn't notice it himself; the odor of farms was the odor of his childhood, and even if two hundred souls in close living quarters amplified the odor, it still didn't hold a candle to the stench of the Sandbox.

That stench either didn't bother Melanie Clement and her boyfriend, Greg Mills, or they hadn't been around enough for it to be an issue. While Melanie had been a scavenger, Mills was a gate guard on the east wall. Pete couldn't help but think how *that* particular intersection of careers offered all sorts of interesting possibilities. Had Mills ever been working the gate when Buck's crew came back through? It wasn't like they had detailed work records, so it was impossible to know for sure. It was within the realm of reason. It would have been the simplest thing in the world for an incoming salvage crew to pass off illicit goods to a gate guard before heading to the warehouse to unload.

Pete could tell the concept troubled Vir, and he could even understand that to some extent. The guys on the wall should be their first line of defense, not enablers for drug dealers. In a sense it was like finding out someone was a dirty cop back in the old days; the betrayal went above and beyond the normal perception.

They'd taken a short detour out of their way to speak with Mills' supervisor. Gary West had indicated that he was working graveyard shift this month, so he more than likely was asleep in his apartment. *All the better. Get him talking while he's still waking up, maybe he'll give something up without realizing.*

This barn was one of the smaller ones on Gary's property and had only yielded up enough floor space for four apartments when it had been rebuilt. If they hadn't known which apartment they needed to check, the blankets draped over the back window were a pretty good sign.

Charlie peeled off and leaned against the wall next to the window. He crossed his arms over his chest and nodded to Pete as he and Vir stepped toward the main entrance.

"Remember," Pete said under his breath as he held the door open for Vir. "Calm and friendly. We don't want to spook him."

"I understand," Vir said.

It was a few hours before dinner, and the other occupants of the apartment were most likely out and about. Pete wasn't sure if that made this easier, or harder. The lack of bystanders was one less potential check on Greg trying something, but if he was the type to do that, would he even care about bystanders? Pete mulled that over for a minute and decided he did *not* like this aspect of policing the community. *Miles and Larry can't be back at this soon enough.*

They stepped up to Greg's door. Pete resisted the urge to hammer his fist on it and knocked. He hit hard enough to make them loud but kept the rhythm slow and polite. He waited and listened for any movement inside the small apartment. After a moment, he heard the rustle of covers and a faint voice. "Just a second." Pete gave Vir a thumbs up. They didn't have to wait long; Greg opened the door enough to stick his head out and blinked at them in the light. "Yeah?"

"Greg, right?" Pete said, forcing the grin onto his face that he'd once worn when speaking to clueless Majors.

"Yeah. What's this about?"

Pete stuck out his hand. "Don't believe we've met, but I'm a bit of a hermit. Pete Matthews." He indicated Vir. "Believe you know Vir Singh, right?"

"Sure." Greg glanced back at Pete. His expression was more confused than wary, and Pete chalked that up as a good sign. "Sorry, I'm on nights right now and I was sleeping. What can I do for you guys?"

"I don't know if you've heard, but Larry Vance got hurt pretty bad last night. I'm helping the other deputies on an active case while he's laid up."

Greg rubbed a hand across his face and yawned. "Sure, man, we all heard about that. He going to be okay?"

"Should be," Pete affirmed.

"Good, good. He's an all right dude."

"Right. Greg, the reason we stopped by today, we wanted to talk to you about Melanie a bit."

The man in the door frowned. "What about? I mean, we were a thing, and all, but, you know — she ain't around anymore."

Well, aren't you just the big softy. "Right, this isn't about the accident, it's about some things she involved herself in beforehand," Pete explained. Something flashed across Greg's face. *Got you.*

"How do you mean?"

Pete glanced at Vir and cocked an eyebrow. "The drugs, mate," Vir said. "We have reason to believe that Melanie and some of the people on her crew were part of the supply chain for the people who've been cooking and selling meth."

Greg looked at Vir for a long moment. *Does he know that Vir was on that mission? I bet he does.* He looked back at Pete, and muttered, "I don't like where this is going."

Pete avoided his urge to glance at Vir and focused his attention on maintaining eye contact with Greg. "I'm not sure what you mean, son. We're not saying you did anything. We're just thinking that you might have seen or heard something, considering your relationship with Melanie."

"I don't think I should say anything. I think you guys need to leave."

"Greg, that isn't how this works anymore. You don't get to have your tears wiped away by a court-appointed lawyer who will protect you from the big bad policeman. If Vir and I decide we want to beat the ever-loving hell out of you, nobody around here would say a word. It's our word against yours."

The other man shook his head in a fierce denial. "No, no, you don't get it. I don't want a lawyer, I don't want to go down to the station, and you guys need to get the hell away from me before . . ." Greg caught himself and glanced behind the two of them. "Look, nobody saw you guys coming in, right? If it gets out that you wanted to talk to me, I'm a dead man."

Pete couldn't help it; he gave Vir a look of surprise. "Greg," Pete said. "What I said before goes the same way for whoever you're afraid of. If you know who's peddling this poison, we'll take you into protective custody. After that, I'll go and put a bullet in the bastard's head myself. You can trust me on that. We're not going to give him a lawyer or a cutesy little trial. He took it to the next level last night, and he's going to reap the whirlwind." Hanratty and the Marines wouldn't like it, but tough. They didn't get to show up out of the blue and start dictating legalities. That *might* come later if they were true to their word about working together.

Greg gnawed on his lip. "There's a story they tell about you. I've heard it a lot over the years."

I've got him. "Which one's that? Lot of gossip around here."

"Story goes, you and a few of the other guys went out on a scavenging run. On the way back, you saw Val and a bunch of kids trapped in the school. They said you shouted to them that you'd be back to help them. And that when Pete Matthews says something, you better believe it, because sure enough, you came back and every one of those survivors made it to safety."

"Yeah, pretty much. But that's not about me keeping my word."

"It's not?"

"No, it's about what's right and wrong, Greg. And what's going on here is wrong. If you help us, we'll keep you safe until we take care of the situation — because that's the *right* thing to do."

Greg stared at the ground for so long that Pete half-wondered if he hadn't fallen back asleep. But then he raised his head, looked Pete in the eye, and told him everything.

After the gruesome discovery on the ninth floor, the return to the server room was almost anti-climactic. They abandoned any pretense of stealth and sprinted through the office. The lack of attention the chair of the zombie sentry, if that was what it had been, had garnered indicated that the floor was either clear or that any other occupants were also immobile. Despite that, they double-timed it back to the elevator and were back up top before Miles had begun to catch his breath.

The doors opened into a darkness that was just barely lit by the power indicators of hibernating systems. Miles kicked himself at the piercing beeps of the power supply alarms. The batteries had been old enough or underutilized to the extent that they weren't able to keep the system running. They were going to have to switch back to panel power to complete the mission. Ross caught the issue immediately.

"When we switch the power over, the elevator drops back down to ground, correct?"

"Right," Miles said. "Even if there's power in the system to run it up and down for a bit, default setting is to go to the bottom."

Ross considered it for a moment, then toggled his MBITR. "Chief, you saw the evolution to switch the power over, correct?" He paused for the other man's answer, then responded. "Good. We're going to disembark, get the information we need, then you reverse the procedure when we're ready to come back out." He winked at Miles. "I'd rather play it safe on the way out than have to climb out again." He motioned Miles and Janacek forward. As the three of them stepped into the auxiliary server room, the lieutenant concluded, "When you're ready, Chief, we're clear."

Relays clicked in the server room at the same time that the elevator doors slid shut and the cab began to descend. The lights in the room flickered on, and Miles let out the breath that he hadn't even known he was holding. "All right," he said. "Let's get this done."

He removed his backpack and took his time to unlace the server blade. He didn't want to rush things and jab a knife through the housing or something just as stupid while trying to cut the paracord holding it in place. He hummed to himself as he lifted the server and slid it into one of the open receptacles in the rack. Whoever had been in charge of putting this room together had at least had the foresight to build in expandability. He connected patch cables, double-checked his steps, and pressed the blade's power switch. After the nerve-racking "will I boot or won't I" delay that seemed sadistically endemic to computers, the lights on the server's front panel began to light up.

"Touchdown," Miles said, and stepped over to the desk. He repeated the process to boot the NUC, inserted his badge into the reader, and tapped the desk in impatience. Finally, it was up. "Here we go."

In the end, it was almost anticlimactic. He entered his password. After an interminable delay as the computer consulted the authentication server, the login screen cleared to a rather vanilla desktop with the generic company wallpaper installed on all the deployment system images.

He was only vaguely aware of Ross and Janacek standing at either shoulder as he opened up the taskbar and looked through the most recently used programs. He wasn't sure after all this time, but it looked like this system was set up much like the machines in the research and development division. He thought he recognized the names of some of the software applications. R&D already had their own secure file archives, so why the redundancy here?

The two most-used applications were the e-mail client and the project database software. He opened both of them and drummed his fingers as he waited for them to load. The e-mail must have been on a local mirror because it came up first. He clicked on a message and studied the header, curious about who the sender was.

"The 'Guidestone Project?'" Miles read, then frowned. Why did that sound familiar? The odd thing was, he didn't think he'd heard it in a work context. For some reason it made him think of watching the History Channel with Pete. These were the times when he missed Google. He turned away from the screen. "Mean anything to you guys?"

Ross let out a long burst of air. "That'll be it," he said, with a hint of what sounded like triumph in his voice.

"Your source, again?" Miles guessed.

"Need-to-know," Ross said, his voice firm.

"Guess I don't."

Miles' eyes started to glaze over as he glanced through one or two of the e-mails. He had a feeling that the SEALs didn't appreciate his doing so, but neither man spoke up. Either way, it read like Sanskrit, with all sorts of medical terms that he didn't recognize. Many of the e-mails had attached PDFs, but he didn't push it and open any of them. "All right," he said. "I'm guessing you want it all. What do you have for me?"

Ross opened a pouch on his harness and dropped a literal fistful of thumb drives on the desk. "If you need more, we've got a bag upstairs."

Miles picked up a drive and chuckled. "All right, then." He inserted the drive into the port on the side of the keyboard. After a few clicks, he set the e-mail program to dump its contents onto the drive. It was a top-of-the-line model for 2017, and he wondered how big they would have gotten by now if things had kept going. As it was, the drive was filling rapidly. There was a *ton* of data just in the e-mail program. While he was waiting, he pulled the database window up and tried to remember where the archival function was. As he looked, he noted the subject of one of the folders and stopped in mid-click.

The folder read *'Deployment and infection strategies'*. He swallowed and glanced at a couple of the other folder headings.

Projected spread rate.

Viral life-cycle timeline.

Miles lifted his hand from the mouse and swiveled in the chair to face the SEALs. The two men stared at him with impassive faces, and he thought, nonsensically, *At least this chair doesn't squeak.*

"I'm getting the feeling you guys haven't been straight with me," Miles said.

"You sure you want to go down this rabbit hole, Mr. Matthews?" Ross murmured.

"If you say something like, 'you can't handle the truth', I'm going to scream," Miles replied.

Ross shook his head. "It's not so much about handling it as it is being able to sleep at night."

"I haven't had a good night's sleep in over eight years," Miles shot back.

"Fair enough," Ross sighed. "The first thing you have to understand is, up until recently, we were content to wait things out. Infected activity was dropping down in most areas. The remnants of the CDC calculated that no more than 36 months from now, the majority of infected in the continental United States would be non-ambulatory. We planned for Atlantic Fury to kick off right around that time. We were intent on building up our logistics train before that point, so that when we *did* deploy, we'd have everything we needed."

"But you moved up the schedule. What changed?"

"Over the past 90 days, researchers have noticed a shift in infected behavior. This isn't universal across the board, but it has happened at multiple, segregated sites so the thinking is the change is not due to anything the research teams themselves have done."

Miles frowned. "What kind of *shift?*" Then he thought about the legless zombie on the ninth floor, content to look out the window rather than attacking to feed, and he thought he knew.

"Reduction of aggressive tendencies toward visual stimuli. Diversionary actions. Manipulation of environment."

"What Lieutenant Ross is trying to say, they look at you and it looks like they're thinking. When they think you aren't watching, they try to get out of their cages." Janacek said. "We've got triple redundancies in our lab facilities — which are *not* on any manned ships — or we might have had renewed outbreaks."

"Shit," Miles breathed. "They're what, evolving?"

"Evolving," Ross drew the word out, sampling it. "In a way, I suppose. But that's not the worst of it," Ross said. "While the initial effect is not universal, it eventually spreads to all captives in an enclosure. Limited testing has shown that unaffected subjects introduced into a, well, evolving enclosure will soon exhibit the same tendencies."

"It's airborne, isn't it?"

Ross shared a glance with Janacek. After a moment, the other SEAL shrugged. The senior man gave Miles a long, uncomfortable stare, then said, "It's not a virus. It never was."

"I don't follow. If you don't need data, why are we here?" He gestured at the project files on the computer screen. "This sure as hell looks like it's talking about some sort of virus."

"Rate of initial spread and contagion effects were analogous to a bio-terror attack originating in Brazil — for the *first* stage. That threw us off, at first. With some variance, the final stage of the 'outbreak' — what you call Z-Day —occurred within a sixty-minute window around the world. That's *not* how diseases work. They spread geometrically. If this had acted like that, we would have gotten a quicker handle on the response, instituted quarantines instead of trying to fight a thousand brush fires at once. By the time CDC figured it out, it was too late to do anything about it. The people who came up with this thing created the crisis in Brazil, then lobbied to get their vaccine distributed far and wide. But instead of a vaccine, they were spreading a form of the same virus."

"And the same corporation produced every tainted batch," Janacek added.

"GenPharm. What the hell . . ." Miles thought back, to the last time he'd walked into the building and to the banner hanging down in the lobby. Every Wednesday during flu season the company offered a free clinic and flu shots. He'd never gotten one, and he hadn't *been* here any Wednesdays before Z-Day to get one.

The asshole who'd cut his hours had probably saved his life.

He held back the hysterical bubble of laughter that threatened to break free and instead asked, "All right, so what is it?"

"They're nanomachines — cybernetic viral organisms. Only partially organic, self-replicating and generally detectable in a blood screen. Significantly larger than an actual virus, but still light years beyond anything any surviving scientist we've been able to find can figure out. On Z-Day, someone flipped a switch, and the nanomachines went active as the signal propagated. NSA intercepted the signal, but at the time, they didn't know what to make of it. It was an ultra-wide bandwidth, low-frequency signal that did one thing — tell all the nanomachines to be fruitful and multiply." Ross shook his head. "Remember how I told you that all the bunkers staffed to ensure continuity of government got compromised? In the months before Z-Day, there was a government-wide flu shot drive, provided by, you guessed it, GenPharm. That was the first thread that we started pulling at, and it led to, well, here. It was one hell of an effective decapitation strike."

"Partially organic," Miles repeated. "Like what, some sort of cyborg nano-virus?" He shook his head and marveled at the nonchalant shrug the SEALs offered. They'd had much more time to digest the implications. He laughed, this time, and didn't bother to try and keep the shock out of it. "So they're not zombies at all, they're . . ." He fell silent and considered whether to say it. "They're *zyborgs*."

Ross rolled his eyes as Miles snickered. "You can understand why the brass prefers infected."

Miles composed himself and cleared his throat. "Who?" he demanded. "Who in hell would do such a thing? God, man, there were some real assholes working for this company, but not *evil*. We're talking true blue psychopath stuff, here."

Ross shook his head. "Doesn't matter, now. They thought they got away with it, thought they were safe for the duration. They were planning on waiting until the infection burned out to restart civilization the 'right way'."

"Past fucking tense," Janacek growled. He drew his thumb across his throat.

"So yeah, we aren't exactly here for vaccine research. But maybe if we can get the data from the sick freaks that designed this to the right people, they can figure out how to stop the infected from passing on their . . . software updates, I suppose." Ross shrugged. "Humanity is hanging on by a thread, all over the world. If these things start working together, even exhibiting the cunning of a wolf pack, we're all dead. It's just a matter of time. There are too many of them and not enough of us." Ross rubbed his face with one hand. "We thought we had the advantage of time, but we were running out all along and didn't even know it."

Chapter 31

Pete pulled open the door to the station's lone holding cell. It wasn't much of a prison door, or even a holding cell, for that matter. In the end, he supposed it was the psychology of the thing more than the actual fact of solidity. Rather than going with bars, the team that had put the building together had reinforced a solid oak interior door with two-by-fours on either side. Heavy carriage bolts with the ends ground down and smoothed secured the timbers. Finally, they'd bolted a pair of drop-bar brackets to the reinforcing frame. This allowed the officers to drop a square steel tube to bar the door closed when someone was inside.

Chris Naylor blinked and stared at Pete as he sat up on the cell's lone cot. The room was empty save for that and a repurposed five-gallon bucket for a toilet. The only light came from a small, non-opening window high on the ceiling.

"Move," Pete barked. "You're evicted."

Naylor stared at him with a dumbfounded look, then said, "What the hell?"

"You heard me, sunshine, hightail it out of here. I got someone a hell of a lot more important than you who needs to be in here. Keep your nose clean, or you and I will have a much more serious chat."

Naylor didn't take much in the way of convincing, and he had no personal possessions to collect. He shoved his feet down into his work boots and shot out of the holding cell as though it were on fire. Pete stepped aside just in time to avoid getting run over.

Greg Mills watched the entire process with a bemused smirk. His smile faded when Pete turned back to him and barked, "In you go."

The other man blanched. "Are you serious? You're going to lock me up in there and call that safekeeping?"

"This is the best I can do at short notice. You want it, or you want me to cut you loose and see how long it takes for Dantzler to figure out that you ratted him out?"

"All right then," Greg said, and stepped inside the holding cell. "I do believe I'll take a nap."

"Sounds like a plan to me," Pete agreed. He closed the door after the younger man, though he didn't throw the bar across the door. In Greg's case, his own fear was prison enough. He wasn't going anywhere.

"What . . . . what is going *on*?" Jaid Sims demanded. Pete turned and gave the secretary a sidelong glare. He'd never had much personal interaction with her, but the secondhand impression he'd gotten from Miles, Larry, and Tish hadn't been the greatest. Definitely a cutie, though. His appreciation for his nephew's common sense rose a notch as he considered the fact that Miles had been brushing Jaid off for years. *Maybe I didn't do such a bad job of child-raising after all.*

"Come along, and I'll fill you in, miss," Pete replied in an even tone. He stepped over to Larry's office and regarded the interior with a frown. "This everything?" He waved a hand at the array of weapons that lined the folding table. While he'd been stashing Greg in the holding cell, Charlie and Pete had unloaded the contents of the police station's single gun safe. It paled in comparison with the arsenal Pete had just stashed in his own house. *Going to have to fetch some of that, I suppose.* The wall guards were usually the ones packing the heavy firepower; for the most part Miles and his deputies were just there to keep folks honest. He considered the weight of the Russian shotgun Larry had given him. That, at least, was liable to be a difference maker.

Jaid looked at him with incredulous eyes. "Of course, that's *it!* What are you even doing in here? You're not a deputy." She glanced at Charlie and Vir. "And neither are these two." Her voice raised in pitch. "And who in the world authorized you to release prisoners?"

"Look, I don't expect you to be abreast on current events, kid, but Larry's down for the count and Miles is gone. Am I an official sworn-in deputy? No, of course not. But I've been looking out for this place for just as long. Longer than this building has even been standing, in point of fact. We don't have time for Norma's little bureaucratic niceties."

"Larry's all right?" The frantic air about her reduced somewhat as she digested that nugget of information that he'd just provided. "That's . . . that's great."

"He's going to be just fine, and so is Carter. Look, Jaid, like I said, this is time sensitive. So stop giving me static and call the rest of the deputies in, even the ones who are off shift. This is going to be an all hands on deck evolution. And tell them to bring their personal weapons."

As Jaid stepped over toward the radio, Pete turned back to the table. He picked up a Remington pump shotgun and began to feed shells into the magazine.

"Pete, shouldn't we bring Gary in on this?" Vir said. "These are his guys, and he's going to hit the roof if half of what Greg had to say pans out."

"Nope," Pete said. He sat the loaded shotgun down on the table and grabbed the next in line. "Is Gary a solid guy? As far as I know, sure. What I don't know for a fact is how squared-away the guys around him are. We've just found out that an entire bunker has gone rogue. You were one of the wall guards, can you tell me for sure that any one of them — except for Gary — is not involved with Dantzler and his crew?"

Vir's jaw worked as he chewed over the question. "No," he admitted. "Until an hour ago, I'd have thought Dantzler was straight up, too."

"Exactly," Pete said. "I trust you two. I trust the judgment of Miles and Larry, so by extension, I trust the rest of the deputies. That's as far as it goes. The seven of us will be enough."

"Enough for what?"

Pete turned. Despite what was an early hour for them, the third shift deputies — John Keogh and Trey Peters — looked wide-awake and raring to go. Of course, both were also holding their personal rifles not-so-subtly in his general direction. He grimaced, and wondered just what it was that Jaid had said over the radio. They'd made good time.

"We've got a line on our drug dealers. Your boss is out of town and Larry's laid up. You interested, or you want to go back to sleep?" He kept his voice calm and made a point to ignore the barrels of the Garand and AR-15 clone they were sweeping him with. On the bright side, they had the guns angled low enough that an accidental discharge would hit him in the prosthetics, if at all.

Keogh and Peters glanced at one another. The former was the older of the two, and generally unknown to Pete. He'd seen him around, of course, but he'd never sat down to have a conversation with the man. He'd been some sort of mid-level manager in one of the nearby factories on Z-Day and was generally a bland, unassuming sort. Miles had never had much to say about him other than that he was dependable.

Trey was a different story. On Z-Day the recently graduated high school senior sought shelter in the break room of the Lowe's where he'd been working as a cashier. When Pete and the rest of his motley crew had rolled up to clean out the lumber yard they'd rescued Trey in the process. Since then, he'd shown himself to be dependable and hard-working. Which, Pete assumed, was the main reason why Miles had wanted them on third shift. That time of day was usually so quiet that it required a certain type of person who could keep themselves awake and aware. Being a night owl these days wasn't as common as it used to be when lighting was cheap and easy.

Trey nodded after a moment of consideration. Keogh frowned but took a cue from his younger partner and slung his rifle over one shoulder. "All right, then, what have we got?"

"I'm holding out the big briefing until Brett and Jenny get in," Pete admitted. "To make a long story short, we've got a source who dropped a dime on the source of our drug problem." He met Keogh's eyes and watched for the reaction as he said it. Should third shift have noticed something? Pete wasn't sure, but he wasn't going to take any chances either. Depending how the man reacted to the information, he might have to draw down on him. *Could use you right now, Larry. You were always a damn sight better with a pistol than me, even on my best days.*

Keogh smiled. "Well, hot damn. I'm in. Let's get this mess cleaned up."

Pete gave him a crooked grin. "Well, all right then. Let's gear up. We're rolling out ASAP."

Redundancy was the name of the game. The full data export was just shy of two terabytes. Ross had brought along dozens of 512GB thumb drives. The SEALs must have stopped at a Best Buy or Staples and stocked up. Whatever the case, Miles made good use of the extras and sorted out a full backup set for each man in the party. He stuffed his clutch of drives into one of the smaller pockets on his pants and Velcroed it shut.

The lieutenant had a bemused look on his face as Miles looped the lanyards together to bundle the drives. "I like the way you think. Two is one, and . . ."

"One is none," Miles finished, then grinned. "You forget, Marines raised me. Half of my bedtime stories were about logistics."

"Fair enough," the lieutenant said. "We done here?"

Miles took a last look around the server room. Part of him ached to bring *some* of it back home. His pragmatic side noted that everything in this room was a relic of another time and would be of limited utility. *Once a computer geek, always a computer geek.* If anything, the solar panels on the roof and the battery packs up above would be of more use — if they could find some way to haul them out. He smiled and nodded. "Yeah, let's get out of here."

The climb up and out of the elevator cab was trickier than getting down. After Miles braced his feet on the handrail around the interior, he was able to shove himself up on top. He tried to imagine having to make the same climb under duress, with grasping hands trying to tear you down. The woman who'd died on top of the elevator should have had a chance, somehow. The ladder molded into the side of the elevator shaft ran all the way. Even in the darkness she should have stumbled upon it at some point and found her way up and out. There was no sign that she'd slipped and fallen. Had she just given up? From all appearances, it seemed so. Which led him to consider the family in the farmhouse. In a sense, they'd given up, as well, and it was an action that he could in no way fathom. In all the years since Z-Day, through all the pain and terror, he'd never once considered quitting. There was always a chance, and you never gave up without giving it everything you had. *Charlie Mike, boy.* Pete had hammered the sentiment into him from the time he was old enough to get it. *Continue Mission.*

Trouble grasping algebra? Charlie Mike. Got cut from the basketball team? Charlie Mike. There was a time when Miles thought he hated Pete and had even told him as such. As he grew older and saw how his friends and others of his generation reacted to the slightest hardship, Miles understood the purpose behind the method. His uncle had inculcated in him a resolve that was far beyond that of his contemporaries. Pete had never refused to help, but he'd never let him give up, either. Miles supposed those lessons would have paid off if the world had never changed. But even after the change, those lessons had served him well. *Zombies eating the neighbors? Charlie Mike, boy.*

At the top, Miles slid through the railing around the elevator shaft. The three SEALs stood in a loose cluster at the top of the shaft. They didn't acknowledge his presence, which he supposed was a step up from the outright contempt Janacek had started with. *Small victories.*

Chief Foraker waved his hand at the power array. "What should we do with this, Mikey?"

Ross frowned and rubbed his chin. "On the one hand, I'd say leave it as is with the elevator at the top, just in case. On the other, I know you said that the controls at the top lock it out, Mr. Matthews, but I hate leaving something like that to chance."

Miles shrugged. "I'll be the first to admit that I'm not an expert. There may well be a console down there that can run the elevator. Why, are you worried about a zombie learning how to punch buttons?" He fell quiet when the other men gave him only grim stares in response. "Right. Bad joke."

Ross held his thumb and forefinger apart at a distance sufficient to slip one, but not two, sheets of paper between. "Somewhat funny. Chief, Janacek, pull the plug."

"Aye aye, sir,"

Ross opened his mouth to say something else but flinched suddenly. He held up a finger to quiet them as he stepped through the double doors onto the roof and then pressed the transmit button on his MBITR. He listened, then cursed with his finger off of the transmit button. He tapped it and said, "Roger that."

"What's wrong?" Miles asked. With nothing else to do, he'd followed the other man outside. Nosy? Sure, but it wasn't like Ross had ordered him to stay put. After the ordeal downstairs, a little sunshine seemed in order, if only to help him forget the oddness of the corner office zombie.

"Chopper just radioed in. Chip light came up on their way here. That's a sensor that picks up metal shavings in the oil — not a good sign, for obvious reasons. They're going to have to set down on the other building for a few hours so Castillo can filter the oil and check it. Best case, it's just a flaky sensor and they can swap it out. If not, we're grounded. No matter how things work out, we won't be leaving before dark. In that scenario we're headed out at first light." He shrugged. "Worst case, we camp out for a while and hold out for another chopper."

Miles fingered his pouch full of thumb drives. "At least it happened now, and not on the way home. All things considered, I'm much happier stuck up here than I'd be hoofing it out in the Wild. Any word from Camp Perry?"

"Not at the moment, but I'm not particularly worried. I'm sure they're just too preoccupied to be reassuring us." Miles thought he detected a hint of dithering in Ross' words, which was understandable. How would Miles himself be reacting if he knew that his home was under attack? He doubted it would be anywhere near as well as the SEAL.

Foraker and Janacek stepped out of the elevator shack. The Chief joined their huddle and said, "We've got everything rewired and the elevator dropped back down. Chopper on the way?"

Ross handed each man a handful of drives and pocketed his own. "Stash those, Chief, Brian. And we're on hold for maintenance."

"Well, shit," Foraker said.

The thumping of the helicopter's rotors rose in volume as the Black Hawk got closer. At first, Miles felt tempted to watch it all the way in, but then he remembered the sentry on the 9th floor, and he began to scan the ground. He might as well have been looking down on a still photo for all that he saw. He leaned over the edge of the roof a bit to look down at the base of the building. If there had been one in here, there had to be others. The noise outside was sure to rouse them.

Nothing.

The helicopter passed between the admin and executive office buildings and flared as Cartwright pulled the nose up to slow down. Miles turned his head to watch. The Black Hawk was a bit larger than the helicopter the CEO had preferred, but there was still plenty of room around the helipad. With the wheels down, Cartwright cut the engines and the rotors began to slow. After a few moments, one of the side doors slid open. Castillo leaped out with a two-wheeled cart holding a pair of metal bottles. Miles frowned. "What's that?"

"Oxy-acetylene rig," Foraker said as he stepped up beside Miles and made his own assessment of the ground. "Same one we used on the fire door up here." The SEAL extracted a can of Skoal from a pocket on his vest and tamped it down. He offered it to Miles, who declined. Even if he felt inclined to partake, the writing on the can was so faded he wondered if the tobacco had any kick left to it. "Suit yourself," Foraker chuckled and tucked a dip into his mouth.

"Did you guys clear the executive building last time around?"

The Chief shrugged. "Chopper didn't land. Dropped us off, then picked us up after we radioed back in." He grimaced as something seemed to occur to him. "Don't know that they have another drop bar they can install. Then again, if the door starts to give way they can just take off." He winked at Miles. "We ain't got that luxury, 'less you got a parachute in your ruck, there."

Miles shook his head. "Why, do you?"

The Chief grinned. "Naw."

Miles jerked his chin at the ground below. "I don't like that, for the record."

The older man looked down at the ground and sighed. "It is what it is. I'll take a few moments of peace when I can get them, I suppose."

"Where do you think they went? North with the rest of the ones that we've seen lately?" Miles grimaced. "How good are your walls? They able to stand up against thousands, or tens of thousands?"

"Doubt it." Foraker shrugged. "And there's not much I can do about it here." He glanced over toward Janacek and Ross. The other men were digging rations out of their rucksacks and setting down for an early dinner. "Come on, kid, enjoy it while you can get it. Let's grab a bite and take a load off."

Miles followed the big SEAL after a moment of hesitation. He couldn't help a look back at the ground and the opposite rooftop, where the flare of the welding torch was visible despite the brightness of the late afternoon sun.

At this point, Alex was so filthy that the extra mud he acquired crawling up the creek bank was moot. He paused near the top and eased his head up and over.

Cara's sense of direction was right on the money. The faded brick buildings in front of him weren't familiar, but the weed-choked playground equipment was. He looked back and forth across the back of the school several times. Nothing stirred.

He brought his head below the bank and looked down to where Cara and Twigs stood. The creek was narrower here, and there was no dry area to walk on, so they waited in water that came up to Twig's knees. "It looks clear," Alex whispered.

They stared at each other in silence before Twigs shrugged and said, "Hey, we made it this far. Let's quit wasting daylight and saddle up." He scrambled up the bank and over the edge without so much as a look back.

Cara looked at Alex and raised an eyebrow. "Saddle up?"

Despite the seriousness of their situation, he grinned. "What can I say? The kid likes westerns."

Alex moved to follow Twigs. His second ascent was a bit steadier than his first, but every time he slipped, he couldn't help but look at Cara out of the corner of his eye. She didn't seem to have any problems as she clambered up the steep, slippery bank with a dancer's grace. He felt awkward and clumsy in comparison. Halfway up, she noticed his glances and smirked at him.

Cheeks burning, Alex snapped his eyes back to the task at hand. *Focus, dummy.*

They crested the top of the bank and joined Twigs.

For a moment, the three of them froze, overtaken by the spectacle. To one of the adults, it might have been of little interest, but this was their first look at something from the world before that wasn't contained within the safety of the fences.

The rear of the school didn't look as though it had been through a battle. Alex supposed that most of the action had taken place at the front, though he saw a few broken windows. For the most part, it just looked abandoned. The overgrown grass hid most of the facility, though the faded hulks of playground equipment sprouted up here and there. The expanse of blacktop was free of grass, though it had a multitude of weed-choked cracks.

Tall, metal poles sprouted around the perimeter of the cracked blacktop. For a moment, Alex was unsure what they might be, but he realized after he examined them. At one time they'd supported chain link fencing, but the survivors had stripped it to use on their own fencing. He didn't remember much if any of the playground, but he supposed that didn't mean anything. He'd only been a few months into his preschool career before Z-Day.

A pair of double doors led into the school off of the blacktop. A prone, skeletal corpse held one of the doors open. It was too big to be a kid; Alex supposed that was a small blessing. A dead kid was a bit too close to home. *Don't get too used to it. You know most of the kids didn't make it.*

"Through or around?" Cara whispered. Alex jumped and turned to her. Before she'd spoken, he hadn't realized that he'd been staring at the doors for so long. Maybe the body was a bigger deal than he wanted to admit to himself, though he wasn't sure why. The creeps didn't bother him, though it felt a heck of a lot safer when they were on the other side of the fence and he had a rifle. Alex reached up and pulled out his baseball bat, then turned back to look at the doors.

He could see light through the windows in the twin doors. The hallway they opened into had an exit on the opposite side of the building. He glanced left, then, right. The wide, brick structure of the school was uneven. The school corporation had added rooms and wings over the years until the conglomeration of red brick stretched for hundreds of feet. It would save them time to go straight through, but . . .

"Let's just say no for now," Alex muttered, then pointed to the portion of the building to his right. "Let's go around that way. Fewer windows."

"Follow me," Cara whispered, and stepped forward before the others could say a word. Twigs looked at Alex with a raised eyebrow. Alex just shrugged and waved his hand after her.

Cara stepped on the edge of the blacktop, but she kept her attention on the knee-high grass surrounding the buildings. As Alex trotted along behind the other two, he kept his eyes on the grass as well. It stood uniformly tall, which he assumed was a good sign. Nothing seemed to hide in it, and nothing had been through recently. It wasn't like he'd made an intense study of the behavior of long grass, but it was something Miss Val and some of the other teachers had stressed in lessons. 'Always watch out for crawlers.'

Don't know why they bothered. It's not like they ever let us go outside.

Cara reached the end of the blacktop and turned right along a sidewalk paralleling the building. Alex stood back to let Twigs filter ahead, and assumed the final position in line. He tried to walk sideways, although it was awkward, to keep his eyes to their rear. The world was motionless around them save for the flutter of the ground cover in the wind.

The sidewalk turned to follow the building, but Cara held them back at the corner. Alex imitated her and stuck his head around to study the side of the building. A parking lot half-full of faded, dusty cars sat on this end, and a sagging split-rail fence separated it from the sidewalk.

Alex's eyes followed the sidewalk to the T-intersection where it paralleled the road, across, and to the houses on the other side. His breath caught.

The house across from the school was an unremarkable red brick, but it was the sight at the rear of the house that caught Alex's attention. A tall board fence surrounded the backyard, and just over the top, he could see a faded play set supporting a yellow tube slide.

His father's face was as much a blur as that of his mother's, but he remembered that slide. He remembered helping his dad build it — though he supposed that his help back then had consisted of getting in the way. But that was his house, he was sure of it!

Cara grabbed his arm as he moved out from behind the corner of the building. "Slow down," she hissed. "We haven't come this far to blow it now."

His heart pounding, Alex paused, then nodded. She was right. He knelt down and did his best to contain his excitement. After a few nerve-racking moments of silent study, Cara whispered, "I don't see anything."

Alex didn't figure he had a right to chime in after what he'd almost done, but Twigs felt no such compunction. "Me, either."

Cara cocked an eyebrow at Alex. "Okay," he said.

She smiled. "Let's do this, but like a team, all right?" Cara stood and crept down the sidewalk, leaning over to duck under the windows. A few of the windows had brownish smears that Alex assumed were blood, but nothing stirred inside as they moved forward.

At the next corner, Cara peered around and pulled back. "Nothing," she said, though there was a strange tone to her voice.

"What, you disappointed?" Alex joked.

She didn't return his smile. "This is weird. Shouldn't we see something?"

"Some of the adults have been saying they haven't seen as many creeps," Twigs chimed in. "Maybe they're all gone."

"Maybe," Cara replied, but she didn't sound convinced.

"We're not going to accomplish anything talking about it," Alex murmured. "Let's get this over with and worry about where they went when we're back home."

Cara nodded. "Right. Slow and easy, stop at that sign, okay?" She pointed to a large decorative sign in the middle of some landscaping at the center of the entrance to Alex's old neighborhood. Dead weeds choked the sign, but he could still make out the letters that read 'Stone Creek Farms.'

As the trio trotted across the road, Alex realized that the further they got away from home, the tighter they clustered. He couldn't speak for the others, but he knew that the knowledge that he wasn't alone in the Wild helped a lot. It was funny. Just the other day, he'd thought that he was alone in the community, and here he had two friends who were willing to put their lives at risk just so he could get some pictures. Three, if you counted Trina. He stepped up to the sign and crouched down.

"This is your house," Cara whispered in his ear. "You make the call."

Alex swallowed and tried to look at everything except his house. The other houses along the street were much like the school – choked with weeds and fading. Here and there, cars sat on flat tires in driveways. The most vibrant thing he saw, besides, were the bright swipes of spray paint on the front doors of the houses and on the sides of the cars. The sun had faded most of the marks, but some on the cars were brighter, where mechanics had recently scavenged parts to keep community vehicles running.

All was silent and still. He turned to look at his front door, and the sight of the spray-painted X inside of the circle elicited a lump in his throat. A place where he'd once felt safe and happy reduced to nothing more than a repository of survival goods. What, he wondered, had they been able to take from there? He thought that he remembered his mother cooking almost every day. Had his mother's pantry provided supplies of food to help feed the survivors that had taken in her son?

"Okay," he found himself saying, and he soft-stepped across the road, up his driveway, and onto his front porch. His palms were sweaty on the tape-wrapped grip of the baseball bat, and he forced himself to take a deep breath.

Alex peered in through the shrouded front windows. Shadows cloaked much of the room, but enough light trickled in from the windows around the perimeter of the house that he recognized his living room. Sudden tears welled in his eyes, and he scrubbed at them with the back of his hand.

He took hold of the doorknob and tested it. It turned without resistance, and the door came open with a faint scuffing sound as the door and weather stripping separated. He listened for a moment, then stepped inside.

A fine sheen of dust coated everything, and if not for that, Alex thought he might have been able to make himself believe that nothing had changed. But as he looked, he could see the sagging tape in the seams of the ceiling panels and the stains of water leaks down the walls. His first home was succumbing to entropy.

There were a few toys on the floor, coated with dust like the rest of the interior. For a moment he turned back and forth in an internal debate on what to do with his baseball bat, but Twigs came up beside him and took it away with a gentle care that seemed far beyond his years. "Get what you need," Twigs whispered. "We're here if you need us."

Alex gave him a thankful smile and crouched down on the floor. His nose twitched at the cloud of dust as he picked up one of the toys and brushed it off. If he was looking for any sort of meaning in it, it failed him. The toy was a stuffed orb, gone squishy with damp, with a stylized bird's face embroidered on the front. The bird was snarling and heavy lines over its eyes gave it a fierce look. It had to have been his, but Alex couldn't remember it.

This wasn't what I came for, he reminded himself. He stood up and searched the walls. The only decoration in the living room was an art print of some fruit in a basket. Alex turned away and moved further into the house.

The dining room and kitchen showed the most signs of the salvage team. The cabinet doors hung open and empty, and a ransacked desk sat in one corner by the dining table. For a moment, he felt the urge to frown at the invasion, but he pushed the feeling away. Maybe what the crews did wasn't kosher by the standards of the old world, but they did what they had to, to keep the community going.

There was a chalkboard on one wall of the kitchen, and a rack that held decorative plates on the opposite side. If there'd been any writing on the chalkboard before Z-Day, the passage of time had rendered it illegible. There were no pictures, and Alex pushed down his sense of rising panic and headed down the hallway toward the rear of the house. He had only a vague sense of Cara and Twigs following in his wake; his focus was on what lay before him.

The first room he checked was a bathroom, empty and scavenged save for some moldering bath toys. The next was a small laundry room, and he forced himself to remain calm.

There were more doors, he hadn't gone through the entire house yet.

The next-to-last door had the standard circle-with-an-X that he'd come to expect, but it boasted some neat lettering as well. He stared at it and tried to wish away the lump in his throat.

The letters read 'BITER-KIA', and he didn't have to think for long to discern what the notation meant.

Alex realized then that knowing your parents were dead and finding actual physical evidence of it were two different things. His mom was behind that door, where she'd been on Z-Day until one of the men from the salvage crews had stilled her. He stared at the doorknob and tried to force himself to raise an arm to open it.

His hand trembled, but he couldn't do it.

Check the other room, he thought. If there's nothing there, then check this one.

Miss Val made sure that all the children attended frequent church services. As such, Alex was not completely unfamiliar with the concept of prayer. He'd prayed for lots of things, in his life, and none of those prayers had ever been answered. In an adult that might have inculcated a reluctance for prayer, but Alex took a more pragmatic view. God wasn't a wish-granting genie. No matter how many times he prayed for his mom and dad to show up at the gates and take him home, it wasn't going to happen. He'd known that even as he prayed for it to happen. Those prayers had come from sadness and angst, and out of a child's desire for there to be magic in a world that was far too frightening.

Please, Lord, he prayed. *I don't want to have to see her like that.*

Alex opened the door to his bedroom. Even with the passage of time, the barrage of bright colors assaulted his eyes. The frame of the child-sized bed was a stylized, bright-red fire truck, and shelves full of toys lined the other walls. A desk with an angled chalkboard for a surface sat in one corner. This room was sufficiently free of dust that Alex could read his own name upon it, rendered in a child's hand with a backward 'L'. Despite himself, he laughed. And then, on top of the shelf closest to the fire truck bed, he saw it.

Large, multicolored letters decorated the front of the picture frame and read 'FAMILY.' Alex recognized a much younger version of himself sandwiched between the hug of two smiling adults. As he saw them, he felt an overwhelming sense that was both relief and a realization that he hadn't truly forgotten their faces. He just needed a reminder of who they were, and this did that for him. *Of course, that's my mom*, Alex thought. *And I would know my dad anywhere.* A weight lifted from his shoulders as the guilt he hadn't realized he felt dissipated. He rubbed his thumbs across the smooth glass of the picture frame and favored the image of his parents with a wistful smile.

He unzipped his backpack and tucked the picture frame inside. He took one final look around the room. None of these things, even what little he recognized, meant a fraction of the treasure he now held. He turned around. Twigs and Cara stood outside of the door, as though they were afraid to violate what had once been his sanctuary. He gave them a content smile. "I'm good," Alex declared. "Let's go home."

He shrugged into his backpack as they walked down the hall, then accepted the baseball bat from Twigs. "Thanks, buddy."

"No prob," Twigs said. "You know what *is* a problem, though?"

"What's that?" Cara wanted to know.

"If we tell anyone about this, we are so grounded!"

"There is that," Alex agreed. He reached out and pulled the front door open. "But we can tell . . ." He trailed off. He sensed rather than saw Cara and Twigs stiffening at his side.

The creeps stood in a half-circle in his front yard, facing the door to Alex's house. His stomach twisted, and he thought, *They followed us. They followed us and now they're waiting for us.*

"Boss."

The word came through the haze of sleep. For a time, he didn't recognize it as something external to his dream, and carried on. Then the noise repeated itself, accompanied this time by an insistent shake.

Dantzler jerked awake and snatched the hand at his shoulder. His other hand was reaching for the knife at his belt before he realized that Lloyd was leaning over his cot. "Boss, wake up, we got a problem."

He blinked and tried to clear his mind of the vestiges of a dream that was already slipping away. He was sweaty under his clothes, and there was a sour taste in his mouth. It had been a fitful rest even before the interruption. "What?"

"We got a problem, boss."

Dantzler grunted and waved his hand for Lloyd to spit it out. He levered up, sat on the edge of his cot, and massaged his eyes with the balls of his hands.

"I ran into Chris Naylor in the cafeteria. He said Pete Matthews cut him loose and shoved Greg Mills into the holding cell. Said Matthews told him he 'had bigger fish to fry' and that he was free to go."

Dantzler stared at Lloyd and tried to remain calm. "That's it? For this, you wake me up like the hounds of Hell are nipping at your heels? Damn, boy, you have got a *severe* sense of paranoia. Have you been sampling the product?"

Lloyd squirmed under the intensity of his gaze. "No, no, don't you get it, boss? Mills was shacking up with Melanie, on Buck's crew."

"And again, I fail to see the problem. The Buck issue is a dead end, there's no one left alive to link us and him." The facial expression Lloyd assumed in reaction to that comment caused Dantzler to fall silent. Lloyd squirmed under the intensity of his gaze. "Talk."

"Melanie, she had a big mouth, boss. I know Buck had to shut her up one night in the bar because she was joking around about our product, asking if anyone had tried it, that kind of thing. Just . . . just stupid stuff, you know, but if she was that free in public, who knows what she'd tell the guy she was sleeping with."

Conjecture, sure. But 'bigger fish?' What kind of coincidence would it take for Mills to know something about his girlfriend's involvement? Dantzler hadn't lived this long leaving things to chance. If it had been some other nobody off of the street, yeah he could make himself believe that it had nothing to do with him, but this was too close. *Damn it.* "You knew this. Buck knew this." Dantzler was wide awake now. "Why was I not told, Lloyd?"

The other man stuttered. "Buck swore to me he had it under control, boss. He knew you'd freak out if you found out, but he took care of it. And hell, I thought the same as you, the crew is dead, so no loose ends, right?"

Back when he'd been new in the outfit — and low on the totem pole — one of the mid-level guys had made a comment that stuck with him. "Crooks that get caught are stupid. That's not hyperbole; it's fact. The average prison inmate has an IQ ten points lower than the average person in the general population. If somebody in your crew is going to get busted, more likely than not it's going to be the idiot of the bunch."

"So what's the solution?" Young Dantzler had asked.

"Keep the idiots at arm's length and in the dark. And keep the smart ones well-paid."

Now, he wondered if he hadn't overlooked the first part of that equation in favor of the latter. It was becoming evident that he had some serious deficiencies with his crew. He stared Lloyd down and decided that the man was moving to the head of the class for headcount reduction. The only question was when and how to do it, so that Victor and Ben didn't get too suspicious.

He decided that Lloyd had squirmed long enough in the silence and spoke. "Tell the others the plan has changed. We're getting out of here right now."

"Okay, boss, but . . . won't we get spotted?"

Dantzler considered that. If Pete was cutting prisoners loose, he wasn't up in the tower. That helped quite a bit. Of course, the other gate guards were sure to see something, even if it was to notice that no one was standing watch on the southeastern bunker. They needed a distraction. After a moment of thought, he smiled.

"Not if we leave after the fuel dump blows up, Lloyd."

The other man's jaw dropped. Dantzler could understand his shock. The diesel fuel the community processed from their soybean crops at a nearby bio-diesel plant wasn't guarded like gold, exactly, but the large tanks near the motor pool stayed chained and locked with redundant padlocks so that no one person could draw on the fuel stores. "Boss . . . They need that gas for runnin' the tractors and for the salvage crews. If we do that, well, hell."

"Problem, Lloyd?" Dantzler inquired as he pulled on his boots and began to lace them up.

"They'll *starve* to death, boss. They won't be able to plant crops, or haul anything over any sort of long distance."

"Maybe. Maybe not. You in, or out?"

The other man grimaced and swallowed. "I'm in, boss. I've still had about all this place I can stand."

"Good. Tell the others to get anything together they don't want to leave behind. I'm going to sneak out to the culvert and build us a bomb."

Chapter 32

The front door vibrated in its frame as Alex backed away. He'd thrown the deadbolt, but as he watched the door shake and heard the repeated thumps as the creeps launched themselves at the closed door, he couldn't help but think that it wasn't going to hold for long.

"How many?" Twigs whispered. Alex didn't know why he bothered to keep his voice down. It wasn't like they could hide from the things.

"A lot," Alex said.

"Back door?" Cara asked.

"Nothing," Alex said, then turned and pointed. "Just the patio. The fence goes all the way around." The long, rectangular kitchen table sat next to the sliding doors. He supposed that it had made for a nice view during meals, but he couldn't remember. Maybe his parents had kept the drapes closed.

"Better than nothing," Cara replied. She stepped over and checked either side of the sliding glass door. "Fence still looks tight. There's nothing in the backyard. Climb out?"
Before Alex could answer, he heard the sound of splintering wood. When he turned, the front door had popped partially out of its frame. Light shone in from the upper corner,

opposite the hinges. "We have to slow them down," Alex thought out loud. "Help me!"

He grabbed the first chair at the table and hurled it toward the front door. The chair was heavier than he'd first thought, so it landed short of the door in the living room. Better than nothing.

"Flip the table over!" Twigs gasped.

Alex threw a second chair before giving his friend a confused look. "What do you . . ." he started. Then he got it. "Right! Open the slider!" As Cara fumbled with the latch on the patio door, Alex slid his baseball bat into his backpack and got both hands under the table. He heaved with a grunt but accomplished nothing. Like the chairs, the table was solid and heavy.

The patio door slid open a bare few inches, then stopped. Cara cursed and closed it. She tore the drapes the rest of the way open, then bent over to pull the sawed-off broomstick out of the lower track. Twigs stepped up beside Alex and added his strength to Alex's next heave. This time, they got it up on two feet before the weight become too much and the table slammed back down to the kitchen floor with a hollow boom.

As though in accompaniment, the front door rattled again, and wood splintered. They had moments if that. Cara had the patio door open now, and she joined Twigs and Alex. The three of them heaved as one. The table balanced on two legs, and Alex cringed, waiting for it to come back down, but their combined strength got it past the tipping point, and the table slammed down on its side with the surface facing the slider.

The front door gave up the ghost and fell inward along with a pair of creeps. As soon as the blockage was out of the way, another handful rushed the door. With dawning horror, Alex realized that these creeps were faster and more agile than any that he'd seen before. He reached up for his baseball bat but Cara yelled to stop him.

"Outside, pull the table with us!"

Twigs ducked under a table leg and began to pull on that end. Alex had to step around, which took far too long. By the time he got to his own corner, the first wave of creeps was almost on them, emaciated claws reaching out.

But they weren't alone. Cara stepped up between the two of them with her suppressed carbine and began pulling the trigger. Her first few shots were ineffectual, and Alex heard the slight ping of ricochets. If the .22s weren't going to work, they were in big trouble.

That concern vanished as Cara settled down and found her rhythm. A creep slumped into the table in front of Alex, its life snuffed out. Then the next, and the next, and suddenly they had breathing room.

Her rifle clicked empty as Twigs pulled the table flush against the wall next to the door frame and stepped outside. Alex had his as close as he could get it without pressing himself against the window, so he sidestepped and backed out, then tried to pull his side flush.

The creeps inside the house were advancing at a more deliberate pace now, and Alex heard wood creak as others tested the strength of the fence on the side closest to the front door. *They're not supposed to be that smart. They're supposed to be single-minded.*

Cara's voice was high-pitched, and he realized that she was just as terrified as he was. "Their heads shouldn't be that damn hard, it's rotten bone!"

Twigs was the only member of the group that didn't sound like he was freaking out. "Just need a bigger bullet." His slingshot hummed, and one of the creeps inside of the house jolted sideways with a massive hole bored in its skull. "See?"

"Less talky, more runny," Alex managed. One of the fence boards near the house burst in, and a creep got an arm and shoulder through.

"What he said," Cara added, and sent a trio of shots into the creep trying to get through the fence. It fell still, then slid backward as the creeps behind it started moving it out of the way.

Alex sprinted past his playset and put his foot on the bottom horizontal rail of the fence to boost himself up. He didn't see anything to the left or right on the other side, so he pulled himself up and straddled the fence. The pointed tops dug painfully into his crotch, but he'd take that over being eaten alive any day. "Twigs!" he barked, reaching down.

The smaller boy grabbed his hands, and Alex heaved. For a moment, he tottered, but he clamped his thighs tighter on the fence and kept himself from falling over. Twigs' shoes scrabbled on the fence as he tried to get a foothold. Alex had enough momentum that he had the other boy halfway up before his feet got a grip and added his own leg strength to the movement. Twigs released one of Alex's hands and grabbed the top of the fence, then repeated the motion with his other hand. With Twigs steadied, Alex reached down and grabbed Cara's hands. She'd already slung the carbine over one shoulder, and as Alex pulled her up she jerked her head over her shoulder and stared at the creeps who were tumbling over the kitchen table barricade and into the back yard.

"I got you," Alex managed through gritted teeth as he heaved. Cara's longer legs helped even more, but instead of pausing at the top like Twigs, she kept moving, rolling over the top of the fence and landing lightly on her feet. Despite the situation, Alex had to marvel at the move. He unclenched his legs and swung his inner leg over the fence, then dropped down to the grass below.

A couple of creeps had already rounded the corner and were heading their way. Twigs missed low with his first shot, and the ball bearing took a redundant chunk of flesh out of the creep's neck. Cara swung her carbine over and started pulling the trigger. By the time her fourth shot brought the maimed creep down, Twigs' next shot had nailed the last creep in the forehead and stopped it in its tracks.

"I'm never making fun of that thing again," Alex promised.

A grin flashed across Twigs' face. "Less talky, more runny," he laughed. He got a running start and hopped the drainage ditch between the edge of Alex's house and the road.

"Kid's got a point," Cara said, and they moved to follow him. There was no stealth in their motions now; they were running for pure survival. If there were creeps behind them, Alex didn't care. His vision had narrowed into a cone of what was right in front of him. They sprinted across the road and down the sidewalk between the parking lot and school. He had the vague sense of a looming presence in the parking lot, moving to cut them off. But then they had run past it and were sprinting through the overlong grass. They didn't have time to take the long way. Speed was their only salvation.

They angled through rusting hulks of playground equipment, and past the poles sprouting from the blacktop. "Keep going!" Alex shouted. "Jump the creek! That'll slow them down!"

None of them replied, but if it was possible, they bent their heads low and redoubled their efforts. Alex's side burned with exertion, and his heart thundered in his chest. The edge drew ever closer.

Twigs was the first to jump, and his arms cartwheeled in midair. He was going to come up short, Alex realized as he jumped himself. With a squeal that was part terror but mostly exhilaration, Twigs arced into the opposite bank and splashed into the mud. Even as Alex and Cara made their own jumps, Twigs was sinking his hands and feet into the side of the bank and scrambling to the top.

Alex landed halfway up the bank with a grunt. He shook his head to clear it, then imitated his friend. He rolled over the edge onto the opposite bank and landed on his hands and knees. He stayed in that position, trying to catch his breath. Finally, he raised his head and looked for his friends. They were both there, and both stared at the opposite side of the creek. Alex followed their eyes with his own.

Behind the school, the grass waved peacefully in the breeze. Other than that, all was still.

"Where did they go?" Twigs whispered. No one answered, as though afraid that speaking would break the illusion on the opposite side of the creek.

"I don't know," Alex managed. "But let's get the hell out of here before they come back."

They'd completed the mission, but Miles had a vaguely unsettled feeling. It was the kind of sense he'd gotten in the old days when he left the stove on. If the SEALs felt the same way they weren't letting on. Janacek rested on his bedroll in a shaded part of the roof with his baseball cap pulled over his eyes. The Chief sat on his own pack but had forgone rest for the moment. He thumbed through a battered paperback mostly held together by strips of duct tape.

Ross stepped up beside Miles and took in the tableau for a moment. "Welcome to the Navy, kid. Hurry up and wait."

Miles grunted. "How do you just turn it off?"

"Practice, I guess. Take a load off, Mr. Matthews. Time moves slow when there's nothing going on." Ross gave him a knowing smile. "The morning flew by in comparison, huh?"

"Yeah." Miles eased out of his pack and leaned against the outer wall surrounding the edge of the roof. He glanced down, but the streets remained empty. He shuddered. He knew he shouldn't complain, but he'd never expected *emptiness*. This felt more like being back home, without the long sight lines the open fields around the community offered. Sure, what little he could see looked empty, but there were any number of places within easy view that could hide watchful eyes, waiting for . . . . something. That thing on the ninth floor had been there for a reason.

Miles shrugged. He couldn't do anything about it. Being ready for any curve balls that the universe decided to throw *was* something he could control. He dug a box of ammunition out of the bottom of his pack and began to replenish the rounds he'd used earlier.

Just down the wall, Ross sat down and took his own glance at the ground. He worked his mouth for a bit and finally spat over the edge before turning back around. The officer seemed content to lean his head back against the knee wall and enjoy the fading, late afternoon sun. Miles didn't know if the other man had taken any shots before they'd boarded the helicopter. From the calm demeanor the man exhibited, he assumed the SEAL's magazines were in full working order.

The silence was getting to him, so he spoke up. "So how long have you guys known?"

Ross lowered his head and gave him a puzzled look. "Known what?"

"About what really caused the outbreak."

"Ah." Ross brought his head back and closed his eyes. "Couple of years, I guess. We found the survivors, first. If you're going to while away the end of the world on a tropical island, it's smart to shield your light and thermal signature. It took us a while, but as soon as we finagled a connection to the Keyhole reconnaissance satellites, they jumped right out at us. We were pretty excited to find survivors. But that didn't last." Ross made a face. "We started doing radio intercepts — out of habit more than anything, I suppose. There was some weirdness in some of the things they said, so we proceeded with caution, you know? Did a covert insertion and observed for a few days." He sighed. "There were kids there, which shouldn't be a surprise. Sometimes even monsters have families. But they had a school set up, and the things they were teaching those kids . . ." He shuddered. "Command made the decision to capture the place. It didn't even take much interrogation for the whole story to spill. They were proud of it. They did it for the 'greater good.'" Ross' eyes went distant with memory. "We had a tough time with that."

The two men sat in silence for a long time, each absorbed in their thoughts. Finally, Miles mused, "Did it make it easier, knowing why it happened?"

"Not so much. There's still a world full of the infected. We've still got loved ones we'll never see again."

"It's just weird, I guess. We went back and forth for so long over what they were, zombies, you know. It wasn't like we had current events to talk about, you know?" Miles laughed. "One guy I know was sure that they were voodoo zombies, and he almost got into a fistfight with someone who thought it was part of the Rapture." He shrugged. "Maybe knowing would have been better. We still would have been helpless, but it wouldn't have all felt so futile."

"They are just . . . animated dead flesh. They're puppets — meat machines. There's no greater story behind it, other than the insanity of the people who created and spread the plague. No, the real story is about you and the rest of your people. *You* guys endured. So much of the rest of the world just gave into fear or terror, but you fought back. You weathered the storm. I can't even fathom what those early days were like for you folks."

"Why? Was it so different for you and your people?"

"You know, it's funny," Ross remarked. "I mean, we heard the stories about the flu. The situation in Crimea was such a disaster that the initial outbreak was just a blip on our radar. We were so concerned about the Russians kicking off another world war that we didn't realize things were already on the brink. Hell, when the second stage began we thought the Russians had escalated things with some kind of nerve gas. How about you?"

"Not what I would have expected, I guess," Miles said. "Things never came to a complete stop, but it kind of sputtered. It got hard to find stuff in the grocery stores, a lot of businesses were short-handed. Lots of doom and gloom in the press but people just lowered their heads and went on with their business." He huffed a short bark of laughter. "It was easy to ignore when the infection was just a lot of people laid up in the hospital or images on the screen. After Z-Day, not so much."

"That was the make or break moment," Ross agreed. "I know a lot of hard-core guys who saw it and just . . . locked up. They weren't mentally prepared for something out of a horror movie." He shrugged. "Some of them came out of it, some didn't make it."

"Right. Same thing with some of our people, I guess. You can . . . What was that?" Miles got onto his feet and looked around. He'd heard a strange noise, and it came again — the distant concussion of something hard on metal. Beside him, Ross abandoned his relaxed pose and stood as well. The noise came again, and Miles turned his head to look across the span between the two buildings. "It's over there," he said, pointing toward the helipad. He wasn't the only one who'd heard it; two members of the helicopter crew scrambled around on the opposite roof with a frantic air.

Ross got on his radio and said, "Whiskey, Hatchet. Status report, over." He fell silent, then cursed. Now there were three figures on the opposite roof; one had been behind the helicopter. "No helmets — they're not receiving." The other men clustered near the door that Castillo had welded shut earlier. The sound repeated, and the three men reacted as though electrocuted. Without hesitating, they sprinted back across the roof toward the helicopter.

"Shit," Miles whispered. "They're at the door, aren't they?"

"It's got to hold," Ross muttered. "Solid steel, welding bead all around? No way in hell they can crack that."

493

Foraker and Janacek stepped up beside the two of them, curious what the fuss was about. Ross jerked his head toward the maintenance shack. "Chief, Brian, rear guard. Listen up for anything out of the ordinary."

"Aye, sir," the Chief said, and the two men trailed backward.

"There's a dogleg in the stairs on this building. You have to turn almost immediately after entering the stairwell. How about over there?" Ross jerked his chin at the other building. The aircrew had buttoned up inside of the helicopter, and the rotors were beginning to turn as they fired up the engines.

"Straight shot from the landing below," Miles said. "But it's a damn *staircase*. How could they get enough of a head of steam to . . ."

With a final crash, the fire door on the opposite building jerked part of the way open. The weld held for the most part, but the force was pushing the door frame out of the surrounding block wall. Chunks of concrete splintered off and danced on the roof. "Mother of God," Ross whispered. "How many are there?"

The block wall gave up the ghost, and the entire door frame slammed into the roof. Almost immediately, what Miles could only describe as a sheer torrent of gray flesh poured out onto the roof. Literal piles of zombies crawled over the roof and each other with one destination in mind.

"They're so fast," Miles whispered, "Why are they so damn fast?" They must have filled the stairway from floor to ceiling. They enveloped the chopper from the surface of the roof to just below the rotors. Even as the whine of the turbines raised in pitch he could hear the squealing of metal and the cracking of safety glass under the pressure.

"Come on, baby," Ross said. "Fly, fly fly."

The rotors faded into one continuous blur as the Black Hawk's engines screamed under the load. The helicopter began to lift from the helipad. The uppermost zombies who pounded on the sides began to fall as the surface of the airframe shifted beneath them. The mass beneath the chopper surged as one, as though it were a single organism rather than hundreds — maybe even thousands — of individuals.

The surge came up under the helicopter's nose, and the rise accelerated sharply. The tail began to dip toward the helipad, and Ross cursed.

Miles didn't know who was at the controls, but he reacted with smooth precision. The helicopter pivoted forty-five degrees and the rise steadied into a more even horizontal plane. It was still slow going — he couldn't make out the bottom half of the helicopter through the tidal wave of gray flesh that tried to rip it out of the sky — but it crept up, inch by inch, rotors straining.

At once, the mass beneath the chopper parted, hundreds of arms releasing their grip, and the chopper bucked. This is what Vir had seen, Miles realized, and he tried to imagine the terror the other man must have felt as the encroaching horde lapped at his heels.

The helicopter lurched, and Miles' breath caught in his throat. Staccato impacts of bone on metal sounded across the gap between the buildings. A fresh torrent of the dead had erupted from the stairway. They sprinted up the ramp formed by the bodies of their brethren and launched into the side of the chopper. A few went too high and the rotors dismembered them, but most stayed low enough. The repeated strikes pushed the chopper to the side. He realized that the Black Hawk was no longer rising, but the effect of the repeated impacts combined to push the vehicle across the roof.

"Shit, no, no no no!" Ross shouted.

The outside edge of the horde had reached the lip of the roof, and they began to trickle over, lemming-like. Some lost their grips on the helicopter and plummeted to the ground below. Most of them did not.

The helicopter began to tilt. The turbines screamed in a last ditch effort, but the fall of the helicopter accelerated as the rotors went from horizontal to vertical. At one moment it was hanging in midair; in the next, it had inverted and headed toward the ground. Ross grabbed Miles and pulled him down behind the knee wall. "Everybody down!"

The initial impact of the helicopter wasn't much; a subdued thump accompanied by the sound of crumpling metal. Miles could only imagine what it looked like, but his imagination went blank at the thunderclap of the explosion. He didn't know how full the fuel tanks had been, but even empty the fumes would have been explosive. Who knew how much fuel remained in the welding rig? The combined blasts vibrated the building for a long moment, and after all was still, he became aware of the pounding of his own heart.

Ross eased his grip on Miles and the two men straightened. A thick, twisting cloud of black smoke rose from the still-burning wreckage at the base of the opposite building. Miles stared at what had once promised to be their ride home, then raised his eyes to look at the roof across the way.

The mob was no longer as frenetic as they had been, and they trickled back into the staircase to a destination that Miles felt he could guess.

No need to hurry, right fellas? We aren't going anywhere, after all.

There'd been an old guy in the outfit by the name of Deacon who'd been the go-to guy for anything and everything explosive. When he'd started working his way up the ranks, Dantzler had worked a few jobs with the old man. He'd paid enough attention to pick up a few things by osmosis, but the old fart never, *ever* shut the hell up. Ivan figured if he was going to talk anyway, he might as well steer the conversation toward something more interesting. Deac was like a walking Wikipedia of explosives. If he had access to commercial or military grade stuff he knew how to use just enough to get the job done without overkill. One time their supply contact had gotten caught up in a prostitution sting and time was of the essence. The old man had walked into a hardware store and in a few hours had improvised explosives ready to go — all from the contents of a few shopping bags.

"It's just chemistry, kid," the old man had explained. The conversation was concurrent to Deac's slow, careful assembly of the pipe bomb Dantzler was going to conceal under the seat of a dirty judge's convertible. "Exothermic reaction. Any damn fool can get shit to blow up. Takes someone smart to keep it under some appearance of control."

"*Appearance* of control?" Dantzler questioned, curious.

"Entropy rules the world, son. Nothing remains static. Time wears us all down, one way or another. Chemical compounds like this, in a way they're an affront to nature.

They're mixtures of things that never would have come together on their own. So they don't like being together — over time, they'll change states, become less stable and more volatile. So a smart bomber, he doesn't keep a stash on hand, be makes what he needs as he needs it. Anything else is a shortcut to launching your house into the moon. Now, your high-end stuff, your RDX, that's a beautiful thing. Nice and stable, you can light the shit on fire and it won't explode on you. But it's laced with chemicals that the man can use to trace its origin, so that's out. But it is what it is. At least we don't have to mess with dynamite."

"Why's that?"

"Dynamite, in the old days, had tons of nitro in it, and that stuff sweated like you wouldn't believe. The guy who taught me screwed up and dropped a couple old sticks . . . Boom, see you later, guy."

Not long after that job, the BATFE rolled Deacon up in a sting when he went to buy from one of his suppliers who'd turned state's evidence. Unfortunately for him, his penchant for talking was well known. As soon as word got out that ol' Deacon was behind bars, he'd become a problem rather than an asset. He'd breathed out his last on the tile floor of a shower room in lockup with a toothbrush shiv lodged in his kidney.

Post Z-Day, Dantzler didn't have to worry about a reputation for being chatty *or* the long arm of the law. Among the more interesting things Buck had discovered had been the contents of the demolitions locker at a nearby rock quarry. They'd stashed most of it off site — it wasn't like you could hide a few hundred pounds of explosives under your bunk — and never reported the find to the rest of the community. But Ivan always kept a little bit around, replenishing it every so often as Buck used it to access secured areas in warehouses, gun safes, and the like.

In retrospect, it was amazing that no one had ever questioned the sheer quantity of gear that Buck had been able to provide. If they'd known the extent of what he'd been holding back it would have blown their minds.

It had been a good run, Dantzler reflected. But all good things must come to an end.

He didn't need much of the Semtex for what he intended; the fuel tanks weren't fenced, so could place the bomb right against one. He did need some shrapnel, though, and he molded a fist-sized chunk of explosive into a length of cast-iron pipe. When he detonated the bomb, hot shards of the pipe would punch into the thin-skinned fuel tanks and spill hundreds of gallons of fuel before it caught fire as well.

Dantzler had always loved fireworks, and this one promised to be cooler than most.

Lloyd was right, of course. With the loss of the vast majority of their fuel supplies, the community wouldn't be able to haul loads of soybeans to the bio-diesel plant, much less plant and harvest them. More than likely he was sentencing nearly 200 men, women, and children to slow death by starvation. The gardens and greenhouses only provided so much. If they didn't have the large amounts of feed required to raise cattle, the community's only source of protein when the meat ran out were the canned goods. When winter arrived, they'd have to rely on food stores, which would run out fast with the loss of half of their potential supplies. Without the industrial farming methods made possible with machinery, there was no way to feed so many people just on produce with their small amount of secure acreage.

He doubted it would get that far. Starving people would get desperate long before that. In a way, his bomb would kill them all, just not at the time of the explosion. He considered that aspect again and shrugged. Heck with them. They deserved it for not being smart enough to spread out their critical supplies.

Dantzler screwed on the first end cap. This was the easy part; the next was trickier, despite all the practice and instruction he'd had.

Unfortunately, he was out of wireless detonators. This was going to be old school — a spool of wire with a hand-crank activator. That meant the crawling feeling in his stomach was only partly diminished as he fed the detonator wires through the second end cap. He nestled the detonator down into the Semtex and twisted the final end cap onto the pipe. He had to stabilize the wires as he did so, lest he twist them and tear them out of the detonator.

In the depths of the culvert, he heard the sound of movement.

Dantzler froze and cocked his head to one side. He listened for the span of a dozen heartbeats but heard nothing more than the sound of his own breathing.

He licked his lips and set the pipe bomb down on the work bench. With one hand he reached down and grabbed one of the small electric lanterns he used to light up the work area.

The cooking equipment sat further inside of the culvert, shrouded on either end with heavy, translucent plastic tarps. This kept the acrid emissions of the cooking process somewhat contained until it could trickle out. To shield the work lights in the interior, they'd hung heavy, wool blankets on the outside end of the culvert. He drew the first plastic tarp aside and panned the light across the tarp on the other end. Dantzler tried to stare through it to the rear of the pipe as he waited, but the noise did not repeat. The interior was empty, and all he could make out through the plastic were unmoving shadows. He licked his lips and shrugged. *Jumping at ghosts.*

He leaned back over the workbench and finished assembling the pipe bomb. He taped over the exposed ends of the wire and wrapped the excess length around the body of the bomb. Once it was in place, he would connect the ends of the wire spool to the detonator, reel it out as he got behind cover, and set it off with a quick crank. No fuss, no muss, and the distraction should be big enough for him and his boys to make their break for it.

Again, the noise, and Dantzler stiffened.

This time, he realized his mistake. Sound echoed strangely within the confines of the culvert. What had caught his attention came not from the rear, but from the front. He set the bomb back onto the desk and brought his hand down to his waist to reassure himself that his sidearm was still there. The pistol, an M9 Beretta from a fallen National Guard roadblock, lacked a threaded barrel for a suppressor. It was loud, but it had fifteen rounds in the magazine and one in the chamber.

He stepped over to the blanket and listened for a moment. The noise did not repeat. With a frown, he drew the covering aside and looked out.

To his credit, Dantzler didn't flinch. "Son of a bitch," he whispered.

A dozen or more whip-thin figures at the end of the culvert obscured his view. The cannibals stood and stared back at him with unblinking gray eyes as Dantzler swallowed.

He hadn't been this close to them in years, and the first thing that struck him was the lack of smell. In the beginning, blood and voided waste smeared the cannibals, but time and exposure to the elements had washed them clean. There was little left to mark them as having once been human. Though they varied in height they were essentially identical in appearance — naked and gaunt, with thick, dark scars lining their patchy, leprous skin.

Well, shit. This is going to mess up the schedule a bit. Maybe I can disassemble the workbench, start crushing heads with a table leg or something . . .

Dantzler froze.

One of the cannibals lowered its head and almost seemed to be studying the gate latch. After the span of a few heartbeats, it raised its head and stared at him.

The thing didn't have any lips left to speak of, but Dantzler could have sworn that the death's head grin widened. It raised an emaciated arm and extended a finger.

Tink, tink, tink. With a slow tympanic rhythm, it tapped the finger along one of the bars. With each tap, it lowered its hand until it rested atop the hoop of the locking mechanism. Slowly, it drew its arm back and opened the slide bolt.

He realized with a start that there was a hot warmth trickling down one leg of his slacks. He'd pissed himself in sheer terror. Dantzler opened his mouth to scream but all he could manage was a gasped "Huh, huh." He clutched at his pistol with fingers that had turned nerveless and clumsy. The lead cannibal slid the locking bar to one side and pushed the door open. The hinges were oil-soaked and as quiet as a whisper. The door swung into the side of the culvert with the dull sound of metal on metal.

Who needs a padlock, I said to the boys. They're too dumb to open doors. "Idiot," Dantzler whispered, and as though a switch had been thrown by the sound of his voice, the press at the end of the pipe burst into action. He couldn't tell them apart, really, but he thought that the one that had opened the gate backed up and moved out of the way as the others lurched inside.

He was already stepping backward when he realized that something else was horribly wrong. Though they still staggered, they were moving too fast. Not as fast as an uninfected human, but much, much faster than he'd grown accustomed to. *Well, that's not fair.* A hysterical whimper escaped his mouth.

Dantzler set his feet and raised the Beretta with shaking hands. His first shot went wide and sparked a ricochet off the side the culvert. He cursed and adjusted his aim. His second shot was true, and one of the lead cannibals fell. Usually, that was a good way to stagger or roadblock the ones behind, and a few did stumble, but just as many avoided the sudden trip hazard and kept coming. He backed up again and fired. He took down two more, then missed three in a row.

Keep it together, damn it! He tried to slow his breathing as he kept stepping back. He paused to fire, but it was no use. The Beretta locked open on an empty magazine as his butt slammed into the edge of the workbench. If they hadn't been so nimble, he'd have been able to plug up the culvert with the fallen, which would have given him an opportunity to fort up or even melee out. But they just kept coming on with that implacable, patient gait. The ones he hadn't been able to take down, if anything, were more graceful than the ones he had. With dawning horror, he realized that they were toying with him. He couldn't explain it, but they knew he had no way out, and they approached with a collective, almost shark-like, blank-eyed stare that chilled him to the bone.

No. No. Not like this.

Dantzler slid around the workbench and grabbed the pipe bomb. He glanced up but they were still a dozen steps out of reach. He unscrewed the end cap on the bomb and grabbed the rest of the plastic explosives. He'd wanted the pipe bomb to be just big enough to do the job before.

This, he wanted to be freaking *Biblical.*

He mashed the leftovers onto the end of the pipe. It was far more than could fit inside, which gave him something shaped like a stylized bouquet of flowers or an overflowing ice cream cone. Dantzler laughed hysterically and tucked the device under one arm as he picked up the detonator. With quick twists, he had both wires attached to the crank. He glanced up again; the leading edge would reach the workbench in seconds. He stepped back to get a little more separation and knelt down in the bottom of the culvert. One way or another, he wasn't going to let them touch him.

At the workbench, the passage narrowed so that there was only room for them to walk two abreast. Dantzler began to turn the crank to charge the detonator. As the leading pair reached the opposite end of the desk and reached out for him, he spoke. "Looks like I decided to leave this town one damn day too late, boys."

He pushed the button.

The explosion flashed outward, channeled by the culvert as it followed the path of least resistance. The supplies and equipment that Dantzler and his team had stored were either consumed in the blast or pushed along before it. Ivan's body — what little was left of it — shot into the gate and slammed it shut. If he had still been alive after the impact, the debris that followed after would have put an end to that. Shreds of fabric and pieces of metal and wood peppered the corpse and gate. A blast of flame seared the opposite bank of the creek, but the explosion-borne debris piled up to make a temporary but effective stopper. Stymied, the blast rebounded backward.

On the opposite end of the culvert, flame belched through the vertical drain at the side of the highway. This opening was even smaller than the gate and was stopped up even more quickly by the storm of blast debris.

Capped at either end, pressure began to build inside of the culvert. If the explosion had merely been the result of Dantzler's bomb, its energy might have died down at that point. Amongst the supplies had been stores of diesel fuel — plenty of it, after his wheeling and dealing — alcohol, and kerosene. Aerosolized and consumed by the blast, the force increased in an exponential fashion. The culvert had essentially become a massive pressure vessel hundreds of feet in length.

The dirt cradling the culvert bore up well. The workers who'd installed it had done excellent work, compacting the channel and lining it with gravel to aid in drainage. Had it not been co-opted as a clandestine meth lab it might have lasted for decades.

By way of comparison, the dirt on top of the culvert was only a few inches deep. It bulged as the tube swelled, then finally ruptured as the tortured metal gave way. The southern half of the eastern wall was flash-lit by a vertical sheet of flame. The guards atop the bunkers recoiled; those that weren't flash blinded were thrown to the ground by the concussion. The sound faded, but every building in the compound vibrated in its passing. Pictures fell from walls, books from shelves, and sleepers snapped awake.

Pieces of shredded culvert rained back down to earth followed by lighter pieces of burning debris, dirt, and gravel. If there was any luck, it was the fact that most of the burning debris landed on ground that was somewhat damp from the spring rains. This limited secondary fires.

The explosion had holed out a massive trench running parallel to the eastern wall. As much of the blast went upward, there was little damage done to the wall other than some scorched paint on the aluminum sheathing.

At the southeastern corner, though, the dogleg in the drain brought it within eighteen inches of the wall. The blast pressure that hit there was little different than what hit the rest of the wall, except for the fact that there was much less dirt supporting it at that point. The wall leaned in, then rebounded.

The crew that had erected the wall had been in a hurry, but not so much of a hurry that they skimped in their work. They'd sunk the telephone poles that formed the bones of the eastern and western walls four feet deep. The timbers and metal paneling attached to them represented a not-insignificant amount of weight. Supported across the entire width of the wall, this didn't present an issue.

The fence sagged forward. Timbers splintered and metal squealed. Enough of the wall still stood that the fall didn't continue, though the last two vertical supports swayed outward at a 45-degree angle. For the most part, the wall remained strong. But the southeastern corner stood wide open.

He made it over the fence and was about to flop on his back when he remembered the photograph in his backpack. Alex settled for flopping onto his stomach and savoring the feel of the grass on his cheeks.

"Never thought I'd miss the fence," he said as Cara dropped down inside next to him.

"Next time you get a crazy idea, count me out," Twigs announced. Alex pushed himself up onto his hands and knees before settling into a seated position. He grinned at his friend.

"I know you don't mean that," Alex observed.

"Yeah, maybe not," Twigs admitted. He flashed a broad smile in return.

"We need to tell someone," Cara pronounced.

Alex glanced at Twigs before meeting her eyes. "I know," he said. "But who? You realize what's going to happen to us when we admit we were outside of the fence?" She shrugged. "I know. But I'll take getting grounded or some extra chores over something like that sneaking up on us. They were *smart*, Alex. Too smart. We almost blew it."

She was right, of course. That had been too close. Alex didn't even disagree that they needed to tell someone what they'd just seen. The main problem with that was finding someone who'd believe what they said, and not pass it off as a child's prank.

"Will Pete believe us?"

She didn't hesitate. "Yes. Him, more than anyone else, I think."

"Okay," Alex agreed. He climbed to his feet and sighed at the loss of comfort. His legs still burned from the sprint back along the creek bank.

"Guys!" Trina hissed a stage whisper. "Are you okay?"

The group turned to see the girl emerge from behind a tree.

"Hey," Alex said in greeting. "Yeah, we're cool. Just had some weird stuff happen. Coast clear?"

"Yup. Everybody is busy and quiet. I think you did it."

"We need to get away from the fence," Twigs interjected. "I don't know about you guys but I'm sick of wet socks."

"All right," Alex said, "let's go."

As Twigs and Trina headed away, Alex turned to follow, but a hand on his shoulder held him back. He turned to see what she wanted.

As he turned, she got her free hand on his opposite shoulder and drew him close. "That was intense," she said. "And I wanted to thank you for the adventure. And not wimping out on me."

And then, all at once, Cara's lips were on his, warm and soft and mysterious. At first, Alex was so shocked that he didn't know how to react, but she jerked him closer, and he settled for bringing his arms around her, to pull her even tighter. His hands fluttered as he tried to decide what to do with them – go high, go low, don't touch? She kissed him first, so where should he . . .

And then, in the middle of Alex's first kiss, the ground vibrated and a flash lit the late afternoon sky.

They pulled away from one another and turned toward the sheet of flame along the eastern wall.

"What was *that?*" Trina exclaimed.

"We need to get up the Nest," Cara announced. "I don't know what that was, or if it had anything to do with us, but we need to move, now."

"Uncle Pete's not up there," Trina said.

"Doesn't matter," Cara snapped. "There's a radio. One way or another, we can track him down."

One moment, Pete was walking toward Dantzler's shack and hoping that he didn't look as out of place as he felt. The next, he was lying on the ground and watching flaming debris arc across the sky.

The booming echo of the explosion faded in his ears, and he blinked several times in an attempt to clear his head. He sat up as he became aware of distant screams and shouts. No — not so distant. His ears still rang from the blast that had literally taken his legs out from under him. The screams were all around.

Charlie was lying face down on the ground just in front of him. The other man didn't stir. Pete was about to check him for signs of life when he noticed Dantzler's shack, and the wall it abutted.

"Mother of God," he whispered. He could hear himself, at least. Slow improvement. But it wasn't looking like he was going to get much time to recuperate.

The more heavily-built eastern wall had fallen out of true. That and the explosion had shredded the building where Dantzler and his men had been living. That was an afterthought, though, given the rest of the situation.

The sag hadn't created much of an opening, but it was there. If Pete hadn't known what lurked in the woods to the south he might not have been so concerned. His blood ran cold at the sight of the breach. He abandoned all thoughts of bringing in Dantzler and his crew in a frantic rush as he struggled to his feet. He looked around in desperation. Charlie was beginning to stir. Vir had been behind him. As

Pete turned in place, he saw the other man standing on shaky legs, brushing off debris.

The help from the rest of the group would be of limited utility. Trey Peters was on his knees, loudly throwing up. What remained of John Keogh sat on the ground not far away, with most of the upper torso messily removed. Pete didn't know what had hit him, but he hoped that it had been going fast enough that John hadn't felt it.

Jenny Faqir was pale with shock, but her face was set in determination. She'd be all right, Pete judged, though Brett Simmons had a glassy, thousand-yard stare that didn't look promising.

Well. If you're going to die fighting back a horde, you're going to have some company. Horatius Cocles had held a bridge with two companions against an army and received the thanks of a grateful Rome.

Somehow, Pete didn't think he'd be as lucky.

"You good?" Pete snapped at Vir as he pulled the walkie from his belt and inspected it. Hopefully, his head had taken more of a whack than the radio. Vir gave him a thumbs-up and Pete nodded. He crossed mental fingers and hit the transmit button. "Gary, you read me?"

Static, a heart-sinking pause, and then: "Yeah." The other man sounded shaky. "What the hell was that?"

"Be damned if I know," Pete admitted. "We got bigger problems, boss. Wall breach, southeast corner. All hands on deck."

Gary must have been cursing off-channel because the pause was much longer this time. "Right. How big?"

Pete studied the gap in the wall and fingered his pistol. "Bring two of the salvage buses." If they could arrange them just right, they could park the armored sides in an L-shape and block the breach off long enough to get some equipment together repair the damage. At the moment, that was moot — he glimpsed slow, furtive motion behind the dissipating smoke. He let up off of the transmit button and barked, "Up and at it, Charlie. Danger close."

"Right. We're on it," Gary responded.

"Gary," Pete said as he flipped off the safety on his shotgun. "Make it snappy. We're going to need some firepower here, and quick. Got some unwelcome visitors, and they ain't Girl Scouts."

Chapter 33

Grady tapped his knuckles on the doorframe and announced, "Frannie's back. I'm heading over to grab supper. Want me to bring you something?"

Tish considered for a moment and then shook her head. "Nah, I've been snacking all morning. If anything, I need to crash, I feel like somebody taped sandpaper to the inside of my eyelids."

Grady gave her a thumbs up. "I'll be quick, and then you can hit the sack and recharge. Want me to see if I can talk someone into watching Trina?"

"Thanks, but no." She put her hand over her mouth as the reply threatened to turn into a yawn. "I'll track her down after you get back. She's a good kid, she'll be happy enough to curl up with a book while I sleep. Hardest thing to do will be getting her to go to sleep at a decent hour before she gets too engrossed."

He nodded his understanding and headed for the exit. "Back soon," he promised. Tish gave him an absent-minded wave as she resumed studying their inventory of supplies. Even with Vir's bounty, the sudden inrush of patients had put a serious dent in their stocks. She chewed on the cap of her pen. *Maybe when Miles gets back we can arrange another run,*

512

and do it right this time. If the Marines provided security, maybe they could get a big enough work crew to the river crossing to put a more permanent bridge in. Even if that didn't work, they could help keep the cargo trucks secure while they ferried supplies back and forth. The main concern other than the crossing was safety. A vehicle that the infected — her husband's term had never quite worked for her — couldn't breach was a nice thing to have.

The door whispered as someone stepped into the building. Without looking up from her lists, Tish commented, "They run out of food already?" When there was no answer to her greeting she looked up and resisted the urge to jump in surprise. She hoped her recovery was smoother than it felt. "Jaid, how are you? I thought you were Dr. Scott."

The woman looked as poorly put together as Tish had ever seen her. There were dark circles under her eyes and she'd pulled her hair back into a messy ponytail. She wore khaki slacks and a faded red sweater under a light rain jacket, but her pants had wrinkles. Mud stained the cuffs. Tish forced herself to make eye contact, but it was a pointless effort. The other woman had a vacant, thousand-yard stare. Finally, Jaid seemed to compose her thoughts and met Tish's eyes.

"I didn't have a chance to come down before now," she said. "It's been so busy in the office . . ." Jaid fell silent.
Tish cocked her head to the side, confused. "Jaid, is everything all right?"

"Well . . ." The other woman stopped and sighed. "We've been keeping it quiet, just for privacy's sake, you know . . ."

Panic rushed through her, and Tish resisted the urge to clench her fists. *Good God, she's not going to tell me that she's having an affair with Miles, is she?* She laid her pen down and stood up.

". . . But Carter and I have been seeing each other for a while."

The tension went out of Tish all at once, and she resisted the urge to sigh in relief. "That's . . . that's great, Jaid. And I can understand the privacy thing. This place is worse than an old ladies' knitting circle sometimes."

Jaid gave her a faint smile. "Right. Well, we had words, last night, something stupid, and he stormed out. I guess he must have gone to have a few drinks, and then, you know." The corners of her mouth turned down. "Is he going to be all right?"

Despite herself, Tish found herself stepping forward and grasping the other woman's hands between her own. "Oh, Jaid. We've still got him under. He's stable, so that's something. I can't make any promises to you, but that's a good sign. If we can keep him from getting an infection, he should be fine." *I hope.* Tish wasn't ready to out and out lie to the woman; everything she'd said was technically true, but Carter's injuries were worse than, say, an appendix. And she wouldn't have discharged Todd Jenkins unless she had desperate need of the room.

An unrecognizable series of expressions flashed across Jaid's features until she composed herself and said, "Can I sit with him for a while?"

Tish didn't hesitate. "Absolutely. He's in the exam room." She took Jaid by the elbow and guided her in the right direction. "There's even a chair in there. Stay as long as you like."

"Thanks," Jaid murmured and stepped inside. Tish stood and watched her for a moment, then shook her head and turned away to the patient beds. She was due to check on her charges. What a strange world, in which someone she'd once perceived as competition and an enemy would come into her domain and she'd be able to treat her kindly with little or no effort. Any interactions they'd had before had been tense and filled with subtle, feminine venom. She'd been able to discard that without consideration and look at the other woman with unjaundiced eyes. *How about that?*

Empathy was the one aspect of the medical field that Tish had always struggled with. Maybe it was the way her dad raised her. There wasn't anything necessarily *wrong* with the outlook that Larry had instilled in her, but it also wasn't one that fit with the more touchy-feely aspects of the medical profession. His concepts of discipline, self-control, and hard work had been a great help in the coursework of medical school. They weren't so great when treating someone suffering from, say, lung cancer, without making a snide comment about their lifelong cigarette addiction.

Not that there was much of an issue with lung cancer these days.

Tish smirked as she stepped into the patient room and glanced at her dad. His eyes were open, she was happy to note, but he was deep enough in thought that there was an aspect of a daydream stare to his expression. It broke as she crossed his plane of view and he grumbled, "What are you smiling about?"

Her smile widened, and she replied, "For such a big bad Marine, you are an *awful* patient." Across the room, Frannie was performing physical therapy on Bob Gentry to keep his arms and legs from drawing in. She tried to stifle her own laughter but failed.

Larry sighed with the air of one long abused and replied, "Whatever."

"Lizzie, how are you feeling?" The woman had polished off the bottles of water they'd brought her earlier, but she'd abandoned a mug of canned chicken soup on the bedside table. Tish measured it with a practiced eye and estimated the woman had eaten half of it, which wasn't bad, all things considered.

"Better. Sleepy." She squirmed slightly. "Which is weird, isn't it? I'm going to have to pee here in a bit."

"Do you want the bedpan, or do you want to try and walk?"

The woman grimaced. "If you want to let me, I'll try to walk. I want out of here."

Tish smiled. "Sounds good to me. You done over there, Frannie?"

"Give me just a minute."

"All right, I'll go ahead and prop the door open."

She turned around and headed back to the break room. The clinic had one bathroom, mainly used by the doctors. It was a strange mixture of familiar technology and jury-rigged pioneer hardware. The outflow went to a septic tank — and was eventually used for fertilizer, something that still grossed her out if she thought it too much — but they didn't have true running water. When they'd built the clinic, the attic space had been set aside for a large water storage tank. It had been necessary to place the structural walls in specific points to support the weight, but having clean water was a necessity for a clinic. They'd plumbed in a connection to one of the windmill-driven wells to keep the tank topped off. The water smelled strongly of rotten eggs, but it was clear. They still didn't have enough electrical capacity to install a hot water tank, so they boiled and stored water as needed.

Inside the break room, Tish propped open the bathroom door and dragged a couple of chairs out of the way to make a clear path for Lizzie. Despite the other woman's eagerness, she knew that she and Frannie would have to be there for more than moral support. She was stiff and weak from her ordeal, but she wasn't as bad as Bob and his neighboring patient, JT. At some point, they were going to have to decide if they were throwing good after bad. The two men had overdosed weeks before Lizzie, showed no signs of coming around, and were requiring more and more physical therapy to fight against tendon contracture. Eventually, the demands of their care was going to surpass the capabilities of the medical staff unless they got some extra help. Even that might be more trouble than it was worth, as they'd have to watch the newbies like hawks until they learned the job.

The space was as open as it was going to get without moving the tables, she judged. As she turned to head back, the entire building shook. It didn't last long, but it was strong enough to rattle the entire place and knock items off of the shelves. As the vibration faded, a loud *thump* sounded — far enough away that the sound had to travel, she judged, but not so far that there was more than a hair's breadth of a delay.

"What the hell?" Tish exclaimed. She stepped out of the break room and headed for the doors. Frannie sprinted out of the other room to join her and the two of them studied the view through the front of the clinic. A few of the people outside were pointing to the south and east. Other than that, everything looked normal. Whatever had happened was out of view. Tish stepped forward to open the door and go out for a better look but stopped at the sound of a cold, firm voice.

"Don't."

Frannie and Tish turned. Jaid stood in the doorway of the exam room, and her demeanor was so changed that Tish wondered what in the world had happened to her. There was a manic light in her eyes, and her hand was tucked in one pocket of her coat.

Tish's heart sank as Jaid removed her hand and pointed the small semiautomatic pistol. "I think everyone else is going to be busy for a bit. Which gives us a perfect opportunity to have a little chat, doesn't it?"

Hanratty snapped awake at the sound of the explosion. Before he could stop himself, he jerked upright and slammed his forehead into the bottom of the LAV. The dull thump reverberated all the way down to his toes. "Damn it," he cursed. He flopped back to the ground and rubbed at his forehead.

A shout came from atop the vehicle. "Captain! You need to see this!"

Hanratty rolled out from underneath and climbed unsteadily to his feet. His head throbbed. He could already envision the bruise he was going to be sporting later. *Couldn't sleep in the compartment, could you?* He shook his head, climbed inside, and moved up to the vehicle commander's hatch. Rivas was already up in her own turret. He stuck his head up and out and stopped dead. Chunks of burning debris described falling ballistic arcs across the sky, and a line of smoke traced the southern half of the eastern wall. "What the hell, Rivas?"

"Got no clue, sir," she said. "Sheet of flame shot up along the entire front of the wall. Looked like napalm, almost. Are we under attack, sir?"

"Given my luck lately, who knows," Hanratty grumbled. He snagged a pair of binoculars and studied the far end of the wall. Ant-sized people ran around, and their demeanor was anything but calm. The distant crackle of gunfire came to him and he leaned forward in the turret and propped his elbows on the edge. "Oh, hell," he said.

A group of men and women ran by. Hanratty lowered the binoculars and followed the movement. They were all geared up with rifles, and a few carried battered surplus ammo cans. One of them noticed his study and paused long enough to shout, "Wall breach, Captain!"

"Damn," Hanratty cursed and dropped back down inside the LAV. His eyes, unfortunately, hadn't been deceiving him. "Where's Patterson?" He demanded as he closed and dogged his hatch.

"Grabbing chow, Cap."

"Well, he's going to miss the party," Hanratty said. "Looks like it's just you and me. I'll drive, you shoot." If anything, the crackle of gunfire from the corner was intensifying. He pulled the rear hatches and dogged them. Pete's swarm had lurked in the shadows all this time — would they keep lurking after the wall breach? Somehow, he doubted it.

"We're light on machine gun rounds, and we've only got a handful of flechette rounds for the 25mm." The LAV's main gun was of limited utility against even massed groups of infected. One of the first innovations the surviving military had tinkered together was a modified 25mm sabot round that held a bundle of small tungsten darts. They were wickedly effective against infected hordes, but the primitive nature of their assembly line kept supplies limited.

Hanratty settled into the driver's seat and cranked the engine. "Well, there's always the Patton method."

"Sir?" she said, confused. Hanratty grinned and dropped the LAV into gear.

"We'll grease our tracks — or wheels, rather — with their guts, Rivas."

"Anything?" Ross said. His kept his voice pitched low — all the better to avoid disturbing Janacek, who crouched in front of the fire door with one ear pressed up against it. The younger man hesitated, as though he were willing any sounds to pass through the metal door and into his ear, and then shook his head. Miles let out a breath he hadn't realized he'd been holding.

"Nothing, sir," he said, finally. "Quiet as a—" he caught himself, then shrugged with a sheepish smile. "You know."

Ross smiled crookedly. "Let's just hope it *stays* a tomb. Shout out if you hear anything." He wheeled around and stepped inside of the elevator shack. Miles followed though he felt like even more of a third wheel than usual given Ross' energetic motions. "Anything, Chief?"

Foraker gave a slight shake of his head, then shrugged. "Don't know if we'd hear anything, anyway. We left the hatch closed." He rocked back and forth on his heels and finally said, "What's our move, Mikey?"

"I'm working on it, Chief," Ross promised. He turned to Miles. "Mr. Matthews, what do you know about long-range communications?"

"Zip," Miles admitted. "Other than a general 'turn the radio and it gets this channel' kind of thing."

Ross rubbed his head and looked thoughtful. "The MBITR's don't have enough range to reach Camp Perry, but we've got a portable Blue Force Tracker in our supply ruck. Maybe we can, I dunno, hack some sort of antenna together to boost the signal."

"Which assumes that there's anyone left to actually *receive* it," Miles murmured.

"Well, yeah," Ross admitted. "Short of zip-lining off the roof, we don't have a way out of here without going through the building. And I'm not too enamored of that option at the moment."

Miles considered the opposite rooftop and shuddered. "Yeah. Wait, zip line?"

Ross waved a hand. "Bad joke. Antenna?"

Miles sighed and looked around the elevator shack. "I wouldn't even know where to start," he admitted. "I mean, there's more to it than just hooking up a big wire, right? That might help *receive* a signal, but I'm pretty sure you need to boost the power to extend the transmission range." He made a face. "If I had Google and access to Fry's Electronics, no sweat, given the time, but hell, Lieutenant. I'm not MacGyver."

The other man rubbed his face and sighed. "Shit. All right. I'm going to park the tracker up on top of the roof. If I set it on repeat, maybe the signal will get through at some point."

Ross ghosted through the doors. Miles frowned and leaned on the railing surrounding the elevator shaft.

"Don't sweat it, kid," Foraker murmured. "He's just grasping at straws."

Miles glanced up at him and smiled. "I get it," he assured the other man. "Feeling a little out of sorts myself. I've spent the last few years trying to avoid getting into no-win situations. This is a bit out of my comfort zone." He frowned and craned his neck over the edge of the shaft. Foraker followed his eyes and stepped forward to mimic his movement.

"Is that . . . ?" the Chief said.

"I think it's the hatch. It has to be, right?"

At the bottom of the shaft, a faint square glowed. Disaster planning — send all elevator cars to the ground floor and lock the doors open. The doors to the *lobby*. The lobby that was completely walled in with *glass*.

The light from below flickered and Miles caught a vague sense of motion in the distance. "Shit," he whispered. The light faded out, obscured by a press of who knew how many bodies. Could they climb?

Of course they can climb. *They just crashed a fucking helicopter, idiot.*

"Mikey!" Foraker shouted. Gravel rustled outside as Ross leaped down from the top of the elevator shack. "We got problems!"

"The power," Miles snapped. "If we bring the car up to the server room, there's no access from below. It'll cap off the building."

Ross and Foraker stared at him for a long moment, then shared a glance between one another. "That cuts off our best egress," Foraker pointed out.

The lieutenant's mouth worked. "Do it," he spat finally. Miles snapped into action.

"Pull the cable!" he shouted to Foraker as he jerked their jury-rigged connector off of the shelf. He fumbled for what felt like an eternity and finally got it seated into the elevator control system. He turned to pick up the other end, but Foraker had already pulled it over to the battery system and connected it. The SEAL hammered the switch to bring the power back up and turned to Miles with a look of anticipation on his face.

"Come on, come on," Miles whispered. The charging cycle was no longer than it had been before, but it felt like an eternity, now. Finally, the display lit up and he pounded frantically on the buttons. "Get up, get up."

"Guns up, Chief!" Ross barked. "Who knows how many have already gotten through!" The two men trained their rifles over the railing.

The motor kicked to life. The smooth purr from before was gone; now, the motor sounded strained. Miles realized with dawning horror that there were already enough zombies inside and on top of the car to overwhelm the system's weight rating. He racked his mind and tried to remember what the sign bolted by the panel inside of the cab had said, and failed. It had never *mattered*, before. He urged the motor on, mentally. The sound hadn't gotten any worse, but it hadn't gotten any better, either. Whatever the case, it was pulling the car up. This was doable. He'd stop the car a few floors down and they could take out any hitchhikers from higher ground. The cables continued to wind smoothly, and he let out a sigh of—

The strained roar of the motor escalated into a high-pitched whine, and the cable spool suddenly reeled into the housing at more than double the prior rate. At the same time, a sharp snapping sound echoed up the elevator shaft. Miles recalled his earlier concern about the integrity of the cable. It had been strong enough for the car and three of them, but the weight of untold numbers of zombies, both inside and on top? Too much. He dove for the floor as the cable blurred through the pulleys. The arrangement *should* keep the whipping, broken end away from them, but he wasn't about to risk the worst. Across the shaft, Foraker pulled Lieutenant Ross to the ground as the end of the cable appeared at the top of the shaft. It oscillated wildly and smacked into one of the railings as the motor drew it back into the housing. With the cable fully withdrawn, the motor ran for the span of several racing heartbeats until it shut down. It was either damaged or had somehow recognized that a fault had occurred in the system.

"What's going on?" Janacek hadn't left his post. His shout was just audible over the fading echoes of the elevator's catastrophic death.

"Stand by," Ross barked. He got back to his feet and peered down into the elevator shaft. Miles joined him, hoping beyond hope that the falling car had somehow blocked off the open doors to the lobby.

Luck wasn't with them — if anything, the lighted opening below them was even larger, as though the roof of the car had ruptured when it hit the ground floor. Foraker kicked his gun light on and panned it over the bottom of the shaft. Gray-skinned bodies milled about, but there was a sense of order and purpose to their movements. Slowly and steadily, the clot of infected humanity separated into a stream of undead flesh that moved inexorably up the ladder on the side of the elevator shaft.

The slide locked back on Pete's pistol and he stepped sideways and back. The calm resolve of his voice belied the frantic tempo of his thoughts. "Vir, go."

The other man stepped up and began to take slow, aimed shots at the horde that lurched toward them. The breach in the wall was small; narrower at the base than at the top. They'd stacked up enough of the undead that it slowed the newcomers, but their advance was inexorable. The attackers had already forced them to step back, which widened their perimeter even more.

Vir missed his first two shots; his third stuck the zombie crawling over the crest of the mound of dead flesh and knocked it back and out of sight. Another replaced it as soon as it fell back.

Pete dropped the magazine out of his Colt and replaced it with his next-to-last one. The VEPR shotgun was empty and abandoned somewhere under the leading edge of the pile.

Shouldn't have changed your mind about taking the time to get more firepower, boss.

"Where the hell is Gary?" He muttered to himself and thumbed the slide release to chamber a round.

"It's getting a little sporty here," Vir shouted, and began rapid-firing. Pete glanced up; a massive clot was pushing up and over the mound of the fallen.

Charlie was sporting one hell of a shiner where some debris had hit him, but he stepped up without a prompt and added his own fire to the crescendo.

Pete waved an arm at Trey, Jenny, and Brett, and shouted, "No more than three at a time shooting! We can't afford to be all caught reloading."

"Are you nuts?" Brett screamed, hysterical. He clutched his emptied rifle in front of him like a holy talisman. "We need to get the hell out of here!"

Pete licked his lips and hesitated for the barest of moments. He stepped over to the other man and jerked the rifle out of Brett's hands. "Go," he said quietly. "But leave your mags."

Something cracked through the younger man's terror. He opened his mouth to speak, then closed it. Confusion flashed across his face. "Wait . . . what?"

"I don't have time to babysit you here, son. If you can't hack it, fine. But don't create obstacles for the rest of us. Go — but make yourself useful and raise the alarm. Start getting everyone into the shelter." He glanced over at the pile at the breach. The fear and the stress was contagious. His team was missing more shots than they hit, and their actions grew more frantic with each step of retreat. Pete turned back. "Move it, soldier!" he roared.

Simmons jumped in surprise, but he moved. When he was a handful of steps away he stopped and shrugged off the strap of an old, military-surplus musette bag he wore across his chest and tossed it in Pete's direction. Pete caught it automatically and gave a crooked smile at the solid weight inside.

Brett's courage may have failed him, but he'd at least come prepared. *Hell, I bet this came out of Larry's store,* Pete thought as he ran the strap across his chest and let the bag hang on his hip. He tapped the magazine release with his trigger finger and slammed a fresh one home. "I'm out!" Vir shouted.

"Charlie, Vir, reload! Trey, Jenny — pour it on!" Pete screamed as he clicked the M-4's fire selector onto burst and dumped the magazine with ten quick trigger pulls. The onrushing horde crawled over each other and the bodies of the fallen. Arms and legs and torsos intermingled into one continuous press of gray flesh. They'd been waiting long enough, Pete supposed. Their opportunity was at hand and the beasts were going to take it. *Over my dead body.*

His ears were ringing from the cacophony of the gunfire to an extent that he didn't hear the sound of their salvation. He dropped the mag and fed another one home. He slapped the bolt release with his left hand as soon as the magazine was in place and shouldered the rifle to keep firing. The boom of an amplified shout over speakers interrupted him, and joy surged in him at their moment of salvation.

"MOVE!"

Hanratty's voice was deep and authoritative face to face. Boosted via loudspeaker over the diesel roar of the LAV's engine, it was like the roar of some ancient deity come to wreak havoc. Pete waved the others aside even as he joined the scramble. The electric whir of the cannon turret was almost subdued compared to the massive thump that he felt more than heard. Even as he tried to cover his ears, Pete turned toward the wall breach in time to see the center of the horde collapse.

Whoever was manning the turret made a slight adjustment to the cannon's aiming point, and it barked again. The cannon shot washed away the crawlers on top of the heap, and Pete couldn't resist his shout of elation. "Pour it on! Get some, Marines!"

Another cannon shot, and then the coaxial machine gun joined in. He was so fixated on the joys of destruction that he flinched when Vir grabbed his arm. "Pete, we've got to move! The buses are here!"

He glanced up. Sure enough, both vehicles were picking their way through the grass parallel to the eastern wall. The LAV maintained position, and he moved along with the rest of the survivors behind it as the armored personnel carrier continued to fire. The rate was somewhat reduced now, and Pete wondered if they'd taken a big enough chunk out of the horde to reduce the pressure at the breach. He mentally compared the stack of bodies they'd piled up to the gruesome specters he'd been watching. He couldn't help but think that they had only seen a small sample of what lurked in the woods.

The first bus came straight on and nosed up against the southern fence to put the armored side toward the breach. The other bus had to move more carefully. The driver swung wide to line up the rear of his own bus with the eastern wall and began backing up. The driver of the second bus was Gary, and Pete raised a hand in greeting. The other man was too focused on what he was doing to notice.

As Gary's bus came into position, the LAV ceased fire. If they hadn't reduced the numbers at the breach, the pause might have been fatal. As Pete peered around the edge of the armored vehicle, the breach was empty save for the bullet-wracked bodies of the fallen. And then, with the high-pitched tones of the backup beeper, Gary's bus edged back and blocked that port. Metal squealed against metal on the driver's side as he cut the wheel over to make sure the buses made a solid block. There might have been a gap of a few inches between the rear of the first bus and the side of Gary's, but Pete doubted that it would be enough to be a problem. They'd used this method before, and it had worked well at the time. *Just hold*, he mentally urged the buses. *Just hold long enough for us to fix the damage.*

The squeal of metal was his cue to relax. He slung Brett's rifle over his shoulder and strolled out from behind the LAV.

Gary pulled the bus doors open and hopped out. He looked around a moment, then headed in Pete's direction upon spotting him. All they'd been able to hear moments before was gunfire, shouting, and the LAV's engine, but silence — or something close to it — now reigned. The remainder of his team stood wherever they'd ended up, looking as though they were unsure of what to do. One second they'd been in a fight for their lives, and in the other, safety had descended back upon them. It was a weird feeling. Pete knew; he wasn't unfamiliar with the experience. He'd once described combat to Larry as 'minutes of sheer terror followed up by hours of boredom.'

"Everyone all right?" Pete asked, and winced. His ears were still ringing and he'd spoken more loudly than he intended to. The others gave him nods and other gestures of understanding. Despite the knock he'd taken on his head, Charlie stood tall and looked as focused as ever. Of the others, Trey in particular still looked a little queasy.

Going to have to talk to him later, Pete judged. Any other assessment of their condition was on the back burner, though, as Gary walked up with a frown on his face.

"What the hell, Pete?" The other man's voice was firm. "Don't get me wrong, I'm glad that you and your people were here, but last I checked this sort of thing ain't their job."

Pete gave him a level stare, then murmured, "We got a pretty good tip that Dantzler and his boys were the ones running the meth lab, Gary. That's why I didn't involve you and your guys. I couldn't risk word getting out to them before we had an opportunity for an arrest."

Gary rocked back on his heels, eyes wide. He glanced back over his shoulder at the buses. The now-demolished guard shack was inside the new, temporary perimeter they'd created. Maybe they should have checked for survivors, but Pete doubted that there was anyone still alive in there. If they had been, the racket from the gunfire and fighting would have roused them right into the horde.

Stranger things have happened, of course, Pete allowed. *As soon as we fix the breach, we'll have to take a look.*

"Leaving aside the fact that you didn't fill me in on this, why did it just so happen that an explosion damn near takes the wall down right at the same time that you're going to arrest some of my boys, Pete?"

He sighed and rubbed a hand through his hair. "Best guess, they set up shop in the drain culvert and screwed something up. They used to say on the news all the time how explosive those labs were. I didn't think they were *that* bad, but maybe so. Who knows, Gary? It is what it is."

The other man stared at him for a long moment. When his shoulders slumped Pete knew that Gary wasn't going to keep raising hell about the issue. "Good grief. What are we going to tell Norma and the rest of the council? She's going to have kittens."

Pete grinned at the thought. "Well . . ."

Jenny screamed. Before he could turn his head to see what she was screaming about, Gary lurched forward and carried Pete to the ground. The other man tried to speak, but despite his Herculean effort, all he did was aspirate blood down Pete's front. As he pushed himself up onto his elbows against Gary's dead weight, Pete saw the pale, wrist-thick length of wood projecting from his friend's upper back. The incongruity of it made him stop and stare for a moment. It wasn't until his eyes traveled down the length of the shaft that he realized what it was.

Whoever had made the weapon had repurposed some sort of tool or gardening implement. It was too straight and uniform to be anything but a machined piece of wood. Whatever had once tipped it was gone. A long, gray cylinder now sat on the end of the shaft, lashed to it with some sort of fibrous gray cord. As Gary's body slid off of his chest,

Pete realized with a sinking feeling in the pit of his stomach what it was.

A tube of bone tipped the spear, sharpened and shortened somehow. It was too thick and straight to be anything but a leg bone. As Gary's body began to twitch and spasm with renewed, unnatural life, Pete realized that wasn't their only problem.

Whip-thin figures vaulted onto the tops of the school buses, assessed the ground beneath, and hopped down. Some paused long enough to hurl still more spears, and the screams and shouts began to spread.

"Shit," Pete whispered. "They learned how to jump."

Chapter 34

Two hundred feet seemed an interminable distance when it loomed beneath you and promised unthinkable agony or outright death at the end of the fall.

When it was all that separated you from another, more intimate death, it seemed to be nothing at all.

Miles licked his lips and mentally counted off as Chief Foraker pumped rounds out of his SCAR in a steady, robotic rhythm. You could have set time by the measured pace at which the senior enlisted man aimed and fired.

At the count of thirty, the Chief stepped back. He pulled the empty magazine from his rifle as Ross stepped into firing position and began his own measured fire into the elevator shaft.

Despite the inhuman marksmanship of the SEALs, the undulating gray wave of infected flesh moving up the elevator shaft was gaining.

They're too fast, Miles despaired, and then immediately after — *forget how fast they are, they're* climbing, *idiot!*

The dead had behaved the same way for so long that Miles had never given any consideration to the thought that the situation might change. Ross and his men were similarly accustomed to the 'meat machines.' Though each man moved with a calm ease, there was a sense of panic in their words and facial expressions. Despite their accuracy and the dozens of undead they'd sent to the bottom of the shaft, the distance between the leading edge of the climbers and the rim of the shaft continued to shrink.

Another count of thirty, and Ross and Foraker exchanged positions once again. In the short time it took them to move, the leading edge surged forward, and was now past the halfway mark to the top.

Ross pressed a hand to his ear to better hear his MBITR. Despite the sound suppressors on each rifle, the racket of firing and falling bodies echoed around the walls of the elevator shaft and created a hellish cacophony in the shack. "Come back, Brian — all clear, you say?"

Foraker grimaced and shouted, "Pull him in!"

If Ross heard the Chief, he didn't modify his command. "Stand by; we can't afford to get flanked." The Lieutenant raised his head and glanced at Foraker and Miles in turn. "Options, Chief?"

"Explosives."

Ross grimaced and slapped the base of his rifle magazine to ensure it was properly seated. "We don't know the architectural structure of the building. Is the shaft the main support? I sure as hell don't want to surf the whole works down if we implode it."

Foraker went dry, and the men exchanged places. "Server room. There's not enough room for more than a dozen or so of them on the landing at a time, if they can even make the jump across. We hole up in there and wait it out."

"Limited food and water," Ross mused aloud. "That's plan C, Chief."

"We may not have time for anything else, Mikey," Foraker pointed out. "We pussyfoot around for too long and we won't be able to get in there."

Miles grimaced. The Lieutenant had given him a hard look before they'd begun firing and told him to keep his rifle on his shoulder. Sure, he was nowhere close to these guys in skill, but wouldn't *something* be better than nothing? He was about to step forward when Janacek screamed outside. For a moment Miles thought it was a scream of pain, but the words that came next proved that they were anything but.

"Lieutenant! The BFT is buzzing up a storm!"

Ross emptied his rifle and stepped aside. To his credit, the distraction didn't slow Foraker in the least, and he resumed his shooting position. The leading edge of the climbing undead was now perhaps eighty feet from the roof. "Talk to me, Janacek!" the Lieutenant shouted.

The younger man abandoned his position long enough to pull himself up onto the roof of the elevator shack, retrieve the Blue Force Tracker, and return to his position at the door. The portable device looked like an old 90's-style cellular phone, only larger, with a swiveling whip antenna on one side. Janacek presumably read something he liked off the device because he gave a whoop of celebration and shouted. "They've retaken the airfield, sir! Dust-off is fifty minutes out!"

Foraker's rifle clicked empty. As he and Ross exchanged positions the Chief gave the Lieutenant a significant glance. "We ain't going to hold this position for fifty minutes, boss."

Ross grimaced, but didn't look particularly surprised by the revelation.

The situation was immediately obvious to Miles. To get a line of fire on the entire ladder, the SEALs had taken a position at the rear of the elevator shaft. If they remained there, when the climbers crested the top they would cut the shooters off from the door. They could shift positions to the opposite side of the shaft, closer to the door, but they'd be firing directly down on the ladder and would be less effective.

We just need to buy some time. To get this close, only to end up getting overrun — Miles pushed down the despair. There had to be something in here that could help them. He tried to ignore the shooting and rushed over to the workbench and rummaged through drawers and shelves. He paused over the wiring harness they'd cobbled together. Could they wire together some sort of net or fence or something, across the railings, to keep them out? He discarded the thought. They didn't have nearly enough cable to manage that. But maybe — he looked over his shoulder to study the exterior doors, then grinned.

"Hey," Miles shouted. "Any of you guys see Lord of the Rings?"

Gary's eyes had just gone gray when Pete awkwardly pushed his body off and put a double-tap into his head. "Sorry, bud," he murmured. "I know you'd have done the same for me." He grabbed the crude spear jutting out of his friend's back and levered himself back onto his feet.

Getting tired of falling on my ass.

More spears arced out; some hit flesh and elicited screams while others plunged harmlessly into the turf. The clot of wall guards that had gathered after what they'd thought had been the end of the breach had scattered. A handful of them were down for now with spear wounds, while others had run for it.

A few — too few — stood, and fought.

Pete slid his Colt back into his holster and pulled the radio off of his belt. His motions were slow and lethargic. Everything felt surreal and muted, almost like a dream. *Keep it together, Marine. This ain't over yet.*

He licked his lips and pressed the button on the walkie. "This is Pete at the southeast wall. We have a major breach. Everyone to shelters, now! Wait for the all clear. Confirm receipt and cascade." He lifted his button off and listened. There was a receiver set in each of the common buildings. This time of day, most people would be eating supper, which should streamline things a bit. Anyone who wasn't, well, the volume of fire should have been a pretty obvious clue. A handful of voices acknowledged him. The order to cascade meant to pass on the information on the other frequencies they used — by the other wall guards, for the most part. If they weren't engaged in their own fight, at least they'd now know what was going on. It wasn't much, but Pete had done his part. For the sake of his family and friends, he hoped the warning had come soon enough.

The sudden eruption of fire from the LAV's turret drowned out the crackle of gunfire from the surviving guards. Metal shrieked as the heavier cannon raked the top of the school bus. Pete noted with a sinking feeling that the fire wasn't as effective this time around as it had been against the first wave. These zombies ducked and dodged. Their movements were awkward and off-sync, but they did their best to evade the fire. In a way, it looked like a sped-up version of one of the old monster movies Pete had watched with Miles back in the day. Sinbad, maybe, by Harrywhatshisface.

The 25mm barked again, and once more the Marine manning the turret added the coaxial to the mix. Glass shattered and the roof of the blocking bus took the brunt of the rounds that didn't find flesh or bone. *If we make it through this we're going to have one hell of a lot of work to do to keep that thing from leaking like a colander.*

If.

Pete knelt and retrieved Brett's M4 from the ground. After the gunner inside adjusted for the difference in tactics, the LAV was now sweeping any zombies who popped their heads up off the top of the bus. The most pressing concern was the group that had made it down and across. Some were already down, taken out by those who had stood their ground. Still more stalked across the ground with what — frighteningly — looked like a canny sense of animal wariness.

As he watched, one of the wall guards who'd come with Gary fell, flanked on either side as he focused his aim on targets to his immediate front. One zom raked the side of his face with fingers that were little more than bones and dark tendons sheathed in leathery gray flesh, and the other stabbed him in the side with one of the crude spears. The guard fell with a cry, and Pete's mouth went dry as he watched both of them leave the guard where he'd fallen and rejoin the slow advance across the grounds. The injured man cried out for aid, but he was behind the advancing line. Pete recalled what had happened to Gary after the spear took him down. *They're not feeding. They're waiting for him to turn and provide reinforcements.* The bones themselves carried the virus — smeared with blood, or tissue? — and the smallest injury now presented the threat of infection.

Pete raised the rifle and shouted, "Survivors, to me! Defensive formation!" He had to repeat himself twice before the others heard him and pulled back to the side of the LAV. He pushed and prodded and got them into some semblance of a semicircle. "I don't know why and I don't know how, but they're acting smart," Pete fired a single shot at one of the approaching zoms. Its head jerked back but the thing kept its feet. A streak of white showed where the 5.56mm round had creased, but not penetrated, the skull. *Damn poodle shooter.* He fired twice more. This time, he hit straight on, and the zom went down in a heap. "Slow rate of fire!" Pete barked. "Watch the spears — they spread the infection!"

One of the wall guards, Carter something, Pete thought, was having none of it. "This is insane! We need to get the hell out of here!"

I could use a First Sergeant right about now, Larry. He pitched his voice into a harsh growl and said, "This is what you signed up for, soldier. You run, people are going to die!" One of the zoms had crept a bit too close for comfort, so he gave it a double-tap to the forehead. As it crumpled, one of its compatriots lunged forward and collected the spear the other had dropped. That was something, at least. If every member of the attacking horde carried a ranged weapon, the survivors would have lost already. Their accuracy sucked on an individual basis, but a mass of spears coming at their defensive grouping would have been fatal.

The zoms ceased their slow advance, freezing in place. At once, their heads began to twitch rapidly back and forth. Pete didn't know what they were doing, but the perfect synchronization of the movement left him with a tight, nervous knot in the pit of his stomach.

"What are they doing?" Jenny whispered. He could barely hear her over the intermittent staccato fire of the LAV's machine gun.

All at once, half of the attacking force peeled away and headed toward the center of the community. "Shit," Pete hissed. "They know they've got us bottled up here. They're not going to waste any more time with us — they're going raiding." He turned and fired half a dozen aimed shots at the departing group. Two or three fell, but they were moving too fast for effective fire. All things considered, he would much rather face the limping automatons of the last few years than this new wrinkle.

"Look out!" The shout came right in Pete's ear, and strong arms clamped on his shoulder and pulled him fiercely back.

The spear whistled in on a low ballistic arc that left a hiss of air in its wake. Despite the crudity of its construction, it was well-balanced and flew true.

Pete's assessment of it ended when the spear struck him and took his legs out from under him. *Here we go again.*

The others began to scream and shout as the remaining zoms charged forward. He got his rifle out from under his torso and added his own weight of fire to the mix.

A few moments later, silence reigned once more. Metal scraped on the back of the LAV. Pete glanced up as Hanratty stuck his head out. The younger man nodded at him, but when he saw the spear sticking out of Pete's leg, he mouthed a curse.

"No worries," Pete called as he levered himself into a sitting position and grabbed the shaft of the spear. "It hit low." He grimaced at the feel of the spear shaft; it was greasy and cold. Was that from the hands or some remnant of outdoor storage? He pulled the spear out after a moment of tugging, threw it aside, and inspected his prosthetic. "Damn. This was my good set."

The spear had gone in right above the artificial knee joint and wrecked the mechanism. As a result, the leg stuck straight out as though placed in a cast. On the bright side, had it gone a few inches higher into the stump of his thigh he would have had a different problem. The prosthetics were almost as irreplaceable as *he* was. His backup set wasn't as comfortable or easy to use. With luck, the damage was repairable. Pete glanced up and winked. "Good looking out, Vir. I owe you one."

The other man looked relieved. "When you fell, I thought I was too late."

"Nah. Help me up, would you?" He was going to be walking around like a pirate captain for a bit, but needs must. He glanced around and assessed the group. Carter, the one who'd complained earlier, seemed to have settled down. What remained of his team were up and ready.

Pete's eyes flickered over the rest of the wall guards. He recognized most of the faces but not well enough to put names to them. He was most familiar with Pastor Dave, who was leaning over another man. The second man was on both knees, his right arm clutched on his left, covering . . . oh.

He stepped forward and reached for his pistol. Dave saw the motion and raised a hand to still his movement. "It's all right," he murmured. "We've just finished praying." Pete stopped and nodded. Dave stepped back, and the man on the ground rose. As he pulled his hand away from the wound on his forearm, Pete saw the shallow scratch and the angry black lines crawling up toward his elbow.

That quick, and from a scratch? Pete swallowed. *We're all going to die.*

The injured man removed his gun belt with his uninjured hand and passed it to Pastor Dave. He gave the rest of the group a faint smile as he raised his pistol with shaking hands and pressed the barrel into his temple.

As one, they turned away and awaited the shot. Call it post-apocalyptic courtesy. They remained there as company, not as an audience.

The shot was their signal to turn back. The others stood in silence as Dave murmured a few more words. When he finished the prayer he collected the pistol from a cooling hand. Waste not, want not.

It occurred to Pete that he not only didn't know the dead man's name, he didn't know if he had a wife, or children, or anything. Part of him piped up and said that was a consequence of having so many survivors, but another part offered dark disagreement.

You cloistered yourself up in your little nest and told yourself it was to watch over these people. You saw this coming and did nothing. This is your fault.

The renewed thunder of the LAV's machine gun shattered Pete's reverie. Even more shocking was the fact that the gun fell silent after only a few seconds of fire. He turned to look in the direction the gun had been aiming. He greeted the sight with more resignation than shock or fear. The reactions of his compatriots testified to the fact that there was plenty of the latter to go around.

All along the southern fence line, zoms clambered out of the creek bed. Many of them slipped and fell back, but their increased agility combined with the dogged, mindless persistence that they'd always possessed gave them the final edge they needed to overcome the line of defense that had protected the survivors for so long. Once up and out of the depression, they leaped forward with what Pete could only describe as eagerness to scale the wire fence. Their combined weight was starting to pull it down. Even if the wire stood up to the assault, they trickled over the top in ones and twos. In a contained area, that would have been manageable, but the breadth of their line of attack was such that Pete knew immediately that they only had one choice. "Fall back!" he shouted. "Get to the shelters!"

At first, no one seemed to respond to his command; they froze in place at the spectacle before them. Finally, Hanratty added his own weight to the order and broke the gridlock. "Get in! Get in!"

The mad scramble that ensued was almost laughable. They'd grown so used to dealing with the creeping doom of the slow undead that this new, quicker variant was more frightening than it should have been. Pete held back and observed the fences as the rest of the group pulled themselves up into the armored personnel carrier in ones and twos. The majority of the fence jumpers were ignoring them and heading toward the center of the community. *Why not? They've got the numbers; they can come for us at their leisure.*

There was a fierce tug at his shoulder and he turned. Charlie jerked a thumb over his shoulder at the LAV; the two of them were the last ones outside. Pete nodded and let the man help him up inside before reaching down and pulling Charlie in as well.

The interior of the LAV was claustrophobic, to say the least. In many places, the survivors quite literally sat on top of one another. "What are we doing, Pete?" Hanratty shouted back from the driver's seat. "We're dry on the cannon as well as the belt-feds. Best I can do is run the damn things over, but our fuel situation is starting to get a little iffy."

"Get to the silos by the observation post," Pete replied. His damaged leg wouldn't bend enough for him to sit. He settled for standing up and holding onto the row of seats running down the middle of the vehicle. "That's the main shelter point — we can gear up and figure out what we're going to do."

Larry came up on his elbows after the explosion rocked the compound. The reverberation carried on longer than the initial blast. The contents of the room shook in sympathy before the aftereffects died out.

In the bed beside him, Lizzie Johnson muttered, "What was that?"

Larry didn't have time to answer her; he was too busy trying to listen for whatever came next.

The popping sound of gunfire wasn't as audible as the thunder of the explosion, but he'd experience enough firefights in his time to peg it almost instantly. He sagged back into his bed and tried to gauge the chances of getting out without his head pounding off of his shoulders. It was already kicking up a fuss in response to sitting up, so walking didn't look good.

Tish and Frannie marched into the room, guided by someone he couldn't initially identify. For a moment, Larry was the only one who noticed that anything was wrong. Then Lizzie spotted the gun in Jaid's hands and shouted out.

"What the hell?"

Larry forced calm into his voice. "Jaid, everything all right?"

Her face twisted into something recognizable, then morphed into laughter. "That's all you've got? Good God, you're an idiot, Larry."

The crackle of gunfire intensified to the south and east, but he resisted the urge to break eye contact. "You'll have to forgive me," he said in an even tone. "But I'm suffering from a head injury, and I'm not as quick on the uptake as usual. Do we have a problem?" He jerked a thumb in the direction of the gunfire.

"No problem at all," she said, airily. "Just taking advantage of the opportunity to clean up a mess."

Despite the pounding in his head, he grasped her meaning almost immediately. "That was you, last night. And you killed Ronnie, too."

"Of course I did! None of you people *get it*! Staying quiet is the only thing that's kept us safe! Night and day, it's all I can do to get you to do anything about it." Her voice quivered with rage. "If you'd had the damn courtesy to tell me you were setting up an ambush for Ivan I'd have stayed in bed, but no, I had to go and almost get caught." She shoved the barrel of her pistol into Tish's back and pushed her forward. "You think I want this? You people are quieter than most, you're not part of the problem, but I know you won't understand me." There was another boom from the southeast, and Jaid cocked her head to one side and considered the noise. It hadn't been as pronounced as the explosion that had kicked everything off, but it was still enough to shake the building again. "From the sound of it, though, I don't think it matters."

"Jaid, what have you done?" Tish demanded before Larry could will her to silence with a look.

She scoffed, and pushed Tish again, driving her to her knees. "Don't blame me. I don't know what's going on, but

I do know that it's going to attract the wrong type of attention." She grimaced. "I've been trying to tell you people, but does anyone ever listen?" Tish remained on her knees, but she twisted around so that she was facing the other woman. *Stay right there, kid,* Larry mentally urged her. *Don't take the risk.* "Every day I make note of the people who can't keep their stupid mouths shut at night. Every day I mark down the noise complaints. And what do you do? You slap them on the back and have a good laugh about it. Laughing at *me!*"

He noted then that Frannie and Tish had arranged themselves so that they were between Lizzie and Jaid. She'd pushed them too far into the room for them to shield him in such a way. His sudden rush of pride was out of place for the here and now and was immediately tempered by the fear he felt for his daughter. Larry forced his emotions down and spoke. "All right, Jaid," he said. "I may not agree with what you're doing, but I understand it, at least. What do you want?"

She shifted her point of aim toward Larry, and he relaxed. It was crazy, but it was much less nerve-racking with the gun pointed away from his daughter. "There's no room for negotiation, here. I don't think you understand this at all."

"Jaid, don't be . . ." He almost said 'crazy' but decided that was *not* the way to go. ". . . Hasty. We can figure this out. If you've got a problem with me, that's fine. We can go talk about it. But these people, my daughter — they don't have anything to do with what happened last night. They don't see the noise complaints. That's all me."

"*You're still not getting it!*" she shrieked, and he winced. "I need to clean things up. The only people who might know about what I did to Ronnie, what I did last night, are in this building. Even if your precious daughter didn't know about it before, she knows now. Sorry, but that's how it goes." She took a deep breath and flipped the safety off.

"Jaid," Tish said, "What did you do to Carter?"

"He's not a problem anymore," Jaid said, and Frannie picked that moment to make her move. She lunged forward and tackled Jaid, driving her to the floor. The other woman pulled the trigger as she fell, but the gun discharged into the ceiling as they grappled.

Tish straightened and shoved Larry's bed to roll him out of the way. He snapped, "Forget me, get the gun, get the *gun!*"

She jerked away and leaped for the floor. As Tish descended, the gun fired again, only this time the round hit something. Frannie screamed in pain. From his position, Larry couldn't make out what was happening. Jaid was on the floor, Frannie was on top of her, and Tish was sweeping down to join in the scrum.

Jaid shrieked, but it was a noise of frustration rather than pain. Tish got back to her feet, and this time, she held the small black automatic in her own hands. She kept it aimed at Jaid as Frannie rolled off of the other woman.

"Talk to me, Frannie," Tish said in a steady voice. The other woman groaned as she clutched her side.

"Through and through," Frannie said through clenched teeth. There was a spreading bloodstain on the right side of her scrub top. "Don't think it hit anything vital, but *damn it*, that hurts."

Larry held back a sigh of relief.

"Scoot back, idiot," Tish barked, and directed with the pistol. Her face was hard and furious, but Jaid crab-crawled backward and leaned up against the wall. Tish wheeled and pressed the pistol into Larry's hand. "Cover her, dad."

Bemused, he switched it from his left to his right and kept it trained in Jaid's general direction. Ruger LCP, he noted. Chambered in .380, which was not only hard to find these days but underpowered. He imagined that Jaid had snagged it from a bin of similar odd duck weapons in the warehouse and no one had ever been the wiser.

It looked and felt new enough that it just might have come off one of the shelves in his shop. How was that for irony?

His daughter paused in the doorway and announced, "Keep some pressure on it, Franny — I need to grab some stuff."

Chapter 35

The doors opened *in*, and that one decision by an anonymous architect might just save their lives.

Miles hadn't paid much attention to the doors when they'd entered the elevator shack. He'd gained an intimate familiarity in the last few minutes. They were solid, heavy steel, supported by four hinges and latched in the center. The lower half of each door featured a three-foot square metal ventilation grate, to keep the interior cooler in the summer, he supposed.

Janacek stepped back and muttered, "Think it'll hold?"

"It has to," Miles said. "But only for a little while."

The exterior handles of the shack doors were squared-off 'C' shapes. They were longer than they were deep and bolted to the door at top and bottom. Each handle had a push-button locking mechanism at the top. Even if the SEALs hadn't drilled one out to enter the shack, it would have been a moot point. The handles on the inside were of the type that unlocked when pulled for safety reasons.

While Foraker and Ross made their own preparations, Janacek and Miles repurposed the cable they'd made up to power the elevator.

They'd spanned the door brackets with a pair of long adjustable wrenches and interwoven the heavy cable in and around them. It looked ridiculous, but when they pushed the doors in, they opened a few inches before the wrenches hit the surface of the door and jammed up against the handles. Frodo and the Fellowship had used halberds in the mines of Moria. Miles would have been happy with a shovel or two. The wrenches would have to do.

Since the doors opened inward, the jamb would do much of the work of keeping the door shut. The press of undead flesh coming their way should hold them tight and keep them from pulling the door open.

As they'd seen in the other building, though, enough pressure against the door would blow it out of its frame. This was one of the two weak points of their plan, but the small amount of space between the doors and the edge of the elevator shaft should help. They shouldn't have enough room to build up the mass required to break the frame itself. Of greater concern were the ventilation grates, as it wouldn't take much force to push them out of their frames. If there was a mob pressed up against the doors, they'd find their way through the grates sooner or later.

The smaller gaps would slow them down, but they couldn't depend on that giving them the time they needed. For that, they had Ross and Foraker, and their own preparations.

Each SEAL carried a pair of claymore antipersonnel mines in their load out. While Miles and Janacek secured the door, the other men staged the mines in pairs, with each set placed further back on the roof. The ductwork and heat exchangers of the building's HVAC system made convenient mounting points for the mines and kept the point of aim for the explosive force at head height.

Their job finished, Janacek led Miles away from the doors and to the edge of the roof. Miles' skin crawled as they passed through the kill zones created by the angled claymores, even though Ross was still running the firing wire back to their final position. They'd make their last stand here, on the roof's edge.

As defensive terrain went, it was lacking. The bulk of the solar panels and their mounting frames secured one flank, but the other was only partially blocked by a heat exchanger. They had no cover to the front.

When their attackers breached the doors, at some point they'd spread across too wide a front for the SEALs and Miles to cover. They'd chewed it over as much as they could in the time they had left, but there was nothing they could do about it.

Ross had shrugged it off. "If they're smart enough to climb, and they're smart enough to get through the blocked doors, then they're smart enough to come at us from multiple directions. But my hope is, they'll come at us just like they did the helicopter. Yeah, they've got some new tricks up their sleeves—" Miles had refrained from pointing out that few of the undead had clothes of any sort at this point, though it was tempting. "But I don't think they can overcome their baser . . . Programming, I guess. I don't think you can call it instinct. If they see a target in front of them, they *have* to go for it. I blow the claymores, row by row, spreading it out as much as possible. We just need forty minutes."

"What the hell," Foraker said. "Beats dying in bed."

Now, as Miles knelt at the edge of the roof, he pulled his gloves out of his backpack and put them on. He'd promised his daughter that they would keep him safe, but that wasn't looking so good at the moment.

Who's going to take care of my family if I don't make it home?

The first clang of flesh against metal sounded and derailed his train of thought. "Don't worry about the future," he whispered. Miles pulled rifle magazines out his vest and lined them up on the ground in front of his position. He had one in his rifle and eight spares. At 30 rounds per, he had a total of 270 loaded rounds. There was a bandoleer of stripper clips with another 210 rounds in his backpack, but he didn't know if he'd have time to reload his magazines once they were empty. With the mag in his pistol and the spares in his pouch, he had another 52 rounds of .45.

Janacek settled down next to him with a nod and began to line up magazines of his own. The thumps against the door came with a growing, persistent frequency, but each man ignored them for the moment. They had time yet; the numbers they faced weren't great enough to overcome the obstacles they put in place.

"Scoot over a bit," Janacek murmured. "You anchor up against the solar panels on the left flank and I'll cover you on the right."

Miles looked at him for a long moment and tried to read the expression on the SEAL's face. Janacek was as cool as always, but he thought he detected a hint of something other than disdain in the other man's eyes. For what it was worth, he didn't think that he'd ever call Miles 'nugget' again. "Thanks," Miles replied, and shifted. "It's been a privilege."

"Don't get all sappy on me," Janacek growled. He went prone on the gravel, supporting the barrel of his SCAR on top of his rucksack.

Foraker and Ross fell back as well. The lieutenant knelt on the far right flank and began to wire each pair of claymores into a separate clacker. "Slow, aimed fire on my call, gentlemen. Brian, Mr. Matthews — focus on the left vent opening. The Chief and I will target the right. Once there's a buildup in the kill zone, I'll call fire in the hole. Conserve your ammo until after the explosion. We don't have the bullets to double- or triple-kill them as they're taken out by the claymores. Same goes for zone two. After zone three we may need to fall back in a semicircle." He glanced at his watch. "Thirty-seven minutes, fellas. Time *is* on our side here."

"... need to grab some stuff."

Tish scrambled down the hallway before Frannie acknowledged her words. Her friend was a good, if not great, nurse, but Tish didn't like the speed at which the blood had saturated her side. Maybe the bullet *hadn't* hit anything vital, but she didn't have the luxury to take Frannie's self-diagnosis for holy writ. She lurched into the break room and tore open the storage cabinets. As she rifled through the supplies, it occurred to her that she was spoiling all the effort they'd just spent cataloging and arranging.

She loaded up her arms, tucked her chin on top of the stack to hold it in some semblance of order, stepped back out into the hallway, and . . .

Tish froze as she met the eyes of the infected standing outside of the clinic.

Let's use glass doors in the clinic, they said, Tish thought wildly. *Natural light will be good for the patients, and will save electricity for more important equipment.*

Well, shit.

Neither of them moved, and Tish got the unnerving sense that it was studying her just as much as she was studying it. She'd been up close and personal with them before, of course. They'd just been . . . fresher.

On the Day, she'd collapsed at the end of forty-eight hours straight and passed out. The flu had been running hospital staffs ragged, and little niceties like breaks had been catch as catch can. When she'd started slurring her words, the other staff pushed her inside the physician's sleeping lounge and closed the door.

The screams in her nightmares had chased her from sleep, but she hadn't escaped them when she'd returned to the waking world. The screams had been right outside the door.

Tish had survived that day, but the door of the staff lounge had been solid oak. Glass in an aluminum frame just didn't have the same gravitas.

Outside, the infected cocked its head and inspected the doors.

Miles said something about them acting differently. Something Charlie said. She'd forgotten it until now, lost in the tumult of his departure. This was for sure different, and it was a change she didn't like. A look of cold calculation from a thinking predator was far more terrifying than that of a mindless automaton.

She kept her eyes on it and eased forward. It didn't seem to pick up on the motion, but if it did, it didn't react to it. As she got a little closer, she began to notice other differences.

As she was one of only two doctors, the community had, for the most part, wrapped Tish in bubble wrap over the last eight years. When their numbers had been fewer, she'd gone on her share of supply runs. As soon as they had the population to take that over, the community forced her and the other medical staff to remain behind the walls. Despite that, she was familiar with the physiological changes the infected had undergone over the years. She'd examined more than a few bodies that Pete or the wall guards had brought her, in hopes of determining what sort of time frame they were looking at until the infected rotted away.

Rotting was the wrong term, of course. After reanimation, they did *not* rot, in point of fact. Whatever process kept them up and moving made them almost literally antiseptic. The bacteria, insects, and fauna that would reduce a body in the open to bones had no effect while the infected was up and moving. Remove the head from the equation, though, and they rotted away — fast. Tish had no way to tell whether it was an accelerated rate or the impact of the already degraded tissue, but it was measurable.

Wild animals had learned to leave the infected alone. Tish had once observed several coyotes collapsing and succumbing to seizures shortly after attacking an infected and biting it.

The most recent examples she'd seen were little more than skin and bones — gray skin the texture and consistency of leather wrapped over the skeletal structure. Withered musculature that had uncanny strength despite its appearance drove them along. She didn't have the skills or training to perform an autopsy, but she'd observed the same dark structures anchoring the teeth and striating the muscle. She and Grady had long theorized that whatever *it* was, it was what did the work of muscles. The remaining tissue, more often than not, was more akin to the long-term bedridden than that of a person who could get up and walk around.

This infected was different, and it was a change that was rather disconcerting, the more she thought about it.

It still had the wiry frame and build of its brethren, but it looked more robust, somehow. The musculature of its arms and legs was more pronounced, and there was enough muscle on its torso and shoulders to give it an admirable V-shape. The surface of its skin was still the gray of the grave, but she saw darker patches, here and there, that looked for all the world like healed scars. And, unless the infected had been in the habit of suffering severe bite wounds before dying, she theorized these were the bites that had felled it.

She'd have called the thought crazy if she'd put it spoken word, but the thing looked like it was *healing*.

But it was dead — that was impossible, right?

The thing reached out and tapped a forefinger on the glass. Tish bit back the urge to scream.

"Tish! What's going on?" Frannie called. She resisted the urge to call back out. Her hands were too burdened with supplies to wave her friend off. Tish settled for shaking her head.

The infected put a palm on the glass door and gave it an experimental shove. The door separated from the sill seal with a sucking hiss and bounced inward. The double doors were on free-swinging hinges and could open inward or outward. *Had to have the damn glass doors.*

It reared back, and she could tell that it was preparing for another, more robust shove, and she made her move. She swept her hands out from under the medical supplies. Rolls of gauze and bandages bounced off the floor as the cauterizer landed with a sturdy clatter of metal and plastic on the floor.

Tish jammed her foot in front of the center of the doors to keep them from swinging in and fumbled for the lock with hands that suddenly felt absurdly clumsy. *Get it get it get it.*

She sighed in relief as the bolt slid home, locking the two doors together. She kneeled and threw the locking bolts at the bottom corner of each door to secure it even further.

The infected burst into action and its hand slammed into the glass again with a boom that rattled the doors in their frame. "Frannie," Tish said with a calm that she didn't feel, "We've got a problem."

It was a close-run thing, even riding in the LAV.

Pete directed Hanratty off the blacktop and through the gravel around the grain bins. Hanratty had pushed the LAV to what felt like ridiculous speeds, and the rear wheels slewed around as he made the turn. Despite the rush, trickles of zombies already trickled around either side of the facility. A slowly-collapsing circle of guards covered the main entrance to the storage warehouse.

Pete swallowed. *Did I make the call soon enough?*
He shook off the question and shouted forward to Hanratty. "Can you back it up to the doors?"

The Marine didn't answer, but he gave a thumbs-up. Rooster tails of gravel shot out from the big vehicle's wheels as he cut the wheel over and gunned it. Pete clutched his rifle and shouted over the roar of the engine.

"We can't take much time — we need to unload and get inside. If it looks like we aren't going to make it inside, we've got to go down *hard*. I ain't lettin' these sons o' bitches anywhere near my family, ooh rah?" There was a vague chorus of replies and nods, and that just would not do. Funny. Despite all the years and injuries behind him, he fell right back into his squad leader persona. He mimed screwing a finger into his ear and shouted, "I *CAN'T hear you!*"

That worked — if their replies weren't in the proper verbiage, they at least had the proper tone. He glanced out the rear hatch as Hanratty began to back up. The guards at the door grasped their intent and shifted to allow the bulk of the armored vehicle to form the third wall of their defensive front.

Hanratty cut it close; Pete might have argued about the distance, but he couldn't complain. As the engine cut off, he leaned over and threw open both crew doors. The vehicle was *just* far enough from the silo for them to open. So close, in fact, that several of the guards who'd been covering outside had already withdrawn inside. The others looked to be assessing the possibility of doing the same. "Move, move, move!" Pete shouted. "Cover to the side of your door!" He put words to action, pushing off with his working prosthetic before he could wince at the thought of the drop.

The stiffness of the damaged leg threatened to pull him over as his opposite foot hit the ground. He reached out and grabbed one of the flanking guards to support himself. The man jumped in surprise, but Pete put his mouth close to the man's ear and shouted, "Fall back inside, we'll cover you as we dismount!"

The guard gave him a frantic nod and pulled away. Pete staggered at the sudden loss of support, but he regained his balance and ground the ball of his stiff leg's foot into the gravel. Thus supported, he flipped his rifle off of safe and began shooting. The trickle was thickening. They didn't have long before there'd be more surrounding them than they had guns to hold off, but they didn't need long. He hoped.

The volume of fire intensified as the men and women inside of the armored vehicle dropped down and joined the lines of defense flanking the door. Pete dropped an empty magazine and slammed a replacement home as he turned his head to shout, "Start pulling inside, closest to the doors! Smooth and steady, people!"

Hanratty hit the ground behind Pete and shouted, "Last man!" Pete nodded and kept shooting.

Slowly, the lines of defense thinned. This was the trickiest part. As they fell back inside of the warehouse, the volume of fire they put out lessened and allowed their approaching foe to come closer and closer.

It wouldn't have been so bad, Pete thought bitterly in the midst of another magazine swap, if they'd acted like they always had. If they'd just come straight on, the piles of their fallen brethren would have built up a bulwark. These were cagey, dashing forward in fits and starts. They fell back as the defenders took down groups of their attacking forces. It was almost as if they were trying to assess the relative strengths of the living defenders. And, to make things even worse . . .

"Down!" Pete roared and knelt as far as he could. Spears whistled overhead. One of the guards wasn't quick enough. He fell to the ground, speared in his stomach. Before Pete could open his mouth to order the coup de grace or perform it himself, Charlie lowered his shotgun and silenced the man's screaming with a single shell. "Thanks," Pete said with a grimace. He raised his head to find that he was one of only a handful of remaining defenders. "This is it, inside now, move!"

His stiff-legged stagger ended as Charlie wrapped arms like iron bars around his waist and lifted as he dove for the door. Pete would have cried out at the indignity of the whole thing if the press of the other man's arms hadn't driven the air from his lungs.

Inside, Charlie staggered and took them both to the ground as he fell. Pete caught as much of his weight as he could, but Charlie took the brunt of the fall. With a hysterical laugh, Pete rolled sideways and faced the door. They needed to get it shut, right . . . he relaxed.

Hanratty slammed the door and stepped aside as a couple of the others took up a heavy iron bar and slotted it into brackets on either side of the door. The first was in place just in time; heavy blows sounded on the reinforced aluminum. Dust vibrated out of the door frame as the assault continued. The second and third bars above and below the first stiffened the entire assembly, but the strikes continued.

"Well," Hanratty said, his voice drained. "I hope they haven't rediscovered the can opener."

Pete held back the nervous laugh; they weren't out of the woods yet. "Buddy check," he snapped. "We're looking for scratches. Anyone get a spear wound?"

In the beginning, it had been a tense occasion, but over the years they'd winnowed out the ones who were of the sort to rabbit when facing potential death. They patted each other down. The guard who checked Pete took a long stare at the rip in his slacks until Pete rolled his eyes and knocked on the prosthetic. "'Tis not even a scratch, Sir Knight." The other man relaxed, but the continued pounding on the outer door was putting them all on edge.

Pete was about to declare they needed to move to the central silo when a quiet stand-off at the edge of the huddle boiled over.

"Drop the shotgun, asshole!" One of the warehouse staffers yelled. He had his pistol pressed up against the back of Charlie's head.

"Ah, hell," Pete muttered, and hobbled over. Charlie's face was turning red with suppressed anger, but he kept himself still. "What's the problem here?" Pete studied the warehouse guy for a moment and said, "Foster, right?"

He must have been correct because the kid didn't correct him. His hand shook as he hissed, "This guy didn't even try to help Malcolm, he just *capped* his ass!"

Pete tried not to sigh. "Foster." The other man didn't look at him, so he repeated himself with a firmer injection of command tone. "*Foster.*" Their eyes met, and Pete barked, "Things have changed, son. They got, hell, smarter, I don't know. They climb fences and they throw spears. And they're dipping their spears in infected tissue. It does the same thing as a bite and they don't even have to get close. All right? Malcolm was turning, even if he didn't know it yet."

The other man stared at Pete. He opened his mouth to speak, but said nothing. Finally, he lowered the gun from the back of Charlie's head and tried to slide it back into the holster at his waist. His hands shook so much it took him several attempts before he brought it home.

Silence reigned in the warehouse. Pete was about to open his mouth to suggest they move into the main silo when his radio hissed with low volume static. With a frown, he brought it up and adjusted the volume knob. "Come back," he transmitted. "Last not copied."

"Mr. Matthews?" a young voice said in a quiet tone that was just this side of a whisper. "Is that you, sir? It's Alex, Alex Worthington."

Ah, hell. Pete rubbed his forehead. He keyed the radio and lowered his voice. "Alex, where are you?" He released the button and prayed for a different answer than the one he expected.

"I'm up in the nest, sir, with Cara. And, uh." His voice faded out for a moment, as though he were speaking to someone else near him. "A couple of the younger kids, sir, Twigs." There was the sound of a scuffle and a different voice came over the radio as someone else claimed the transmitter.

"Uncle Pete?" Trina's voice was shaky with fear. "They're starting to climb up after us. The covers are closed, but . . . they're still coming."

Chapter 36

The ventilation panels hadn't lasted as long as Miles had hoped they might. The press of flesh had jammed up against the doors and created an eerie silence as the zombies ran out of elbow room to strike. A few scant minutes later, they'd discovered the openings at the bottom of the doors and hammered their way through.

The first few through had cut themselves to ribbons on the steel fins, but the mass behind had pulled away enough to pull the first casualties back through. That didn't bode well for their expected timeline. If they couldn't depend on the bodies of the dead to create some sort of temporary barricade, Ross was going to have to fire off the first rank of claymores that much sooner. They'd angled them as much as possible, but Miles didn't know how well the shack doors would stand up to the blast. For that matter, every shot they missed was liable to go through the doors.

The quartet settled into an easy rhythm; one man on each side shot while the other waited or reloaded. Miles wasn't ashamed to admit he was the worst shot in the group. At this range and with the window he needed to fire through, that just meant he wasn't nailing a headshot every time. So far, it was enough.

Ross cursed on the right as his SCAR locked open on an empty magazine and the final bullet bounced off of the skull of his target with a high-pitched pinging noise. "Got it," Janacek said, and calmly sent a heavier 7.62mm round into the zombie crawling through the opening on that side. Whatever boosted their capability and intellect seemed to have made their bodies more robust. At this range, a 5.56mm armor-piercing round from Ross' SCAR 16 should have gone through bone like butter. All too often, the sound of a ricochet was their only reward for Ross and the Chief as they hit their targets. *Meat machines*, Miles reminded himself bitterly. The survivors had allowed themselves to dream and look forward to the future with the assumption that the hordes arrayed against them were withering in the face of time. Confronted with the opposing reality, he couldn't help but feel more than a little helpless. He hadn't been this scared outside of the wall in a long time.

The heavier rounds from Janacek's rifle and Miles' own custom job were more than up to the task of taking their attackers down. That firepower was also focused on the left side. As Foraker began to fire, Ross called out, "Janacek, swap with the Chief when he drops his mag."

"Roger that," Janacek called back. Foraker shouted his own curse as his second shot of the session came tumbling back at him.

"Mine," Miles said, as he lined up his shot and pulled the trigger. It didn't take him long, but it was enough of a delay that the zombie was completely out of the door and on its knees before he took it down. *Damn, they're so much faster.*

It was a strange sort of tension, Miles reflected. There was no frantic edge to their motions, but the low-grade undercurrent of terror defined every action. They were holding the tide back, if only just, but any hesitation on their part was an opening.

"Shit, shit, shit," Foraker said. "What's he doing?" The following zombie reached through the ventilation hatch and seized the one Miles had shot, but rather than pulling it back through, it rolled the lifeless body onto one side as it started to slide through. Foraker fired steadily, but the fallen body acted as a shield. It jerked under the impact of the Chief's fire, but there was enough cover there that he couldn't get a direct headshot. It crab-crawled sideways, as though trying to get out of the line of fire.

"Mind your sector!" Ross barked, and Miles jerked his eyes back over to the left opening, where a pair of smaller zoms had crawled out at the same time. The first put its back to them and ducked its head down.

Miles' mouth dropped open. It was acting as a shield for the second, which slid between the first and the door and started tugging at the cable they'd used to secure the handles together.

"I see it," Janacek said and flipped a switch on his SCAR. Even suppressed, the three-round burst made for an impressive concussion in Miles' chest. The shielding zom spasmed as the heavy bullets struck it in the back and neck. At least one of them got the spinal cord because it went limp. Janacek's follow-up burst messily removed the second zom's head from its shoulders before it could do any more than tug on the ends of the cable.

"I'm out!" Foraker announced and came up on his knees as he pulled his magazine and replaced it. He and Janacek flip-flopped positions as Ross began firing. The Chief propped his rifle up on Janacek's rucksack and grimaced. "I can smell your dirty socks, you animal!"

Janacek laughed. "It's not my fault you only change yours once a week, old-timer!"

Despite his fear, Miles laughed. This time, when he spotted movement in the left opening, he didn't hesitate. The target of his fire flopped, suspended halfway between the interior and exterior of the shack. He waited for the one behind it to make a move . . .

Silence reigned for the span of half a dozen heartbeats before Miles realized that everything inside of the shack was still. "Is that all of them?" he whispered.

Foraker was silent for a long moment, then muttered, "No way. They're up to something." The big man fell silent and cocked his head and stared at Ross for a long moment. The two men held eye contact until the lieutenant gave an oblique shrug.

Foraker levered off of the ground into a low crouch. He tucked his rifle into his shoulder and crept forward. The only sound in the silence was the light click of gravel against his boots.

The Chief paused just behind the final line of claymores and stared at the openings in the shack doors.

Tink.

"Did you hear that?" Janacek muttered.

"Shut up," Foraker hissed. He pressed his ear up against a ventilation duct.

Tink.

The Chief straightened and looked back, brow furrowed in confusion. He placed a hand against the air duct.

Is it big enough? Miles wondered. *It's got to go sheer vertical at some point, how the hell can they get a grip to climb that, even if it is big enough?*

Tink.

Foraker pulled his hand away from the duct and whispered, "Ah, shit." He began to step backward, faster than he'd advanced with no concern for the noise he was making. "We got problems," the Chief sang out. Confused, Miles looked over to Janacek and Ross; the other two men looked as baffled as he felt.

"Chief . . ." Ross began, but the other man cut him off with a pointing finger. A pair of hands reached through the upper part of the ventilation holes and took hold of the right door.

"The doors open in, Mikey, which means the hinges are on the *inside*. They popped the pins."

Metal scraped as the gray hands *pulled*.

The cable and wrenches kept the doors together, but with no support at the right side, the doors swung open as one, and the horde burst forth.

Tish didn't know what was worse; the knowledge that there were a dozen or more infected milling around in front of the clinic, or the fact that they weren't trying to break through the doors.

"What do we do?" Lizzie whispered. Tish bit her lower lip and glanced at Frannie, who shrugged. Tish had bandaged the entry and exit wounds and wrapped gauze around her waist to secure them. It wouldn't do for a long-term fix — they needed to clean the wound channel, if nothing else, to get any debris out before stitching it — but it would do for now. Frannie was pale with pain, but she'd accepted the small pistol from Larry and was keeping a close eye on Jaid. The other woman sat slumped in the corner of the room and seemed oblivious to what was going on around her.

"Dad?" Tish murmured. "How are you feeling?"

Her father didn't answer right away, but his sigh told her all she needed to know. "I don't know how much good I'm going to be in a fight, kiddo." He pressed a hand to his forehead and grimaced. "Where's my stuff?"

She leaned over beside his bed and pulled a plastic laundry basket out from underneath it. Tish had reduced his clothing to rags when she'd cut them off in surgery. She'd gotten him a clean pair of jeans, a shirt, and underclothes from his house and laid them inside. His belt with his holstered handgun was underneath. "Here," she said.

He opened one eye and regarded the basket. "And, like an idiot I had to give Pete my shotgun. Anything else in the building?"

She licked her lips and tried not to curse. "No." *Sure, it's a clinic — but you're Larry Vance's daughter, you should have known better.* Now it was an oversight that might just be fatal.

"Damn it," Larry muttered and winced. "So we've got the LCP with what, six rounds in it, and my Glock and a couple of spares?" Tish glanced at Frannie; the other woman nodded in confirmation.

"We just hole up, right?" Frannie said. "They'll start sweeping the interior soon, won't they?"

Tish glanced at her dad. He wouldn't meet her eyes.

"I don't know, Frannie," Larry admitted. "That was one hell of an explosion — I'm guessing something breached the wall. Did they get it contained? We haven't heard gunfire for a bit." He hesitated. "And that doesn't even begin to consider who or what breached the wall, if that's what it was. Could be raiders."

"No way can we fight our way out," Tish said. "We have to wait."

Her dad glanced around. "This isn't the room to do it in." The windows were high up, as they were in all the settlement's new construction, but what did that really mean? She remembered Vir's description of how the infected had piled up on top of each other to get at him and shuddered. It wouldn't take many to get high enough to push their way inside. These windows were ordinary residential glass, nothing fancy. They wouldn't last long under a determined assault.

"The surgical suite," Tish said. It was the only room in the clinic without a window. The door wasn't the most solid, but at least it wasn't glass. Maybe they could put some shelving in front of it . . .

"Get moving," her dad said. "Start with Lizzie."

Tish nodded. "Right." She stepped over to Lizzie's gurney and kicked the locks off of the wheels. It had been a colossal pain to get the hospital beds back to the settlement, but right now, she was glad she'd fought for them. There had been serious consideration to using simple, stand-alone cots — that wouldn't have rolled.

Frannie stepped aside, closer to Jaid, as Tish wheeled Lizzie's gurney around the foot of her dad's bed and toward the door. She tensed as she neared Jaid, but all the fight seemed to have left her. The other woman settled for staring Tish down with sullen eyes as she passed.

Tish negotiated the gurney through the door into the hallway and resisted the urge to push as fast as she could. The last thing she wanted to do was lose control and shove the gurney through the glass doors. "Don't look," she whispered to Lizzie, but the other woman either didn't hear or didn't want to look away. The infected outside pressed themselves up tight against the glass doors as she wheeled the gurney by, but they did nothing other than stare.

Lizzie whimpered, but she remained silent. Tish whispered a silent prayer in thanks for that. She didn't know *what,* if anything, would set them off. A scream had to be at the top of the list.

She wheeled Lizzie through the door and shifted her sideways to clear the doorway for the other gurneys. "Sit tight," she said and turned to return to the other room. As she crossed the glass doors, one of the infected ran its fingertips down the glass with a slight scraping noise.

Just a few more minutes, she told herself.

"I'm taking you now, dad," Tish said as she kicked the locks open on his gurney. "Hold tight."

He was closer to the door so her path was easier. She swung the foot of the bed toward the door, moved to the headboard, and started pushing.

She tried to ignore the infected at the doors as she pushed him by, but something nagged at the back of her mind as she did so.

Are there less of them? Where did they go?

"Jesus, Mary, and Joseph," her dad whispered as they crossed. "They look different."

"They're sure *acting* different," Tish managed through gritted teeth. Her shoes squeaked on the floor as she pulled up to slow the gurney down. She moved around to the front to turn it, then pushed it further in. It was going to be tight in here with all four gurneys; maybe they should put JT and Bob on the same gurney for this last run? She considered it for a moment and almost abandoned the idea. Frannie was in no shape to be pushing, and she didn't think she could move a gurney with that much weight on it.

Maybe Jaid would help? She snorted to herself. Regardless, she needed to move them. "Be right back, dad."

Tish started talking as soon as she crossed the threshold into the other room. "Frannie, we need to shift Bob and JT into the same bed."

The nurse grimaced and nodded. She was opening her mouth to reply when Jaid chose the moment of distraction to make her move.

"You two are idiots," Jaid snapped, then jumped on top of Bob Gentry's gurney. "You can stay in here all you like; I'm leaving." She threw open the latches on the window above the bed and lifted the sash. Tish turned to Frannie and opened her mouth to tell her to shoot, but the sudden shriek from the open window cut her off.

She turned back and stared. Jaid had gotten halfway out the window. Now, though, she shrieked odd, wet screams and tried to pull back inside but couldn't. As she twisted, Tish understood why and tried not to retch.

Something had shoved some sort of wooden shaft into and through Jaid's shoulder. If she'd pulled in the right direction, she might have been able to slide it out, but in the frantic urgency of her agony, she was pulling straight back. The length of the shaft slammed into the outer frame of the window and pinned her in place. A pair of wasted gray arms appeared at the bottom of the window frame and put Jaid in a choke hold. Her screams cut off, and a sudden, surprisingly strong yank pulled her body the rest of the way through the window. Save for a spray of blood, there was nothing to declare that the woman had ever been there.

"Go," Tish whispered as a pair of hands grasped the bottom edge of the window and began to pull. She saw a bald head outside, just outside of view, and heard the scrabbling of feet against the side of the building. "Go, now!"

Frannie only hesitated a moment before sprinting out of the room and down the hall. Tish stared at those grasping hands, cursed herself for a fool, and leaped onto Bob's gurney.

Her skin crawled at her proximity to the thing trying to climb in, but she forced herself to reach up and seize the top of the window. She put all her weight into it; bone cracked as she slammed the window home on the grasping hands. One released and pushed up on the window, but she pulled down again. This time, the bone splintered enough to tear through the desiccated flesh. The fingers plopped down inside; outside, she heard a thud as the climber hit the ground.

How much time do we have?

She twisted the locks on the window. It wouldn't keep them from busting through the glass, but it should slow them down. She hoped.

Tish climbed down to the floor and stared at the two men in their hospital beds. Despite all the commotion, neither had reacted. If not for the slow rise and fall of their chests, they could pass for dead.

Would the infected be fooled? Somehow, she doubted it. Despite their stillness, the bodies were warm. It would take no more than a touch to tell the truth of their state.

She couldn't save them both, but she couldn't leave them for the infected to eat alive.

Could she?

Be honest with yourself, a calculating part of her whispered. *Neither one of them was ever going to wake up, even if this didn't happen. But that doesn't mean you can't give them some small mercy.*

A decision this momentous should have the benefit of more time and more discussion. It shouldn't be the call of single, desperate woman. Outside, something bumped against the wall.

You don't have time for this. Do it.

Tish pulled a large-gauge syringe out of the supply cart between the two gurneys. She tore it out of the packaging as something thumped against the wall outside the window. She watched it out of the corner of her eye as she drew the plunger back and filled the hypodermic with air. She jabbed it into the port on JT's IV drip and pushed it home.

God, forgive me.

They didn't have heart monitors, but JT jerked up in the bed, then sagged back down. Death by air embolism wasn't a certain thing, but she hoped that she'd dumped enough air into his system to make it so. She pulled the syringe out and refilled it with air and repeated the process in Bob's IV. He didn't react as JT had, and she wasted a handful of seconds attempting to find a pulse. He was gone.

Tish left the syringe in the IV and sprinted down the hallway as fast as she could. More of the infected at the glass doors had peeled away — moving around back, perhaps? — but enough were there to eliminate the front doors as a possible escape route. There was a crash of breaking glass behind her as they breached the first window.

She stepped into the surgery suite and ducked to one side as Frannie slammed the door. There was a lock on the doorknob, but it was a light-duty one intended, like the windows, for residential use. She doubted it would stand up to a determined assault.

"The gurneys," Tish said. "We'll jam them up against the door. It's better than nothing."

Frannie nodded and stepped over to Larry's bed. He'd heard Tish and was already trying to climb out.

"Let me help him, Frannie," Tish said. "I don't want you straining yourself with the wound." She looped one of her dad's arms around her neck and lifted, helping to support him as he stood up beside the bed. "Floor for now, dad," she grunted and eased him down.

The gurney was easier to roll without any weight on it. They rolled it tight against the door and engaged the locks. Tish eyeballed the distance between the foot of the bed and the opposite wall. A slight smile broke across her face. Maybe they weren't sunk, after all. "I think it's just enough room, Frannie."

The other woman cocked her head but said nothing as Tish helped Lizzie to the floor. They put the head of the second gurney at the foot of the first. After a few moments of pushing and heaving, they had the second gurney wedged up against the wall.

Exhausted, she collapsed into a sitting position on top of the second bed. Frannie stood in the center of the room, one hand pressed to her side and the other clutching and unclutching at the leg of her scrub pants. "Tish," the other woman whispered. "In the other room — what did you do?"

She looked in turn at each of the other three people in the room and sighed. *Shouldn't I be crying?* The only thing she felt was a deep fatigue and a desire to curl up into a ball and sleep until this was over. *I just killed two men. I just killed two patients.*

"What I had to," she replied, and the first set of fists began to pound on the door to the surgical suite.

Pete hobbled as fast as he could through the passageway into the central silo. A few of the guards stood aside and let the others through before closing the outer door and throwing the locks. The zombies outside had stopped beating on the door, but they weren't taking any risks. Pete approved of the sentiment even though he had other things on his mind.

At the end of the corridor, a pair of men beckoned the group forward. Pete stepped to the side to let the rest by, though Vir, Jenny, and Charlie stayed close to him. As they stepped through, the men at the door threw it shut and heaved bars into place. Standard procedure — secure every area at every possible point in case of further breaches.

On one hand, it sucked pretty hard for anyone left on the other side, but it also ensured that any small breach wasn't going to turn into a full-fledged outbreak. Pete turned away from the door and scanned the interior of the ground floor.

The floors of the emergency shelters were donut-shaped. A pair of central metal support cylinders rose from the ground floor and stretched all the way to the top. On the ground floor, they'd cut the right-hand cylinder open, and Pete could see people clambering up the ladder welded to the inner wall. On the floor above, the ladder was in the opposite support. Welded caps interrupted each segment so that the furthest one could fall was about fifteen feet — painful to be sure, but survivable. The initial proposal had been to use a single support column with a single, continuous ladder from floor to roof. They'd abandoned it for safety reasons. It was still a lousy arrangement for the elderly and the — ahem — handicapped. It was also the best they could do in the absence of niceties like elevators or enough concrete to cast an actual staircase. He muttered, "Let's go," to his entourage and hobbled that way.

To no surprise, most of the people milling around on the ground floor were the older folks who didn't get around so well, along with Val and her walking wounded. She spotted Pete and sprinted in his direction.

She grabbed his arm and fell in line beside him as he headed toward the first ladder. "Pete, have you seen Larry or Tish?"

He almost stopped in surprise, but he caught himself at the last moment and kept hobbling. "No, but I've got bigger problems. Trina and some of the other kids are up in the nest, and they've got climbers coming."

Val brought her hands up to her mouth. "Oh, God. This is insane. I had to fight with Norma to keep her from having the exterior doors sealed before you guys got here. I don't know if we're short, it's chaos in here."

Pete gritted his teeth. No wonder the guys at the door had been in such a hurry to shut everything down. "Did they do a head count or anything?"

"No."

"Damn it," Pete cursed. He glanced around the room. "Get everyone calmed down and get a count. Send somebody up to the next floor and have them do the same, and so on. We need to know how short we are — we can't just leave people out there. Larry should still be in the clinic." He thought about the double glass doors they'd scavenged out of a strip mall and tried not to let his emotions bubble through to his face. Val was smart; she'd already done the math. "He's not unarmed," Pete said in what he hoped was a reassuring tone. "Worst case scenario,

575

kid, we'll make enough noise here to have every one of those bags of pus coming for us. Who knows, Larry may just nap through the whole thing."

She gave him a doubting look but finally nodded. He watched her go and turned to his group. Hanratty and Rivas sidled up and joined the crew. He imagined the Marine felt like a third wheel without something to do.

Good. I have a feeling I'm going to need some backup.

"I want everyone to go up before me," he said. "Things have gotten bad enough without Norma and her people losing their marbles. But I have no time to deal with this shit right now. I have to get to the Crow's Nest."

"Pete," Vir interjected firmly. "Not to belabor the obvious, but you're staggering on level ground. How are you going to climb out onto a catwalk six stories in the air and not fall and break your bloody neck?"

Pete clenched his jaw and tried to resist the urge to punch him in the face. But Vir had a point. His shoulders sagged as he admitted, "I don't know. But I have to try."

"I'll do it," Charlie rumbled. He looked at each member of the group in turn. He paused the longest on Hanratty and Rivas. Finally, he shrugged and said, "Not like I need to worry about the spears."

"You hope," Pete spat. "Everything else has changed, who's to say you're still immune?"

Hanratty hissed a low curse. Pete gave him a crooked grin. "Merry Christmas, Adam. Charlie has had more than his fair share of bites over the years and is no worse for wear." He turned back to Charlie. "Hell if I'm letting you go out there alone, big guy. I've got your six, even if I have to do it from down below." He looked around. "Rest of you can keep Norma and her people in line, ooh rah?"

Hanratty and Rivas replied in turn, and the others chorused in. *Not bad*, he judged. *It'll do.*

He gestured, and the others began climbing up to the next level. He hoped by going last he could streamline the process of going up. Anything would be faster than the entire group bunching up behind him as he tried to negotiate the ladder. He assessed his damaged prosthetic and decided he was better off not even trying to use it. As Vir cleared the next floor and left the ladder open, he slung his rifle and hauled himself up with both hands, planting his good leg on the second step. He paused and repeated the process. He had enough upper-body strength to take two steps at a time, but by the time he accepted Vir's outstretched hand and stepped out onto the second story, his arms trembled with fatigue. *Suck it up, Marine.*

This floor was much the same as the last, though most of the people milling around or sitting were family groups or other folks. He didn't spot anyone that he recognized as a wall guard or any of Norma's normal hangers on. He grunted to himself. Typical. Their defense plan hinged on getting everyone but defenders up to the top floor, then guarding the second. In the old days, that was the definition of safety. Norma and her people had not only abandoned the less able on the bottom floor, they hadn't bothered to mount a defense in the event the zombies breached the ground floor. *They're up top*, he realized, and Pete shook his head. He'd always considered Norma a flake, but this went beyond the pale.

But . . . in a way, it made a strange sort of sense. Many of the wall guards hadn't had the mental flexibility to deal with running, spear-throwing zombies. How could he expect the likes of Norma and the rest of the council, who hadn't been outside of the walls in years, to react with anything less than panic?

Given that, he could almost feel sorry for them. Almost. But the fact that they'd left people downstairs made him shake with rage.

He turned to Vir and Charlie. "Check the weapons locker, see if they left anything. I'm betting they stopped to haul it up with them but you never know."

The two went to inspect the tall, metal cabinet bolted behind the two main support columns. They hadn't stored their cream-of-the-crop weaponry in there, but the stuff was capable in a pinch.

Pete turned to the crowd and barked, "What the hell are you doing just *standing* there?" The reaction rippled through the crowd, but he didn't give them time to digest it. He jerked an accusatory finger at the ladder to the ground floor. "A couple dozen people down there who can't climb a ladder and you're sitting around fat and happy?"

Someone shouted back, though he couldn't see them. "They're going to bust in here!"

"Yeah, and if they do, anything that happens to the folks below is going to be on your conscience. Well, not for long. The zoms can climb now, after all. So after they go through the ground floor they're coming up here. I'm going to do something about it, though — busted leg and all. What's *your* excuse?" He swept his gaze across the room. Most of them avoided eye contact, but a few stood straighter and met his gaze. Most of the latter nodded and moved toward the ladder. Good. That was enough. He hobbled around to the next support and the ladder up to the third floor just as Vir slammed the cabinet door in frustration.

"There's sod all, Pete."

Pete shrugged. "That's all right. We'll get what we need when we track them down." He waved the others on and unclipped the radio from his belt. "Alex, you there?"

The boy came back almost immediately. His voice was shaky, and Pete mentally urged the others in front of him to climb faster. "We're still okay, sir. They're getting closer. Almost to the walkways."

Catwalks, Pete corrected, but he didn't speak. He winced. The hatch at the top of this silo exited directly onto the catwalk. They needed to pick up the pace. "We're on our way, kid. Hang tight. And hey, Alex?"

"Yes, sir?"

"You're a dead shot, kid. You guys are going to be just fine. Be right there."

Pete clipped the radio back onto his belt and repeated his process to climb the ladder. The third floor was much the same; a few people milling around or sitting, and an empty gun cabinet. Pete didn't even have to yell as much this time. His speech below had echoed up here and they'd gotten the gist of it, even if the wording hadn't been clear. He wasn't doing a head count as he went, but there didn't seem to be just under two hundred people in here. Half that, maybe. *Not good.*

Outside the last ladder, Pete gathered his people together and muttered, "Sling your rifles and keep them that way. We don't draw down. Unless I miss my guess, they're going to try and stop us. But I don't think it will come to violence. Norma would rather filibuster us to death than be in the middle of a gunfight." He waited for nods or murmurs of confirmation and continued, "Same drill, you all go first. When you get up top, act aloof. A couple of you need to go over by the stairs to the upper hatch; the rest get over by the weapons locker. Okay? Let's roll."

As before he waited, listening as his team clambered to the stop and stepped out one by one. It didn't take long before the yelling started.

Pete couldn't help himself; a crooked grin broke across his face. He whispered under his breath. "Norma, Norma, Norma. You are nothing if not predictable."

He took a deep breath and steeled himself to climb the ladder. He'd had enough of a break that his arms had stopped shaking.

They were back to shaking as he accepted Vir's hand once again. He willed them to be still as he stepped out onto the top floor and entered the zone of Norma's wrath. She put her nose an inch from his face and began her rant.

"I don't know what you people think you're doing. We are *not* going to open *any* of these exterior doors until the infected have lost interest and wandered off. We have ample supplies in here, but some foolhardy rescue mission is *not* the best use of the supplies we do have!" Inhale. "Furthermore, you are in *no* position of official authority to be leading either the police or the wall guards. Frankly, *sir*, you are a self-entitled kook we allow to sit up in your little nest because we much prefer you up there instead of bothering us down *here*. You *will* turn over your rifle and stand down right . . ."

Pete cut her off with a lifted forefinger and a fiery look. "Jim," he called out. "What's the count?"

The man stood a bit behind and to the left of Norma. He looked a bit nonplussed at the sudden attention. "Ah . . . I'm sorry, Pete, I don't follow."

"When we put together the evac protocols," Pete hissed through clenched teeth, "One of the first things we agreed to do was a full head count of everyone in the shelter, to see if we were missing anyone. What's the count, Jim?"

He stammered. "Well, I, uh, that is, we, I mean . . ."

"How short are we, Jim?" Pete hissed. "Cause right off the top of my head, you incompetent morons not only left people in the clinic, there are kids up in the observation post radioing for help." He raised his voice. "Anybody still got their radio on, in here?" He waited, got no answer, and shook his head. "Good God, people. I'm almost glad Gary didn't make it because this shit would have killed him."

"I don't appreciate your tone!" Norma stepped forward and jabbed a finger into Pete's chest, punctuating each word.

He looked at her and tried to keep his tone indifferent. "The only reason you're not laying on the floor unconscious is because my grandma raised me to respect a lady. But you are *rapidly* approaching the limits of my patience."

Norma smirked and opened her mouth to retort, but before she could get out the first word, a fist snaked in from Pete's side and slammed into her chin with a dull thump.

The council member collapsed to the floor in front of him with all the grace of a dropped bag of groceries.

Pete cocked his head down at Norma's unconscious form and turned to look at Jenny Faqir. The deputy shook her hand and grimaced. "Oww. That hurt a hell of a lot more than I thought it would."

Pete tried not to grin as he replied, "Well, next time try not to tuck your thumb inside your fist." He raised his voice and stared Jim down. "Mr. Piper, we're going to have a temporary change of command for the duration of this crisis. I'm top dog, here, and, uh, Vir, Jenny, and Charlie are my secondaries. You don't like it, you can take it up with Jenny." A titter of laughter chorused around the room. He waited for any outbursts. Hearing none, he turned to Charlie. "Let's go shopping, buddy."

He couldn't tell if the guards had taken the better weapons from the other two cabinets and left the dregs in this one, but what was there wasn't all bad. He just wasn't sure that what remained was appropriate for their situation. There were a couple of scoped bolt-action rifles, a few older pump shotguns, an M-1 Garand, and a lever-action .44 Mag Marlin 1894.

There was, at least, plenty of ammunition. He glanced over at Charlie and the rifle over his back. It was an M-1 Carbine, chambered in a relatively slow 110-grain round. It would do, in a pinch, but how would the round-nosed .30-caliber rounds do against these newer, better zoms? Some of the rounds from his M4 hadn't been completely effective, after all.

"Hell," Pete said, then shrugged the sling of Brett's rifle off of his shoulder. He held it out to Charlie. "Roll with this. Here, I've got plenty of mags."

Charlie looked at the proffered gun for a moment and frowned. Finally, he unslung the Carbine and set it inside of the cabinet. He took a moment to check over the M4 before slinging it over his shoulder.

Pete transferred his mags out of his musette bag and into Charlie's waiting hands. As the other man tucked the magazines away in the pockets of his jacket and his web gear, Pete filled the musette bag up with en bloc clips for the Garand. "I'm going to hold the hatch," he said. "I'll cover you. You get to the ladder that leads up to the nest and keep it clear on that end. Between the two of us, we keep that segment open long enough for the kids to get inside here, then you fall back in and we figure out our next move. Sound good?"

Charlie considered it, then grabbed the Marlin out of the rack as well. He found an empty pocket and dumped a box of shells into it. "Think I'll start off with this," he rumbled. "I'm old school."

Pete grinned and leaned the Garand against the gun cabinet and pulled out one of the bolt-actions. "I like the way you think." He slid a box of rounds — .308 Winchester — for the scoped rifle into the bag and decided if he had any more weight to carry he was liable to topple over. "You ready?" He slung the .308 over his shoulder and picked up the Garand.

Charlie gave him a quick nod.

They drew a crowd as they headed for the staircase, and Jim Piper emerged and stepped up beside Pete. "We're getting everyone up from the second floor onto three now, Pete. Should we bring them up here?"

"No," Pete decided. "Get everyone consolidated on three. See if you can't wedge the cabinet in the shaft down on two, that will cut down the possible entrance points to this up here. These damn things have gotten too smart, I don't know how long our defenses are going to hold. And we can't count on them giving up and going away like we could back in the old days."

"Okay. Okay." Jim gulped. "The count is, ah, the count is, one hundred and twenty-six."

Man. Pete closed his eyes and tried to think. Their total population was 197 — but no, that was wrong, wasn't it? Hanratty and his Marines were in here. So out of an even two hundred, they had seventy-four unaccounted for. That was a terrible, potentially crippling blow. How many had they lost at the breach? Ten, maybe twelve? God help him, he couldn't remember; it was all just a blur. "Once we get the kids back in here, we need to figure something out. We can't just leave our people high and dry out there."

"How you fixed for belt-fed 7.62mm, Pete?" Hanratty interjected. "Get us some ammo and some shooters to man the gun ports and we can start cleaning this place out from the LAV. If they've got a few of us to pay attention to, it's going to split their focus. "

A chorus of cheers rose up and out of the surrounding group, and Pete couldn't help but grin. "I don't think volunteers are going to be a problem. Piper, how about it?"

The warehouse manager rubbed his balding head and thought about it. "Pretty sure we've got at least three, maybe four ammo cans full. Figure out who's going and what they're carrying. We'll cut through the warehouse and hook them up with all the rounds they can carry."

"Any chance I can talk you into swinging by the clinic to pick up my daughter-in-law and the others?"

"We can do that," Hanratty agreed.

Pete grimaced as another thought occurred to him. "Adam, what about getting back into the vehicle? We didn't exactly clear the area when we left."

Hanratty gave him a long flat stare, then murmured, "Pete, as soon as you step out on that catwalk and start ringing the dinner bell, do you think they'll be wasting time trying to claw through a steel building?"

Pete blanched. "Yeah. Good point." He patted the musette bag at his side to reassure himself that it was still there, checked the action of the Garand one final time, and gave Charlie a direct look. "You ready? Let's do this."

Chapter 37

The roof seemed to heave below Miles as Ross lit off the first wave of claymores. For one heart-stopping moment, Miles thought Ross had frozen, but he was demonstrating a cold-blooded level of patience that Miles could never have duplicated.

The press of bodies behind the now-breached door scrambled over the bodies of the fallen as they caught sight of Miles and the SEALs.

It was quieter than such a moment should have been, quiet enough that Miles heard Ross' bark of, "Fire in the hole!" before Foraker grabbed him by the neck and pulled his head and upper body down.

The boom of the anti-personnel mines was a bit like a pair of massive shotguns going off. He was close enough that his ears were still ringing when Foraker shook him roughly and screamed, "Up and at 'em!"

Miles lifted his head and got his rifle back into line. They'd angled the claymores at an angle to sweep the area in front of the dual doors. Firing both off at once was nigh-cataclysmic. The claymores had shredded the initial horde of infected, with many decapitated or dismembered. A bulwark of dead flesh lay between the defenders and the opening. Though a few bodies jerked weakly, the majority were down for the count. Those who'd come through unscathed were quickly put down by aimed fire.

The results, unfortunately, weren't all positive. The storm of ball bearings from the mines had punched into the shack after wreaking havoc on the attackers. The upper half of the metal doors resembled nothing more than metallic Swiss cheese. Another blast or two, and they were liable to fail completely.

Save for the weakening twitches of a few mangled bodies, all was still. "Anyone have a clear sight line into the shack?" Ross called out.

"I got nothing but shadows," Foraker called out.

"Zip," Janacek added.

Miles licked his lips. *Come on.* In the old days, any survivors would have rushed them mindlessly. The four of them might have been overrun by the sheer force of numbers, but at least they would have known what was coming.

"Anyone else want to recon?" Foraker joked. "I had my turn."

"Stow that, Chief," Ross said and eased himself to his feet. He moved forward in a half-crouch, with his rifle shouldered and aimed toward the doors. He hesitated a beat, then stepped back. "Here they come."

They'd either learned from the initial rush or they were trying something different. The infected ducked down as they came out of the door and attempted to use the bodies of their fellows as cover.

"Hold fire, left," Ross barked. "Janacek and I." The two fired as one in evenly-timed single shots that could have been the product of a machine.

A decade of combat in this world, plus whatever training and experience they'd had before — Miles doubted they even had to think about aiming. "When we switch," Foraker murmured, "you take the ones coming out of the door. I'll go for any you miss that get behind cover." Miles nodded.

Janacek's heavier rifle had a lesser capacity than Ross's, but shortly after the enlisted man's gun clicked empty, the Lieutenant's fell silent as well. "Reloading," Ross barked, and Foraker began firing.

Miles missed his first five shots before he adjusted to the different motions of the infected. It was as if they knew that their heads were their weak point, so they ducked, hunched, or bobbed their heads back and forth as they moved. Once he grew comfortable, it was smooth sailing at this range. His bullets were heavy enough that any hit on the head was sufficient to take them down, whereas Foraker's lighter bullets needed to be perfectly placed. With the Chief, it didn't matter. If anything, his accuracy was more preternatural than that of his compatriots, despite the growing mound obscuring the doors.

Miles and the Chief clicked empty within a few moments of one another, and Janacek and Ross took up the defense again as the other men reloaded.

"Take a drink, kid," Foraker said and hauled out his own canteen. "This is going to be an endurance race."

Miles nodded and took a drink. It was a good recommendation — he hadn't realized how parched he was, and even lukewarm well water tasted like Heaven going down.

"Out," Janacek reported, and Miles took up his own rifle. A heartbeat later, Ross reported, "Reloading," and Miles and the Chief began firing again. Everything blurred into a pattern; lay the dot of his sight on a head, squeeze, verify the hit, and repeat. He only missed three shots this time, but as he dropped his second magazine, Miles couldn't help but frown.

"This is too . . ." He began. He was going to say 'easy', but a sudden impact slammed him to the roof, and the sudden, squirming weight on his back told him that their position hadn't been as secure as they thought.

"Flankers!" the Chief roared, and the volume of fire exploded.

Miles rolled onto his back, shoving the weight off to one side. The naked and hairless infected had lost the flesh on one side of its face at some point. The death's head grin left it devoid of any identifying features that might have proclaimed that it had once been human. It staggered, caught its footing, and lunged for him.

He got his arm up and wedged his forearm into its throat. He tensed the muscles of his arm and held the snapping teeth a few bare inches short of his face. He had enough time to note the new wound on its head — they'd hit it, but not straight on. Had it played possum and crawled around to climb up onto the solar panel array? Had this been their plan all along? He heard a sound of impact on the other side, and one of the SEALs shouted, though the sound quickly faded away. He started to turn his head to look, but a renewed assault on his chest reminded him that inattention was fatal. He jerked his head back around.

The infected clawed at Miles' jacket even as it tried to push his arm down and get to exposed flesh. His left hand found the grip of his pistol and he jerked it out of the holster. He was a lousy — hell, *terrible* — shot with his left hand but that made no difference at all as he jammed the barrel into one of its eyes and pulled the trigger. As he did, he instinctively turned his head and closed his mouth.

"Not today," Miles muttered.

He threw the body aside and got up on his knees. Two of the SEALs were dumping rounds downrange as fast as they could; Janacek was nowhere to be found, and Miles realized with a sick feeling what that fading scream meant.

"Huddle up!" Ross shouted. "Fire in the hole!"

He squeezed the clackers on the second set of claymores, and the roof shook again. Miles didn't have time to appreciate the effect of the explosives. He'd turned to the left and spotted the half-dozen infected crawling on top of the solar array in their direction. Their motions were disconcerting; spider-like, jerky, scuttling. He clicked the safety selector on his rifle to FULL and held the trigger down as he let the recoil pull his point of aim to the right. His wild fire took down four of the infected, but before he could reload, the Chief stepped up beside him and fired two bursts down range to take the last two.

"You all right?" the older man shouted. "No scratches?"

"I think so," Miles said, his voice shaky. He hadn't even taken the time to check himself. *I'd know if I'm infected, wouldn't I?* Celia had known, so many years ago, and warned him away. Even if the infection had changed, could it change *that* much?

It didn't matter — there was no time for introspection. He slammed a fresh magazine into his rifle and noticed that he only had three left. *Doubt we're going to have time to load them, either.* He glanced to the right.

The second line of claymores had stopped that charge from the center, but they'd also done a number on the doors. Both were down, now, with massive chunks torn out of the surrounding frame of the shack. The infected had a huge gap out to pour through. As Miles watched, they moved to either side as even more picked their way forward through the debris of the first few assaults.

"Concentrate on the sides!" Ross shouted. "Once we build up enough in front of us, I'll hit the last line."

Where Miles stood, he didn't have a good angle on the infected before they were actually on top of the solar array. They seemed to recognize this fact, and more and more began to move over to that part of the roof, although the panels remained clear.

"They're going to hit it *en masse*," Foraker muttered. "They figured it out last time." He glanced at Miles and said, "It's been real, kid."

"Fire in the hole!" Ross announced, and triggered the last set of mines. By now Miles was almost inoculated to the concussion of the blast. He shouldered his rifle and waited.

"Turtle up, boys," Ross said evenly. "Let's show them how hard a frogman dies."

"Hooyah, Mikey. Let's do this thing." Foraker said and stepped over to press up against Miles' side.

The three remaining men compressed into a pseudo-triangle at the edge of the roof. The frantic rush that had overtaken the infected had faded. Their movements were slow and unhurried, now. More and more of them cascaded out of the elevator shack. As the roof in front of Miles began to fill, climbers moved up onto the solar array. A line of attackers crept their way.

Ross began to fire single shots, picking off leakers on his side. Miles took that as a sign. He flipped his own rifle back to semiautomatic and began engaging the advancing line. Foraker alternated, taking a few shots to Miles' side, then turning and directing fire to the front.

Miles licked his lips and wished he had time for one last drink. It was funny, really — as a kid, he'd hated the smell and taste of well water and now, on the brink of death, it was all he wanted. He smiled to himself and dropped his empty magazine. Two more and he was down to pistol. He hit the bolt release to chamber a round, then frowned.

The roof was shaking. Were there that many on the roof, that . . .

He heard it.

The staccato boom of engines. The thump-thump of rotor blades whipping through the air.

The sound of . . . . trumpets?

With a roar and the rush of wind, the single-largest helicopter Miles had ever seen swept over the elevator shack. Every head on the roof turned to look at it, even the undead ones. Foraker whooped in exultation as the helicopter slowed and banked. The massive, slate-gray helicopter looked like a Greyhound bus with wings, and Miles cheered himself as the massive machine gun sticking out of the open door behind the canopy opened up. The weapon had the familiar boom of the wall-mounted Browning machine guns on the walls back home, but the rate of fire felt like double or even triple compared to what the M-2s could put out. Debris flew as bullets slammed into the roof and the ring of infected.

If anything, the sound of trumpets got even louder as the music cascaded into a familiar tune. Even as Miles recognized the song he took note of the massive, cylindrical speakers under the helicopter's wings.

"Is that . . . *Ride of the Valkyries?*" Miles managed, and Foraker just laughed.

"Gotta love crazy Marine aviators, kid!"

The gun on the side fell silent, and the helicopter rotated in place. A hydraulic ramp descended from the rear and revealed another cannon, manned by a helmeted soldier. Miles and the SEALs hit the floor as the gunner swept the barrel from side to side, clearing the roof. As he fired, the helicopter descended, and Foraker yelled in Miles' ear. "Shift forward, kid, or you're going to get crushed!"

The lip of the ramp slammed onto the edge of the roof. Ross yelled, "Let's go!" and crab-walked up the ramp, keeping under the gunner's line of fire.

Miles glanced back; the fire from the helicopter had shredded most of the infected, not to mention the elevator shack, which was collapsing. The rubble settled for a moment, then continued to fall as it trickled down the elevator shaft. One way or another, the way blocked. Moments ago they'd faced certain death; now, salvation was at hand.

He turned away and scrambled up the ramp with Foraker as though it might disappear at any moment. He sprawled out on the deck, and the whine of hydraulics filled his ears as the ramp lifted back up and the helicopter pitched forward and away.

"We did it," Miles whispered to himself. *I'm going home.*

As soon as they'd begun, the strikes on the surgery room door ceased. Whether the infected discerned that there was no way to get in or the press at the door was too tight to allow for movement, Tish didn't know. In a strange way, she hoped for the latter. A mass of dumb, unthinking monsters was easier to contemplate than intelligent and cunning ones.

Tish turned away and moved to Frannie's side. "Why don't you lie down," she suggested. "I think I should be able to scrounge up enough in here to get that cleaned up and stitched."

Frannie gave her a wan smile. "Sounds fun, especially since the painkillers are in the other room."

Something thumped against the wall, away from the door. Tish turned back and frowned. They were in the exam room. She moved over to the wall and put her ear up against it. She expected the pounding of fists against the wall, but what she heard was far different.

What are they doing? Tish gasped after she listened long enough to identify the noise. She stepped back to her dad.

"Dad, you helped build the clinic, right?"

He pulled his hand away from his eyes and blinked at her. "Yeah, why?"

She pointed. "How solid is that wall?"

He grimaced and glanced at it as more thumps sounded. "That wall and the opposite wall in the patient room, those are the internal bearing walls. Sixteen inches on center."

Tish rubbed her forehead. "The walls are plywood, at least. That's something. It should slow them down."

Larry frowned. "Slow them down?" He trailed off as she grimaced.

"They're clawing through the walls, Dad."

Pete cursed himself for a fool as soon as he stepped out onto the catwalk. The walkway was little more than a narrow strip of perforated steel planking bolted on top of the pipes that had once carried soybeans and corn between silos. Vertical supports sprouted every few feet and supported a pair of flexible wires that served as hand rails.

It reeked of danger if you had *two* good legs.

"On the bright side, I just have to cover you," Pete muttered to Charlie as the other man closed the hatch they'd just passed through. He pounded a fist on the surface. The scrape of metal on metal was just audible as Trey and Jenny slid the interior crossbars back into place.

Charlie assessed the path and grimaced. He started to move, then stopped and pointed.

Pete had thought the security covers on the ladders would have been more of a barricade, but these advanced zombies had just shifted to the outside of the safety cages. As he and Charlie watched, the first in a line that stretched all the way to the base of the silo grasped one of the horizontal support cables and began to pull itself onto the catwalk.

He bit back a curse and leaned back into the dome of the silo. He wedged his damaged leg against the nearest vertical support to give himself some support. Pete shouldered the Garand, ready to start shooting, but Charlie had already rushed forward, blocking his line of fire.

"Damn it, Charlie!" Pete yelled, but dropped his point of aim to the lower climbers and started pulling the trigger.

Charlie couldn't remember the last time he'd been afraid to die. Not having to worry about biter bites was one thing. Looking down and seeing that stomach-wrenching space between you and the unforgiving ground? Altogether different.

He almost froze, but when the first climber reached the catwalk, a surge of anger pushed the fear away. In his rush, he didn't even bother to grab for one of his weapons. He stutter-stepped across the narrow walkway, yelling an inarticulate roar the entire way.

The climber was on its feet and headed toward the ladder to the Crow's Nest when Charlie began his run. He didn't know if it was the sound or the shaking, but it hesitated and turned toward him. He lowered one shoulder and slammed into it. The thing was more robust than the norm, but for all that he still out-massed it by more than two to one. The impact sent the biter sprawling backward. Its thighs slammed into the support wire and flipped it over. It plunged headfirst to the ground.

Eight stories down, bone met the concrete pad and splintered into ruin. He would have smiled, but there were more where that one had come from. Across the bridge, Pete's rifle pinged as he emptied the magazine of his big rifle. Another quartet of bodies was down at the base of the ladder courtesy of the old man's shooting.

Another reached up and took hold of the catwalk. Despite the denial of the high ground, they came on in utter disregard of individual safety. Maybe they'd learned to climb, but they were stupid as hell. Or maybe they just realized that their biggest strength was their numbers.

Charlie unslung the lever-action and jammed the barrel into the biter's face. At this range, there was no chance of missing, and he added another body to the growing pile at the base of the ladder.

The ladder at his back vibrated, and he glanced up. One of the kids from up in the nest was starting to come down.

He slammed his hand against the side of the silo three times until the kid met his eyes. Charlie shook his head and pointed back up to the top.

Let us clear this out first, he thought, but the kid got the gist of it from his gestures. He started climbing back up. Charlie resisted the urge to sigh and turned his attention downward.

Pete was getting a bead on the climbers. The stack of bodies around the ladder was making it more difficult for those on the ground to climb up. Charlie jacked another round into the lever-action and took aim. The next-highest biter was a good twenty feet below. He missed the head, but the impact of the bullet into its shoulder shook the thing loose, and it fell to the ground.

He saw the motion out of the corner of his eye before he heard the rush of the body falling through the air. Before he had a conscious realization of what was happening, he leaned sideways and grabbed hold of a support wire.

The biter clipped him on the shoulder, slammed into the side of the silo, and crumpled to the floor of the catwalk.

What the hell?

Charlie straightened and put a quick shot in the back of its head. He swept his head around as he tried to discern where it had fallen from.

He saw the next one before it duplicated the maneuver the first had attempted. The smaller storage silo across from where Charlie stood was a twin of the one that had been set up as the shelter. The external ladder, though, was on the opposite side.

They'd reached the top of the ladder and gotten onto the rounded dome of the bin. From there, they could turn and look down on the position Charlie held. It would have been faster to come at him on the catwalk from their silo to the Crow's Nest silo, but he would have seen that coming. With his attention focused down, an attack from above was canny.

Maybe not so dumb after all.

The second jumper didn't have quite enough speed, and it described a long, slow ballistic arc that terminated at the base of the ladder.

If they were climbing this one, then . . .

Charlie turned to look at Pete. He waved his arms over his head to get the other man's attention. Pete raised his head from the rifle with a puzzled look on his face before he caught Charlie's motions. He turned in place as the first biter slid down the curved face of the shelter silo. Pete yelled out and swung the barrel of his rifle into its head to push it to one side. It slid past the hatch and into the open air.

But that was just the first — more and more began to pop up. A few of them hammered at the air vents in the top of the silo to gain access, but others crept toward Pete. They'd figured out that each silo had its own ladder, and that they were all interconnected at the top.

"Come on!" Charlie yelled-gargled. He shouldered the lever-action and began firing. At this range, he hoped that the bullets wouldn't punch through and ricochet.

Pete cursed and started to lurch across the catwalk. With his leg locked out straight he had to almost move sideways. Behind him, the next biter slid down the side and made a grab for the rail before falling to the ground. The one after that made the drop just right, though, and the catwalk shook under the impact. Even worse, the following biter took an identical approach. It was as if, Charlie realized with a sinking feeling in his stomach, that each, in turn, learned from the mistakes of the others and adjusted their approach.

My God — are they talking *to each other?* He turned and glanced — case in point; the ones atop the opposite silo who'd been trying to leap across the gap had disappeared. The catwalk encircling it was empty so far, but presented with their new intelligence, he felt sure that they'd be seeing an attack on that front soon.

He couldn't keep firing without hitting Pete. Charlie opened the action and fed shells into the Marlin's tubular magazine. He still had the M4, but he couldn't shake the sense that he was going to need the firepower, and soon.

Halfway across, Pete turned and aimed his rifle across his body. The empty clip pinged out, but at least one of his shots hit home. The first biter in line behind him sagged down and created a temporary blockade. While the others wrestled at the lifeless corpse to clear the way, Pete crossed the rest of the bridge and met Charlie at the base of the ladder.

"Up," Charlie said and jerked his thumb in the same direction.

Pete hesitated, but Charlie just shook his head and frowned.

"I'll make it snappy," Pete promised. "When I get up top, I'll cover you to climb." He slung the empty rifle over one shoulder and started climb-hopping up the ladder.

The live biters finally lifted their lifeless counterpart and tossed it over the side. Charlie bared his teeth.

Let's do this, then.

He aimed and took methodical shots. The narrowness of the path helped him, but the oncoming biters still bobbed and weaved. Years of easy shots hadn't prepared him for a walking corpse that tried to avoid gunshots. The

Marlin clicked empty after he'd taken down only three of them. That was enough of a blockade to give him some breathing room, though, and he fed more shells into the weapon. He'd thought his pockets were overflowing with rounds, but he was emptying them fast. He glanced up — Pete was halfway up the ladder.

Hurry up, you old fart.

Charlie shouldered the lever-action and resumed firing.

Hanratty dropped the can of linked ammunition to the floor with a grunt. Jim Piper had led them on a meandering route from the shelter to the warehouse, then back to the where they'd entered the complex.

Charlie and Pete should be up top by now.

They needed to get a move on and provide a distraction, or every infected in the damn compound was going to be crawling over each other to get to them. He turned to Rivas, Patterson, and the handful of people who'd volunteered to come along. "All right. Patterson, you lead the way. Get into the driver's seat and get the engine started. Rivas and I will cover you." He turned to look at the motley collection of men and women who'd come along, and immediately regretted the judgment. They looked scared, to be sure, but their faces were also determined. *These people are* survivors, he reminded himself. What they lacked in military discipline and uniformity they made up with tenacity and capability. "We load up in twos." He glanced at Jim Piper and fixed the man with a fierce glance. "You're on the door. Drop the locking bar as soon as you see the doors slam on the LAV. Worst case scenario, we can hold up in there." On top of weapons and ammunition, they'd loaded up on bottled water and rations to supplement what was in the vehicle. It wouldn't last forever, but if they got stuck inside at least they would have something to stave off dehydration.

He cocked his head at the sound of gunfire. The metal walls muted much of it, but it was recognizable. "That's our cue. Let's do this."

Chapter 38

Wood splintered as the sharpened bone at the tip of the crude spear punched through the interior wall of the surgical suite.

Tish licked her lips and raised the Glock, but her father said, "Wait. Wait for it."

She glanced over at him; with the wound in her side, Frannie wasn't of much use, so she was leaning against the wall in the open corner of the room. Her dad was sitting up, once again, in defiance of her advice. The queasy expression on his face and the slight side-to-side movement of his upper torso would have given her a sense of 'told you so' satisfaction if she weren't so terrified.

"Just a little hole," Larry managed. "Give them a bit longer. Wait till you see the grays of their eyes."

Lizzie laughed, though there was a frantic tinge to it. "That's your great advice? Man-eating, walking corpses are digging through a wall to come at us and that's all you got?"

Larry grimaced and gave her a look. "Yes, sorry to say, that's all I got. I . . . ."

"Shut up," Tish hissed. The other three looked at her with varying degrees of confusion and annoyance. "Don't you hear it? What *is* that?"

The survivors had four cans of linked ammo that worked in the LAV's machine guns — 800 rounds, all told. Not a little, but not a lot. If they wanted to make a dent in the horde, they needed to be . . . creative.

Hanratty couldn't help but think that he might have erred in expressing that to Corporal Patterson. The Corporal whooped in joy as he gunned the LAV's big diesel and jerked the wheel to steer toward a clot of infected. They froze, unsure whether to flee or to attack. That indecision came at a price as the front of the armored personnel carrier slammed into them. A few might have been lucky enough to pass beneath the undercarriage, but the LAV's big tires ground just as many into the dirt.

Bone thumped on metal as a cast spear bounced off of the vehicle's sides. For now, Hanratty had decided to keep all the firing ports sealed. When and if they did start firing, he'd stick to the machine gun in the turret. He didn't want to risk a lucky toss plunging a spear through one of the side gun ports or taking him down from the cupola. In the last encounter maybe one in every four or five had carried a weapon, now every other one seemed to be hauling something around. He wondered with a sick sense of curiosity what they'd done with the infected they'd gotten the bones from. Maybe they'd been the dumber, slower ones?

"Corporal, if you roll this thing, I'm going to kick your ass between your ears," Hanratty shouted. "Get over to the clinic."

"Ooorah, Captain," said Patterson. He pulled off the blacktop and made a broad turn through a freshly-planted garden. Hanratty winced, but a few crushed vegetables were of little concern compared to survival.

"Ouch," he said as the LAV came around and the clinic came into sight through the viewing slit. The crowd of infected were packed around the building three and four deep.

Well, at least that indicated there were survivors inside.

"Patterson, make a run in front of the building and thin them out. Rivas, if you get a good angle with the 240 after that, take your shots. Just make them count, friendlies inside." He turned around and glanced at the civilians who'd tagged along. Most of them were unknown, but one of them from the fight at the fence — Simmons, he thought his name was — seemed to have taken the lead. "Your people ready?"

The other man swallowed and gave him a thumbs up. "All right. We're going in hot. We'll clear as many of them off as we can, but we're going to have to open up and help any wounded back inside."

One of the other men slapped Simmons on the back and shouted, "Just get us there and back, we'll do the rest, Captain!"

Hanratty pulled back around and smirked. He didn't know if it was the sudden change of management or the psychological support the presence of the Marines and the LAV offered, but the demeanor of the survivors was completely out of phase with what he'd seen when they first entered the shelter.

I'll take it.

Patterson gunned the engine and steered the LAV close to the clinic. The staccato thump of bodies on the frame filled the cabin. In the sudden noise, Hanratty almost missed the alert chime of the BFT. He glanced down at the screen and had to read through the message three times before he comprehended what it read.

A smile crept across his face. "Step on it, Patterson!" *Sounds like we're in for a show, and I don't want to miss it.* He began to key in a reply.

The interior of the helicopter — Foraker informed Miles that it was a CH-53K 'King Stallion' — was claustrophobic despite its imposing size. There were a bare handful of seats bolted along the left bulkhead. A series of crates that looked fabricated from odds and ends filled much of the remaining floor space. Miles could have sworn one patch of metal had a Chevy badge on it, though the entire assembly had been spray-painted the same shade of olive drab.

Ross noticed his interest and leaned over. He had to scream into Miles' ear to be audible over the thunder of the engines. "They designed these bad boys to be heavy lift choppers. One of these suckers can haul an LAV. We don't have much use for that, so they retrofitted it to carry as much as ammo as we could cram in."

Miles shook his head in amazement and gave the SEAL a thumbs-up. Despite what had to be literal *tons* of ammunition in the belly of the helicopter, the ground was a blur. The Black Hawk had been fast, but this was the next level. Ross elbowed him and pointed. There were machine gun stations immediately behind the cockpit to either side. The gunner on the right — starboard, he supposed —

beckoned to Miles. He unstrapped his harness and made his way forward, though a sudden shift of the deck beneath his feet made the movement more difficult.

The gunner handed Miles a headset and gestured for him to put it on. After Miles did so, the sound of a rough Southern drawl in mid-sentence replaced the sound of the helicopter's engines.

". . . Coming up on the objective now, you got the civilian on, Chambers?"

The gunner spoke into his own microphone; the sound was just out of sync with the movement of his lips. "He's right here, Captain."

"Howdy, son, Captain Billy Heppel, U-S-M-C. We lost contact with our Marines at your camp for a bit, but we've got them up. Hate to say it, but looks like your walls got breached. I'm going to do a flyby and see if I can pique the interest of the deadheads. You take a look and let me know the best place to shred 'em."

The sense of relief Miles had felt at his own survival washed away in a sudden surge of terror. He swallowed past the sudden thickness in his throat and said, "You got it."

He turned to look out the side of the helicopter. The gunner had the handles of his machine gun to hold onto, but the bank of the chopper left Miles unsteady on his feet. He searched around for a moment before he saw a canvas strap bolted to the ceiling. He grabbed on and looked even as he prayed that Heppel was wrong.

They'd circled around and come in from the east. The thunder of the engines faded as the pilot slowed, giving Miles an opportunity to take in a sight he'd hoped never to see.

The grounds of the settlement were overrun, and as best as he could tell, every creature on the ground below moved with the same brisk motions as those they'd faced in Cincinnati. A ripple seemed to go through the crowd as the helicopter passed overhead.

The largest concentration was around the silos, and he let out a sigh of relief. So some of his people *had* made it. The dead wouldn't have paid attention, otherwise.

His breath caught in his throat — there were *people* in the Crow's Nest, shooting down at a mass of zombies on the lower catwalk. As he watched, more cascaded over the top of the nearest silo and dropped down onto the catwalk to join in the assault. Still more hammered at the ventilation grates leading into the shelter. Knowing that they could climb had been terrifying on top of the building, but he hadn't made the next mental leap. If they could scale an elevator shaft ladder, how hard would a chain-link fence be?

We might as well have had no walls at all.

A couple of people in the Crow's Nest noticed the helicopter and began pointing and waving. Miles leaned forward, and his jaw dropped.

Trina was up there. For a moment he was almost convinced that they'd locked eyes, but they swept by and the moment was gone. Miles turned to look toward the cockpit, though the pilots couldn't see him.

"Some of my people are still alive! They're clustered on the west side of the compound." He craned his head to try and see more as they passed over the western gate. The helicopter turned to come back about.

The eastern half of the community was barren, compared to the area around the silos, which teemed with zombies. "Can you pull them to the east side, and keep your fire north and south?"

"Sho'nuff," Heppel replied. "Johnson, warm up the flare dispensers. You heard the man — keep your fire north and south, we don't want any blue on blue. Whose turn is it to pick the playlist — Nash?"

The gunner standing next to Miles shook his head and rolled his eyes. "Tim, if you roll with Drowning Pool again, I'm going to scream."

The gunner across the way turned and erected a middle finger. "Just for that, I should, you dweeb. How about we kick it old school, Cap? Start 'em off with Paradise City."

"I like it," Heppel drawled. "Going to hover. Roll flares. Let's *rock*."

The last en bloc clip pinged from the Garand, and Pete laid it aside with a curse. He fumbled the bolt-action off of his shoulder. Before he could bring it on target, one of the dead surged forward over the mound of its fallen brethren and stabbed at Charlie with a spear.

He twisted, but the head of the spear still skated along his side and opened a bloody gash. Charlie stabbed the Marlin forward and discharged it at point-blank range into his attacker's head.

The half-dozen attackers on the opposite side of the catwalk hesitated, as though waiting for something.

Damn, Pete marveled. *They know.*

Charlie jacked another round into the Marlin and fired, taking down the first in line. The remaining attackers seemed almost taken aback that he was still fighting.

Pete preyed on the still moment and fired at the next in line. As it fell he worked the action to chamber the next round in the magazine. At such a short range, .308 was bound to over-penetrate, but at this angle, his fire was more likely to go into the ground than the silo.

"Charlie, get your ass up here!" Pete screamed.

Below him, the other man jumped as though startled. For a moment, Pete worried that Charlie's immunity didn't work on this new strain, but he looked up, met Pete's eyes, and nodded.

As soon as Charlie's foot was on the first rung of the ladder, the attackers ended their pause and surged forward. Beside him, Cara pumped rounds out of her M&P, but the .22s had even less effect than the higher-velocity rounds out of the M4 had earlier.

Great, they're not only smarter and faster, their heads are harder.

"Alex! Under my bunk," Pete snapped. "There's a footlocker with an AR and a bunch of mags." It was a custom 300 Blackout job like Miles', though Pete had gone with a plainer setup. Miles liked to hang every 'kewl' accessory he could find on his guns. Pete had put his foot down when he'd shown up one day with a rail-mounted bottle opener. There were some lines you just didn't cross.

Alex scurried away to find the gun as Pete fired again. Two rounds left. Charlie was halfway up the ladder. Shoot — miss — one round left. Zombies at the base of the ladder.

Pete leaned over in an attempt to get a bead on the first one. Fired — hit. He laid the bolt action on the floor next to the Garand and reached out to help Charlie up through the hatch. "Get that M4 up, Charlie." He turned back toward Alex, "Damn it, where's my — ah." Alex slapped it in his hands. He pulled back the charging handle and looked back at Charlie. "Now we're cooking with gas. We can hold them off longer. Alternate fire. By the time we clock out of

608

rounds there should be enough bodies in the way they won't be able to climb up."

"Right," Charlie rasped. Pete glanced down at his side.

"Hell, you're bleeding like a stuck pig. Cara! Get the first aid kit."

"I can help!" A little kid Pete didn't recognize at first chimed in. He glowered, but the kid refused to shrink under the weight of his glare. *Of course.* Pete had seen that stubborn expression before.

"Twigs, right? I'll ignore why you're up here, but if you can help, you do it."

Pete turned away, leaned over the opening and took aim. The thwack of the 220-grain subsonic slamming into the head of the first zombie up the ladder was *much* more satisfying than the whine of a ricochet. "I'll cover this. . . ." Pete trailed off and cocked his head to one side. "You guys hear that?"

Even as he asked it, he realized both what the sound was, and the fact that most of the kids would never have heard it before. He glanced at Charlie. The other man frowned, then mouthed, "Chopper?"

Pete turned to follow the noise. On the horizon, a speck came into sight. It swelled larger as the thump-thump-thump of the rotor blades grew more and more overwhelming. They were booking, whoever they were.

The helicopter followed the path defined by the county road. As it got closer, he could make out the 'USMC' painted on the side in bold, black lettering.

"Yes!" Pete shouted. "The Marines are landing, kids!"

The helicopter slowed. For a moment, he could make out of a pair of faces in the gunner's station behind the cockpit. One wore dark goggles and a helmet, but the other — his heart leaped into his throat.

My boy's alive. Thank you, Lord, my son is alive.

Trina recognized the figure as the helicopter rushed past and shook the entire nest. "That's my dad!" She threw a celebratory fist to the heavens and ululated a cry of sheer joy.

It was a shout that, in point of fact, one could almost describe as laughter.

The helicopter was moving away as fast as it had approached, but he felt no fear — the Marines wouldn't leave them behind. Not his people. Just over the eastern fence, it turned to come back around and came into a hover thirty feet from the ground. He glanced down; for the moment, their attackers had paused. Was there just too much sensory input for them to decide where to attack?

Pete grabbed Trina and hugged her tight. "Watch this, kiddo. It's about time you learned about fireworks."

Twin arcs of glowing flares shot from the sides of the hovering monstrosity and tumbled through the air. At the same time, the gentle chords of an electric guitar began to pulse from massive speakers mounted on the stub wings. A smile crested Pete's face, and he recalled his conversation with Hanratty. What had the man said? 'We've got a few helicopters with those big psyops speakers on the side'?

He'd scoffed at the time, but as the drums joined the guitar solo and Axl Rose's melodic snarl boomed out, he couldn't help but laugh, himself.

The zombies committed themselves to the attack now. The horde flowed away from the silos and the other besieged buildings. They stormed toward the emission of light and sound that must have seemed irresistible. The attackers on the catwalk melted away, leaping over the side like lemmings. By this time, there were enough bodies on the ground below to serve as a cushion that many got up and joined the new assault. Just as many leaped to their end. The dead became a living, surging mass beneath the chopper. *"Oh, won't you please take me home . . ."*

And as the guitar solo began, the heavy machine guns on either side of the helicopter opened up. The laser-light of tracers joined the flash of the flares, and sure enough, it was one *hell* of a fireworks show.

A wave front of shredded flesh and bone cascaded away from the lines of the gunfire. Still, the zombies came on, heedless of the fact that they sprinted to their destruction. Pete let out a Bronx cheer and shook his rifle in the air. "Close air support, baby! How do you like *that*, you half-rotten pieces of shit!"

The helicopter slowly rotated in place, revealing a third gun mounted on the lowered cargo ramp. The rate of fire was nowhere close to continuous. Pete assumed that the pauses and rotation provided time for the guns to cool and for the gunners to find the densest clusters. All the while, the music pumped and throbbed — now something electric and fast by ZZ Top — but at this point, the flares seemed unnecessary. Everything on two legs within the fence line that could get eyes on target had focused either on salvation or destruction, according to their own perspective. As Pete watched, the LAV pulled up to the edge of the helicopter's killing field and added its own fire to the fray. Compared to the high-speed destruction of the helicopter's .50-caliber machine guns, the ground vehicle's fire seemed superfluous. He half-wished he were down there putting steel on target himself, though.

And then it happened. It was something he hadn't seen in the years since Z-Day, though it was not an unfamiliar sight when one fought the living.

611

Hundreds, perhaps even thousands of their brethren were down, obliterated from above. Where once they might have stood their ground, seemingly unaware of the consequences, these were different. For better or worse, they had changed. They had grown past what they had once been, and so confronted with potential destruction, the survivors turned away from what should have been their final demise and fled.

It wasn't a fast run, which gave the armored personnel carrier and helicopter more time to whittle at their ranks, but it was fast enough. They made it back to the fence, and to the school buses, and at that point, the settlement fell silent as the firing ceased. Perhaps it would have been worth it to try and destroy even more of them, but Pete understood the thinking. Why damage the barricades they had left? Yes, the enemy had shown they could scale them. Pete also knew that their bland acceptance of the security offered by fences and walls was a thing of the past.

More than the infected had changed. Yes, their enemy was not as close to collapse as they'd dared to hope, but they'd been vigilant once before. They could be so again.

And this time, they weren't alone.

Chapter 39

The vibration shook Charlie awake.

For the second night, he'd slept a deep, dreamless sleep. He eased up in bed and tried to reduce the pressure on his side. Tish had sewn his wound shut in the clinic the night before, after they'd made the final sweep of the settlement and ensured the interior was clear.

As always, fights with the biters ended in binary probability. There were those who survived and those who were infected. They'd found plenty of the former. There had been, oddly enough, none of the latter. There were twenty people missing and unaccounted for. Presumably, they'd succumbed to infection and were destroyed in the final attack or had fled with the others. It could have been worse. Most of the shelters had held. Most.

The engines growled outside, shaking the floor a bit more.

The first road convoy from Camp Perry had shown up around midnight. The heavy-lift choppers had already been ferrying troops and lighter supplies back and forth during that time frame. He hadn't been there, but he'd heard how poor of an initial welcome the rest of the community had given Hanratty. The new arrivals didn't have to deal with that. The town was ecstatic, in an almost celebratory mood despite the pain of their losses.

Charlie stood up, prepared to wince. The motion felt smooth and natural, though, and he twisted to the side to present his flank to the mirror on top of his dresser. In the absence of a sink and faucet in his cabin, he made do. He'd left various bathroom clutter spread across the top of the chest — a pitcher of water and a large, ceramic bowl, as well as other toiletries.

The bulge of the bandages wrapped around his middle was visible beneath the threadbare t-shirt he slept in, but other than that, nothing. It looked, for all the world, as though it were freshly applied.

With a groan, Charlie doffed his shirt and studied his side again. Surely there'd been some sort of seepage over the night — but no, the bandage was clean.

His curiosity unraveled into gnawing worry. He fiddled with the bandages in search of a seam, but gave up and cut them off with his pocket knife.

The gauze pad came away from his skin with ease. He glanced at it before discarding it on the floor. The pad had a faint discoloration of blood, but that was it.

The gnawing worry transited into shock.

Charlie fingered his side even as he stared at the reflection in the mirror with wide eyes.

The seam of his wound had healed over. There was some scarring, as he might have expected, but it was a thin, puckered seam in his flesh, dotted here and there with extraneous bits of stitches. He supposed at some point he'd need to have them removed, but that was a small concern at the moment. Of more importance was the fact that the seam in his flesh was a dull, silvery gray.

He recalled the slight quaver in Miles' voice the night before as the other man worked his way through a tumbler of Pete's celebratory Scotch.

Nanomachines.

Charlie's mouth went dry, and he poured a measure of water from the pitcher on the chest of drawers. As he took a deep drink, he almost immediately began coughing. Most of the water ended up on the mirror, but he bent over and continued hacking into the bowl. He had the sense there was something in the back of his throat that hadn't left enough room for the water to pass. He coughed and coughed. It occurred to him that he might be about to suffocate when something liquid shifted and splattered out of his mouth into the bottom of the bowl.

He gasped for breath; great, heaving wheezes of air — clinging to it like something he'd lost for years and not mere moments. Charlie wiped his mouth with the back of his hand and leaned over the bowl, studying the mass he'd coughed up. It looked like nothing else but raw, stringy meat, shot through here and there with bits of pale white.

"What the hell?" he whispered, and fell silent. The voice was his own, just not the one he'd heard since Z-Day.

He stared at himself in the mirror, forcing his eyes as wide as they could go, but they'd not yet betrayed him. They were white — a little puffy from sleep — but recognizably human.

"What's happening to me?" he said, louder this time.

"You sure about this?" Miles asked.

Pete hefted the duffel bag at his side. He seemed to weigh it as though trying to discern if it held too much. "Yeah," his uncle drew out. "I'm sure." He turned to face his nephew. "You going to miss me?"

"Not a bit," Miles assured him, though he felt certain that the thickness of his voice bore witness to the lie.

Pete laughed and dropped the duffel to throw both arms around him. "Well, I'm sure as hell going to miss you, boy," he whispered into Miles' ear. He pulled back. "It's a bigger world now, and from the sounds of it, Hanratty's people could use all the help they can get. This is always going to be home base, though." He shrugged.

"Well, where you headed first?"

"Got a meeting with General Vincent. He's the head honcho behind this herd of cats. From what Hanratty tells me, I'm liable to end up in planning or logistics, most likely." Pete turned and waved a hand at the bustle of activity on the eastern end of the camp. Bulldozers pushed the bodies of fallen zombies into hastily-dug trenches even as semis brought in prefab housing and other supplies on lowboy trailers. Everywhere he looked, people moved with purpose, though there was an air of frenetic disorganization to the entire thing. Miles had to laugh. Yeah, it was a herd of cats, all right, but that was a lot better than the emptiness of the alternative.

"Why do I suspect," Miles mused, "that you're not going to settle for some sort of cushy desk job?"

Pete did his best to look innocent. "Who? Me?"

"You."

His eyes twinkled. "Swift, silent, deadly, kid."

"Well, you got two out of three, at least."

Pete laughed and slapped his damaged leg. "Sounds like they've got some good techs up at Perry, I'll be bouncing around before you know it."

Over the wall, the echo of a helicopter became audible as another approached. It was funny, Miles thought. They'd spent so long hiding and being quiet. The enemy had changed, though, and hiding and being quiet were no longer effective. What *was* effective, though, was providing them with too much feedback. Enough sensory input, and the part of them that had learned animal cunning lost control. They could herd them — they could destroy them. He smiled. If you couldn't hide from the enemy, being bold was a good alternative. Somehow, that seemed more palatable than cringing behind a wall. They could laugh, now. If for no other reason, that made it all worthwhile.

"There's my ride," Pete said. "I'll be in touch."

He hefted the duffel bag and hobbled toward the area they'd designated as a landing zone for the incoming choppers. When he was halfway there, Miles called out, "Nobody blames you, Pete." Last night, when they'd gathered together, family and friends, to commemorate their triumph and to remember the fallen, he'd admitted to them that he'd known of the nearby horde for some time. The revelation had stunned them into momentary silence, but for the most part, as each examined it from their own perspective, they agreed with his judgment. The community hadn't been ready. They'd been in denial, complacent. If he'd tried to tell them, they wouldn't have listened.

The hardest truths made the best lessons. But only when made painfully and evidently obvious.

Pete turned back and looked. He smiled, but sadness tinged it. "I know, son. But I do."

There was plenty of room in the clinic, so overcrowding wasn't an excuse to try and get out. Even if he'd wanted to give it a try, Tish had put a preemptive foot down.

Larry was feeling a hell of a lot better, though he was still somewhat sensitive to light. So, instead of fighting it, he accepted his daughter's medical advice and remained in bed. That didn't mean he wasn't receiving visitors, though most of them rushed away in reaction to Tish's protective scowl. She was getting to that stage with Jim Piper, but he was either unaware of her dark looks, or didn't care. "I can't believe you didn't know."

"In case you missed it, I've been a little busy the last few days," Larry said and rubbed his forehead with his fingers. It was still throbbing a bit, but he refused to voice any complaint to Tish.

"Fair enough. We finally got enough serious suggestions to name the town. Norma wanted to announce it the other night during the town meeting. But, well, the Marines showed up, and that didn't work out." He dug a much-folded piece of paper from the pocket of his jeans. Jim grinned. "How about we make a double announcement of it? You taking the position and our name." His grin faded. "The rumor mill has already spread the *name* far and wide, but I've been able to keep a lid on Norma's replacement."

"You keep coming and going like this, they're going to figure it out." After Norma had regained consciousness, the survivors in the shelter had informed her that she was stepping down. There'd been more than enough survivors present to form a quorum. The spontaneous motion had passed with unanimous consent. There'd been some bickering back and forth about her replacement, at which point Jim had suggested a secret ballot of the most popular nominees. When they tallied the results, it was close, but Larry had been the top choice.

Larry took the paper from Jim and unfolded it. "If you guys named it Woodbury, I'm leaving." He folded a corner of the washcloth on his forehead up so he could see a little better.

Jim didn't reply, but if anything, his grin got bigger.

Larry looked at the list of names and the number of votes next to each and smiled despite his headache. "Huh. How about that."

Once again, Vir was outside the wall.

This time, though, heavy equipment and ever-growing piles of construction supplies surrounded him. Dozens of sharp-eyed Marines lined the perimeter, watching for incoming threats.

"You Singh?"

He turned and nodded at the man in the odd-looking camouflage, made up of patterns of blues and blacks. "That's me."

The other man stuck out his hand. "Lieutenant Commander Rick Ferris, US Naval Construction Forces. I hear you're a structural engineer?"

Vir shook his hand and beamed. "Yes, indeed I am. I must say, I hadn't expected to get the opportunity to build much more of anything in my lifetime, so this is definitely a happy occasion."

Ferris laughed. "Well, I'm glad we're finding survivors, Mr. Singh. I've got a few of my team leaders and supply folks waiting in the command track. If you'd care to join me, we've got a rough sketch of the planned wall expansion and we'd love to get your take on it. We've got plenty of supplies. You guys did one hell of a job with what you had, but it would surprise you how quick we can build up something with Conex trailers and heavy equipment."

Vir smiled again. "I can't wait. Shall we?"

For the first time in a long time, Charlie was completely alone. It was strangely exciting.

He hadn't asked permission or told anyone of his intent. He'd walked over to the last Humvee in the motor pool, topped off its tank, and drove away. The crew at the west gate hadn't questioned it. Perhaps they'd assumed he was running around assisting in the recovery effort. Maybe they'd seen Charlie at the wheel and figured he could move about as he pleased. Whichever the case, they'd lifted the gate and he'd driven on.

Once, if forced into absolute honesty, Charlie Maddox would have proclaimed that hope was something lost to him. It had shriveled up and died inside of his chest on that day so long ago. On Z-Day, he'd not only lost the two things that gave his life purpose but those things became something that wanted to destroy him.

Neither Corey nor Dalton had said anything to him about the tote of supplies he'd left behind. Such was Charlie's credit in their bank of trust. If he wanted to leave a box of salvage out in the middle of a housing edition, who were they to judge?

He touched his throat, then rubbed it. They were good men. He hoped that they'd be working together in the future. Charlie had carried little out the gate with him. The holstered pistol at his hip wasn't for his own defense. If he felt his faculties began to slip, or if the sclera of his eyes turned from white to gray, he hoped that he'd have time to put himself down.

In the chaos of the last few days, he hadn't much time to think about the possible survivors in the subdivision, but when he had, his thoughts had been self-deprecating. If possible, he'd questioned himself far more than his teammates ever would have.

Finally, he'd felt foolish about the entire thing and resolved to put it from his mind. The world had changed, had moved on. What little good that remained was fleeting and sparse. Who was he to expect?

Who was he, to hope?

After yesterday, he couldn't help but think that he'd gotten his answer.

The damage to both the settlement and its population remained, but there was a new undercurrent in the air. An excited buzz that had never been there as long as Charlie had lived there.

It ranged from excited whispering to bold gossip. Hands that had been idle unless forced to labor were suddenly there, offering to help in the cleanup.

We're not alone! More Marines are coming! They want us to expand, they want to help!

Miles saved us all — Miles helped find a way to stop this. Could it be . . . ? Could things someday be back to normal?

They told tales of their own people as well and made heroes of ordinary men and women.

Norma went crazy, she was threatening some kids — Jenny *Faqir tackled her and saved them all.*

When he heard the words about the last stand he and Pete had made at the Crow's Nest, he couldn't decide whether to be embarrassed or laugh at the absurdity. The now-healed wound at his side had reached epic proportions in some of the telling.

On such anvils are heroes forged. Horatius at the bridge; Leonidas at the Hot Gates. Charlie on the catwalk.

It wasn't so much the stories, he knew — it was the emotion behind them. Dead men tell no tales, but neither do dying societies. If there is no hope for a future, why remember the past?

As Charlie listened to the words, as he saw the excited faces, something kindled within him. Something grew inside, until it settled — not unlike a lump in his throat — and made him wonder, what if. What if?

And so he drove now, navigating through the country roads, driving past scavenged houses and the rusting hulks of farm equipment. Little stirred as he moved through the countryside. The smarter, faster biters had gathered their army to them and left little behind. Somewhere, of course, there would be more, but for today, it could have been a bright spring morning in the past. The windows on the Humvee didn't roll down, but he could open the top hatch and let in the cloudless blue sky and the fresh air, alive with the scent of growing things.

His excitement grew and grew, and when he pulled into the entrance of the subdivision, he couldn't stop the smile that flashed across his face. The tote was no longer where he'd left it. Little else had changed in the subdivision save for that, but that one small thing was enough to maintain the spark inside his chest.

Charlie pulled to a stop and put the Humvee in park. He waited, and the newfound thoughts of possibility dueled with the cold pessimism that had ruled him for so long. Overwhelmed with the emotion of it, he closed his eyes and lowered his chin to his chest.

Please, Lord, he prayed. *Grant me just this one thing. Forgive me for doubting you, Lord.*

He raised his head and looked at each home in turn. Then, at the third house, he saw her.

The girl was dirty; her clothing ragged and overlarge. She stood silently in the open door of the house and studied the Humvee and Charlie. Her hair was short, blondish-brown and raggedly cut.

It had been a long time since Charlie had looked at a child and considered their age. He thought this girl might be a short ten-year-old or a tall eight-year-old. Either way, she'd spent the majority of her life in this changed world. Was she maybe a little bit like Charlie? Did she know what hope was?

He eased the door of the Humvee open and stepped out, standing behind it so as not to spook her. She didn't stir, just kept studying Charlie. "Hello," he called out and winced at the volume of it. He brought a hand to his throat and rubbed it. His mind was telling him there should be pain, but he felt nothing. *Just this one thing.*

She cocked her head to one side, looked around, and finally spoke. Even then, she kept her voice pitched low, and he had to strain to hear it. "Why did you help us?"

Charlie pushed down his surprise. "That's what grownups should do," he said, finally. "Make sure kids are okay."

The girl stepped forward, and Charlie realized there was another child standing behind her — a boy, with the same, ragged hair, but smaller. Perhaps half her age. He clutched the raggedy girl's jacket with one hand and had the thumb of his other hand planted in his mouth.

"That's what Pap-pap said," the girl murmured. "We hid from the monsters for a long time with him until the bad men came. Pap-pap told us to run and hide and he would come find us." She looked at Charlie in consideration, and when she spoke again, there was a faint note in her voice. It was almost pleading. "Are you one of the bad men?"

"No," Charlie said. "No, I'm not."

The three of them stood, staring at each other. Finally, the girl looked down at her companion and whispered to him. The little boy looked at her, then Charlie, and back again. He nodded. His sister looked back at Charlie, but he could see the doubt in her eyes. She wanted to believe, but life hadn't given her many rewards for her faith. He could understand that.

"Come with me," Charlie said. "There's a safe place like I said in the note. You can come stay. There are other kids, a school. We have animals." He fell silent. He didn't know what else to say but finally, he smiled and said, "For a long time we argued about what to call it." He laughed, despite himself. "We finally decided, though. We named it Hope."

Word of mouth is the most cost-effective advertising there is for a new author.

Critiques are even better. Whether you enjoyed this book or not, please consider leaving a review at Amazon. If you did enjoy it, please feel free to follow me on Twitter (@NerdKing52) for updates, snippets of works in progress, and other randomness. If social media isn't your thing, you can check out my blog on www.daniel-humphreys.net.

I'd also like to give a huge shout-out to my awesome crew of beta readers at AoSHQ. You helped make this a better book, and I am forever grateful.

ABOUT THE AUTHOR

Daniel Humphreys geeks out for movies, target shooting, and football. He has worked in Fortune 500 IT for over two decades, and resides in southern Indiana with his wife and children.

Made in the USA
San Bernardino, CA
29 April 2019